IN MY FATHER'S
GENERATION

12/25/01

Merry Christmas to you & your
family — Peace & joy throughout
the year!

From the Lee Container family

Best Wishes —

James Martin Rhodes

IN MY FATHER'S GENERATION

James Martin Rhodes

toExcel

San Jose New York Lincoln Shanghai

In My Father's Generation

Published by toExcel Press,
an imprint of iUniverse.com, Inc.

For information address:
iUniverse.com, Inc.
620 North 48th Street
Suite 201
Lincoln, NE 68504-3467
www.iuniverse.com

ISBN: 1-58348-324-1

LCCN: 99-62833

In order to have John Warren take part in certain historical events at particular stages in his life, I have had to alter the correct dates for those events. I apologize to the historical purists, and I want them to know that I was raised better than to do such things.

To my father and mother,
James and Ruth Rhodes
with my admiration, respect
and love always.

Acknowledgements

I wish to thank the following people for their contributions to the making of this book. I take responsibility for any of its shortcomings, and I want them to receive recognition for the strengths that it may have.

Judge Folks Huxford of Homerville. *His History of Clinch County Georgia* (Huxford, 1916) was both research tool and muse. Also, my thanks to the people whose labor of love it is to sustain the Judge's Huxford Genealogical Library in Homerville.

A.S. McQueen and Hamp Mizell for their 1926 book, *History of Okefenokee Swamp* (Jacobs and Co., Clinton, S.C.). I am particularly indebted to them for a photograph in their book that inspired the story of Cau Au Ra and Au Eve.

Mr. Grady Lacy of the Modern Foreign Language department at Valdosta State University, Valdosta, Ga. for the quick lesson in Latin.

Professor Chris Trowell of South Georgia College and of the Okefenokee Swamp for his generous sharing of time, maps of the great swamp, and information on a wide range of topics, including the Suwannee Canal Company. You may have forgotten those long-ago conversations, but I certainly haven't.

Mr. Luther Thrift and Mr. Leonard Thrift of Waycross, Georgia. Thanks for several days' worth of conversation back in the 1980's that fired my imagination. I stand in awe of the men, women and children who lived the adventure that I can only write about.

Melvin Crandell, past historian at the Jekyll Island Authority, Jekyll Island, Georgia (circa 1983) for research assistance on matters that did not make it into this work, but that will play a large role in the lives of the next generation of Warrens and Stokes.

My mother-in-law, Ann Robbins, for entrusting the papers of her father, Charles W. Pittard, to me and for her interest in this endeavor over the years.

I am grateful for the support of family, friends, and past students who have endured the seemingly infinite promise of "The Book". My special thanks to my beloved Jan, Luke, Emily, and Drew, who not only make all things seem possible, but also make all things worthwhile.

Finally, to Mr. Charles W. Pittard, I acknowledge and celebrate the living of a life with such integrity and dignity that you would inspire one to write a story about it. I apologize for putting you off to tell about your father's generation, but you made the end of this book, and the next one is all yours.

"I returned and saw under the sun, that the race is not to the swift, nor the battle to the strong, neither yet bread to the wise, nor yet riches to men of understanding, nor yet favor to men of skill; but time and chance happen to them all."

Ecclesiastes 9:11

Prologue

"John Warren was the best friend I ever had. The first time we met, he was fighting Ned Worthington and a couple of his gang near Mr. Ben Taylor's sawmill. I held off Ned's cohorts long enough for John to beat the fire out of him.

"John and I used to hunt and fish together a good bit, and we had some great arguments about every topic known to man. We made all sorts of plans and pacts over the years.

"A lot of people around here don't understand why I haven't been laid in the lap of luxury since John made all that money and since we were best friends.

"Well, sir, I could've had it made a number of times, but I've never needed or wanted much in this world, so John and I got along fine. I was someone he could always turn to for a shot of liquor and a little quiet conversation. He was a good man."

Excerpt from interview with Gray Hampton,
The Jacksonville Times, April 29, 1917.

"Now that Mr. John Warren dead, he roasting in hell! You hear me? Tell that to them city folk what reads your paper. And you know why? He killed my man Jeeter thirty year ago! He tied Jeeter and Janie's Samuel to trees out in these here piney woods, and he poured camphor oil to 'em, and he laughed and screamed and pawed the dirt like old Scratch, and then he throwed the fire to them and burn them up alive! We heared the screams all over these woods. That man, John Warren—he gone to the pit of hell!"

An old woman of Shakerag

1

"Mr. John Warren? Until I was sixteen years old, I thought he was God."

A young man of Magnolia, Georgia.

"My mama used to tell all us children that lest we was good, Mr. John Warren would get us. I thought he was the devil hisself 'til I was most of twenty years old."

A young lady of Shakerag.

"My husband was a powerful man, and because of that power, many people lost sight of the fact that he was subject to the emotions common to us all.

"John's family died in the siege of Atlanta in 1864. As a result of that loss, he was never again free to open up completely to other people. He tried. He tried to allow all of us into his heart, but he lived with the constant dread that the children and I might be taken from him as suddenly as his parents and his brother and sisters.

"He wasn't so wrong to feel that way, was he? John came closest to letting down his guard with our youngest daughter, and she was taken cruelly from us. I wish people could have seen past his exterior. I wish he could have let himself break through the aloofness that he wore like armor. My husband loved as he could."

Excerpt from interview with Kathleen Warren,
The New York Times, April 29, 1917.

"My father's relationship with John Warren was a once in a lifetime phenomenon. Think of it. At the time they met, the war had just ended, and there was a tremendous amount of resentment directed toward black people. At the time Mr. Warren and my father went into business together, about 1866, the white man had seen his slave property slip away, without reimbursement. As a matter of fact, he not only lost his property, but also he had to pay it a wage. Despite the feeling of the time, my father befriended a white boy and was bold enough to take him into his business.

"There were many advantages for my father in forming a partnership. For one, John Warren was educated far beyond anything we knew at the time, despite the fact that he never even graduated from high school. His knowledge of legitimate business was invaluable. He also provided easier access to the white market, and he could travel freely, particularly at night.

"Most importantly, my father saw something that he admired in Mr. Warren. It was the will to excel in spite of tribulation. Not merely to survive, but to prosper and to grow in spite of circumstances."

Excerpt from interview with Leander Stokes,
Wall Street Journal, April 27, 1917.

"Yes, my father was pretty hot-tempered throughout his life. Most people were afraid of him because of that temper and his size—and because of that story. That's right.

"I was only six years old when my sister was killed, so I can't tell you much about the incident. I can't believe my father would've taken revenge on her killers the way that people say he did. I think he would've turned those people over to the authorities. The old man was a fairly straight arrow."

Excerpt from interview with Harry Warren,
The Jacksonville Times, April 29, 1917.

"John Warren was life blown all out of proportion. He lived in epic times, from the War Between the States until his recent death, and it seems that he was a man suited for his era. He was a big man physically, and he was a big man at heart. Therefore, he loomed over epic events as few men did.

"Mr. Warren was probably everything people say he was and a lot of things some of us never knew him for. He probably was a coward, an agnostic, and a murderer. He probably was an adventurer, a great benefactor of the church, and a loving husband and father. He probably did lie and steal and cheat his way to the top. He probably did employ half of the men in Clinch County and support widows and their families without the least expectation of gratitude or repayment.

"I don't doubt that John Warren could have been and done all of those things. The potential for the worst and best of mankind is in each of us, and John Warren was susceptible to the extremes of human nature. I think his ability to live on a grand scale was due to his forceful personality and to the times in which he lived, for men and events were different in my father's generation."

Editorial written by Charles Warren in
The Atlanta Journal, April 27, 1917.

I

John heard them in the distance long before he saw them. He heard the clatter of equipment and the clamor of the drayage animals first. He and two other boys set aside their rations of cold beans and walked to the dusty street directly in front of their tents. In the heat of the late July twilight, he removed a handkerchief from his back pocket to wipe the sweat from his face, to mop brown hair back from his eyes. As others joined John and his companions on the street, the noise of the approaching army increased. They heard the steady creak of wagon wheels and the terse orders of company commanders.

"Must be Hardee's Corps," a boy said. "They're coming right down Peachtree."

"Yeah, here comes the camp flies up yonder," an old man said.

Everyone looked off to the northwest where the man indicated. An odd assortment of men, women, and children proceeded toward the city hall square where John's militia unit was camped. Some of the women drove covered wagons, a few of the men rode gaunt, sweat-stained horses, but most of the people trudged down the dust-plumed street in the heart of the city.

Two boys from John's unit walked out to meet these camp hangers-on in an effort to glean information of the approaching army. Eight or ten small boys dashed about the square, hunting the best vantage point from which to view the imminent line of march. As John watched his companions walk back toward the square with the camp flies, a tumultuous cheer rose from the north. Above the darkening outline of nearby stores, a billowing red cloud of dust, intensified by the last red rays of the setting sun, reached tree top level and suspended in the heat. It was a pall that followed the thousands wherever they went.

"Don't know what they're cheering about," an old man said. "I bet our whole durned army is fixing to hightail it out of here, and we'll be left holding this here baggage."

"Well, that's all right with me," one of the youngest boys countered. "Atlanta's mine, and I'm willing to fight for her, be it against Sherman or the devil hisself."

"Ain't you heard, boy," the old man said, "Sherman is the devil hisself. That's a pretty speech somebody filled you full of, but we ain't nothing but Joe Brown's melish. I'm seventy-one years old, and you ain't no more'n thirteen. Them real soldiers would eat us alive and wouldn't leave much to spit out behind them."

The boy's rebuttal was lost on John who stepped out into the street with several others to meet the two boys returning from their talk with the camp flies.

"It's Hardee all right," one of the boys said.

"Is there any word of how we fared north of the city?" John asked.

"Seems we took a pretty bad whipping," the other boy said. "We held the line, but the Yanks are all across the Chattahoochee, and they say we lost a lot of men up on Peachtree Creek."

"What is this movement that's coming toward us now?" John asked.

"They ain't sure," said the first boy. "Some say it's an all out retreat and that we'd better be at the head of it. Others say Sherman can't get past the defense lines up north, so he's flanking to the southeast and Hardee's going to cut him off over at Decatur."

"Either way I expect they'll be picking us up to replace their losses," John said. "We had better get ready."

Even though he was only fifteen and a mere militia conscript, John commanded respect from those around him, young and old alike. He possessed an air of quiet confidence far beyond his years that people found compelling. The face that now at fifteen was merely attractive with a pronounced jaw and prominent nose would soon be handsome and strong to the point of intimidation. His eyes held the promise of the power that was to be.

At six feet three and one hundred ninety pounds, John towered over his fellow soldiers. He was lean, and he carried himself in a way that one knew on first sight that this was a man who, even at a young age, did not back down. Both the boys and the old men followed him back to the square to pack their scant provisions.

As he rolled his mildewed blanket, John thought of the contempt in the old man's voice for "Joe Brown's melish". *What did Governor Brown expect of such an assortment of humanity as comprised the militia—boys of fourteen and fifteen and men of seventy and better? Even the most able-bodied troops would be ineffective if they were outfitted such as we, John thought. No two men have the same uniform and most of the issued clothing and bedding is in poor condition at best. Almost three in ten of us have no weapons, and those of us who have a firearm have precious little ammunition.*

As he finished gathering his gear, he heard the advancing army more distinctly and thought how strange it was that an entire army should be marching through streets once traveled only by buggies, surreys, or freight wagons. He tried to picture his family at home on Mitchell Street only four blocks away to the southwest and his father at the Medical College about the same distance to the northeast.

On a normal Thursday at this hour, we would be waiting dinner for father, John thought. Surgery or some conference that couldn't wait for morning would hold him up. We children would be feigning starvation for mother who would hold us at bay with her calm, confident smile. Or perhaps father would have been on time for once, and we would be seated around the table in the dining room now, holding hands at prayer and discussing the day's news, guided by father's expert commentary. He even insisted that little Elizabeth join in those conversations, though most of the time she had no understanding of what we were discussing.

Against his will, he remembered the family home as it had been for the past six months, as the number of wounded coming into Atlanta escalated by the hundreds each week. Several dozen wounded men and what meager fare they carried with them littered the once immaculate yard. Small circles of charred wood marred the ground where the cook fires lay. The house and grounds were falling into a state of depressing disrepair. The trees and a high wooden fence had been mutilated for firewood. All night the sick and wounded moaned for water or for a tender touch. The house reeked of disinfectant and of dead or dying flesh.

All family routine was lost as John's mother, Mary, took more and more wounded into their care. Each day was consumed by tedious duty, all directed to the care of the soldiers. The children gathered and cut wood for the cook fires. They hauled water ceaselessly and changed bandages grown putrid from gangrenous wounds. Mary and her thirteen-year-old daughter, Susan, wrote letters for those too weak or illiterate to let their families know of their conditions.

John was so lost in his musing that he failed to see the first ranks of the tumultuous army round the final corner from the north and trudge into view of the militia in the square. When he did look up from his bedroll, the sight was nowhere near as impressive as John had assumed it would be.

Four men on horseback led the army down Peachtree Street. A Colonel's bay mare looked as if she were coming up lame, and two of the other men lagged behind to study her gait. All four men were covered with red dust, and their faces were tracked where sweat had cut through the stain.

Behind these officers the first company of infantry rounded the corner some fifty feet distant. To John they looked more like a mob than they did an army. Forty or fifty men and boys surged around the street corner with no semblance of rank or file that might enable a bystander to distinguish where one platoon started or another ended. From his vantage on the square, John watched the number of soldiers turning the corner swell into the thousands. As the head of the formation passed him and neared the far end of the square, the command to halt echoed up and down the line.

Each company's commander appeared on horseback, dismounted, and made a brief speech about resting for half an hour, gathering water, and remaining in the area bounded by the storefronts on either side of the street. As the Captains rode away toward the head of the column, three men from each platoon loaded themselves with canteens and left in search of a convenient pump. The rest of the men scratched around for a place to stretch out.

John saw that most of them fell asleep in an instant. A few men pulled books or writing material from a knapsack or coat pocket, while others tended to some little habit of personal care, but the largest number simply closed their eyes and momentarily were away from the filth and sweat and parched throat of a soldier on the move.

Minutes later, as the water bearers returned to the troops, Major Jackson rode into the square, and the boys and old men of the militia gathered into a ragged formation. The regular soldiers nearest the square looked up from their canteens as the militia fell in to ranks.

"Old Sherman better look out now," one of the soldiers yelled. The others took their cue from him.

"Does your mommy know where you are, boy?"

"Come get my musket, grandpa. I don't want it no more."

"You'll be sorry!"

Major Jackson waited patiently astride his horse until the clamor subsided, then addressed the one hundred or so militiamen.

"This is it. We'll be joining General Hardee's corps. For now, the less said about our objective, the better off we'll all be. As soon as the column moves out, you'll fall in behind the second company that comes by the square here. Squad leaders, you are to keep your men at parade rest until we move out. Captains and Lieutenants, front and center!"

The square was shrouded in darkness so that John could barely see the Major conferring with the other officers at the front of the column. Shortly after the Major rode away, the regulars stirred from their rest, the company commanders bellowed orders, and the beast of an army gathered its various parts into a body. In the vicinity of the square the beast stretched and swayed here and there, hesitated as the impulse to move traveled slowly down its spinal column, and finally lurched out of the square following Decatur Street to the southeast.

§   §   §   §

"Hey melish, you got any tobacco on you?"

At first John didn't realize that the question was directed toward him. They were out of the city, and he was still struggling to get the rhythm and feel of marching in the dark.

"I'm talking to you, big boy. You got a chaw on you?"

John twisted awkwardly to see the man who spoke and lost his footing on the rutted road. He fought to keep his balance, but the shifting knapsack and bedroll on his back dragged him down to a sitting position. The first two ranks of the platoon behind him surged around the bulky obstacle in the road. A soldier in the third rank stopped, extended a hand to John and hauled him to his feet. Amid the hoarse, mirthless laughter of those around him, John felt his face burning an extra measure in the July heat.

"Does that mean you ain't got no chaw or you ain't willing to give it up?" the voice asked from the front of the platoon—more laughter.

"I don't have one," John said. The statement came out much louder than he had intended.

"Well, now I know and so do the Yanks," the voice said.

John felt the heat on his face intensify. He let his broad shoulders slump, hoping that he would be a little less conspicuous. He had thought of catching back up to his platoon, but now the desire for anonymity held him in place beside the soldier who had helped him. He tried to discern the man's face in order to express some visual token of gratitude, but the moon was not yet high enough to provide the necessary light.

"Yes sir, I feel a whole lot safer now that we got these here militia boys with us. How about you, Sam?"

"You bet. If I thought I'd get a chance to sleep tonight, I'd sleep a heap better for it."

"These fellers may not be able to fight, but you fellers back there ought to see them march. Whoooo-ee!"

"Yeah, all 'cept that big feller what hit the clay back there a piece."

John silently suffered another round of laughter.

"Hey big 'un," a new voice called to John, "What you doing in a militia outfit, anyway? A man your size ought to a been regular army a long time ago."

"My mother and father wouldn't let me enlist until week before last."

"Whaaat?" the new voice asked. "What do you mean, your ma and pa wouldn't let you? What's your ma got to do with it?"

"Governor Brown didn't call fifteen year olds to the militia until the first of the month, and my mother felt as if I were needed at home to help care for the wounded."

"You mean to tell me you're fifteen years old, man? It ain't that dark out here that I can't see the size of you."

"I don't blame you for doubting my word, sir, yet I am fifteen, and my parents were within their rights to withhold me from service until the age of induction was lowered."

"He don't talk like no kid, does he, Billy?"

"Yeah, sure he does—like a fifteen year old lawyer," Billy said. "But all this jawing back and forth ain't gonna solve nothing. Wait 'til that moon breaks the tree line over yonder, and we'll have a good look at this young bull. Then we'll know something or other. And that's all of that quoth Dancing Bill."

As if by decree, the infantrymen stopped taunting the militia. Men and boys marched on wearily to the southeast of Atlanta. They passed the rolling steel mill, winding out past Oakland Cemetery until they out-walked all remembrances of the city. As the moon began its ascent of the eastern sky, John looked out over the familiar fields on either side of the road. The field to the south there belongs to Mr. Kinship, he thought.

"You gonna bust your ass again if you don't quit looking out across them fields."

The voice shook John from his thoughts. "Sir? Were you speaking to me?"

"Yeah, I'm speaking to you, but I ain't no sir. You are fifteen, ain't you?"

"Yes, I am," John said.

"Well, I'm barely seventeen myself, so don't be calling me sir. My name's Ned."

"How do you do, Ned. My name is John Warren, and I want to thank you for helping me up back there."

"Never you mind the boys' little jokes, John. They don't mean nothing by it. We're all a little jumpy, that's all."

John didn't reply, and they walked on in silence for a moment.

"You from Atlanta?" Ned asked.

"Yes. I was born and raised here."

"You know much about the countryside out this way?"

"Sure. We know the man who owns that farm over there. My father and I used to ride out this way often."

"Don't some rivers start up in here and run south?" Ned asked.

"There are plenty of little creeks that start up here and feed into the South River, and the South eventually runs into the Ocmulgee. Are you familiar with the Ocmulgee?"

There was no reply, so John looked over at Ned. The boy was straining to see the unfamiliar territory to the south. He was a dirty hulk of a boy who almost matched John in height and weight. His hair was shaggy and matted, and he had a scraggly beard. His nose was slender and a wad of chewing tobacco distended his right cheek.

"Yeah, I've heard of the Ocmulgee," Ned murmured. "It runs right through Macon."

"The pale lady of the night shares her charms with us, Mr. Worthington," said a voice that John recognized as that of the man known as Dancing Bill. His choice of words betrayed an educated mind that earlier had not been evident.

"What is your pronouncement concerning the young man who stumbles by night?"

"I believe him when he says he's only fifteen," Ned replied.

"Sound enough judgment for now, quoth Dancing Bill," the voice said. "Gentlemen, the matter is at rest. Should the harsh glare of reality, which must come with the morning light, reveal Mr. Worthington to be a hopeless gull, judge not him. The cold temptress who now glitters above us shall ultimately make fools of us all. Be it in love or in war, she shall surely snare us one and all."

John looked quizzically at Ned, who smiled and winked. They marched on through the moonlit night, a weary and silent army traveling the way of destruction south of Atlanta.

II

John Warren surveyed the desolate landscape around him. It consisted not of hills and trees, but of hundreds of bodies which lay about him on the cruel, red earth. His legs were stiff from the twelve-mile march they had just completed, his shoulders tense and raw from bearing the weight of his knapsack throughout the night. His face and arms were slick with a mixture of red dust and sweat.

Even lying perfectly still did nothing to staunch the flow of perspiration. The delicate wings of mosquitoes whined in his ears, irritating him almost beyond the limits of endurance. Every few minutes he flailed hopelessly at his head, then shifted his weight in an attempt to settle into a semblance of comfort. Within seconds the mosquitoes were back, and he discovered new sources of discomfort beneath his body, prompting him to repeat the process.

"Care to be anointed with hog, John?" a voice next to him asked. Ned Worthington sat up and rummaged in his knapsack. He pulled a packet from the bag and offered it to John.

"What is it?" John asked.

"A soldier's best friend. Smear some on your hands and rub it anywhere skin shows."

John accepted the packet. It was greasy to the touch, and he recognized the odor immediately.

"Why this is bacon, Ned."

"That it is. Skeeters don't seem to appreciate it, though."

John was repulsed by the idea of smearing himself with the greasy pork rind, but he noticed that Ned seemed unperturbed by the little pests, so he rubbed the palm of his hand on the soft slab and applied it to his face and neck.

"You had any sleep?" Ned asked.

"Not a wink," John admitted. "How about you?"

"I was out the second I hit the ground. What time do you suppose it is?"

"Judging by the moon, I'd say it's about three or four."

John leaned on one elbow and looked at the army sprawled on the earth about him. The scene fit his image of how a battlefield would look moments after the clash of two armies. He looked over at Ned who sat cross-legged to one side of him.

"Where do you think we're headed, Ned?"

"Home," Ned said.

His reply was so preposterous that it confused John. "My home is back the other way. What are you talking about?"

"What? Oh, you mean where is the army going? We're there. Wherever this place is. The Yanks can't be more than a few miles off, or we wouldn't be stopped yet."

"You think we are about to see battle then?" John asked.

Ned glared at him. "Damn the way you talk, boy! We ain't about to "see" no battle. We're about to be ass deep in one. Do you know what that means? Have you even got enough sense to be scared? I know what your idea of a fight is, and it ain't worth two cents. You're seeing us on one side of a big field and them on the other. And you're seeing a little shooting here and there along the line and maybe a man getting hit way off down one flank or the other. Then, seeing as how you're so educated, maybe you've even thought of a charge by a company or two, a little advance that takes them out to the middle of the field. And maybe you've seen how the Yanks come out too and how there's a dance out there in the middle of that field. And then we're whupping and the whole army comes pouring in behind us, and we whup them Yanks all the way back to hell where they come from. I know how you see it."

Ned lapsed into silence. He sat pulling at the wisps of his beard and breathing heavily through his nose.

The accuracy of his tirade intimidated John. He wouldn't look at Ned now, but leaned on his right arm and stared at the red clay at his side. He knew that the ground was a dark red hue, but no color was distinguishable in the ghostly pale moonlight. "What is it like, Ned?"

"It's all confusion," he said softly. I can't hardly get it sorted out to tell you. It starts out pretty much like you think. We're all over here, and they're all over there. But you can't always see all of them because of a patch of woods or a hill. Just when you get to thinking it's going to be all right, cause there ain't that many of them, you'll see nigh about two or three hundred men come out of a thicket."

Ned paused a moment as if remembering something specific. "It ain't enough to see a battle, boy. Seeing ain't the half of it. First you hear it. You hear them cannon thundering from behind you when we fire at the Yanks and then their guns rumbling right back at us. All hell breaks out right in front of you 'cause they ain't got the range yet. Hunks of dirt and grass get ripped up and come pouring down on you, and saplings and tops of oaks and pines are splitting and cracking everywhere. Then Captains and Majors are twisting and turning big old horses up and down the line right off your tail and yelling orders that half of us can't hear for the racket and the other half of us don't even want to hear.

"All the time you're firing in the general direction of the Yanks and reloading, praying that a pile of them don't end up in your lap before you can get ready to shoot again. And then you hear them coming. The Yanks are big on drumming and blowing horns when they're coming at you. I guess they figure it gets their men all excited and works on our nerves to hear all the commotion rushing toward us. Anyway, you hear all that pounding and them horns and by then the field is so smoky and burnt, you can't tell which direction they're coming from 'til they're a few hundred feet away. The men falling down ain't on some flank neither. They're right beside you, and that's when you damn sure 'see' battle.

"Up on Peachtree Creek we was getting ready to advance one time when this shot come awful close to me. I looked around to tell this old boy beside me how close that one was and he was already on the ground, deader than your great-grandma. He didn't have no face no more, John. I was wearing some of it on my shirtsleeve. I puked my guts up and went on about my business."

Ned fell silent. He reached into his pocket and took out a small pouch. From it he extricated a dark lump. John didn't recognize it until Ned removed a knife from his other pocket, cut a portion from the lump, and stuffed the tobacco into the side of his mouth. He held out the remainder of the twist to the younger boy. John had never chewed tobacco, but now he felt obligated to accept the gift as a token of understanding between Ned and himself. He sat up, took the lump, and without hesitation, popped it into his mouth. The tobacco landed on the back of his tongue and, before he could gain control, it almost slid down his throat. He gagged and broke into a fit of coughing.

"Why don't you two give your durn jawbones a rest," someone said. "I'm waking up every five minutes over here and all I hear is a bunch of mumbling and farting and carrying on."

John suppressed several more coughs, his chest convulsing from the effort.

"Push it over between your cheek and your teeth like this," Ned whispered. He showed John his distended right cheek.

John shoved the sodden mass over to his cheek and immediately felt the soft tissue burning. For the next few minutes, he alternated between chewing, drooling, and spitting. The burning sensation spread quickly to his nostrils, his tongue, down his throat, and into the pit of his stomach. His head felt light and the world was slightly off balance. On his next effort to spit, he turned away from Ned and surreptitiously let the tobacco slip from his mouth. He lay back against his knapsack and closed his eyes, attempting to let everything internal settle down.

"That's a mistake, boy," Ned murmured.

"Taking that stuff in the first place was the mistake," John replied.

"Set up here and wash your mouth out with this water."

John ignored Ned until he felt something vile and nauseating in his stomach. He sat up abruptly, grabbed his canteen and rinsed his mouth.

"Glad to see you're such a reasonable fellow," said Ned. "You owe me some talk, anyway."

"What do you mean?" John asked sullenly.

"I mean that I told you about fighting and now I want you to tell me about something. It'll take your mind off your stomach."

John didn't answer.

"Tell me about Atlanta. I'm from a little old place down in south Georgia, and I don't know nothing about living in the city."

"What do you want to know?" John asked.

"Start off telling me about your family, and we'll see where she goes from there. What's your pa do for a living?"

"He's a surgeon at the Medical College."

"No wonder you talk like a lawyer."

John went on. "I have two sisters and a brother. Susan is thirteen, Charles is ten, and little Elizabeth is five. We live in the southwest part of the city only a few blocks from where my militia unit was camped when we joined y'all yesterday."

"What are they staying in Atlanta for? Them siege guns ain't making things hot enough for them?"

"It's obvious why my father is staying and if you knew my mother, it would be obvious to you why she's still there. She's a proud and independent woman. Her father was a railroad superintendent here back when Atlanta was called Terminus because that was where the railroad ended. Mother grew up with the city and when father tried to talk her into leaving a few months ago, she made a speech worthy of Ben Hill's best day in the legislature. We started taking in wounded over a year ago when the hospitals started filling up, so I can promise you that right now my family are all sleeping with aching backs and a full day's work ahead of them."

"What about this area? On the march you said y'all used to come out this way a good bit."

"Yes, a neighbor of ours, Mr. Kinship, owns several hundred acres of land out this way. Father and Charles and I used to come out here to a cabin with Mr. Kinship for several days at a time to hunt and fish."

"Where's the cabin?" Ned asked.

"About three or four miles southeast of here where Intrenchment Creek flows into the South River. It's odd to think that we haven't been down there in almost two years. Up until then I had gone there with the men for five years running. I wonder if the Yanks or some bummer hasn't burned it by now."

Ned turned away from John so that he had a better view of the terrain to the south. John lay back against his knapsack, idly searching the sky for the old, familiar constellations.

"Have you ever been to south Georgia?" Ned asked without turning around to John.

"No."

"You ever heard of Clinch County?"

"Clinch," John repeated. "That's around the Okefenokee Swamp, isn't it? I vaguely remember it from school."

"Clinch is a big county," Ned muttered, as if thinking aloud. "And if it ain't big enough, the Okefenokee is one more big swamp."

"Big enough for what, Ned?"

He looked around to see that no one listened to their conversation and moved his head to within inches of John's face.

"When that sun comes up and this army starts fighting another army I know of, I'm heading home. Clinch County is big enough to hide the likes of me and the likes of you, if you're of a mind to come. Even before I left home, I heard tales of men hiding out in the swamp. You know this area pretty good. If you could get us through the Yankees to that cabin on Intrenchment Creek, we could rest up and get some food for the trip. Once we hit the Ocmulgee, I could get us the rest of the way. We wouldn't have to go into the swamp right off— maybe never. I know a couple of places in the county we could go." Ned reared back on his haunches and sat looking at John. "Well, what do you say?"

John studied Ned's face for a moment. At the same time it was the face of a predator and of prey—a fox perhaps with his slender nose and narrow, almond eyes staring hungrily. The pale glare of the moon played tricks on John's eyes, and he thought he saw Ned wink. So that's it, he thought. This is Ned's idea of a joke. What a peculiar sense of humor! But Ned had not winked, so he sat expecting an answer.

"You're serious, aren't you?" John said.

"We could do it," Ned said. "It ain't gonna be easy, 'cause we'd have to stay away from our own people as well as the Yanks. It wouldn't take somebody long to figure out what two able-bodied men was doing heading south, but we could do it. I figure to get on the Ocmulgee and stay on it all the way down. The roads would be too risky to travel. It'll take a lot longer by river, twisting and turning like they do, but we got nothing but time. What do you say?"

"I haven't known you very long, Ned, but I don't think you're a coward. Why are you talking about desertion? How could you turn your back on your country? Don't you believe in what we're fighting for?"

"Believe in it?" Good God, boy, I don't even know what we're fighting for! You tell me. Am I fighting so's some rich bastard can keep him a bunch of slaves out in his fields? That ain't nothing to me. I ain't never owned no darkies, and I ain't got prospects of getting none. I ain't got no rich daddy."

"It's a lot more complicated than that, Ned. But the best reason for staying here and fighting is camped about four or five miles down this road. My family is back there in Atlanta. I grew up here and now my home is under attack. I intend to defend it."

"Well, that's one big difference between me and you," Ned said. "You're here defending your home, but I'm here, and my home is wide open. You're right about one thing though. I ain't no coward. I been with this army for almost a year now, and I figure I done my share of fighting. I stood between them Yanks and your home place all the way down from Chattanooga. I done froze my butt off up in them hills, and I've ate enough of this here red clay to last me a lifetime. You stick with it for a year and get enough gray backs crawling on you and start smelling like dead hog and dodging shot every other day, and then you come tell me about what you're fighting for. I'll be down in Clinch County when you're ready to talk."

Ned stood up and stretched. "It's finished, John. I've retreated all the way down from Tennessee with this army, and I can tell you, we're just wasting time, men, and money here."

"That's not true," John said. "If you've made up your mind to desert that's one thing, but don't try to justify your decision by saying that we're beaten."

John stood, expecting the verbal confrontation to escalate into a fight. When Ned turned toward John, his face was sad and worn, not belligerent.

"I don't expect you to believe me. If my folks was in Atlanta, I wouldn't want to believe that we're whupped either. But look at where we stand, John. Atlanta is almost surrounded by Yanks. We just got it good up on Peachtree Creek, and now we've marched clear to another side of Atlanta to fight some more. I know these men. They're gonna give those Yanks all they want, but all that means to me is that they got more guts than they got sense. We all hemmed in here, and them siege guns is playing hell with your city—just like Vicksburg. You ask around in a little while when they start getting up. I don't know if they'll level with you or not, but most of them know that Atlanta is gonna turn out just like Vicksburg. And they oughta know."

Ned took his knife from his pocket. Kneeling on one knee, he began to scar the red clay with the point of the blade. John heard the harsh scraping, but he couldn't see if there was a pattern emerging from the work.

"You do what you have to do, Ned, but I hope you think it over and change your mind. There won't be any coming back."

John lay back down, his head resting on his knapsack, and pulled his hat low on his forehead. The sound of Ned's knife working in the clay softened as the earth loosened around it. John felt his back relaxing, his legs melding to the hard earth. "If you run from this army, Ned, don't let me see you do it. I'll shoot you down."

III

The gray body of the beast lay undulant among the hills next to Intrenchment Creek south of the city. Below, a creek bed lay largely exposed, victim of the intense summer sun, which at seven a.m. already shimmered with waves of heat. A thread of water trickled past the soldiers' position, broadened from one bank of the creek to the other further downstream, only to narrow once more in the distance.

In the middle of the men on the hillside, a lean, young man of fifteen years sat studying the creek bed. He made careful mental notations of its composition—water level negligible, creek bed predominately rocky, dense vegetation on the low banks.

That will be his route, John Warren thought. He can travel the creek bed in the dark and even in the daylight there are plenty of places to hide in that brush. I have to maneuver behind him somehow if we move out to the north. Have to keep him in sight.

John sat on the flank of Smith's Militia next to the soldier he knew only as Dancing Bill. He was a slight man with thinning blonde hair. A perpetual smile was on his face, and his every movement was lithe. He seemed perfectly at ease, as if he were out with his friends for a stroll in the country and not on the verge of hell.

"Go easy on the water there, boy. We fixing to light out, and you ain't gonna get another shot at that branch water down there."

"Sir?"

"I say when we get to work here shortly, you gonna be spitting cotton, and you about to drain that canteen already."

John stared stupidly at Bill until the man's advice slowly registered. War would be thirsty work, and he had drunk almost half of his precious water supply. Before John could think of a way to get back to the creek, the order came to fall in, and the army moved north.

For the first mile the going was difficult. Many of the regulars had fought at Peachtree Creek north of Atlanta the previous day, then had marched fifteen miles to their present position at Intrenchment Creek. Now they fought a thick tangle of vines and brush back to the north only a few miles east of their previous line of march.

"Fore God, it does appear we are headed back the way we just came."

"Indeed we are, Sam," Bill said. "Ain't you seen them Yanks out-flank us enough to know what's going on? We have flanked way to the south and something tells me the church social is about over."

They struggled on through the woods until they reached a small valley. In the distance to the north they heard the thunder of the Yankee siege guns, thick in the early morning air. There was a brief hesitation along the line as the army split into two divisions. The first division continued north while John's division angled off to the north-east. Struggling on for another thirty minutes, they reached a cross-roads and took the Fayetville Road toward Decatur. Scarcely a quarter of a mile up the road, the column turned to the northwest and plunged into the wilderness once more.

The terrain gradually flattened, and marching became easier until the men bogged down along the margins of a pond. For better than an hour they fought against poor footing and the dense tangle of creepers and thickets until at last they arrived at the upper end of the pond.

Throughout the march John kept an uneasy watch on Ned. The older boy showed nothing of his intentions. He pushed on as if in silent desire for the fight that lay ahead. The regulars sensed the imminence of battle. Earlier everyone was intent on the difficulty of the march, avoiding the line where the undergrowth was thickest or the briars were rank. Now, as the troops reached the pond's apex, the mood was tense and withdrawn. The routine of past battles alerted some extra sense, which John and the rest of the militia lacked, and all of the regulars became lost in thought and last minute adjust-ments of equipment.

Just before noon the Babel of warfare swelled from the direction of Cleburne's division off to the left flank. The sharp report of the Yankees' rifles sliced through the soft puff of the Confederate muzzleloaders. The thick woods between the divisions muted the rallying cry from the adjacent division.

Dancing Bill nudged John. "Any minute now, boy. Be on your toes and stick to me. Don't get in no clinch with a Yankee or you're a dead man." Bill pointed toward the head of the millpond at a group of men on horseback. "Look there, John. I do believe that's General Walker and his staff."

"Which one's the General?" John asked. As if in reply, an officer astride a stallion in the center of the milling horses pushed his hat to the back of his head and raised a pair of binoculars to his eyes.

"That's him," Bill said, "The one looking through the eyepieces." As Bill spoke, the General's head snapped back, spraying the surrounding officers with a fine mist of blood. His hands and arms arched up and out in seeming exaltation, the field glasses tumbled into the air, and his body pitched back onto the horse's spine, bounced once, his feet catching in the stirrups. The horse was pulled back momentarily with the impact. The General bounced up, back down and then fell to one side off his mount.

"Good God," Bill yelled, "They got Walker!" Men along the line turned to Bill and John to see what was happening. They followed the line of Bill's gaze and saw a confusion of officers scrambling first away from a riderless horse, then dismounting and running over to the spot from which the horse had bolted.

The word of General Walker's death swept down the line east and west. As it passed from one company to another a restless stirring of men passed with it, a murmur punctuated by the clatter of weapons and the rising echo of curses and threats. Several men nearest the pond and the position of the dead officer began to fire into the undergrowth ahead, and the word passed quickly that these men had sighted the northern pickets who had killed Walker.

John watched the huddle of officers around the corpse and was surprised to see them recover so quickly. Within minutes a detail had the General on a makeshift stretcher, bearing him back beyond the northern reach of the millpond. A slender officer took charge, and soon couriers were rushing up and down the line, relaying messages to the company commanders. Within ten minutes of the General's

death, the order came to move out, and John's company stumbled
into Sugar Creek Valley.

Advancing, John realized he had forgotten about Ned in the confusion of the moment. He hurriedly checked his left where Ned had been
and was relieved to see him not fifty feet away, walking into the valley
slightly ahead of him. Maybe now he sees a reason for staying, John
thought. He surely had the opportunity to take off just now.

From the moment they left the pond it seemed to John as if
Sherman's entire artillery was turned against his division. It was even
more chaotic than Ned had said it would be. As the division meandered through the woods, picking its way around the thickest parts of
the undergrowth, the security John felt in their numbers dissolved
into pathetic patches of visible platoons here and there. He labored to
keep pace with Bill who followed closely on the sergeant's heels.
Gunfire popped all about him from the Yankee pickets and from the
return fire of his platoon. Panic swept over him, and he stumbled forward, fighting the desire to huddle behind a nearby oak until he could
create some order from the surrounding bedlam.

The men in his platoon fired and somehow reloaded as they
slouched from ravine to thicket, but John had yet to fire. He couldn't
see anything to shoot. The Yankee cannonading moved swiftly from
his distant right to a range terrifyingly close to his own position in the
line. The tops of huge pines snapped overhead sending a shower of
bark and needles down only a few feet from where the platoon
regrouped.

Already, not a hundred yards into the advance, men were hit and
lay moaning or crying out for aid. The combination of noon heat and
fear parched John's throat and soaked his shirt through with sweat.
His pack was a terrible burden and the canteen sloshed unmercifully
at his side. His breath came in short, ragged bursts. His eyes stung
from heat and smoke and from the fear that with a single soothing
blink, he might miss seeing the Yank who would shoot him dead.

Crouched low, stumbling through the soft debris of the forest floor,
John finally caught up to Bill and the others. He fell behind a fallen
sweet gum trunk next to Bill and sat with his back to the tree, gasping for breath. To his astonishment, Bill and some of the other men
chuckled at him.

"What's so funny?" he demanded.

"You are," Bill said. He slapped his knee and the easy laugh changed to a roar of gut-shaking intensity. "We ain't even near the Yanks yet, and you look like you been through half the war."

This set off a fresh wave of laughter from the men nearby. John stared incredulously about him, blinking to clear his eyes.

"If we aren't near them yet," he said through clenched teeth, "who's doing all that shooting at us?"

"Them's just the Yank pickets, boy," the sergeant said. "They're out in advance of the main line giving everyone fair notice that we're coming. We'll hit the main line in a few minutes here and then bidness will really pick up."

The sergeant's words sobered the men so that the laughter changed abruptly to little knowing grins at John, then subsided into solemnity.

"Oh God," John said to himself, "I thought that was the worst of it."

"How's your water, John?" Bill asked.

"I haven't drank any since Intrenchment Creek, so I still have about half a canteen."

"Not that water," Bill said. "Back off out there a bit and get some relief. From here on out there ain't going to be time for it."

Embarrassing as it was, John realized the wisdom of Bill's advice. He crawled back to an oak and stood up. Behind him other platoons were still advancing on the flanks. Just before he turned to rejoin the others, he saw Ned's platoon advancing to his right. Ned Worthington was not with them.

John scanned the woods behind his position, but he saw no trace of Ned. He grabbed his musket from where it leaned against the tree and started toward his right.

"Warren, where do you think you're going?" his sergeant demanded.

"I don't see Ned Worthington with his platoon, sarge. I was going to see what happened to him."

"It don't work that way, boy. We're fixing to move up. You can't go making calls on every platoon what's missing a man. Get your ass back over here."

John hesitated a moment, looking back and forth between the two platoons. He again started over toward the other group of men.

"You keep going and I'm gonna consider you a deserter. Boys, if he passes that stump, shoot him."

John held his ground and yelled to the other platoon, "Where's Ned Worthington?"

The men of Ned's platoon looked among themselves and seemed surprised that Ned was not with them.

"Semmes says he got hit back in the woods a ways."

"Did you see him shot, Semmes?" John asked.

"Yeah," replied another man, "I see'd it."

"Warren, I told you to get back over here. I mean right now!"

He wanted to question the man, but he knew that the sergeant meant business. John returned to his platoon and sat beside Bill. He continued to survey the area to the rear, but Ned was nowhere to be seen.

"Did he tell you he was deserting?" Bill asked. John was about to tell Bill of the previous night's discussion with Ned when the word came to advance. Crouched low, the men of the platoon left the safety of the fallen tree, heading north.

The thunder of the Yankee artillery increased. As they reached the base of a hill, Yankee rifles and muskets set up a furious counterpoint to the steady rhythm of the cannons high upon the hill. One moment John was running with the others, and the next he was flat on his stomach, struggling to retain his composure. Bill lay several yards to his left, firing methodically and rolling over on his back to reload.

"Stay with me, John," he yelled. "Don't just lay there. Give them what for and don't move up until I do."

A chill shivered John's shoulders and for a minute he could do nothing but stare alternately at the dry, dead grass beneath him, at the shroud of forest ahead of him, and at Dancing Bill. It seemed to John as if Bill was part of some grotesque ballet, which was occurring far away. The battle receded in the boy's mind until he had a sensation of passing from the scene altogether. The clamor of war faded all about him. The artillery was a dull throb in his chest, the whine of rifle fire became the irritating pitch of mosquitoes at his ears, and the rallying cry of a platoon was as old men mumbling reminiscences of war in the twilight.

Deny this and it will go away. The strangest thoughts coursed through him in disconnected bits of coherence. DENY. Peter denied knowing Him three times before the day broke. He swore that he wouldn't, but—Susan! My God, where is Susan? My sister is always there when I need someone to talk with. She would understand. DENY. Durn mosquitoes, driving me—Anoint with hog. That's better. They've quit whining in my ears now. The wounded. Oh God, the terrible running wounds come into our house by the hundreds. Where do they all come from? Father sends them from the hospital, and I must be about my Father's business! DENY.

We hunted not far from here. Back toward Intrenchment Creek is where I shot the deer. I waited the better part of an hour and across the creek a doe and her yearling came and drank softly. I waited, and then he came, gliding through the morning mist. My feet were cold and my finger was stiff on the trigger. I tore a jagged hole in his chest with the shot. He went to his knees and then rolled to his side. Cold water splashing about my ankles and my knees and up into my crotch, and then I was across the creek, fumbling at my side for the handle of the knife. He had kicked back from the stream and lay threshing in the sand and when I knelt beside him to cut his throat, he almost gored me. Those eyes! At once passive and defiant, in control even in the throes of death. And I hesitated. Oh Lord, I hesitated and fell back from him, astonished that he would still defy me, and it seemed that those eyes never left me as he choked to death on the bitter taste of blood. How dared I approach such dignity, such spirit? DENY!

John lay shivering in the heat and red dust in the battle for Atlanta.

"Ned," he yelled, "You can't run away from this. We can't deny it, Ned. I'll kill you!" He ran toward the distant hill. Twenty feet into the woods John fell, but he sprang to his feet, stumbled a few steps and regained his balance. The brush and saplings lashed at him until bloody stripes crisscrossed his grimy face.

After another forty feet or so, he fell again. This time he remained on his hands and knees, struggling for air under the oppressive weight of the heat and his backpack. Pushing himself up to a kneeling position, John realized that he was close to the main line of battle. A closer look ahead revealed several men crouched in the undergrowth facing north. He saw Bill and moved up behind him, making just enough noise to avoid startling him.

"What happened to you back there, boy? The way you were shaking and mumbling I thought you were having some kind of fit. Scared the hell out of the sergeant."

"It's in the blood," John lied. "My father has the same sort of attacks from time to time."

"Well, I'm pleased to know you ain't a coward," Bill said.

The sergeant motioned for them to move up. This time John stayed close to Bill and within a matter of minutes, he killed another human for the first time. Under other circumstances he would have been remorseful, would have stayed by the corpse to ponder the implications of such an act, and would have been violently ill. Here on the battlefield, however, he merely reloaded and moved on. He had escaped disaster once while wrapped in self-pity, but then he had been in a position of relative safety. Now the shot ran mortally close and salvation lay in movement.

Throughout the heat of the afternoon, the platoon worked on, unaware of the grand scheme of their actions, aware only that more Yankees were close at hand and had to be reckoned with.

Early in the afternoon a Yank artillery battery was captured on Bald Hill, and the battle looked as if it had swung to the Confederate advantage. Twice John's platoon advanced on the Yankee line, fighting hand to hand when there was no time to reload and fire. Each time the enemy repulsed their charge and each time the valley near Sugar Creek lay littered with the dead and dying men of each great army.

Late in the afternoon the enemy regained their artillery on the hill and by nightfall the order was given to fall back. The remains of John's platoon wandered once more through the darkness and solemn stillness of the night, a stillness broken occasionally by light skirmishing and the bass thunder of the Northerner's thirty pound artillery pieces.

At nine-thirty on the night of July 22, 1864, the men of Walker's Division of Hardee's Corps, exhausted and dehydrated, stumbled into the trenches which constituted the southeastern defense lines of Atlanta. For John Warren, the physical torment of battle was over. The nightmare of war was about to begin.

IV

He danced a light Irish jig along the ridge of hard-packed Georgia clay, his fists jammed against his hips, elbows jutting out to either side. The accompaniment came from somewhere deep inside him, for none of the men safe in the trench below possessed a musical instrument. Step, step, step, jump. Step, step, step, kick. Step, step, step, jump. Step, step, step, kick. Stroll, stroll, and kick to the left. Stroll, stroll, and kick to the right. Then his arms were outstretched, more for show than balance, and he jigged a delicate, full circle.

"Bill, quit that foolishness and get back down here," John Warren commanded. Dancing Bill gave no indication that he had heard. He continued the circle until he once again faced the enemy's line and resumed the gentle rhythmic patter of the dance.

"You're going to get your fool head shot off," John said. Still the dancer made no reply. After another minute or so gliding along the ridge, Bill slowed his movements gradually, then bowed low to his audience. To John's astonishment the Yankee pickets applauded generously, making no effort to fire upon the solitary figure within easy range of their rifles.

"Hey Reb," someone shouted from the distant cover of the forest, "Can you give us a clog?"

"Can I?" Bill yelled. "Are grits home-cooking?" Immediately he stood erect, dropped his arms to his sides, and began a quick shuffling of his feet. His right foot bounced from heel to toe while the left foot kicked forward, then backward, out to the side and then back again. He switched the rhythm effortlessly to his left leg and the right leg jerked about from the knee down, his right foot scraping lightly over the clay.

"He's got it working now," a Yankee yelled from the distance, and Bill acknowledged the accolade with an intricate step that took him

perilously close to the edge of the trench. Small chunks of clay tumbled onto John and several others until they yelled at Bill to watch his
step. Since the morning heat had already drenched his shirt and his
legs were cramping slightly, Bill used their protests as an excuse to
end the dance. He jumped into the air, turned full circle, and landed
in a kneeling position with his arms outstretched for the audience in
blue.

Both armies cheered while Bill took his bows. When the noise subsided, Bill yelled, "I know I can't pass the hat, boys, so my fee is this;
the next time we get together out in the field, don't shoot the Reb with
the red bandanna tied around his head. He's a dancing fool!"

"You got it, Reb," a voice replied. "By the by, how's about a little
bartering today? I haven't had a chaw in three days."

"Sorry boys," Bill said, "you done got close enough to Atlanta to
serious things up a bit. You were lucky to get the dance today."

"Then you try chewing on this!" A rifle shot kicked up the clay within inches of Bill's feet. Before the other shots hit the embankment, he
crashed down on John in the trench below. As the two of them fell to
the floor of the trench, a brief volley of fire set up between the two
groups of pickets. No one's heart was in the exchange and by the time
the two scrambled up for their weapons, the shooting was over.

"Sorry Yank bastards," Bill muttered. "There ain't no appreciation
for true talent these days. That's the first time they ever fired on me,
though."

"The first time they've fired on you? You mean to say you've done
this before?" John asked.

"Hundreds of times in the last few years," Bill said. "My dancing is
a real crowd-pleaser. I may take it up for a living after the war."

"It may take you down for a dying during the war," someone behind
John said. The regulars in the trench recognized the voice as that of
Colonel Talbot, and they snapped to attention.

"Private, you know that such fraternization with the enemy is con-
trary to orders, don't you?"

"Yes sir, I reckon I do," Bill said softly.

"Then I'll thank you not to endanger the lives of these men as well
as your own by such behavior as I just witnessed. Do you understand
me?"

"Yes sir," Bill said meekly.

"All right then. Gentlemen, your replacements on picket duty will be here in an hour. At that time you're to fall back to the second line of pickets a quarter of a mile to the northwest and from there, gain direction to your company's position in the defense line of the city. Is there a Private John Franklin Warren in this platoon?"

"Yes sir," John said. His stomach began to churn as he thought of his militia unit. Could this officer possibly consider his absence from his proper unit as desertion?

"Come with me, Warren."

John climbed from the trench and walked away from the others with the Colonel.

"Why aren't you with the militia, son?"

John's mouth was dry, his hands cold in the heat. "I was separated from my unit in the dark, night before last, sir," he said. "I attempted to find them, but by the time we stopped to rest, they were nowhere near this unit."

The Colonel looked at John intently as if weighing his brief testimony against his facial expression. "I'm finding that to be the case throughout the troops this morning. I've been looking everywhere for you, Warren. When you get back to the defense lines, you have orders to report to General Hood's headquarters at once."

The Colonel saw John wilt a little.

"No need to worry about the fact that you are missing from your unit. I hardly think the General will concern himself with one misplaced militiaman. I understand that Atlanta is your home."

"Yes sir."

"The General's headquarters is at City Hall Park near Decatur Street. Are you familiar with that section of the city?"

"Yes sir."

"Very well, Private, you're dismissed."

When the replacements arrived, John, Bill, and the others began the hike along Fair Street back to the city fortifications. The area through which they passed was on the western perimeter of the main fighting. The level of destruction stunned John. The area was sparsely inhabited, and of the few homesteads they saw, only one house still stood.

It was a substantial brick plantation home fronted by three massive columns. The front of the house was pitted with thousands of rounds of shot and the chimney was completely gnawed away by the onslaught. The grounds of the plantation were wasted as if locusts had ravaged the area, feeding on everything domestic. A wagon smoldered in the front yard, and a grand magnolia prostrated itself before the bomb crater that had brought it low.

Bill noted John's expression, and he felt bad for the boy. "Better get used to this, son," he said gently. "It doesn't get any better."

"How could it get any worse?" John asked.

"Well, for one thing, they've already got the bodies up."

The immediate area consisted of open land, some cleared for farming, but most leveled for the construction of fortifications and for the creation of open fields of fire. In the distance, black patches of woods, still burning, doubled the heat and haze of the July morning.

They soon reached the second line of pickets, stopped for a few minutes for directions to the remains of Walker's Division, and then moved on to the security of the city's perimeter. Within less than an hour they were inside the defense line with their division near the Oakland Cemetery. John stopped long enough for coffee and farewells.

"I suppose I'll be ordered back to the militia, so we'll make this goodbye, Bill. Thanks for taking me under your wing out there."

"It'd take one hell of a wing to get over you, John Warren. I ain't done that much no how."

"Good luck with the dancing. If there is anything left of Atlanta after this siege, I live on Mitchell Street near the park. You be sure and look me up."

"I'll do that, kid."

John gathered his musket and bedroll and began the walk to Decatur Street. The morning had turned off cloudy, dispelling some of the heat of the past few days. As John left the vicinity of the cemetery and turned left onto Decatur, he worried about what he might find at General Hood's headquarters. He knew that his mother had wanted him to stay at home, but he could not believe that she would beg for his return once he and his father had persuaded her to let him join the militia. She would respect their decision.

The shelling of the city over the past two days had been concentrated on Atlanta's center, dangerously close to their home, so as John walked, he tried to prepare himself for the worst news possible. Still, their lives had always been charmed. With honest labor had come all the attendant rewards. He would not believe that even war could touch them irreparably. He allowed the terrible scenery around him to fill his mind, to block the unthinkable.

The stench of death was everywhere. Fetid carcasses of horses and mules lined the street, foam-flecked and fly-covered, their eyes held open by death. Many of them had fallen from the heat—some had ghastly, blood soaked heads. An occasional mule-drawn wagon lumbered past the boy, carrying dead and dying soldiers into the city for whatever last hour ministrations were appropriate.

With Oakland Cemetery at his back, John reflected that most of these men were undoubtedly being transported in the wrong direction. Too often he walked past men in groups of two and three, men with relatively minor wounds bearing their more seriously wounded brethren to one of the field hospitals set up around Atlanta.

Approaching City Hall Park, he heard and smelled all that remained of the previous day's battle. His ears were assaulted by the pain of men enduring gunshot wounds and amputations, by the moaning of men insensible of their surroundings, aware only of their last, feeble protest against the terrible inevitability of darkness. He heard the confused, shrill babbling of doctors and nurses and transporters all attempting their work outside, under the worst possible conditions.

A short distance from where he entered the park, John saw a row of tents which he assumed were either those of the surgeons on duty or those of the headquarters staff. He was glad that he did not have to pick his way through the wounded to reach his destination, for even as he stood searching for his father, several men cried out to him for water.

Near the tents a group of officers huddled around a table where one man sat talking and stabbing his index finger at a map. Off to that group's left, two men sat alone in conference. One man was a civilian dressed in a harsh black suit. The other man was General John Bell

Hood, for almost a week now the Commander of the Army of Tennessee, C.S.A.

The General sat stiffly, his right hand gripping the arm of the chair to provide balance for the legless side of his body. His left arm lay paralyzed and useless in his lap. The civilian sat with his back to John and so did not see him as he approached. Unsure of the proper manner in which to approach a General, John stood at attention and said nothing. Hood looked up.

"What is it, soldier?" he asked.

"Private John Warren reporting, sir."

The civilian turned suddenly to look at him. "John, thank God you're alive!" He was a round, little man with huge jowls and a fringe of rusty-gray hair which encircled the back of his head from ear to ear. He jumped up and strode over to the boy, extending his right hand. "It certainly took them long enough to find you!"

"Good morning, Dr. Westmoreland. I've been separated from the militia the better part of a day now, so I've been difficult to locate." He looked at the General. *My God*, John thought, *I've already admitted that I haven't been with my unit during the battle!*

"John, I know you must be intimidated by the General, but I'm still Uncle Josh to you." The doctor turned to General Hood. "This is the young man I asked you to locate for me. His father and I have worked together for almost twenty years now."

"Private Warren." The General acknowledged him with a nod of his head. "Doctor, I believe you have business with the private. Will you be so kind as to ask my staff to join me now?"

"Yes, of course. I'll see you at three this afternoon then?"

"Yes, at three."

"This way, John," the doctor said. They walked past the officers, and Dr. Westmoreland relayed the General's summons to a young aide on the edge of the group. The doctor's pace was deliberate as they skirted the northern side of the park by way of Decatur Street. To the young man of fifteen, filled with the adrenaline of battle still, it was a maddening pace. To the doctor it was an attempt to prepare the boy emotionally for what the doctor felt sure he already knew. As they walked, each avoided the other's eyes. Doctor Westmoreland spoke first, his speech as deliberate as his step.

"The General tells me that things did not go well out east of the city."

"Uncle Josh, why are we leaving the park without seeing father?"

"He says that General Hardee failed to execute properly last night's flanking maneuver to the southeast, allowing the federals to escape entrapment on their left flank."

"Father is too fine a surgeon to be at the hospital when all the action is out here. I realize that he is terribly busy, but I must see him."

The old man thought for a moment. "Your father cannot be disturbed now, John." he said. "I want you to look at this section of the city for a moment and while we walk, I want some information about yesterday's battle. When you have had time to calm down a bit, I'll take you to your father. Will you humor an old man?"

"Yes sir," John said quietly.

"Thank you. I suppose you recognized the siege guns for what they were when you heard them. You see the results they obtained there at Erdmann's store and elsewhere along the railroad tracks."

The city around them swarmed with activity as people hurried in and out of those stores still standing on Decatur Street. They stepped cautiously amid the rubble that spilled out into the street from the shattered remains of a dozen buildings. Wagon traffic slowed to a crawl at the corner of Decatur and Ivy Streets where the back wheels of a wagon had slid into a bomb crater. The wagon sat at such an angle that the owner had been forced to unhitch the team and now several men strained to push the wagon back onto the street.

At the sight of the partial destruction of his beautiful city, John felt nauseated. The silent acknowledgement of the tightening in his stomach made him realize that he had not eaten in over twenty-four hours. He was easy prey for the hunger and fatigue, the anger and sadness that stalked him. His pace slowed to match that of the doctor, each step an agony to his body and spirit. Although Dr. Westmoreland seemed preoccupied with observing the destruction about them, John knew that the old physician was gauging his strength as he had done with a lifetime of patients.

"What is your judgment of the battle, John?" the doctor asked, motioning the boy south on Ivy Street. "Is General Hood justified in his criticism of General Hardee's maneuver?"

There was no doubting the doctor's intended destination now. The turn onto Ivy took them away from the business district and along the most direct route to the Warren home on Mitchell Street.

"I suppose that there are good enough reasons for the failure of our flanking movement," John said. "It was, after all, a night march over terrain that was unfamiliar to most of the men and probably all of the officers. Most of the regulars were exhausted from the battle up on Peachtree Creek, and I expect that slowed us down so we couldn't travel as far south as desired. And then I'm sure there were other problems of which I'm unaware. For example, General Walker's Division, of which I was part, left Intrenchment Creek headed toward Decatur that morning. For some reason, the General turned us north at Sugar Creek instead of staying on the road to the northeast. First we wandered into a bog around Terry's Millpond and then about the time we made solid ground, we ran straight into federal pickets. I watched the General fall."

"Good Lord, didn't the man have a guide who knows that terrain?"

"Yes sir, he had a guide. That's why I say that there must have been some unusual circumstances. It was pretty late in the morning by the time we met the pickets, so maybe the General thought we had them flanked, and he was trying to save time."

They were only a block from Mitchell Street. Ahead of them on the corner of Ivy and Mitchell, John saw the smoldering ruins of the Lee home. He felt his stomach burning. His house was only one block west of there.

Doctor Westmoreland noted John's expression when he saw his neighbor's house. "So, what is your conclusion, John?"

"The difficulties of the march were surely taken into consideration beforehand. In a military campaign the results are all that matter. General Hardee was given an objective and the manpower to achieve that objective. He failed. General Hood's criticism is justified."

They reached the corner and stood looking at the remains of the Lee home. Neither of them spoke for several minutes.

"That was quite a dispassionate evaluation, John. You seem to understand the views of warfare that your father advocated in our discussions of the past three years. Tell me, boy, are you in complete sympathy with the notion that results are all that matter in a military campaign?"

John was finding it increasingly difficult to be patient with the doctor. He knew what was down the street and the burden of that knowledge was on his face.

"John, you said you would humor an old man. Answer my question please."

"Yes sir, I do believe that. Men are committed to battle with the foreknowledge that a great many of them will die, so human life must be secondary to the achievement of a military goal. General Johnston failed to stop Sherman from Tennessee down to the Chattahoochee. Now General Hood, through Hardee, has failed, and our Atlanta is paying the penalty. How could I believe otherwise?"

"You can believe otherwise by looking beyond the results. It's a difficult task, but we do it or there is no tomorrow for us. You must know by now that I'm no longer speaking strictly of military campaigns. But, they are a part of life, and if you believe that results are all that matter in war, you may believe the same applies to every aspect of living."

"And you're saying you don't believe that results are all that matter?"

"I'm saying that there is much life to be lived on either side of some arbitrary result in a person's span of years. Just because one battle is lost, an army doesn't despair of winning a war. So it is in the rest of life. When one part of your life passes away, you must overcome the loss with the desire to see what lies ahead. You know what lies down this street, don't you, John?"

Their eyes met, tears welling up to the bottom of John's lids. All he could do was to nod affirmatively.

"Your father wasn't at the park or at the hospital during the siege, son. He was at home. They are all dead."

V

John Warren dreamed.

"What is wrong with you?" a voice asked.

"I don't know," John said. "I don't think anything is wrong. No, I'm all right."

"But you aren't," the voice replied. "Something is wrong, or you wouldn't be here—not in this condition. Now answer me! What terrible thing have you done to deserve this?"

The voice came to John out of a profound darkness. It was masculine, harsh, and demanding. The boy could not identify the speaker by the sound of his voice. Nearby, water coursed and broke like waves on a desolate shore. John tried to relate his position to that of the speaker and that of the water, but the darkness confused him and his perspective shifted continually.

"I've done nothing wrong," he insisted. "Why am I being treated this way? Who are you? Show yourself to me!"

The sound of the rushing water increased until it nearly obscured the voice.

"What have you done, John?"

Light moisture, as if from wisps of wind-driven surf, covered him and then quickly evaporated, leaving his hands and arms and his face salty and taut. With his arms extended, he searched the blackness about him, attempting to catch the voice by the throat and demand an explanation. He wanted to fall on human shoulders, to feel compassionate arms encircling him in assurance that he had done nothing wrong. As he inched forward, the water surged at his legs and staggered him. Twisting left and then right, he fought for balance, regained it briefly, but finally fell. He lashed at the water in panic, calling out for help as he went down.

Something soft brushed his arm, wakening him. The grim labor of the past two days had drained him physically, mentally, and spiritually, so that now he lay face down, stared dumbly at his arm, and wondered who was rousing him in the night. Something scratched the rubble near him and rubbed against his legs and his torso. Annoyed, John raised his head to protest the rudeness of these interruptions of his rest. A quick movement to his right startled him. As his mind cleared, horror and revulsion gripped his throat.

"Oh God," he whispered. Thrusting himself to a kneeling position, John groped about for his musket. His fingers scraped over pieces of brick and charred wood, so he hurled whatever came to hand at the intruders around him. The rats scattered.

He took no notice of their retreat, but clawed wildly among the debris for fresh ammunition, spinning wildly on his knees, firing in all directions, crying and ranting at the enemy. Finally, he fought madly against no opposition. The dirt and brick dust rose in a column above him, caking his face and arms, burning his eyes until he could no longer see for the tears.

The dust rose in a great plume and fell to the earth again, covering five makeshift shrouds. John collapsed, gasping for breath in the thick heat and dust.

The rats rested in the shadows of the ruined house, the wounded tending to themselves as runners moved among the troops, assessing the losses. Officers grouped here and there to discuss the set back, to assign blame, and to plan the strategy for the next assault. All were astonished that the enemy could fight with such intensity, and they began to wonder if the campaign might not drag on much longer than had been anticipated. Some favored the abandonment of the campaign altogether in the belief that easier conquests lay all about them in this ruined section of the city.

The commanding officer dispatched scouts to survey the field of battle and to check enemy strength and deployment. Three rats lumbered from the darkness toward John. Hearing their advance, he forced himself to a kneeling position again. The rats eyed him warily.

"You're just out of my range. Come a little closer." Two of the three obliged him, and John let fly another handful of brick. They wheeled into the shadows with their report. Moments later John heard the rats retreat across the ruined brick and wood which only days before had been his home. He rolled to his right and again lay fighting for breath in the summer night.

A blood sun hung just above the horizon in the east, when the first explosion rocked John awake. He clawed at the earth for objects to throw until the second and third explosions made him aware that the siege guns were again shelling the city. Dropping the useless ammunition, he crawled a few feet to the nearest corpse and flopped over it protectively. After the next few explosions, he realized that the cannons were concentrated on a section of the city north of the railroad.

When he pushed himself up from his mother's body, John saw what the rats had accomplished during the previous night. He twisted away from the sight, retching violently until there was nothing left to heave. Averting his eyes from the corpse's legs, John pulled the blood-spotted shroud back into place. Crawling over to what had once been his sister Susan, he replaced a sheet over the upper part of her body. The other three shrouds were untouched by the night foragers. John walked to a well at the back of the yard and lowered the bucket. The odor was less severe there, and the cool water washed the taste of vomit from his mouth.

The sun was well above the horizon now. It was drained of blood, the same pale tormentor it had been yesterday when Dr. Westmoreland brought him home—rather, brought him to the remains of home.

He sat with his back against the well house, mentally rebuilding the rambling two story brick home that his grandfather had designed and built. He remembered the high pitch of the roof, the ornate carvings that decorated the gables, the row of windows running from one corner to the other, the wide cement steps descending to the backyard.

It was the underside of the house that he recalled best. The home sat on columns, creating a three-foot high crawlspace. For the Warren children, this was a natural habitat. John had his own sanctuary up near the front of the house behind the lattice of the front porch. The other children shunned his place after hearing John's stories of gigantic spiders and snakes.

He spent many summer days there in the cool of the crawlspace, yet not there, but pacing the halls of a Danish castle with another boy faced with the death of his father, a king. Or in agony for the love of a Capulet and he a Montague. Could those days have been only a few years gone? It seemed like another lifetime in another place.

He put the bucket aside and stood. That other time was too fine for this terrible life, and he had work to do. With the shovel Dr. Westmoreland had left for him, he began digging the first of five graves in the garden spot adjacent to the well. Though the morning was hot and humid and his hands were raw, the work progressed rapidly. The earth was pliant from the years of gardening, and John dug each grave only to a depth of three or four feet.

He stopped to rest twice. The first time the sun stood directly overhead, so he crawled underneath the one remaining corner of the house and attempted to eat some bread and salt pork that the doctor had left him. The odor of death was so strong in the heat that it was all he could do to choke down a few bites.

He almost regretted having persuaded the doctor to allow him to bury his dead in solitude. Given the three laborers the doctor had hired to dig the Warren family from the remains of their home, the burial would have been finished by noon. His family would have lain in more secure graves. But John felt so strongly that only he should lay them to their rest that Dr. Westmoreland finally relented.

The second time John stopped digging, he fell asleep in the shadow of the well housing. He dozed fitfully for a half-hour until he felt water surging against his legs, threatening to topple him. He heard the voice asking over and again, "Why are you here? What have you done?"

This time, before John could protest, the wave was upon him, and he lost his footing. Swirling under the onrushing tide, his arm scraped a coarse surface. He twisted his body and dug the tips of his fingers into the surface, but water pulled him up and away from the land. He felt that it was hopeless to fight back. He was disoriented in the profound darkness so that further struggle might only take him further from the land.

Let go, he thought. Let it take me where it will. "What have you done? Why are you here?" Even under the water the hateful words sounded in his mind, enraging him so that once again he lashed out, seeking to survive if only for the sake of being alive and resistant.

As he labored for his life, a world of remembrance contended for his attention. Memories and ideas flashed across the surface of his brain, like lightning vivid upon a barren, wet landscape. A deer with a gaping wound in his chest thrashed on blood-spattered sand. A soldier danced maniacally on heaped clay above a trench. His mother kneeled in the soft earth of the garden and pushed a strand of hair out of her eyes with the back of her hand. His father and Uncle Josh stood in the library of his home with the Governor and several other men listening to John's opinion of the progress of the war. Wounded soldiers littering the back yard of his home moaned and called for water in the night. Rats peered at him from dark places. "They are all dead." A man bounced once on the spine of a horse and toppled sideways. John was in a cool, dark place reading when he heard thunder rumble in the distance. No, not thunder, but monstrous cannons and then the house shook violently and then it crashed down around him, and then he dug and dug, and then the deer looked at him and the rats stared at him from dark places, and the men in the library observed him distantly, and his mother laughed gently, and his eyes met those of his Uncle Josh, standing at the Lee home and saying, "They are all dead" and the General falling from a horse glanced at him, and the dancing man stared down at him in the trench, and five corpses stared at him through their shrouds and then in rapid succession: his laughing mother, the deer, the General, the rats, the men, the dancer, the thunder, the house, the garden, the digging, the darkness, the water, the voice, the wounded, and then faster: deer, dancer, rats, darkness, men, wounded, thunder, digging, garden, mother, house, General, voice, water, then slowing: The voice, the water, the voice, the water, the voice, the water, the voice, "Dead, all dead"...DENY!

"John," a voice called. "Wake up, son. You're having a bad dream. John, can you hear me?"

The voice was finally within his grasp, and John seized it viciously at the throat.

"I've done nothing," he yelled. "Why are you torturing me? Leave me alone!" His grip tightened on the throat. He had every intention of choking the last bit of air from his accuser, when he awakened and found himself staring into the shocked eyes of Dr. Westmoreland. The old man sank to his knees and almost lost consciousness. John relaxed his grip and drew back as if in fear. The doctor pitched forward onto his elbows and knelt, gasping for air.

"Oh God! Uncle Josh, are you going to be all right? I'm sorry. I—" John covered his face with his hands and slumped back against the well house.

"It's all right," the old man wheezed. "Be all right in a minute." Slowly the color returned to his face, and he regained enough oxygen to sit up. "Were you dreaming about your family, John?"

John could not speak. His chest heaved with the effort of crying, and he couldn't bring himself to face the old man. He shook his head from side to side.

"I'm going to be fine, John. Just try to calm yourself. You didn't know what you were doing, son."

The doctor's throat ached from the effort of talking. Shaking, he stood and lowered the bucket into the well. He tried to drink, but finding it painful to swallow, he wet his handkerchief and knelt to wash the boy's sweating, tear-stained face.

"I want you to go with me to the Medical College. I'll hire someone to finish up here."

He still couldn't bring himself to face the doctor, so he closed his eyes and shook his head again. "I'm all right now, sir. I'll not have them buried by strangers."

"You are not all right. You're exhausted and dehydrated and very close to a state of shock. You're physically, mentally, and emotionally spent, and I insist that you enter the hospital now."

John pushed up from the wellhouse and stood facing the doctor. "You underestimate me, Uncle Josh. I'm tired, but I'm nowhere near through with what I intend to do. I'll not be going to your hospital." He turned from the doctor, found the shovel, and resumed digging the final grave.

Dr. Westmoreland watched him for a few minutes, suppressing the rebuttals that came to mind. He knew that John was like his father to the extent that further persuasion would be fruitless. While John worked with the shovel, the doctor secured the shrouds about each of the five bodies. Neither the doctor nor the boy attempted further conversation until each grave was occupied.

Finally they stood beside the plot which contained John's father. "Surely now you've done enough, John. It's bad enough you'll have to remember them this way. Let's say a word of prayer, and I'll get a man to finish the work."

"Yes Doctor, let's say a prayer! Here, you stand back there, and I'll pray." John pushed him back from the grave and grabbed the shovel. He jammed it viciously into the mound of dirt beside the hole and threw the first bit of dirt onto the corpse of his father.

"Our most gracious heavenly Father, we commend these souls to your most benevolent and tender mercies." Again he jabbed the shovel into the clay and flung the dirt into the grave. "May you attend them with more care in heaven than you did on earth."

"John, that's quite enough! You don't know what you're saying." Dr. Westmoreland moved to take the shovel from the boy. They struggled until John shoved him to the ground and resumed covering his father.

"Thank you, dear God, for the chastening of our bodies and souls made possible by the advent of war in our land. We give thanks for the slaughter of our people, for the shells that rain down upon our city, day and night, destroying men, women, and children alike. We know we are unworthy of your love and protection here in this life, so crush us one and all that we may be lifted up on high to the glory of your kingdom in the clouds."

He worked in a frenzy now, the dirt falling over three of the five graves, which held the remains of his family. John was so preoccupied with his work that the doctor was able to stun him with a blow to the head. John sprawled on the mound of dirt, insensible for a moment as the doctor attempted to take the shovel.

"It's your Uncle Josh, boy. Listen to me, John. I didn't want to hit you, but you don't know—" John lashed out with the back of his hand and sent the old man reeling back from the edge of the grave. The doctor was unconscious before he hit the ground.

"*What have you done, John Warren? Why are you here?*" *The voice was insistent and louder than ever before.*

"Damn you, I've done nothing to deserve this! Just leave me alone. I've done nothing, I tell you!"

The boy reclaimed the shovel and stabbed furiously at the dirt. He went about his work filling the graves, totally unaware that Dr. Westmoreland was anywhere near him. He ignored the heaving in his chest and the streaming tears in his eyes and kept at the grim labor of burying his dead, yet the voice pursued him. *"Why? Why, John Warren? What have you done?"*

Still he shoveled, cursing the voice, then pleading with it for peace, then cursing it again. DENY.

"What have you done? Dead, all dead. I'm telling you, you did something terrible! What is it?" Blood from the deer, blood from the General, blood from his mother's exposed leg, gnawed by the rats.

He couldn't hear himself scream. Seconds before he began, an explosion ripped through the air, obliterating all other sound. A second explosion echoed the first, a third re-echoed them both and then another explosion and another and another coursed into the heart of Atlanta. John was past knowing or caring that the Yankee artillery was once again pounding the city's interior in the vicinity of the railroad and the city hall.

"John, you must help me." The voice was so weak and tremulous that it was doubtful that it could have been heard on the most peaceful of summer nights. For John Warren, the personal horror, the accusatory voice and rushing water were almost quieted by the horror of the siege guns. His breath came in ragged, rasping torment as the inner demons hushed. As if spellbound, John relaxed his grasp on the shovel and gazed in awe at the flames rising in the sky north of him.

Dr. Westmoreland labored to push himself to his hands and knees. His head was still spinning from the blow. Through filmy eyes he saw John silhouetted against the blaze to the north, his head tilted to the sky, his arms extended upward, fists clenched at heaven. If he made a sound, it was obscured by the concussion of the next shell from the artillery.

With the last of his strength, the old man crawled toward John. When he judged to be a few feet from the boy, the old man pushed back to his knees. "For the love of God, John, I'm going to faint. You have to—" He looked up in time to see John Warren stumbling across the ruins of his home, heading down Mitchell Street southeast of the city. Josiah Westmoreland's body fell silently to the earth.

*   *   *   *

"Hey boy, where do you think you're going?" The voice, stentorian and rough, came from behind him. He made no sign that he heard, but continued walking to the south of the city's defense line.

"James, wake up. Come alive there, man!"

The sentry's companion stirred reluctantly and looked about him in the darkness. "What is it? Yanks?"

"I don't know. Some big feller just walked by here like he was out for a Sunday stroll. Didn't even act like he seen me. This way. Come on!"

James grabbed his rifle, and the two men picked their way through the undergrowth following the sound of John Warren. When they were within ten yards of him, the sentry motioned James off to the right. He turned to the left and by listening to John's progress through the thick growth of brush and vines, made a broad enough circle to position himself in the boy's line of travel. Seconds later, James joined him, but the sentry motioned him back out of sight. As James retreated behind an oak tree, John Warren broke into the clearing occupied by the sentry.

"Hold it right there, boy," he said, raising his rifle to hip level and pointing it at John. He was tensed, ready to fire, as he expected the boy to react quickly, perhaps violently, to his command. He was intimidated by the boy's size. John gazed passively at him.

"Who are you, and just where do you think you're going?" the sentry asked.

"I'm going away from here. I'm going right through there," John said tonelessly, indicating the southeast.

"Like hell you are. I ain't letting nobody pass my part of this here defense line."

"I'm going through there," John repeated and started to walk past the sentry. The man hesitated just long enough for John to reach him, so that in order to stop the boy, he grabbed at his arm. John's right hand flicked across his body, catching the sentry's wrist and twisting his arm behind his back.

"James, he's got me!" The man swung his rifle behind him trying to hit the boy. John grasped the wrist with both hands and jerked the man's arm diagonally across his back until he felt the shoulder dislocate and heard the articulation of arm and shoulder snap. The sound was almost inaudible above the sentry's scream.

James stepped from his hiding place and drew a bead on John. As he fired, John jerked the sentry's arm up again, forcing him up on his toes, and John fell to his left. The sentry would have fainted from the pain had not his friend's shot pierced his skull just below his left cheek. The sentry fell onto the soft mat of leaves in the clearing and convulsed. John crawled from the clearing and crouched in the darkness, waiting for James.

"Albert! Oh God, Albert, I've killed you. Oh, no! Albert!"

The sound of rifle and musket fire echoed through the woods, as other pickets took their cue from James, relieved for the opportunity to shoot at the shadows which had assumed human form and had tormented them throughout the evening.

John turned in the direction he had told Albert that he would take. Crouched close to the ground, he weaved from tree to tree, trying to gauge the density of shot from one area to the next. He had run only a hundred feet through the tangle of woods when the shooting diminished to the point that he could travel upright again.

The encounter with Albert and James had occupied his mind for a few minutes, but now that they were behind him, the old images threatened to return. Something about a deer bleeding in the early morning sun, something about water and a voice from the night, calling to him, "John, you must help me" and "They are all dead" and "What have you done? Why are you..."

No! That was the one he must deny, the voice that tortured him so. He tried to concentrate on his surroundings. Where was he headed? Which direction was away? He had come this far from the city by instinct, but now his mind demanded from him some logical explanation. He stopped walking and knelt on one knee beside an eroded ravine to work out a solution.

South is the only logical direction, he thought, south, away from both armies, away from the remains of Atlanta. For the first time in what felt like years, he thought of Ned Worthington. Of course, the river! Ned had been right about that. It seemed that Ned had been right about many things. Travel would be more difficult on the river than on a road, but it would be much safer, too. And it would give him time to think. Time to be selective in his thinking.

Where would Intrenchment Creek be from here? As he stood to get his bearing, John heard a rustling in the undergrowth to his right. He crouched down again, straining to see who or what approached.

"I'll find him, Albert. I'll find him and when I do, he's a dead man." This second sentry was of medium build and a head shorter than was John. James reached the ravine and paused. John sat quietly, hoping the man would choose to cross the gully or else to travel its margin away to the west. The full moon crested the trees, and John saw the rifle protruding from James' hips. He tried to will the man away from him, an effort that seemed to work in reverse. The sentry stepped back and turned toward John. He seemed to look directly at him, and John went cold in the July heat.

His mind commanded him to run, but something held him to the spot as James approached. John was acutely aware of himself, of the cramped ache in his hips, of the overwhelming rumble of his breathing. James was only a few yards away. He was walking cautiously now, slowly, as if certain that his prey was nearby, but he gave no indication that he saw John. He didn't see him until the boy lunged from the darkness and was on him. As John's shoulder struck his chest, the man fired, but too late. The impact sent both of them careening over the edge of the ravine, the rifle twirling far out beyond them, preceding them to the crusty bottom of red clay fifteen feet below.

James hit the side of the embankment with John sprawling on top of him. Their momentum carried John over the man's head so that he hit bottom first, James sliding the rest of the way down on his back. Both of them were on their feet instantly, doing a mad, spinning dance in search of the weapon. John gave up the fruitless search first and plowed back into his adversary with his right shoulder. They fell against the wall of the ravine.

As John pushed up, the lower half of his face went numb from a right jab. His lower lip felt pulpy and his teeth hurt. He recoiled and James was all over him with short, telling jabs to his head. It was too fast, and he couldn't recover. Confidently now, the older man pursued him across the floor of the ravine, pounding John's head and chest until he drove the boy back against the far embankment. John stumbled and fell to a sitting position, widening a gap between the two of them. In James' eagerness to fill the void, he lost his footing and fell to his knees in front of John. For a second they sat staring at each other.

James cocked his arm to jab again at the blood-soaked face in front of him, but two huge hands at his throat arrested his motion. His right fist struck John a slight, glancing blow. The boy rocked back, pulling the man with him and then abruptly shot forward to a standing position, retaining all the while his grip around his thin neck. James beat furiously at the boy's forearms. John gritted his teeth, and though pain shot through his head and though blood and sweat blurred his vision, he pressed his thumbs tightly into the man's trachea. James gagged and fought to suck the least bit of air into his bruised throat. He threw three more punches at John's battered face. Each blow jerked the boy's head slightly and sent another deep spasm of pain to his brain.

Enraged, John bent at the knees, pulled his hands and James' head close to his chest, and suddenly thrust his legs up and his arms up and out. He felt the soft, ridged pipe collapse beneath his thumbs, heard the final strangling exhalation of air. The head slumped against his hands and the weight of the body, recoiling in air, dragged John to the red floor of the ravine.

He crawled away from the corpse and sat with his back to the dirt wall, his legs trembling spasmodically, his breathing labored and tinged with the taste of blood. He closed his eyes and willed his mind to be still, to drift beyond his will, until it no longer labored with acceptance or rejection of any thought or image. He longed for release, yet not the fearful unknown into which he had sent James.

John's mind linked itself insatiably to the pain of his body and would not loose itself. His lips were torn and swollen. His teeth throbbed and each beat of his heart pulsed around the ravaged nerves. His left jaw ached and as blood accumulated in his mouth and he turned to expel it, the force of spitting sped the raw ache up into his temples and along a line encircling the back of his skull.

He opened his eyes and sweat-diluted blood stung them. Reaching up to wipe his brow, John grazed the tip of his nose. The resulting pain caused him to cry out, and he knew that his nose was broken. The laughter started as a faint quiver of his stomach, rising quickly to his throat and emerging as a series of panting noises, scarcely recognizable as human laughter.

"What else?" John said. "What is your pleasure?" Every part of his face reacted in pain from the effort of speaking. Still, he persisted. "You've pretty well taken care of John Warren. Why not finish him off? Come on now, what is it you want next?" Finally the effort of talking was too much.

John stood and stumbled to the corpse he had made from a man. He rolled it onto its back and saw that a cartridge belt encircled the thing's chest. John grabbed the shirt and pulled the corpse to a sitting position. When it tipped to the right, John lost his grip and the body slipped back to earth, this time lying on its side. The boy maneuvered the cartridge belt up the back and over the head. When he reached over to roll the corpse face up again, the belt came free. John saw an empty knife scabbard at the body's side.

"Oh, you lost your knife when we fell down here, didn't you, James? Well, you just stay right here, and I'll see if I can't find it. And the rifle, too. I'll see if I can't find it." The weapons were easily located, now that they had no immediate use for either the man or the boy.

John looked up and studied the southern constellations for a minute. The brightness of the late July moon obliterated much of the sky. Holding the knife and the rifle in his left hand, he gently raised his right hand to trace the new contours of his nose. "Nothing is quite the way it used to be," he said.

He tucked the knife blade under his belt and walked east until the ravine narrowed and its uppermost edges were on a line with his pelvis. He turned to his right, placed the rifle on the jagged lip of the ravine, and thrust himself up onto the harsh level of earth. He picked up the rifle and squatted there for a moment. Through a thin fringe of trees, he saw a plateau extending beyond the limits of his vision, glimmering softly in the pale light from above. In the distance to the north-east, he heard the meditative, rolling thunder of General Sherman's siege guns. Despite the destructive intent, the guns' insistent bass notes melded with the quiet meadow before him to create in John a feeling of tranquility.

This was the way he must go. That which lay behind him was of the past. Somewhere in the meadow before him Intrenchment Creek wandered down the gentle slope to the south. It meandered, ever turning southward, until it joined with other creeks to form the South River which wandered further to the southeast until it found its brothers, the Yellow and the Alcovey. It was the way John Warren must go. At that point where the three rivers, peacefully wandering above, became as one, they clashed, as brothers often do. From their conflict, from the mingling of their life's blood, from the suffering and the agony of rebirth, trinity became unity. And the great unity flowed on to the south. It was the way John Warren must go.

VI

Gray Hampton's Journal
Sunday, July 24, 1864

Impoverished is the land that is unriven. Ignorant of rivers, it lies barren and desolate, land turned in upon itself, unyielding, defiant, and dead. Unwilling to relinquish a part of itself to water, it forfeits the gain which is made possible only through suffering and sacrifice. For the land that gain may be trivial, unworthy of submission. For man, it is paramount in this life.

The man who cannot persuade the earth to yield to water exists in waste places, and such an existence strips his spirit leafless, leaving him as barren as the soil. There is no solid foundation on which to build, and so he is driven before the harsh and hateful winds of the unyielding land, the unriven land. The land molds the man in its own image. It eradicates his past, negates his present, and vanquishes his future.

Man seeks the riven land. He strives for that region which humbles a part of itself to water, the element of paradox. To the earth, water is at once the great destroyer and the great creator. Where earth and water meet, there earth must suffer loss. In the constant movement of water, the earth must yield more and more of itself. Nowhere is this destruction and creation more apparent than on a river.

A river has a life of its own. No two have the same personality. Like a man, a river consists of two beings in one form, part physical, part spiritual. The river is what it is because of the terrain surrounding it and because of its own internal qualities. Like a man, a river is defined by its limitations, its boundaries. The Mississippi, broad-shouldered and powerful, is not the Suwannee, slim-hipped and delicate as a lady.

Yet all rivers, like all people, have more in common than they have in diversity. They are paradoxical by nature, ever the same in appearance, ever changing from flood stage to the summer's drought. They are wild and free, yet in an abstract sense, a river is set within boundaries that are seldom broached in the march of time. The exorbitant rains of spring may swell a river beyond its limitations, but then it loses its identity for a time, and despite its basic nature, the current at the heart of things, becomes more of a lake than a river. It is due to this basic internal strength, this urge to move, that the river soon reinstates its self, and becomes once more that which the external world would, but could not completely, absorb.

An ocean is too extreme in size for the individual to grasp. Oceans are for those who band together and merge their identities with the herd. A lake provides for today, but lies docile in the sun, demanding nothing of itself or any man. A creek is the river of our childhood and loses its majesty when we ascend to manhood. A man seeks a river.

Poor is the man who senses no river flowing within his soul.

     s   *s*   *s*   *s*

The water stretched around him as far as he could see. At first he thought he was stranded on an island in the middle of some ocean. As the light of the east encroached upon the darkness, it revealed to him in silhouette a towering tree line. The trees swayed gently across his field of vision. Then, as the light strengthened, he saw the water transformed to thick clumps of grass, extensive prairie, and tangled masses of wooden debris, logs and tops of trees scattered about in the water.

He felt uncomfortable in the midst of the water. When the sun rises a little higher, its light will flow from everywhere, and I will be able to find a path across the water, he thought. I'll be able to get off this place. Strange how this water doesn't move, yet it doesn't appear to be a lake. Where am I?

"Why are you here, John Warren? What have you done and why are you here?"

He shifted and looked about him. Only the water and the dark tree line were visible. John looked anxiously to the east, but the sun seemed

*no higher than it had been minutes ago, the landscape no lighter. He
suppressed the old anxiety and waited.*

"John Warren, answer me! What have you done?" The voice was
angry, demanding, loud as siege guns on a city.

"Nothing," he mumbled. Then louder, *"No! I've done nothing! Who are
you? Why do you accuse me so? The sun, where is the sun—only a
faint glow there to the east. Why doesn't it rise higher? Oh God, the
light, where is the light? I've got to get away from here. I've—"*

John wakened abruptly, sat up and looked around. The morning
sun was still below the trees across a creek to the east, but already he
was uncomfortably warm. Still groggy from the night's fitful sleep, he
fanned the irritating mosquitoes away from his head. The movement
was painful, and he became aware of a dull throbbing at his temples
and at the base of his skull. His left eye was swollen almost shut and
what vision he had in the other eye was blurred. His nose ached and
when he crossed his eyes to look at it, he saw more of it through the
watery film than he ever recalled seeing. When he touched his forehead, he flinched and quickly withdrew his fingers from a cut just
above the left eyebrow.

He vaguely recalled the last events of the previous night—the bone-
jarring fall, the vicious jabs thrown into his face, the taste of blood in
his mouth. But who had he fought and to what end—Yankees? Had
he fought in some battle and been left for dead here by this creek?

Where is this place, he wondered? He owned no rifle, yet here was
one at his side. He remembered the musket he carried at Bald Hill.
Where was it? Where had this knife come from? Too many questions
to deal with when his head felt like this. He did remember the dream,
though—the oddly sluggish water; the sun which rose only so far in
the sky, then no higher; the harsh, bass voice that demanded answers
of him. Water. He could barely swallow from the thirst, so the first
order of business was water.

Satisfied that he was alone, John stood in the awakening forest,
stretching until his back popped and his weak limbs trembled a little.
He heard water trickling on stones and was drawn to it. Just below
him the water of a creek ran barely a foot deep. To the south he saw
a pool where the creek bed deepened and accumulated a portion of
the stream.

John eased down the slight bank and walked downstream past the pool. He drank deeply from his cupped hand. Best water he'd ever tasted. On the shallow side of the creek he undressed, laying his clothes, the knife, and the rifle out on the shoulder-high bank. Once naked, he squatted on a slight, fan-shaped sandbar to relieve himself. Idly surveying his body, he was amazed at the number of ticks clinging to his waist and scrotum. Between the tiny wounds inflicted by the ticks and the soft, red mounds of red bugs, John's waist and armpits were a mass of itching sores. Delicately grasping each brown back, he worked the ticks' heads from his body and flicked the tiny parasites out into the stream.

Moving far away from his excrement, he rubbed himself down with sand from neck to feet. His hair was oily to the touch, and his scalp itched fiercely. Returning to the creek bank, he found the knife, and on his way to the deep pool, he held his hair up and eased the knife along a line scarcely an inch from his head. By the time he walked to the pool, most of his light brown hair lay in the creek. He was a hideous sight, his hair ragged and gapped, his face much the same from the previous night's fight.

The water was tepid and soothing to his bruised arms and aching legs. He sat on the edge of the pool, leaning back on his elbows, allowing the gentle current to ripple around his neck. John closed his eyes tentatively, his shoulders tensed, afraid to doze in the heat of the rising sun, fearful of a voice from the darkness. Unable to relax with the temptation of sleep washing over him with the stream, he sat up and slowly massaged the sand from his legs and trunk. He rubbed his fingers lightly over his face, taking special care to avoid pressure around the nose, the lips, and the sensitive left eye. Droplets of blood trickled down to his elbow and chest, mingling with the current and preceding him downstream. The vision in his right eye was much better now, and he could even see faintly from the swollen left.

It was coming back to him now—the nightmare of burying his family, the dark flight from the remains of his home, his Uncle Josh left behind, the struggle with the sentries. He slid farther down into the water and tipped back to scrub the grit from the remains of his hair. He was trying to sort out the awful events of the last couple of days when he heard a stirring in the leaves on the west bank of the creek.

Instinctively he reached back into the shallow water at the upper lip of the pool for his knife. Keeping his hand and the weapon submerged, he fought through the fear in his stomach and eased his arm in a broad arc back to his side. Now that it was too late, he realized that the animal and bird sounds had faded into the distance. He waited, scarcely daring to breathe, straining to hear a repetition of the sound. There it was again. The rifle! He had made up his mind to slide into the water feet first, hoping to throw the first shot off so that he could—

"You done heard me, ain't you?" someone said. The voice was high-pitched, just barely masculine.

John held his breath and slid down into the water, balling up to make the slightest target possible of his large frame. The water remained strangely placid. He turned to his right and kicked upstream until he felt the smooth sides of the pool sloping to the surface. He was running out of air, still the water remained uncut by the expected shots. Two choices—either explode from the water, make the bank and run or come up cautiously so as not to startle the intruder. Whoever it was, they were obviously in no hurry to kill him. Maybe they didn't intend to shoot. Maybe they had overlooked the rifle.

John touched bottom and straightened to his full 6'3" height. As his head broke the surface, water streamed over his good eye, making it impossible to see clearly. The voice was behind him again, only much closer now.

"Be careful now, mister. I done found your rifle over there and I got it pointed at your raggedy head."

John's knees felt weak, but he was too scared to move anyway.

"Are you a nigger?" John asked.

"Naw sir. I'm a nigger with a gun. Now wouldn't you say that's different from being just a plain old nigger? And didn't I just tell you that I'm asking the questions first? Now what you got in that hand that's under the water?"

"I don't have anything in my hand." John heard a sharp, metallic click behind him. He raised his hand with the knife above the surface of the water.

"That ain't no way to make friends. Throw that knife out in front of you there."

Reluctantly John flicked his wrist and watched the blade of the knife flash once in the sun and disappear into the far end of the pool.

"Thank you, sir. Let me see your other hand. That's better! What's your name?"

"John Warren."

"Where you from, John Warren?"

"Atlanta."

"Uh-huh. You got yourself a belly full of fighting, ain't you? Where you headed?"

"Clinch county, down near the Florida line," John said. He had not realized it until he heard himself say it. The last few days had been so confusing that the only plan of escape he had was the one Ned Worthington had outlined for him the night they marched from Atlanta.

"You got folks down there?"

"No. I have a friend I'm going to look for."

"You got kin back in Atlanta?"

"They're all dead now."

"That why you running away?"

"Are you going to shoot me or do you intend to talk me to death?"

"You take your pick, and I'll oblige you. Don't make no difference to me."

"I've had enough of this," John said. "I'm going to get my clothes." He turned to face his captor. In the middle of the stream stood a black boy about John's age. His hair was cut close to his head. His skin was black to the point of metallic blueness like the barrel of John's gun. He judged the boy to be about five feet tall and thought that ten pounds of river rocks might bring him up to one hundred pounds.

"Whooee," the boy said, "Your face look like you come out second in a two man axe fight."

John ignored the remark and walked up the slope of the pool. The boy backed upstream a few feet still holding the rifle on him. Finally John stood on the main level of the creek, the current swirling gently about his ankles. He rushed forward a few steps, but the boy swung the rifle around on a line with his chest.

"You taking this too serious, mister. That's it. Now just turn yourself around and go get your clothes on."

When John had dressed, the boy pointed downstream. "Let's get going."

"Where are you taking me?"

"You want to go to Clinch County, don't you? Well, that suits me. Florida is south of here, and that way goes south."

"Do you think you can keep that rifle on me the length of the state?"

"Oh, we gonna talk about that some. We get along all right, and I might let you hold it on me for a while." He loved his own jokes, and as the two walked in the shallow water of the creek, the boy giggled hysterically. His laughter echoed from the banks.

They walked silently for a mile along the winding stream, John down stream from the boy. At first he looked for an opportunity to attack his adversary again, perhaps some way to slip off through the thickening woods to stalk his prey. Once, when the water deepened, he tried slipping under the surface on the pretext of falling. The boy shot dangerously close to his head so that John quickly surfaced in the chest-deep water. When he turned upstream, the boy stood in the middle of the current with an expectant expression.

"Did I hit you anywhere?" he asked cheerfully, and he looked terribly disappointed when John walked on without acknowledging his question.

They stopped at midday at a bare spot on the western bank, a place worn grassless by the feet and rumps of local fishermen. Immediately John hung his shoes and socks on a tree branch and stretched out on his back. "You rest well, boy," he said, "but you better wake up before I do."

His stomach ached for food too much to sleep, but John put on an elaborate charade for the boy's benefit. He lay still for several minutes and faked a light snore. He tossed around for a while and then, unable to ignore the buzzing of mosquitoes around his face, he shifted his back to the boy and lay looking out over Intrenchment Creek.

"You asleep, John Warren?" the boy asked.

John lay quietly. The boy lapsed into silence, but John heard him whistling softly to himself, so he made no effort for the rifle.

"Lawd, I'm tired. Tired and hungry." The boy was mumbling to himself. "If I put this gun down and shut my eyes, that white boy gonna be all over my head." He whistled softly through his teeth for another minute. "Lawd God, Joshua, what you got yourself into now? Can't listen to nobody. Mighta been up north by now. Might be living free and easy up in some city up there by now. Hush up, belly!"

John listened intently now, trying to get some indication of this Joshua's intentions. He listened despite the insistent rumblings of his own stomach.

"John Warren, wake up now!"

John twisted slightly and then settled down again, snoring a little louder.

"Boy snores worser'n Aunt Ruby," Joshua said. Rather than continue his monologue as John hoped he might, Joshua fell silent. John heard only his own steady breathing and the gentle gurgling of the stream, and he was soon sleeping soundly. When he awakened several hours later, he saw Joshua kneeling out in midstream, washing his face.

"About time you woke up. We gonna get to the South River by nightfall, we got to step lively."

John sat up and pulled on his dry socks and shoes. He stretched luxuriously and slid down the bank to the stream. Walking past the boy, he asked casually, "Have a good rest, Joshua?"

Joshua looked calmly at John's back and followed him downstream at a safe distance. "Played some possum on me, did you?" Joshua asked.

John made no reply.

"What all did you hear?"

"Enough to know that you don't intend to shoot me."

"I don't mean to shoot you if I don't have to," Joshua corrected.

"Fair enough," John said. "Why didn't you run to the north?"

"Started off that way, but it didn't look too promising. Me and another boy got as far as some Yankee troops up north of Atlanta, so we figured we had it made, and we turned ourselves in. He tried to talk me out of it. Said we ought to keep moving, but I went on and walked right in to their camp. Next thing we knew we was out ahead of the troops, digging trenches and clearing brush."

"So you took off again, huh? Where's your friend?"

"Got shot down 'fore we made a mile. I'm a small target, and I run like a rabbit when I scared enough, so I reckon that's why I'm here now. Had to go clear 'round by Decatur to get this far."

"How long ago was it that you ran away from the Yanks?"

"Oh, four, five days ago. I've had to move awful slow to pick my way around all them soldiers."

They walked on in silence, each boy preoccupied with his predicament and the means to escape it. From time to time John stooped, dipped his hand in the water, and dabbed stinging sweat from the cuts on his face. Hardwood trees—oaks and sycamore and sweet gum—shaded the creek, but John still found it necessary to cover his swollen eye with the wet palm of his hand. The dry whirring of insects in nearby brush was an irritant to him, and he was still nervous from the rifle at his back.

They stopped to rest once again in mid-afternoon. John kept to himself and cut short further attempts at conversation. He was unaccustomed to the gnawing in his stomach, his body was tense and aching, and worst of all, there was a big gap in his knowledge of the events of the past few days. Just when did he leave Atlanta? Had he told anyone of his intention to travel south? He was certain that his family was dead, but who of his friends remained?

They walked on throughout the remainder of the day without encountering anyone. Joshua made several feeble attempts at teasing John about the rifle, each of which John rebuffed with hollow laughter, followed by tense silence.

As the sun receded beyond the scrub oaks and sweet gums, the deeper, harsher sound of water reverberating against rocks drifted up to them on the creek, and they knew they were close to the South River, westernmost of the three brothers. Even as the sun fell beyond the horizon and night took dominion over the earth, they pushed on to their first night's goal, the river. Between the death of the sun and the birth of the full moon, in total darkness, they stumbled on with only the obscure boundaries of the creek showing them the way they must go.

When at last they reached the place where Intrenchment Creek metamorphosed into South River, the moon danced along the topmost edges of the trees and the night sounds tentatively breached the dull monotony of the insect sounds of day. The creek bed angled sharply to the south and cut into the earth at the place where creek and river united.

Joshua climbed the steep bank and stood above John in the slight angle between creek and river. John continued all the way down the creek until he had to stoop beneath the trees that extended their branches down over the bed. When he reached the confluence of the two, he stood a moment studying the place in the moonlight.

It seemed to him that two worlds balanced here in the mingling of these waters, and for an instant he savored the time when he would bridge the two. The old world of Atlanta seemed as small as the creek to him now and through the pain of his facial wounds and the longing for that tighter, more secure world of the past, he stepped into the larger world of the first brother. In the distance the siege guns rolled thunderous about Atlanta. He turned his back on them, slipped headlong into the current, and began to swim south.

VII

The water rose up out of the darkness most unnaturally, running verti-
cally into the sky, flowing past him into the night sky. With his eyes he
followed the movement of the stream upward until it diminished from the
inability of his vision to perceive the places where the water ascended
ever higher. Within the limits of his perception, yet miles above the
place he occupied, pebbles lay translucent beneath the surface. They
were the only source of light apparent to him and so defined the bound-
aries of the world.

He felt no foundation beneath him, no lateral boundaries of trees or
rocks, no beginning or end to himself, the stream or time. He had
always been there. The water had forever flowed vertically. The pebbly
bottom had infinitely shone, providing a sense of depth and direction.

He touched the water and, at his touch, a precarious balance was
forever disjointed. The ropy length of water, extending infinitely above
him, began slowly to fold upon itself, looping luxuriously like silvery
ropes of taffy out beyond itself to bend and meet again and redouble
and fall again.

He strove to shield himself from the water, but it came on, dragging
the glistening pebbles toward him, so that their light intensified and
illuminated more and more of his being. At first he felt that this was the
way it must be and that so long as he gradually became a part of the
water, no harm would come to him. But as the light descended with the
water, as the water gained momentum and threatened to overtake him
before he was ready, a sense of urgency grew within his heart.

He saw too much, too quickly. He attempted to withdraw, but it was
too late. The water was upon him, and he was carried relentlessly into
the engulfing stream. The light was almost upon him, but still the water
came on bringing more light, and the light engendered heat, and he

struggled against all sensation. He found himself knowing less and less. Almost mindless and then—

"*What have you done, John Warren? Why are you here?*"

John became aware of sand beneath him, and he thought of the deer with the dark-fringed hole in his chest, the last defiant lunge of antlers. He awakened, raised his head and looked into the solemn eyes of Joshua. The boy kneeled on the sand several yards away and watched him intently.

John sat up and looked around him. They were on a sandbar on the inside cut of a river bend. Behind them lay a broad expanse of sand and the upstream portion of the river. To the right were the woods of the western bank. To the left the river cut into the wooded eastern bank some fifteen feet away. A smooth hump of rock broke the water's surface and round the rock, the current swirled and danced, impeded only for a moment before it broke free to the south.

Looking back toward Joshua, John's eyes caught the gleam of early morning sun on steel.

"What are you looking at?" John asked.

Joshua stared at him silently, as if trying to understand a foreign tongue. "I'm looking at a man with a head full of trouble," Joshua said softly.

"It'll heal up with time," John said, gently touching his nose.

"I'm talking about inside-the-head trouble," Joshua said.

"Then don't talk about it. Are you looking for some sort of show-down this morning?"

"What you mean?" Joshua asked.

"I mean that rifle is closer to me than it is to you. Do you think you're that much faster than me?"

"No. You said yourself yesterday that I got no intention of shooting you. I just figured this morning would be a good time to find out what your intentions is."

John stood and walked over to the rifle. Joshua retreated several paces to the water's edge.

"You're feeling brave this morning, then?" John asked.

"It ain't so much that. I'm just tired. All last night, even hid out like I was, I kept thinking I saw you coming through the woods after me.

Didn't get an hour of rest all night. Besides, I seen enough of you to think you ain't a killer."

"Oh, I don't know about that. There was a time when I was ready to take a knife to you."

Joshua laughed nervously. "Well that was different, 'cause I was holding a rifle on you then."

John reached down and picked up the weapon. He swung it around on a level with Joshua's waist.

"Then there was a time that you shot awful close to my head. Suppose I don't like niggers who have the nerve to shoot at a white man?"

"Then I suppose I'm foolish, not brave. Try to kill me outright, so's I don't feel it too bad."

John raised the rifle to his shoulder and aimed it at Joshua's head.

"I might miss your heart and make you suffer, so I think the head would be a more humane target, don't you?"

"I expect it would," Joshua said in a hoarse whisper.

They stood suspended in time and space on the sandbar, looking into each other's eyes. John lowered the rifle and walked to the river's edge. He looked downstream to where the current bent around the next curve in the river.

"Traveling the river will be harder than wading Intrenchment Creek. The water is too deep for walking and the banks are too overgrown," John said.

Joshua followed him tentatively. "What we gonna do?" he asked.

"We have to find a boat, but until we do, we're going to have to find something to float on. I can't swim with the rifle in one hand that's for sure. Besides, my stomach needs a little encouragement, so let's look for a cabin."

They took opposite banks, working their way downstream through the thick tangle of creepers, brush, and fallen trees. After an hour or more, they had traveled only two miles, but at the end of that time, John heard the sound of something substantial crashing down the steep eastern slope of the riverbank. He worked his way to the river's edge and saw Joshua sliding down the bank to where a log six feet in length lay protruding skyward, half in the water.

"Is that it, Joshua?" he yelled.

"I do believe this is what we looking for," he yelled. "Can you get across here?"

John eased into the water, keeping the rifle above the surface, dog paddling across the river. Together they rolled the log onto the edge of the stream until it lay poised to enter the current.

"Get into the water with the rifle and hook your arms over the log," John said. "It won't hurt to wet the rifle a little, but don't let it go all the way under."

"I can't handle the rifle and stay on that log," Joshua said. "You go first."

He handed the rifle to John and squatted by the land ward end of the log.

"Are you sure?" John asked.

Joshua handed him the cartridge belt and nodded. John stepped into the shallow water by the bank.

"Here, take these too," Joshua said. "Ain't no need of them being in my pocket no more." Joshua handed John three shells. He grinned as John looked foolishly at the empty rifle in his hands. Joshua pushed the log out into the current and began to sing in his finest falsetto voice:

> "Don't know I like living in this life.
> Don't know a doggone thing 'bout living this life.
> But one thing I know,
> And I gonna let it show,
> I ain't ready to die!
> No! I sho ain't ready to die!"

The two boys laughed over the improvised lyrics as they kicked out to midstream, holding onto the log.

"You oughta seen your face when I handed you them shells, John Warren. Whooo boy!"

"I knew you had some trick up your sleeve," John said.

"Yeah? You did not. You thought I was gonna let you shoot me. Whooooee!"

"Get off this log, nigger!" John grabbed him by his scrawny neck and pulled Joshua back into the river. He came up blowing water and sputtering for air and paddled furiously back to the log while John laughed, his head thrown back to the sky. Joshua made it back to the log and they floated on south, their voices lifted in dubious praise of life:

"Don't know I like living in this life.
Don't know a doggone thing 'bout living this life.
But one thing I know
and I'm gonna let it show,
I'm sure as hell not ready to die!
No, I ain't ready to die!"

     *   *   *   *

They lay prone some thirty yards from the cabin and watched carefully for human activity. Not since the middle-aged man had emerged two hours earlier and hurried off up the road leading away from the river had there been a sign that the cabin was still occupied. Shortly after the man left, a decrepit hound dragged himself around the back corner of the cabin and flopped down in the dust of the dooryard.

"I'm telling you, if there was anyone else around they would have come out for something by now," John said.

"Still don't like it," Joshua replied. "Let's just get that boat down there and count ourselves rich for the stopping."

"And I told you already, I'm not stealing their boat. We can work a deal for the boat. They probably have another or can make one easily enough. From the looks of the place, they'd be willing to trade most anything for an honest day's work. Besides, we need something to eat and some flint and steel."

"What good is it gonna do us to make a fire if we ain't got the rifle no more to shoot us some supper?" Joshua asked.

"I told you. I'll get them to throw in some line and hooks for the rifle, and we'll have fish."

Joshua laid his head down on his arms, muffling his voice. "You a crazy white boy!" He looked up at John. "If there's anybody in there, the first thing they gonna do is shoot us. Why not just steal the boat and then give some thought to how to steal food the next time around?"

"We're all human, Joshua. They're going to help us out for that reason if no other. We're away from the war now—away from all the killing lunatics. Now let's ease out there and call the cabin."

"Whatever you say. Only you ease first."

John stood and brushed the crusty leaves from his front. The old dog raised his head and turned to look where the boys stood. The dog growled and Joshua immediately scanned the vicinity for a tree stout enough to bear his weight. John stepped into the clearing and raised his hand to his mouth. "Hello, the cabin," he yelled.

The dog struggled to his feet and barked three or four times, looking as if the effort would collapse him back onto the red hardpan. A faint voice called back from the house, but neither boy could make out the words.

John took several steps across the clearing toward the cabin. The rifle lay propped against a tree behind him. Joshua followed, keeping John between himself and the cabin door. The dog barked feebly again. This time John heard the voice from the cabin.

"Jess, is that you? Hurry Jess!" The voice was feminine and as weak as that of the old dog. John eased closer to the dog who cringed slightly, trotted away a few paces, and resumed the attempt to do his duty.

"Jess, you got to hurry now." Something in the woman's voice was familiar to John. Some urgency he had heard before was there. Now he was only a few yards from the door. He turned and looked at Joshua. The boy grimaced, shook his head negatively and pointed to the river, making little paddling motions with his hands. John ignored him and turned back to the cabin.

"This isn't Jess, ma'am," he said loudly. "My name is John Warren. I'm traveling on the river, and I sure am hungry. I was wondering if—"

An explosion ripped the door of the cabin, the shot narrowly missing John. Startled, he stood and stared at the door momentarily before diving to the ground. The old dog yelped and scurried off behind the cabin. The woman inside the cabin screamed and then all was quiet.

John looked around where Joshua had stood. There was no sign that he had ever been anywhere near. John was about to crawl back to where the rifle lay when he heard something inside the cabin. It was a moaning sound that was all too familiar to him. He had heard it dozens of times while consoling nervous fathers-to-be as his father tended to their wives.

"Ma'am, I'm a doctor. Can I come in there and see about you? I mean you no harm."

"Oohhh Jess. Please hurry!" The voice was very faint.

"Ma'am, don't shoot now. I'm a doctor, and I'm coming in there."

There was no response.

John stood up hesitantly and looked around. "Joshua," he yelled. "Come on back here. It's all right. There's a sick woman here. Come back, Joshua!"

He walked to the cabin and stood to one side of the door.

"Ma'am, don't shoot me. I'm going to open the door." He reached over to a crude latch, flipped it up and quickly retracted his hand. The door swung inward several feet.

The voice came softly into the yard. "Please, doctor!" Joshua was still not in sight. John inhaled deeply and, crouching, took several steps into the cabin. At first he could see nothing and felt terribly vulnerable. The only light came from the door at his back. He blinked repeatedly and finally he saw a table and two rickety chairs. Beyond the table was a stone hearth with kitchen utensils scattered here and there. To his left, on a line with the door, he heard the woman gasping and moaning through clenched teeth.

"Doctor, hurry! I think it's coming!"

John's eyes adjusted to the light, and he saw that the woman who was about to give birth was, in fact, a girl younger than he was. Her head was tilted back into a corn shuck mattress, her back arched in painful effort. John crossed the room to the bed and reached down to push the sweat-matted, black hair from her forehead. He felt surprisingly calm.

"How long have you felt like you do now?"

"Since before Jess left. Don't know how long exactly."

John had watched the man leave better than two hours ago, so he estimated that she had been in labor for about three hours. This baby, he realized, could come soon or it might be long, weary hours yet.

He looked at the horsehair blanket covering the girl's torso. My God, he thought, what is happening under that blanket? What do I do first? Water! His father always demanded lots of warm water. But why? The baby was coming out of her body, he reasoned, so that must be pretty messy. Where was Joshua? John said the only thing he could think of, and it sounded ridiculous coming from someone as scared as he was. "You just do whatever you have to do. Everything's going to be all right."

"Where you going, doctor?" she asked.

John turned to her from the door. "There's someone with me. I'm going to have him get some water. Just take it easy." He turned back to the door and yelled, "Joshua!" The boy stood not two feet away.

"God-a-mighty," Joshua screamed and fell back several steps. "You trying to give me palpitations?"

John leaned against the doorframe to compose himself. "You didn't do much for my heart, sneaking up on me like that. Where have you been?"

"Never you mind where I been. What are you doing in that cabin with somebody that just tried to shoot us dead?"

"There's a girl about to give birth. We need water. See if you can find a bucket and if you have to, get some river water. See if there's a well first though."

"Giving birth! Uh huh, I'm gonna see if I can find some river water. I'm gonna find some, and I'm gonna put it under that boat down there. Nice knowing you."

"I don't have time to argue with you," John said. The girl's breathing became forced, punctuated with little yelps as if to underscore John's statement. "You hear that? That gun of her's is still loaded, and if you're not back here in two minutes with water, I'm going to get that gun, and I'm going to ruin your day."

He turned and walked back to the girl, dreading the next step. Kneeling beside the bed, John grasped the girl's hand and put his right hand on her forehead. "What's your name, honey?"

"Ra—Rachel."

"Okay, Rachel, it's time for me to look for your baby." Her eyes opened wide, and she looked at John for the first time. "Don't be embarrassed. I've done this a hundred times, and it's no big deal. Just trust me." John patted her hand and walked to the end of the bed. He glanced out the door. "Joshua!"

The boy was just rounding the door post lugging a wooden bucket half full of water. The other half soaked his trousers from his thighs down.

"Dammit, John Warren, would you quit yelling at me? I ain't your nigger! I done had to fight that raggedy old dog for this bucket and then I had to fight that river bank to get a half bucket of water back up here, just so's you could—Oh, Lord!"

John had lifted the blanket from Rachel to expose her white, tumescent stomach and thrashing, bloody legs. Pushing with all her strength now, she whimpered in pain. Her body tensed until it was still, yet trembling from the exertion. She collapsed, then lifted her pelvis a little and strained again.

"Get up there and brace her shoulders. Give her something to push against."

"Oh Lord!"

"Do what I tell you, Joshua!"

"What?"

"Push on her shoulders!"

John grasped the girl's feet, gently pushing them toward her body. She strained again and again. He looked up to her face. Her eyes were shut tight, her teeth clamped together in an exaggerated, mirthless grin. The black face above the girl was an exact copy of her face. She pushed again and John sensed movement below him. He looked down in time to see the baby's head and arms emerging from the girl.

"Again, Rachel! Push again, girl! That's it!" She obliged and John pulled her feet down, bent her knees up, and planted her feet firmly on the mattress. He reached down carefully and placed his hands under the baby's neck and buttocks, the bloody sac enveloping his hands like gloves. It came out much easier than he expected. The baby gagged delicately once or twice. Its tiny face contorted in rage, its mouth opened, closed, and then opened again to emit the first contentious cry of life.

Being careful to keep the baby within the limits of the umbilical cord, John stepped over the corner of the bed and laid the bloody, outraged mass of humanity against Rachel's body. The girl lay back on the mattress, exhausted, but laughing softly.

"Joshua, hold her head up, so she can see her little man."

There was no answer, and Rachel remained flat on her back. John looked up and saw the rough-hewn side of the cabin where Joshua had stood only seconds before.

s   s   s   s

"I can't understand where he could be," John said. "He had to know her time was close and, according to Rachel, the midwife only lives a few miles over there."

Joshua made no effort to speculate on the whereabouts of Rachel's husband, Jess. He remained immobile on a stump with his head between his knees, his hands folded on top of his head. John paced about the clearing, pausing to look down the trail that led away from the cabin and off into the woods.

"It's so close to dark she's worried out of her wits, poor thing. Where is he?"

"Maybe he don't like the sight of blood neither—or the smell of it," Joshua mumbled.

John stopped pacing and looked at him. "I'm sorry I had to put you through that, but I've never delivered a baby before, and I needed all the support I could get."

Joshua remained silent and bent over.

"Aren't you feeling better now? Why don't you just try one of these corn fritters?"

"Why you got to keep tormenting me about them fritters? I reckon I'm as hungry as I ever been in my life, but I can't bear to talk food just now."

"Just try a little piece of one or maybe a bite of one of these apples." John held one of the cold cakes out to the boy's down turned head. Suddenly Joshua pitched forward off the stump and landed on his hands and knees. His chest and head heaved violently, but he expelled only a thin, vile saliva. After a minute he lifted his head and glared at John. He formed the words slowly, emphatically. "Get...away...from me...with that...SHIT!"

"All right," John said cheerfully, "but you're making a mistake. I'm going to check on Rachel and the baby. Let me know if you see Jess coming."

His misery was so profound that Joshua did not know how long John had been in the cabin when the man came riding up the trail. In fact, the rider was almost upon him before Joshua was aware that he was coming. His first impulse was to run for the river, but before he could take two steps, the rider was in the yard, pistol drawn.

"Hold it, boy! Where do you think you're going?"

Joshua was too scared to speak. He stood with his arms raised, praying for John to hurry out of the cabin.

The man swung down from the horse and stuck the pistol under the boy's nose. "Where's my wife? What are you doing here?"

Joshua's mouth opened and closed several times, but words would not come out.

"Can't you talk? I asked you where the girl is."

Joshua shook his head rapidly, his jaws still working silently. He pointed a trembling hand toward the cabin.

John Warren yelled from the door. "Is that you, Jess?"

"Yeah, who are you?" He kept the pistol pointed at Joshua.

"I'm a doctor. Rachel's just fine. That's my slave out there, so don't hurt him."

"You show yourself, doc, or I'm gonna do a whole lot worse than hurt him."

"I'm coming out. Take it easy." John stepped outside, his hands held out to let Jess see that they were empty.

"What's going on here? You ain't no doctor, boy, and how do you know my name?"

"Rachel told me your name, and you're right, I'm not a doctor. But if I had just told you my name it wouldn't have meant anything to you. I didn't want you to hurt Joshua there. Come on in here and see your wife. She's pretty weak, but she'll explain things to you and show you your new son."

Jess turned to Joshua. "Lay down there, nigger, and don't move an inch. You—move away from that door real easy."

John obeyed and Jess crossed the dooryard to the cabin.

"Lay face down here where I can see you from the door," he said.

"Jess!" Rachel called. He forgot the two boys instantly and rushed inside. After a minute John stood up and called to Joshua.

"It'll be all right now. You can get up."

"You ain't giving me no more orders, John Warren. I'm doing fine just like I am."

"No, I mean Rachel will be all right. Her husband is going to be occupied for a while, so let's take the boat for our doctor and nurse's fee and get out of here."

"Come to think of it, I'm gonna let you give me one more order, and that's the one! Let's go!"

VIII

He sat with his back against the stern of the wooden boat and took careful aim at the squirrel on the oak limb. He waited for it to move back along the limb so that it would be over the bank when it fell. The squirrel raised its head, looking hurriedly to one side, then the other, and finally scurried back toward the trunk of the tree. John held his breath and firmly squeezed the trigger.

"Good God a-mighty!" Joshua yelled. He kicked up from the bottom of the boat and rolled over the side into the current of the Ocmulgee River. John fought to right the boat and managed to keep it afloat despite the water that poured in over the starboard gunwale. Joshua dog paddled halfway across the river before recognizing John's laughter. By then the current carried him so far downstream that he had no recourse but to continue on to the opposite bank.

"You awake now, Joshua?" John yelled as he climbed out to retrieve the squirrel.

"Crazy white boy! Who you shooting at this early a morning? Damned fool, scare me out of ten year's growth, and I ain't got it to spare. What you doing?"

"Breakfast." John held up the squirrel by its tail. When he reached the opposite bank in the boat, Joshua was still breathing heavily and glaring at him.

"Aren't you hungry?" John asked. "We haven't had anything since the last corn fritter two days ago. I thought you'd be grateful for a little meat." John remained in the back of the boat, skinning the squirrel.

"And just how you plan on fixing that thing with no fire?"

"This isn't the Trout House in Atlanta, Joshua. We have to make do with what we have."

Joshua looked into John's eyes, trying to fathom his meaning. When he understood, he glanced down at the dark red, bloody meat, then back up at John.

"Naw sir, not me. You got to burn that rat a little bit for me to eat him."

John slit the soft belly and deftly removed the guts, dropping them over the side of the boat. "Can't do that," he said.

"Then I'll find me some grapes or something along here." Joshua stood and surveyed the area along the river. Seeing nothing that would serve as breakfast, he turned and tramped off into the woods. He thrashed about in the thick undergrowth, unable to concentrate on the search for food for trying to negotiate the tangle of briars that tore at his face and arms and clung to his clothing. By the time Joshua returned to the bank, John had cut the salvageable squirrel meat into strips and discarded the rest of the body. Joshua climbed into the boat, pushing off from the bank as he did. "Let's get on downstream," he said. "Maybe there's a cabin close by." He sat with his back to John and paddled out into midstream.

"It's a little chewy, but not too bad," John said.

Joshua stared downstream. "Hope you catch something terrible from eating that rat."

John scooped his hand over the side of the boat to wash the bloody taste from his mouth. Having choked down the first bite, he tried another. "You ought to try it, Joshua. It gets between your teeth, but—"

"Good Lord, man!" Joshua protested.

John grinned weakly, but continued chewing. The next several bends of the river brought no cabin into view. Joshua remained resolute, but when the next three hours produced no hope of food, he stirred uneasily so that John thought that he was ready to give in.

"I've saved you some. Are you ready to give it a try?"

Joshua kneeled in the boat's bow. He looked restively from bank to bank, but made no move toward the back of the boat. By noon, however, he was feeling weak and drained by the midday heat. For the first time that day, he turned to face the stern. John started to laugh, but Joshua was in such obvious pain and indecision that it touched John's heart. "It's all right, Joshua," he said. "You can take it."

The boy stared at the dried strips of meat for a while, his breath coming fast and labored through his nostrils. He reached out, then withdrew his hand, and finally closed his eyes and took a piece. He was so hungry that his hand shook and tears streamed down his burnt cheeks. He put the strip in his mouth, gagging for a second and then choking the meat down. As he took the next piece, John averted his eyes out of embarrassment for his friend. He looked off down river and there, coming into sight around the next bend, were the crude pilings and planks of a boat dock.

John casually steered the boat toward the eastern bank, away from the dock that clung to the base of a steep bluff. He looked for further signs that someone was settled there. Joshua remained with his back to the bow and suspected nothing. There was no evidence that anyone lived within miles, but John felt sure that no one would go to the effort to build such a structure unless they intended to use it often. Joshua turned toward the front of the boat and stopped chewing. "John!"

"I know. It was too late to stop you from eating when I saw it."

"Let's get over there." Joshua turned around and grabbed the paddle.

"No." John said. "We'll go on downstream and hide the boat first. Then we'll walk back. If there is a cabin, it's bound to be on top of the bluff. See where they've cut steps in the bank going down to the dock? We'll look the place over first."

When they rounded the next bend, John steered the boat across the river and into a shallow cut that ran into the west bank. On the bank John bent a sapling to the ground until it snapped at the base. He cut it free and laid it in the boat so that its leafy top obscured the boat from the river.

"You take the knife," John said. They walked back to the northwest, uphill through the leaf-strewn undergrowth of the hardwoods.

"How long we gonna sit this time, John?"

"As long as we think we need to."

"Well, that little dab of rat meat didn't go far with me. Let's just crawl in there on our bellies if we have to. Not likely there'll be another young 'un to birth."

As they ascended the bluff, the two boys fell silent and walked cautiously, straining to see as far ahead as the brush allowed. The slope gradually leveled and five minutes away from their boat, Joshua saw the cabin.

They slowed their pace to a crawl until they were within fifty feet of the homestead, then sat down to begin the vigil. The cabin was small, yet well constructed. All of its chinking was in place and the chimney on the south wall looked tight and sturdy. The cabin sat on the edge of a clearing and faced a trail, its back to the river.

The boys' position was such that they could see the front of the cabin and, on an angle, the clearing behind it. In the back, across the clearing from the cabin, was a cord of firewood. A small corral, situated on the opposite side of the clearing in front of the cabin, held a mule. There was no indication that anyone was home.

In mid-afternoon John heard someone on the dock at the base of the bluff. Minutes later a short, stocky, bearded man of about forty appeared, hauling a stringer of fish up the steep trail from the river. He paused at the edge of the clearing and stood looking at the cabin. He took a few tentative steps, surveyed the surrounding woods, and then drew a pistol from the holster at his right side. John lay still, but turned his head slowly to his left to check on Joshua. He was sleeping. It seemed to John that the man stared directly at them, but since he didn't challenge them, John remained still.

The bearded man eased the fish down on the dirt and advanced to the back of the cabin. John lost sight of him until several minutes later when the man reappeared to claim the stringer of fish. He went back to the cabin and the place was silent again. John expelled the pent-up air from his lungs and settled back against a tree.

Hours later, as night descended on the clearing, Joshua awakened and the two of them huddled together as John related the afternoon's one event.

"He must have come from downstream, else we'd have seen him this morning," Joshua whispered. "Do you think he seen the boat?"

"He might have, but then with so many people out wandering around these days, he might be that cautious every time he comes home."

As they talked, the sound of an approaching horse echoed down the trail that led to the cabin. A lean, angry-looking man rode to the corral. He opened a small gate, led the horse inside and hurriedly unsaddled the animal. As he slung the saddle over the top rail of the fence, the bearded man came out and walked over to the gate.

"You take care of that troublemaker?" he asked the horseman.

"Yeah, he won't give us any more problems."

"You didn't have to kill him, did you?"

"Nope, but we're gonna have to tend the patch the next week or two. He's gonna take some time to mend."

"Serves him right," the bearded man said dryly.

"Did the lines pan out?" the horseman asked.

"Did all right. Come inside a minute."

"I got to feed the horse first."

"No, you come on in." The bearded man looked casually toward the road, then the two disappeared inside the cabin.

In the fading light John looked around the area once more. He carefully noted the position of the smokehouse in relation to the main structure and to the place where the man had appeared over the bluff. He estimated the distance from his position in the woods to the cabin and from the cabin to the edge of the bluff.

The horseman walked back out to the corral, entered the gate, and went into a lean-to on the backside of the corral. It was dark enough that John could no longer see the man's facial expressions. He was a mere shadow as he moved about, tending to the animals. He re-entered the cabin and the night grew still except for the occasional stirring of some nocturnal creature and the whine of mosquitoes.

"I'm going to sleep for a while now," John whispered. "If they come back out, wake me." He passed the rifle to his companion and stretched out, face down. Despite the mosquitoes, he was asleep instantly. It seemed mere minutes from the time he went to sleep until he felt Joshua's hand pushing his shoulder. He immediately recalled where he was. "Do you see them?" he murmured.

"No. That lantern has been out a long time, and they not stirring."

"How late is it?" John asked.

"Don't rightly know without no moon, but you been asleep a long time. It in the morning."

John rubbed the sleep from his eyes and sat up to stretch. "It's nowhere near sunrise, is it?"

"No, I don't think so."

"Then we'll wait a while longer." They held their position for another hour without hearing the slightest sound from the cabin. No breeze stirred, and they both sweated profusely, moving only to rub softly at their heads or arms as the mosquitoes kept up a constant attack. John's battered face had begun the healing process, and as he waited, he gently explored the new contours of his nose and probed his cut lips with his tongue. Finally, he leaned over to Joshua. "I don't like it, but who knows when we'll find another cabin, and even then, it may be the same."

Joshua nodded in agreement.

"You take the rifle and cover me. I'm going into the smokehouse and carry out everything I can."

"You too big and white," Joshua said. "I'll be harder to see, and I'm faster than you is. I done studied it out."

"We can't afford to argue about it," John said.

"Then you just do as I say."

John knew that Joshua was right. "Head for the river when you come out. I'll be over there by the edge of the bluff, and I'll intercept you to lead you to the steps. We'll take their boat."

"But John, there's no need of that. They'll help us out just 'cause we all human," Joshua teased.

"Real funny. I wish Jess had gone ahead and shot you."

"Don't know nothing 'bout living this life," Joshua sang softly. "Let's walk to the chimney, then I'll give you time enough to get over toward the river. Go slow."

John picked up the rifle, and they began the torturously slow trek toward the cabin. He measured each step carefully, quietly putting one foot down, straining to see ahead of him, then placing the other foot cautiously forward until he was assured that there was no stick to break, no tree root to stumble on. Joshua followed directly behind him. It took them almost ten minutes to cover the fifty feet from their hiding place to a point about ten feet from the cabin. John turned to look at Joshua, wanting to give him some sign of encouragement, wanting him to understand how much he respected and liked him at this moment. Strange, he thought, that in less than a week this most unlikely of allies has become the closest friend I've ever known. He wanted to turn and embrace Joshua. Instead, he resumed the steady pace in the river's direction.

Joshua waited until he thought John had reached a position near the edge of the bluff. Then he decided to wait a few minutes more. The waiting was agony. Sweat trickled from his forehead, mingled with his eyebrows, and overflowed into his eyes and down his cheeks. He was too afraid to risk reaching up and wiping it away. Nausea growled within his stomach, a combination of fear and acute hunger. His breathing came in gasps, and he almost laughed when it reminded him of Rachel's breathing in the throes of childbirth. When he was certain that John must be ready, he took a deep breath, expelled it through his nose, wiped the sweat from his head, and stepped out around the corner of the cabin.

The cabin's silhouette against the sky provided Joshua a reference point, and as he progressed across the dooryard, he glanced up to keep the same distance between himself and the cabin. He stayed on a line with the peak of the smokehouse as he knew that the door lay beneath the peak.

When he reached the smokehouse door, he paused to wipe the sweat from his head once more and then wiped his hands on his trousers. He strained to hear any sound from the cabin and became aware of the night sounds around him. Frogs sang down on the river. The dry fiddle of crickets dominated the woods around the cabin. A scurrying among the trees marked the foraging of another small animal.

Joshua held his palm flat against the door, high above where a latch might be. He lightly brushed his hand down the rough wood until his fingers found the wooden bar snuggled in the latch. Cautiously, slowly, carefully, he raised the wooden bar and rotated it back. He opened the door an inch or two, testing its hinges. They were leather, and the door sagged but made little noise. Finally he opened the door wide enough to slip inside.

The room was dark and cool and even the air smelled good enough to eat. Only a step or two inside, Joshua sensed the presence of some live thing in the room. He froze for a moment and held his breath, trying to locate his unwanted companion, waiting for some sound or movement. The room remained as still as a grave, yet he knew that something else was there. He wanted to give up the search, to turn and leave immediately, but the smell of ham held him.

He raised his hands above his head and groped another step or two into the thick, black gloom. His arm brushed against a bundle suspended from the ceiling, and he recoiled in fright. It took a few seconds to regain his composure. Reaching up, he felt the bundle, then took the knife from his side. He could barely reach the rope from which the meat hung. He grasped it with one hand and cut the rope. Despite his effort to catch the grease-stained bundle, the ham bounced against his chest and fell to the dirt floor. A staccato rattling sound from the nearest corner made Joshua's heart race.

He snatched once at the ham, caught the rope between two fingers, and backed hurriedly toward the door, dragging the bundle after him. The rope trailed along behind the sack, and the snake struck as Joshua turned. Pain shot up his leg, then returned to his right calf and nested there.

"John! Help me! Oh God, oh Jesus, help me!" He hit the door, staggered for a moment, regained his balance and shot out into the yard. Facing the cabin, he stood bewildered and watched the back door open, spilling a stream of light at his feet. The bearded man held a lantern above his head.

"Nail him, Tucker!"

An explosion shattered the night calm, and the back of the cabin splintered from the impact of John's first shot. The man in the door leaped toward Joshua, hitting the dirt only a few feet away. Joshua saw a pistol in his right hand. He spun, and his wounded right leg gave way, dropping him to the ground. John shot a second and third time, and the bearded man with the lantern screamed and crashed back into the cabin. The lantern broke along the threshold, and fire flowed up the cabin wall.

"Get up, Joshua. Come on!"

Joshua looked toward the river. From the light of the flames at his back, he saw a shadowy form beckoning to him. The nausea was overpowering. He was weak and dizzy, and he began to retch violently. Still, he pushed up and hobbled toward John. He saw John raise the rifle, then hesitate and skip to his left a few paces. As John raised the rifle again, Joshua heard shots and saw John go down, the rifle tumbling into space between the two of them. Joshua reached John as he stood again.

Holding each other's arms for support, they turned and ran as well as they could toward the edge of the bluff. Joshua let the ham drop in the dirt as he strained to support John's weight, and as they tumbled off the edge, two more shots ripped the trees behind them.

"Hold on," John yelled, but Joshua pushed free, fighting for balance as he fell. They hit the river several feet apart. John surfaced first and spun himself around, facing upstream. He started to call for Joshua, but the boy broke the surface before he could. John reached him in three strokes and clasped his hand on Joshua's arm.

"The bank," Joshua said. "Get us to the bank."

"No. Got to get downstream. He'll be after us. The boat."

Joshua was too drained to argue. His leg throbbed and all he wanted was a place to lie down, a place to lay and forget the pain. It seemed to go on and on. *John Warren is mule-headed, he thought. Won't get us out of this river 'til we're halfway to Macon.*

John was watching the western bank for the sapling he had laid in the boat, but it was still too dark. After a minute or so of kicking and dog paddling, he saw the bluff taper down and rather than float downstream of their boat, he pulled Joshua toward the bank. When he touched bottom, he pulled the boy in between himself and the side. He pushed him up onto the bank, then crawled up beside him and collapsed. The ache in his right thigh intensified as his leg scraped on the earth.

"Where are you hit, Joshua? You yelled before the shooting started. What happened?"

Joshua's breathing was fast and shallow. He whimpered softly, "Oh Jesus, oh God. I gonna die, John. I'm scared to die."

"You're not going to die. Tell me where you're shot, and I'll take a look at it."

"Ain't shot. Rattlesnake got me. They had him in there waiting on me. Oh God, I don't want to die out here on this river."

At first John couldn't comprehend what the boy was saying. The men kept a rattlesnake in their smokehouse? That couldn't be. He sat up on the bank, trying to see Joshua in the darkness. "Are you sure it was a rattlesnake?"

"Heard it shake them rattles before it hit me. My leg, John, back of my leg hurts so bad. Help me."

"Where on your leg? Down here?" he asked, touching Joshua's left calf.

"Other leg. Oh, sweet Jesus, I'm really going to die!"

"Quit talking like that." John rolled up the loose trouser leg to Joshua's knee and squinted at his calf. He saw the wound where the fangs had ripped the flesh. "Give me the knife, Joshua."

"Ain't got it. Lost it back there."

John looked back up the bluff and saw a light flickering in the distance where the fire consumed the cabin. His own leg felt warm. He was growing weaker and wearier by the minute. He could never make it back up the bluff or contend with the man who had shot him.

"Joshua, can you get up? We have to find the boat and get away from here."

"No use. Gonna die. Ain't no use to go nowhere."

"You can't give up like that. Now get up and let's go."

"Bad pain in my leg. Make it stop hurting, John."

John stood and tugged at the boy's shoulders. He pulled him to his knees, then grasped him under his arms and jerked him to his feet. The pain in John's leg increased from the effort. He supported Joshua with his right arm and started along the bank parallel to the river. The undergrowth was thick, but John pushed on until he found the cut that held the boat. The sapling that had covered the boat was gone, and the boat lay exposed.

John picked Joshua up and put him into the bow. Wading to the stern, he looked upstream and saw nothing but the quicksilver flow of water framed by woods. When John threw himself up to the gunwale and fell into the boat, Joshua shifted in the front.

"Don't quit," John said. "There may be another homestead around the next bend or two."

Joshua nodded faintly. John pushed the boat back into the stream with his paddle. The current carried the boat sideways until John could situate his wounded leg in an upraised position and steer them straight.

He kept close to the western bank, watching the river for the man he expected to be close behind them. Joshua lay still in the bow, and

John decided to let him rest. He wanted to lay back against the stern, but was afraid to sleep, afraid he might miss a cabin where he could get some sort of aid for his friend. The boat glided past two bends, then a third and fourth without any sign of a cabin. When John estimated that half an hour had elapsed, he called to Joshua. "Are you awake?"

"Hurts too bad to sleep."

"Just hang on. There's bound to be another cabin along here somewhere."

"Gonna be too late for me, John."

John tried to ignore such talk. "At least I don't see that fellow behind us anywhere. He's had time to catch us now, so I don't think he's coming. Probably had to get that fire out and then get his friend to a doctor."

"They was waiting on us, John. They knew we was out there, and they dumped that snake in the smokehouse, and they was sitting up with a blanket or something over that light just waiting."

"I know," John said.

"Let that be a lesson to you, John Warren. Just when you think you got somebody fooled, he be waiting on you. You can't fool this world, so don't you be trying." Joshua began chuckling to himself.

"What is it?" John asked.

"I just heard my Mama talking. 'Let that be a lesson to you, Joshua Brown,' she always said." John realized that he had never asked the boy his last name.

"Joshua Brown," he repeated. "Where is your family, Joshua?"

There was no reply for a minute and then John heard him crying. He tried to say something, but his emotions had the best of him for another minute. Finally Joshua said, "You facing the truth of it now, ain't you? Well, you don't need to do that, John."

"Do what?"

"You tell me."

"They need to know what happened to you, Joshua."

"No, they don't. You'd go there telling some sweet lie about how their boy died saving somebody's life or some such foolishness other'n stealing ham, and my mama'd see right through to your bones."

Joshua fell silent for a moment. John didn't like the signs. Joshua's speech was slurring and he seemed to have trouble focusing on what he was saying.

"She's a conjure woman. Probably knows anyhow. Done killed some old rattlesnake and bit him. Trying to—trying to—"

"There has to be something I can do," John said.

Joshua pushed himself up in the bow of the boat so that John could see his silhouette against the river. "Onliest thing you can do now is look out for yourself. You understand that? Even if we found a place now, it's too late."

John looked down and nodded.

"Seen a man die from a snakebite one time. Sure weren't pretty." He looked to the western bank and was silent for a while. "Promise me something John Warren," he said.

John looked up. Joshua seemed to draw all his remaining strength together.

"You the best man I ever knowed, and I don't think it'll be a hard promise. Don't be too hard on black folks when you around them. I expect this war gonna change a lot of things, but some things is gonna stay the same no matter what. Help black folks out when you get a chance, 'cause one of them came to love you like a brother one time."

They looked into each other's eyes, and John nodded affirmatively. Joshua grasped the side of the boat with both hands and rolled over the side, off into the current. John started forward.

"Joshua!"

He watched the river intently until the boat rounded the next three bends, then failing to see the body, he slumped back against the stern and cried himself to sleep. Light was beginning to show on the eastern side of the river, bringing with it the most beautiful of summer days.

*　　　　　*　　　　　*　　　　　*

The boy in the boat opened his eyes, but couldn't focus them to see the river on which he floated or the surrounding woods. He tried to push up, but weakness and pain held him in place. Time—past or present—meant nothing. This is death, he thought.

In his spirit he stood, as if on high ground, looking down on a powerful column of water that rushed over the edge of a cliff, cascading to the earth below. At each level of the cascade, the water tore at the earth, expropriated a bit, and assumed a new identity, not wholly water, in which to continue its journey.

At first the process was merely interesting, but when he had observed it for a while, the implications of destruction and transition disturbed him. He wanted the earth to resist the water's onslaught, to hold firm and unchanging beneath him. Instead, the process seemed to accelerate. The water gained momentum, the earth yielded more and more readily, vast sections of it fragmenting, readily subsumed by the column of water. He recognized the necessity of retreat, but stood firm, determined to withstand the water, as if he could send down a network of roots into the infirm soil and anchor himself and the earth to some unshakeable core of the universe.

Slowly the water yielded. The powerful surge became a steady flow, the flow an insistent stream, and the stream a gentle trickle about his feet. John lifted his face to the sky, ingesting the bright power of the sun, the light and heat of the heavens. Yet the water trickled around his feet, the tiniest particles of soil moistening imperceptibly.

"Why is light given to a man whose way is hid, and whom God hath hedged in?

For my sighing cometh before I eat, and my roarings are poured out like the waters.

For the thing I greatly feared is come unto me. I was not in safety, neither had I rest, neither was I quiet; yet trouble came."

✶   ✶   ✶   ✶

John Warren came to a place in a season when land meant nothing to him. He had lived in a place on the wealth of his father. He had been driven from that place under duress.

John overcame the hardships of his journey down the Ocmulgee river. Over the course of the next month his wounds began to heal—

at least the physical ones. He endured hunger and loneliness as he traveled by night and rested or foraged for food during the day. He pushed himself to stay busy as he traveled, to work himself near to exhaustion in order to avoid thinking of his family and Joshua. He perceived little of the coastal plain through which he and the river passed. He was millions of years too late for the rolling tide of the Atlantic Ocean that now lay one hundred miles to the east.

John had no thoughts of power and possession, nor even hope of predominance, and so the land meant nothing to him. The vast plain around him excited no visions of arable farmland or milling herds of cattle. The widening and deepening forest tracts, virginal and extensive, spread out before him where the river turned east and where he left the river to continue on foot to the south. The great forest where men were already employed with their sawmills and turpentine stills were an obstacle to him.

From a life of propriety and the pursuits of the mind, John Warren had survived the tests of the battlefield. Having seen his world of secure classrooms and elegant homes laid to ruin, the unendurable corpses laid in shallow graves, he wandered, the inexplicable will to survive, even in extremes of despair, his only reason for living.

John traveled the Ocmulgee from its origins in the rocky upland, across the fall line that marked the boundary between an ancient sea and its coast, down through the sedimentary coastal plain. Now, as he stepped off the river for the last time, he entered the last leg of his journey, out of the gentle slopes and into the perfectly flat terrain of the southernmost part of the land called Georgia. He came in search of an ideal, and he came with little hope of finding it, for he expected its manifestation to come from one whose life he had once threatened.

Without knowing, John Warren came to the land.

IX

"Howdy!"

The greeting startled John, but he didn't break his stride.

"Hello," he answered. The person approaching him along the twilit road was twenty yards away and indistinguishable. They walked on toward each other, prepared to defend themselves. John shifted his eyes, searching the pinewoods for anyone who might be lying in ambush.

"I thought for a minute there that you was my brother, Levi, come to fetch me from town. You a good sight bigger than Levi, though, so I done figured you weren't Levi."

At six-feet, three inches John towered over his new acquaintance, and he was lean from the weight loss he had suffered over the past month. He noticed that the young man studied his face and realized that, although he had healed, he must still look like a prizefighter— misshapen nose, swollen features, maybe a scar above his brow.

"Have you come from Magnolia?" John asked.

"Yeah. Got to playing cards with some fellers, and it got late on me, so I'm gonna catch it from Ma now. Name's Joshua. What's yours?"

The name startled John for a second, and he looked closer to see how this Joshua compared to the one in his heart. The two were face to face now, and when Joshua grinned, John could see only three teeth, coated in tobacco juice. His cheeks were sunken, drawing the skin under his eyes taut. His right eye was fixed, but the left wandered continuously, and John found it difficult to focus on the good eye. The boy extended his hand, and John accepted the welcome.

"My name's John. How far is it back to town?"

"Bout a mile or so. You headed to Magnolia or just passing through?"

"I'm looking for Ned Worthington. Do you know him?"

"Sure. His mama and the kids live a good bit south of town. Doubtful if you could find them tonight. Last I heard tell, Ned was up in north Georgy with the army."

There was an awkward silence between them. John looked down the road toward town.

"You kin to the Worthingtons?" Joshua asked.

"No, I'm just Ned's friend."

"Met him in the army, huh?"

John didn't answer.

"The Worthingtons are all right by me. They've had a hard time since Ned's pa died, and that was ten year ago. Old Cable hung around with Mr. Mac McLendon, and they got on one of their rip-snorters and made out that they both owned the fastest horse in the county. Nothing would do but they found out who was the liar, so they commenced to race.

"What they found out was who was the drunkest, 'cause Cable smacked into a oak limb and broked his neck. Didn't do his face no good neither. I was one of the first what see'd him on account of I was helping the high sheriff back then, sweeping up and all, and Mr. McLendon, he got Cable laid over his saddle and brung him in to the sheriff's office. It were a terrible sight! You ever see'd a man with his natural neck broke?"

"No, can't say I have," John said. His mind was occupied with thoughts of his next move, and he barely paid attention to Joshua's rambling.

"Terrible, terrible sight," Joshua repeated. "But them Worthingtons is all right by me."

"Excuse me, Joshua. I better go on to Magnolia now. It'll be dark about the time I get there."

"Sure. That's right. I'll barely make it home before nightfall myself. What do you plan to do tonight? You might as well come stay with us. Probably gonna be a frost tonight."

"Thanks just the same. I think I'll go on into town."

"Suit yourself. Miss Birdie Leggett's boardinghouse is down by the courthouse. Maybe I'll see you around sometime," Joshua said.

"Yeah, maybe."

John walked the last mile to town in the same steady pace he had used all the way from the river. He stopped on the edge of town within sight of dimly lit houses and shadowy buildings and side streets. There was no money for a boardinghouse. He knew that if he entered town at night, the local sheriff would be his first acquaintance. He didn't want Magnolia's first impression of him to be that of a vagrant, so John walked back out the Pearson Road a quarter of a mile, found a clear spot off in the woods, and lay down for the night. Ned was his only hope.

John Warren dreamed, and in his dream the water flowed around him, high and dangerous. It pulled against his bare legs, threatening to tear him from the preacher's loose grasp, his arm cradling John's back. The gown that he wore lifted and fell in the current and swept out straight as if by a strong wind. Water fell from the heavens, intensifying until the drops splattered on his face and forced his eyes shut. He wanted to see, to escape the terrible darkness. His eyes opened and fluttered, but the onslaught of water was too great, and he was forced to close them again.

The river swirled higher and higher on his body, up around his neck, splashing onto his cheeks. Still, the preacher droned on and on. John's eyes fluttered open again. He saw the shadowy figures standing about him in the water and some on the bank of the river—blessed land. He retreated into the darkness, felt the heavy, callused hand on his forehead, and then was immersed in the swirling rush of the river.

The baptism came without warning, and the water choked him. He immediately needed air, but the preacher kept him under the surface. When finally John could breathe again, he gagged and blew water out of his mouth and nose. The voice he heard was not what he expected, and the words tortured his spirit.

"What have you done, John Warren? What have you done, and why are you here?"

"Nothing!" John yelled. "Done nothing wrong! Don't know why! Where—where am I?"

Back on the riverbank John saw a magnificent deer lying on sand, a gaping wound in its chest. And then there came a voice, familiar and different than the voice of the accuser. "...Not in the park. They're dead—all dead."

"Nothing wrong!" John yelled. "I've done nothing wrong." He thought he perceived light and a new, unfamiliar voice.

"Now there was a day when the sons of God came to present themselves before the Lord, and Satan came also among them. And the Lord said unto Satan, 'Whence comest thou?' Then Satan answered the Lord and said, 'From going to and fro in the earth and from walking up and down in it.' And the Lord said unto Satan, 'Hast thou considered my servant...'"

John drifted again into the darkness and the water.

    s   *s*   *s*   *s*

The next morning John awakened at sunrise and spent an hour looking for a creek to wash in. He rubbed himself down with the smooth, white sand of the creek bed and cleaned his shirt and trousers. By midmorning his clothes were sufficiently dry, and he walked the short distance to town, shivering and nervous in the cool November morning.

The first store he approached was a dry goods operation. Three old men sat in front of the store, weather-beaten as the covered walkway. They were on a wooden bench, chewing tobacco and spitting across three feet of planks to the dusty street below. They seemed oblivious to the early morning chill and to the stranger in their town. Nodding to them, John sidestepped the puddle of tobacco juice and entered the store.

It took a moment for his vision to adjust to the dim interior of the place. It held a bewildering array of goods that spilled over countertops and littered what remained of two or three small aisles. From the door where John stood, it was possible to walk forward just ten or twelve feet before confronting a heap of shoes and boots.

Along the right side of the main aisle ran a counter, two planks sitting atop three barrels. The only open space along the counter was at the far end of the boards, where a man with a stub of cigar jammed into the right side of his mouth leaned over a cast-iron cash register. Across the counter from the proprietor an old man warmed his hands over a potbellied stove. Both men glared at John. There was a musty smell of clothes and stale cigar smoke. He walked to the men and extended his right hand.

"Morning. My name's John Warren."

The squat paunchy man behind the counter reared back from the cash register and turned to dig among an assortment of tobacco goods scattered along a low shelf. That left only the old man to respond, so he reluctantly took John's hand and shook it limply.

"Morning," he muttered.

The man behind the counter turned back to the two of them. He was already in the process of lighting a fresh cigar. He took his time, puffing deliberately at the new stump of cigar, warily surveying the lean, travel-weary boy. "What can I do for you?"

"I'm looking for Ned Worthington." John paused, and when neither man responded, he shifted uneasily. *Coming in here was a mistake, he thought. How do I tell them I know Ned without getting onto the subject of the army?* "I'm his cousin from up around Douglas."

The old man looked as if he wanted to say something, but the cigar smoker silenced him with the slightest of glances.

"You his cousin and don't know where he lives?" It was more of an accusation than a question.

"Mama and the kids and me just moved down to Douglas from Macon. Things were getting pretty hot up there with Yankee cavalry, and we didn't feel safe with papa off in the army. I've never been far from Macon before three months ago." Even as he said it, the story sounded too slick to John. He decided to play it out anyway. "Look, mister, I don't want no trouble. If you don't want to tell me where Ned lives, I'll go see the sheriff or somebody and find out."

"Nothing against you, son," the man said, "but we've had a lot of trouble with deserters around here. It pays to be suspicious of strangers lately."

"I understand," John said. "I'll just find the sheriff and explain things to him."

"No need of that." The man behind the counter extended his hand. "I'm Cyrus Johns. This here's Mr. Lewis Jordan."

John shook hands again.

"The Worthingtons live out south of town on the Griffin Road. Just keep going past the store here and it's out about a mile and a half. It'd be the second house you come to, and chances are there'll be a heap of kids out in the yard. Won't be any trouble to find."

"Thank you, sir."

"Ned's still off with the army, so I'd be real cautious about how I come up on the house. Your Aunt Martha is a pretty good shot."

"Yes sir. That's what mama told me. Thanks for your help."

John walked out the sandy Griffin Road headed to the Worthington place. He regretted having lied to the men in the store about his relationship to Ned, but it was done, he decided, and now he had to push the lie to the back of his mind and think of how he would approach Ned's mother.

He was confused concerning Ned's whereabouts. Most likely he was at home and was hiding out so that the people of Magnolia wouldn't know that one of their own was a deserter. Possibly he had found somewhere to stay on the way back to Clinch County and was hiding his disloyalty from his family as well as the rest of the county. I might have even passed him on the way, John thought, or maybe he decided to go to the Okefenokee until news of the fall of Atlanta.

John realized that he had blocked all thoughts of his home for weeks. His emotions were mixed on that point. He hated the thought of Yankees roaming the streets of his city, but since he had deserted, the thought of stronger men holding on where he had failed was just as repulsive.

He was so engrossed in these thoughts that he failed to hear the approaching horse and rider until it was too late to hide. He turned and saw a big, white-haired man riding directly at him. The man was John's size if not larger, and he was completely at ease, as if headed nowhere in particular. John stood his ground as the rider approached.

"You John Warren?"

John felt light in the stomach and envisioned Mr. Johns leaning over the heavy cash register, chewing on the stump of his cigar.

"Yes, sir," he answered.

"Well, you made a mistake back there at my brother's store, young fellow. Ned's ma is named Sara, not Martha."

John's mind raced back over the conversation with Cyrus Johns. He tried to think of a plausible explanation, but his heart was not in further lies.

"Turn yourself around now and let's get back to town."

John saw the rifle butt protruding from the sheriff's scabbard. He glanced at the woods to his left, then back at the sheriff.

"You could try it, but I'm a pretty fair shot, and those woods don't look as thick to me as they do to you," the sheriff said.

John started the walk back to Magnolia. Ten minutes later as he passed Mr. Johns' store, the sheriff directed him to turn right, and he dismounted to walk alongside him.

"You ain't guilty of nothing but lying yet, so I'm not going to give these busybodies any more to talk about than I have to. You just act like I'm giving you a tour and that's what I'll do."

John nodded and looked at the big man appreciatively. He saw the old men and Mr. Johns standing out on the porch of the store behind him. On up the street a dozen or so men, women, and children were carrying on the morning routine of any small town. Several of them saw John, and in various places up and down the street, activity was momentarily arrested.

"The Baptist church is back there across from Cyrus's store," the sheriff said. "Right here by us is the Leggett House. Good boarding house if you can talk your way out of this scrape. Couple of stores there."

They crossed the road and headed for a large frame building that John took to be the courthouse. It sat back from the street further than the stores on the opposite side, and except for a couple of houses, was the sole structure of one whole block. The sheriff pointed back across the street from the courthouse.

"Bank's over there, hardware store next to it, and then the pharmacy. Across the next road from the pharmacy is the Methodist church, and the school's to the east of the church."

The sheriff stopped in front of the courthouse and tied his horse to a hitching post. His casual pace had the desired effect, as those who had stopped to watch John's arrival went on about their business.

The sheriff turned to face the stores across the street, placed his hands on the small of his back, and stretched until his vertebrae popped. He reached back to his saddle, took the rifle out of its sheath, and pointed east of town with it.

"Hard to see from here, but that's the schoolhouse down past the Methodists. Back on this side there's a stable and Doc Williams' place. Pretty good sawbones. That's about the run of it." He turned and walked toward the courthouse.

Inside, a corridor ran the length of the building. It was cool, and here and there along the length of the hall, shafts of light broke out of office doors, warming sections of the scuffed pine floor. They walked halfway down the corridor before the sheriff made an abrupt turn and entered a doorway to his left. John followed and found himself in an austere room, bathed in sunlight. The sheriff slid his rifle onto a cheap wooden desk. He motioned to a chair in front of the desk as he pulled open a drawer and rummaged in it.

"Left in such a hurry a while ago I forgot to take me a plug. Do you use it?" He took a small pouch from the desk, drew a hefty knife from his trousers, and cut a piece of the tobacco.

"No, sir," John said.

The sheriff shoved the desk drawer shut, sat down heavily, and propped his brogans up on the desk. As he worked the tobacco into his left jaw, he leaned back and shifted in the chair until he settled into a posture that suited him.

"John Warren, huh? That your real name?"

"Yes, sir."

"My name's Amos Johns. Cyrus is my brother. He's a pain in the ass, but he's my brother."

"Why do you say that?"

"Because we have the same mother and father."

"No, I mean—"

The sheriff smiled at John and winked. "You mean why is he a pain. He sells liquor out of that store of his and that about drives the Baptists up the wall. There's one of them in here two or three times a week wanting me to put a stop to his selling it right across the street from the church."

"Don't the Methodists have anything to say about it?"

"Hell, no. They're his best customers." The sheriff thrashed about in the chair for a moment until he found a new position that better fit his back. "Let's get down to cases, boy. What are you doing in Clinch County?"

John took a deep breath. "I'm a deserter from the state militia that was fighting around Atlanta." He said it as if he thought it would be a shocking revelation to the sheriff, then paused, waiting for him to react.

"It wasn't hard to see that you were running from something of the sort. Go on."

"The militia unit I was in was joined to General Hardee's forces after a battle on Peachtree Creek up north of the city. It was late July, and we marched south and then east one night to surprise the Yanks at a hill called Bald Knob. On the march I met Ned Worthington. I guess I must've looked pretty scared to him, because he sat up talking with me practically all night."

"Did Ned desert, too?"

John hesitated a moment, then decided that he had caused enough trouble for one day. "Ned and I were separated in the fighting the next day, and I haven't seen him since." No lie there, John thought.

The sheriff stared at him thoughtfully and rolled the tobacco under his cheek.

"Anyway, that night we talked about a little bit of everything. Ned talked a great deal about home, so when I took off, this was the only place I knew to come."

"How come you to run, boy? You don't strike me as yellow. Lord knows you look big enough to handle yourself in a scrape."

John leaned forward and put his arms on his legs. He saw the ruins of his home and five shallow graves. "I don't have any excuses to offer you, sir."

Amos put his feet back on the floor and leaned over the table. "I'm not looking for excuses. Just tell me what happened when you left."

John's head stayed down, and he fought back the tears. He tried to speak once or twice, but each time he felt the tears coming and he stopped. Finally he took a deep breath and exhaled.

"I don't recall much of leaving. My family lived in town, and the Yankees started shelling the city while I was with the army. They, uh, they were—" The tears started despite his efforts to repress them.

"They were killed," Amos said.

John nodded.

"Do you have any kin left anywhere?"

"Not that I know of. My mother was an only child, and my father never had much to say about his family. I never knew any of my grandparents."

The sheriff stood and walked over to the window. He remained there for several seconds looking out toward the Baptist church with his back turned to John and the rifle. "What do you plan to do now, John?"

"That depends on you, sir. If you let me go, I guess I'll keep going south. I've heard that a lot of those who desert go to the Okefenokee or on down into Florida. Some have even gone on to Mexico or South America."

"And what if I lock you up and turn you in over at Savannah?"

"I guess I'd wind up back in the army."

"No, they'd probably hang you for desertion." Amos leaned against the window frame.

"That might not be such a bad idea," John murmured.

"If I let you go, the sensible thing to do would be to head for the swamp, wouldn't it?"

"I suppose so," John said. "I could probably get something to eat there and figure out what to do next."

Amos turned to John. John was sitting back in the chair, and the rifle hadn't moved from its place on the desk.

"This county has enough trouble with the deserters we have hiding out around here. We don't need one more if we can help it." He walked back to the desk and took a ring of keys from the drawer. He motioned to the door behind the desk. "Through here, boy. Let's go."

They walked down a narrow corridor a few feet. John passed the first of two cells, and the sheriff stopped and opened the cell door. John had never been to Savannah.

X

The town of Magnolia was incorporated in 1850. The founders were families named McLendon, Taylor, Tomlinson, Pace, Johns and Lee. Of these men and women, Mac McLendon, Ben Taylor, Wealthy Taylor, Clarence Pace, and Amos Johns rose to prominence. McLendon and the Taylors derived their power from the accumulation of land. Amos Johns' authority came from his position as the sheriff of the county, and Clarence Pace's from his ownership of the local bank.

Although they worked hard to establish and nurture their town, Mac, Ben, Clarence, and Amos also sowed the seeds of Magnolia's destruction. Many people say that John Warren and Ned Worthington destroyed Magnolia in the attempt to bring each other down. In fact, they only reaped the harvest of bitterness that the others had sown long before John came to Magnolia and Ned returned there in November of 1864.

*   *   *   *

When George Edward "Mac" McLendon migrated from Moore County, North Carolina to South Georgia in the mid-1830s, everything he owned was riding his horse with him. The horse included, his estate wouldn't have amounted to twenty dollars. Mac was a stout man physically and mentally, so whatever he put his mind to do, his body was able to carry it out.

The McLendons were not highly regarded by their neighbors in North Carolina. They owned no land, and as the McLendon brood increased in size each year, the family resources were stretched thinner and thinner. With four children they were strapped for cash, with eight they were poor, and with thirteen children, they were hopelessly destitute.

Mac's father, Michael, would not have had the means to keep a roof over their heads, but as a sharecropper he was entitled to shelter. As his family grew and his fortunes diminished, Michael more and more often found solace with his drinking buddies, leaving Mac and his mother, Molly, to tend to the family.

It was acknowledged locally that as the eldest boy, Mac was the family's best hope for redemption. If somehow Molly could keep the boy untainted by Michael's growing alcoholic episodes, he might make something of himself and thus redeem the family. It would, they all agreed, take a miracle. There would be no miracle for the McLendons.

As each child matured, their father chose the fields and turpentine woods for them over the schoolhouse, and so he lost any opportunity for the family to rise above their current state of affairs. The McLendons were always paying for last year's necessities with this year's labor—except for Michael's liquor bill. That account had to be kept current.

Though he loved his mother dearly, by the age of fifteen Mac was becoming more and more his father's son. Michael considered him to be a man at that age and encouraged young Mac to "knock the dust from your throat with your old man." The first time that Mac came home drunk with his father, a fight ensued between husband and wife that lasted for days. Mac felt too manly to listen to his mother's reasoning and pleading. He craved the attention that his father now gave him.

Over the next several years, Molly reluctantly gave up the hope that her eldest child would rise above their circumstances and pull the rest of the family with him. Out of necessity, she turned her attention to the twins, who were three years younger than Mac. Maybe she could win the battle for their minds.

In 1835 Molly McLendon became pregnant for the fourteenth time. She had not borne a child in almost four years, and she had recently turned forty-three. The pregnancy was difficult, and the worse her condition became the more her husband drank. Rather than leave her with the twins and the younger children, who he considered weak because of their devotion to their mother, Michael assigned Mac the task of looking after Molly in the evenings when he was out on business.

In the early hours of a June morning, Molly hemorrhaged and died. When Michael sobered to find himself a widower, he began to sulk and to drink again. All through the wake, he told every man who would listen exactly where the blame lay for his dear wife's death. He had been out on business that night, it seemed, and had left that oldest boy of hers to watch over his sainted wife. A fine job he had done.

On the third day after Molly had been laid to a well-deserved rest, Michael had been drinking long enough to absolve himself of all blame and to lay the full responsibility for the early demise of his loving wife at the feet of his son. At three that morning, Michael staggered to the bedroom where Mac slept and roused him for the beating he needed.

Mac dressed himself amid his father's cursing and walked calmly from the house. When they reached the barnyard, he turned and listened without protest while his father cursed him for the lowest form of life imaginable.

The tirade went on for almost ten minutes. Michael finally wore down and fished in his coat pocket for a bottle. He turned it up, took a long swig, and as he brought it away from his mouth, a fist caught him full in the face. Mac followed with a right jab, and his father never had a chance.

After Mac beat his father into unconsciousness, he looked around until he found the half-empty liquor bottle. He poured the remainder of it in his father's face, and as soon as Michael came to, Mac beat him senseless again.

All of the children had been through Michael's shouting and cursing so often that, except for the three eldest, they slept through the incident.

"I'll have to leave you awhile now," Mac told them. "This whipping may humble him for a time, but in a few days he'll be drunk again, and then it'll be him or me. I'm not guilty of my mother's death, and I'll not be guilty of my father's."

"Where will you be, Mac?"

"I don't know. I'll head south and see if I can't land in the turpentine woods, since it's the work we know best. I'll write you after the old man's had time to cool off. Never you mind what he has to say about me. You three have to tend to the little ones. If I can get situated favor-ably, I'll come fetch all of you, but you can't count on that. I won't be playing, though. I'm going to work to save my family from this mess."

Two months later, Mac's travels brought him to South Georgia. He homesteaded an area so deep in the pine forest that no one else knew he was there for the first eighteen months. In the late winter of 1836 the white settlers in the area were increasingly coming into conflict with the Creek and Seminole Indians. When a Seminole raider, Red Stocking, and his men massacred a family just south of Alapaha, Colonel Josiah Tomlinson formed a troop to pursue him to the depths of the Okefenokee if necessary.

The Indians had burned Mac out earlier that year, and he had just finished rebuilding his cabin when they came through his area again. Tomlinson heard the gunfire as Mac held the Indians off, and he arrived just in time to save him. Ben Taylor and Amos Johns were among the men with Colonel Tomlinson.

Mac joined up with Colonel Tomlinson to chase Red Stocking, and for the next four days, he, Ben, and Amos became well acquainted with each other, and a mutual respect grew among them.

Although the Indians changed their line of travel from east to west and back again, it became apparent that they were headed south to the Okefenokee. Colonel Tomlinson sent Amos, Mac, and Ben to the east and south and a separate flanking movement of three other men to the west and south, with the main party of nine staying on Red Stocking's trail.

If one of the flanks could intercept the raiders, they were to pick the most fortified spot they could find and attack the Indians to inflict as many casualties as possible. Then they were to fall back and hang on for dear life until the other two parties showed up to catch the Indians in a cross fire.

Amos' group traveled east for three miles, then dropped south to a point southeast of Mac's cabin. They found a shallow pond heavily wooded with cypress that would make for difficult travel unless one had scouted the best way through it. They did just that and sat down to wait.

Within a few hours Amos heard them coming. He, Mac, and Ben slipped to one side of the Indians' route and moved parallel to them.

As they neared the pond, Amos picked the opportunity, signaled the others, and opened fire. Three of Red Stocking's men went down immediately. They scrambled to the pond and made their way in deep enough to hold off the Indians until Tomlinson's main party could catch up.

Another five Seminoles were killed at that point, but Red Stocking was not among them. The militia chased them to within a mile of their Okefenokee refuge where they were able to outflank and surround them. Amos Johns fired the shot that killed the Indian leader, and from that day, he longed for the challenge of the manhunt.

In another year Ben and his sister, Wealthy, settled a mile away from Mac's home site. Each man was deeded five hundred acres from Ware County as their initial homestead. By the time Ben completed his cabin, Mac had attained another five hundred acres and had begun his turpentine operation.

After two years, Mac was established and was ready to bring his family to Georgia. The Indian threat was diminishing with the removal of the Creeks and the Seminoles, and his brothers and sisters would be a great help in the work. Since he could not leave for an extended time, Mac wrote a letter to his younger brothers and impatiently awaited their reply.

When thirty days had passed without an answer, he wrote to the postmaster to inquire of their whereabouts. In another six weeks, he received his answer.

September 8, 1839

Dear Sir:

As I am new at this post, I do not personally know your family, but here is the best information I can attain. I regret to inform you that your father, your two eldest brothers, Sean and Gallegher, one sister named Barbara, and one sister, Mary Katherine, are now deceased by some year and a half. I have been unable to learn the whereabouts of the next two eldest, Thomas and

Michael. It is generally believed that when they reached the age of fourteen, they went their own ways to find work.

The other six underage children were taken into various homes upon the deaths of Sean and Gallegher. I have spoken with the ministers who took responsibility for the placement of the children, and they advise you to leave matters as they are. After almost two years, your younger brothers and sisters have grown accustomed to their new families, and it would be unfair to all concerned to uproot them again.

For your peace of mind, the ministers ask me to assure you that the children are loved and now have the opportunity to become useful members of their community.

Sincerely,
Phineas Brogdon, Postmaster
Carthage, North Carolina

Mac was stunned. He could easily understand the death of his father—a violent death, no doubt. But the twins...Barbara...Little Mary Katherine? And the family dispersed for so long. How could he ever hope to find them—any of them? There was no hope. If he left what he had built up here to search for them, there would be nothing to return to. The realization that he had lost his family burned Mac's conscience.

He couldn't rest anymore. He would come in at dark from the day's work, physically exhausted, but with his mind racing and his nerves on edge. He had little desire for food, and his very soul was anxious. In his isolation he turned to the only consolation that he had known in life. On his next trip to Waresboro for supplies, Mac bought more liquor than he did food. There was food enough in the woods, he reasoned.

For the next ten years, Mac lived for his work. By the time more settlers moved into his section of Ware County, there were a half dozen families who had accumulated most of the land. Of these families, Mac and Ben and Wealthy were by far the largest landowners.

In 1848 they began to talk of forming a new county to relieve the inconvenience of conducting their business in Waycross, some forty miles to the east. By 1850 the leaders in two counties, Ware and Lowndes, saw the wisdom in reducing the area that they had to administer, and Clinch County was carved out from the extreme edges of the two counties.

The leaders of the new county decided to take Ben and Wealthy and Mac up on their offer of adjoining land for the county seat, and Polk, Georgia, named for the President of the United States, was incorporated that same year.

"Polk!" exclaimed Wealthy to Ben. "Good Lord, what a name! And to think we're going to live in a place that sounds like what you'd do to a coon up a tree. It's too hard to say properly. And its downright unpleasant sounding. I won't have it."

The men thought that Wealthy would go on to other things and let them proceed with laying out the town square. Ben Taylor knew his sister well enough to know that they might as well begin choosing a new name for their town. By the time the Methodists had set the pilings for the town's first church, the state legislature had approved the change in name from Polk to Magnolia.

In February of 1851 the church was completed, and Mac disappointed his good friend, Ben, by becoming the first groom to stand at the church's altar. It wasn't that Ben wanted to be the first groom. He wanted his sister to be the first bride—Mac's bride. But Mac had chosen a Sirmans girl instead. By the end of the year she had produced a daughter, Kathleen.

The town grew at a remarkable rate over the next several years. First, Mac's elegant new home for his family appeared, then Ben and Wealthy's new home to keep up with Mac, then a dry goods store, a livery stable, a Baptist church, a courthouse, and a school in quick succession. Then came a half dozen new homes and a bank.

An enterprising young banker from Waycross, Clarence Pace, moved his family over to Magnolia in 1852. His son, Roger, was four years old, and that year Clarence's wife delivered their daughter, Jennifer.

Over the years that saw Mac progress from a solitary squatter in the middle of the south Georgia pine forest to a man of prominence in the state's newest county, he became a good-humored, prosperous version of his father. He even took on his father's physical appearance in his thirties—a squat, powerful body on which perched a round, hairless head draped with a smile. His drinking had started in frustration at the loss of his family and in his loneliness and in the absence of anything else to fill the void in his life. By the time his wife and daughter had come into his life, it was too late to drive out the alcoholism.

Along with the new homes and the churches and all the good things growing in Magnolia came the lesser things, and the least of these was an establishment a mile from town called The Jug.

Having been given the choice of voluntary removal from nearby Valdosta or an assisted move, complete with tar and feathers, Cable Worthington had opted for moving his family of six to neighboring Clinch County. He opened The Jug for business a month later, and Mac was its best patron within the week.

Each man fulfilled the other's need perfectly. Mac was a lonesome man who never had time to develop friendships, in need of an instant friend. Cable possessed a natural friendliness, a charm that, though it was without substance or depth, appealed to men and made them like him immediately. Cable was also an opportunist, and Mac, with his vast land holdings and other assets, was definitely an opportunity.

Together, the two were a study in contrast. Worthington was as slender as Mac was round. His oily hair hung to his shoulders, and his eyes were ravenous and piercing. He didn't merely look at other people. He sized them up.

Unlike his father, Mac did tend to his business and did not let his love of drink or a good bet endanger what he had worked to accumulate. This fact of his character dictated to Cable the necessity for patience in his cultivation of Mac McLendon. It might take a year or longer to get Mac's confidence to the point where he could properly fleece the man, but with the security of his new establishment, Cable Worthington was in no hurry.

A year passed and in that year Mac and Cable became closer. They shared a love for competition, whether it was cards, cockfights, or their newest thrill, horse racing. But that's as close as Mac allowed Cable to get to him. He never invited Cable into town to meet his wife or to be sociable with him. Their friendship never strayed toward Mac's business or to anything outside the whiskey-driven competitions in which they engaged.

After two years, Cable was about to despair of ever getting close enough to Mac to make any real money. He picked up five or ten dollars here and there on a gamble, but it was hardly the amount he had in mind. It wasn't even the money that Cable really had in mind. Land would do nicely—lots of land.

But McLendon wasn't the easy mark that Cable had taken him for. He was distrustful of people and tended to hold them at arm's length. Whenever Cable tried to talk business, Mac deflected the discussion back to tough fighting roosters or fast horses.

Just as Cable was at his lowest ebb, two events transpired which profoundly affected his plans to get to Mac and to a sizeable portion of his assets. First, Mac's wife took a terrible fall down the stairs in their new home, broke her neck, and died. Mac was left with three-year old Kathleen to raise and another reason to drink. That raised possibilities in Cable's mind. Associated with this event were several footnotes.

The county undertaker and coroner, Russell Griffin, was a regular patron at The Jug, and under careful interrogation and a promise by Cable to tear up a two-month bar tab, Russell gave up a precious bit of information. Only three or four other people in town knew that at her death, Alice McLendon was considerably pregnant.

Cable thought it odd. Usually a woman started making a fuss when she was just a little bit pregnant. And a proud, drunk papa wouldn't shut up about his boy and what all he's going to do. And wasn't it odd that Mac hadn't been around as much lately? Cable's naturally suspicious and cynical mind didn't have much trouble leaping to the logical conclusion.

Who had impregnated Mac's wife for him? It was a small town, Cable reasoned. It shouldn't be too hard to figure. With an hour's thought, he had shortened his list to three names. He could be patient now. He had his old buddy right where he wanted him, and very soon, Cable Worthington would own Mac.

He thought he knew which of the three men he should praise the highest when he next had a drink with Mac. It was only a twenty-four-hour wait, and when he got the reaction that he was looking for on the first try, Cable knew that Mac would listen to reason. Murder was such a nasty business that blackmail seemed rather tame by comparison. All he was asking was that Mac help him out a little on his finances, and in return, Cable was going to help Mac avoid execution.

When it came right down to it, Mac agreed that it seemed more than a fair trade, so Mac said that he would get the necessary papers in order and bring them for Cable's signature within forty-eight hours. And he did.

After Mac deeded half of his land to Cable and the papers were secured in Cable's office, the two of them had a grand celebration. Drinks on the house. Cable insisted on it. In the early hours of the next morning the second event happened which was to have an impact on Cable's plans. While racing Mac on horseback, Cable slammed into a low-hanging oak limb, driving pieces of his skull deep into his brain. No evidence of a land transaction between the two men was ever discovered.

     *   *   *   *

Amos Johns was born and raised in the northern half of what would later become Clinch County, Georgia. The Johns family numbered twelve, and they were no-nonsense, Primitive Baptist, daylight-to-dark, south Georgia farmers. The children took what education they could get by the cook fire at night. Their studies were intended to enable them to read the Bible, to cipher enough not to be taken advantage of, and to sign their names in a beautiful, floral script.

The Primitive Baptists gathered at their meeting place once a month. It was the only place away from home where the younger children would come out from behind the skirts of their mother or their eldest sister.

Amos was the second oldest child, and from the age of twelve, he knew what he would do with his life. In June of 1826 Amos and his father were in the town of Alapaha to sell produce. They were driving their wagon down the main street when a drunk staggered out of an alley and fired two shots at them. As Amos' father struggled to regain control of their spooked horses, a big man appeared from nowhere and grabbed the halter. By the time the men calmed the horse, the drunk had reloaded and was cussing the big man. He waved his gun threateningly as he approached, but the other man stood his ground. When the drunk was just a few feet away, he leveled the gun to fire. It looked to Amos that there was no way for him to miss this time. At the last possible second, the big man reached out and simply took the gun away from his assailant. With one swipe of his huge right hand, he knocked the drunk senseless.

As he turned to apologize to Amos' father, the afternoon sun gleamed off of a star on his chest, dazzling Amos' eyes. He had never seen such a display of raw power and such calm in so dangerous a situation.

He was going to be that big, and he wanted a star like that one. The good people would listen to him, and he had just been shown how to handle the bad people. It was a lesson that Amos Johns would never forget. He stayed on the farm with his family for another ten years, but he never lost sight of what he had witnessed in Alapaha that day.

Over those years Amos grew into quite a man. He topped out at six-feet-five inches, and there was hardly an ounce of fat on him. In his huge hands a shotgun looked like a toy, and two of his younger siblings could hang from his arms at one time. He was a gentle, homely giant, with the sad countenance of a basset hound and a bass voice to match.

After the pursuit of Red Stocking, Colonel Tomlinson recommended twenty-two year old Amos to fill a vacancy in the Lowndes County Sheriff's Department.

He remained in that office until Sheriff Gaines recommended him as deputy to Sheriff Charles Cowart of the new County of Clinch in 1850. Four years later Sheriff Cowart resigned his office to enter private business and Amos Johns took the position that he would hold for the next forty years as sheriff of Clinch County.

Amos had only been in office two months on that summer night in 1854, when an agitated Ben Taylor woke him with bad news. Accompanying Ben to Mac's home, Amos inspected the scene that Ben had described to him. Mac sat on the floor in the foyer, his back to a wall and a half-empty bottle of bourbon in his hand. As Amos entered the foyer, Mac took a long drink, but didn't acknowledge the sheriff's presence.

Across the room at the foot of the stairs lay the body of Alice McLendon dressed in a silk nightgown, her neck broken, her body bruised in various places. Amos looked at Ben in disbelief. As good friends as they were with Mac, neither of them knew that Alice was pregnant.

The matter was handled discreetly, even to the satisfaction of Alice's family. It was purely accidental. The poor woman arose late at night for one of the various reasons we all do. She lost her footing, fell the length of the stairs, and died from injuries sustained in the fall. The bereaved husband heard a commotion, investigated, and sought help from a neighbor who summoned the proper authority. Tragic, but case closed.

Then, less than two weeks later, Mac was present at a second death, this one more expected, more understandable, and less sympathetic than the first. Cable Worthington died in one of his infamous late-night horse races with Mac. Although Cable left a grieving family behind, he and Mac had been asking for this for a long time.

The people of Magnolia felt sorry for poor little Kathleen McLendon. Thank God for Wealthy Taylor until Mac could settle down some. Miss Wealthy would make sure that he toed the line until they could get the little girl raised properly. Everyone liked Mac, and they hoped that these blows would sober him and straighten him up. Amos Johns and Ben Taylor certainly hoped so. Amos thought that he had done what was best for everyone concerned, but he knew he couldn't justify it to anyone else. Hell, he couldn't even justify to himself what he had done, but he could live with it.

XI

Whenever Ben Taylor was exasperated, he unconsciously clenched his jaws causing the muscles to twitch. As he reflected on the source of his irritation and on the means of relief, he inhaled and exhaled deeply through his nostrils. When he found the means of relief or if no solution was apparent, he resorted to a verbal attack which, unchecked, might consume the better part of a quarter hour. When his spinster sister, Wealthy, was the source of his irritation, the verbal attack rarely went unchecked for more than a few seconds.

"You need not sit there blowing through your nose like some beached whale, Benjamin Taylor," she said, peering over her spectacles at her brother. "I'm not one of your turpentine nigras, and I don't intend to hear it, not in this house."

"You have the mentality of one of my niggers, woman. Whatever possessed you to take in that stray dog is beyond me. The boy is a common deserter, no better than those bastards out in the swamp who ran away from duty and country to leave their brothers behind, dying on the field of battle."

"Don't try your high-flown rhetoric on me, mister. You've never even seen this boy, let alone heard his pathetic story. The preacher and Amos Johns have talked with him. They are convinced that his story runs true and that he poses no threat to decent folk. They—"

"Oh, so that's it—the preacher and Amos. And I suppose they're going to take full responsibility should this boy rob us blind or murder us in our sleep."

"They'll check up on the boy every week, but he'll stay here on my authority, so I'll take any responsibility for his conduct in relation to us. Amos will be responsible for his conduct in the community. He says that doesn't bother him in the least."

111

Ben stood up from his leather chair and scowled at his sister. She continued her needlework and glared at him over her spectacles.

"I'll wager that in a month's time Amos Johns and your preacher will transfer the whole load to our shoulders and for what? To try to save something that's probably not worth the effort in the first place. I'm telling you, this boy will turn out to be trouble."

"There you go again," Wealthy said, "trying to judge in a matter that you know nothing about. I'm persuaded that with a home life and a good job, John Warren will become an asset to this county."

"Hold it right there. I know that if you're determined we'll have the boy to keep, but I'll be hanged if he's staying in this house!"

The old lady looked up calmly. "That might be arranged."

"What might be arranged?"

"To have you hanged."

"If he stays, he stays in the barn. And don't think I missed that remark about the good job. I ain't hiring! Good night to you!" Ben turned and strode from the room.

"Good night, Benjamin." Wealthy put her sewing aside and watched the last light fade from the window. "I wonder if John Warren has ever worked in the woods," she said softly. "No matter. I'm sure he'll pick it up in no time."

As in any small community, the word of a stranger's presence in town accompanied by unusual events had spread throughout Magnolia and the surrounding countryside within two days of John's arrival. Word had it that Amos Johns had a boy in custody. The stranger had claimed kin to the Worthingtons, but he had not known Sara Worthington's first name.

Though he had plenty of opportunity, Amos Johns said nothing that might alleviate his townspeople's aching curiosity. During the week he kept John in custody, he remained as aloof as his job would permit. When those who considered themselves on good terms with the sheriff dared to question him concerning the boy, he replied vaguely that John was a vagrant from north Georgia.

As the first week of his captivity passed, John and the sheriff fell into a routine of peaceful coexistence. Amos let John out of his cell for most meals. The two of them had long conversations in which they discussed their pasts and the progress of the war.

On the morning of John's ninth day in jail, Amos came to the cell unusually early.

"You have some company, boy. Come on out here."

John followed Amos down the cramped corridor, wondering who would call on him. In Amos' office on the visitor's side of the desk a wiry little man sat stiffly on the front edge of the chair, his hands folded in his lap, every hair in place.

"John, this is the Reverend Jedediah Polk, our Baptist preacher. We had planned to give this a while longer, but something's come up, and I've decided to let you out now," Amos said.

"One of my congregation has consented to take you into her home, John," the reverend said. "Miss Wealthy Taylor and her brother, Benjamin, live across the square in the same block as the church. You'd live in the barn behind their house, and you'd be obligated to work at whatever chores Miss Taylor sees fit to give you."

"I don't want anyone's charity," John said.

"There's no charity involved here," the reverend said. "Miss Taylor will expect—and will undoubtedly get—a full day's labor from you in return for your room and board. And there are one or two stipulations to this arrangement. I trust you realize that, despite our confidence in you, Amos and I are taking quite a risk in letting you go free. By agreeing to take you in, Miss Taylor and her brother share in that risk."

"Yes, sir. I understand," John said.

"In that case, you should readily agree to our conditions. First, Miss Wealthy will be in constant contact with the two of us regarding your conduct. In addition, you'll be expected to report to Amos and me once a week. Agreed?"

"Yes, sir."

"Next, you're not to leave town unless you're accompanied by one of the Taylors, the sheriff, or myself."

"I agree."

"Last, you're to attend services at my church on Wednesdays and Sundays without fail."

"Reverend, I've been raised in the Methodist church, but now I prefer no church at all."

"I only stipulated the Baptist church because Miss Wealthy is a member of our congregation, and I know that she'll insist on some church for you. The best I can do is the church of your choice."

"All right," John said. "I'll go along with that."

"Well, then." Reverend Polk rose as he spoke. "Shall we go out and introduce you to Miss Taylor?"

Their destination was a short walk from the courthouse. As they entered the front gate of the Taylor home, John noticed the order of the place. The picket fence was in good repair and freshly painted. The front yard was barren of grass and swept clean. The house and the barn were in excellent shape.

As the men stepped onto the porch, a frail-looking woman in her mid-fifties opened the front door and emerged. The collar of her severe black dress extended to her pointed chin. Her hair was parted in the middle and pulled into a bun at the back of her head. Her face was angular.

"Good morning, gentlemen."

"Morning, Miss Wealthy," Amos said. "We've brought your boarder."

"Miss Wealthy Taylor," Reverend Polk interjected, "Meet Mr. John Warren. John, this is Miss Wealthy Taylor."

"I'm pleased to meet you, Ma'am."

"And I'm pleased to have you here, John. Won't you gentlemen come in for coffee?"

Amos started to say something about having work to do, but the reverend broke in. "We'd like that very much. Wouldn't we, Amos?"

"Why yes, I believe we would," Amos said.

Wealthy served them in the parlor, a spacious room dominated by a piano and an ornate sofa with two side chairs. John thought that Amos looked uncomfortable and out of place in such a formal setting. His huge hands engulfed the delicate cup and saucer, and he sat stiffly on the edge of the plush chair.

When everyone had been served, Amos spoke first. "The preacher and I have explained the terms of John's release to him, and he's agreed to them. Do you want to add anything to what we discussed earlier?"

"No, I think we've worked everything out quite nicely. I'm sure John's looking forward to your sermon this Sunday, Reverend. All our young folks find you quite an inspiration, and they certainly enjoy the socials your wife organizes."

The men shifted awkwardly. Reverend Polk and Amos exchanged anxious glances.

"Miss Wealthy, about the matter of church—" Amos began.

"Miss Taylor." John said. "I was raised in the Methodist church. The reverend has agreed that I may attend services at the church of my choice."

She smiled sweetly at John. "That will never do. You see, all parties concerned must agree to the conditions under which you'll be placed in my care, and that's one point on which I will not waver."

"I hardly see that it matters where John goes to church as long as he goes," Amos said.

"Let me aid your perception, Mr. Johns. You'll forgive me if I speak too bluntly. I intend to see that John has a proper home and that he matures into a useful, law-abiding member of this community. His spiritual development will be of the highest importance in that process. I cannot do creditable work if John's at one church on a Sunday morning, and I'm at another. That's all I have to say on the subject. Either he attends the Baptist church, or I'm afraid he'll have to return to your jail. The decision is his."

Amos placed his cup and saucer on a table next to the chair and stood. "That's clear enough to me. What do you say, boy?"

John returned Wealthy's solemn gaze, then stood beside the sheriff. "Let's go back to jail, sheriff."

Reverend Polk remained seated and spoke as Amos and John turned to the door. "Let's not be too hasty, good friends. Miss Wealthy, may I suggest a compromise of sorts?"

She nodded.

"John, would you be willing to attend the Baptist church for one year? At the end of that time, if you still insist on it, you may go to the Methodist church."

Wealthy broke in before John could answer. "I'd accept that condition, but at the end of one year, if John decides to return to the Methodists, he must also leave this house."

Reverend Polk turned again to John.

"I'm willing to try it," John said. "But only for six months." His eyes never wavered from Wealthy's.

She smiled almost imperceptibly.

"It's done then," the sheriff said. "It's time the preacher and I went on about our business. Thank you for the coffee, Miss Wealthy."

As the gate closed behind them, Amos nudged Reverend Polk and jerked his thumb back toward the house. "That's a stubborn pair. It's going to be interesting to see who survives out of the two of them."

"My money would be on Miss Wealthy," the reverend said.

"A bet with a Baptist minister's too good to pass up. The boy will be a Methodist in six month's time."

"He'll be a Baptist. And if he is, you'll be beside him every Sunday for two months," Reverend Polk said.

"He'll be a Methodist. And if he is, I'll find a box of Cyrus's best cigars on my desk six months from next Sunday."

"And no one would know where they came from?" The reverend asked.

"Not a soul," Amos replied.

*   *   *   *

Reverend Polk's evaluation of Miss Wealthy Taylor's drive and energy proved all too accurate. From his first day's work for her, John Warren never felt himself to be the object of charity.

The morning started at six with a scant breakfast of toast and coffee. Miss Wealthy observed that she had allowed John an extra hour's sleep that he must not expect every day. He put in the hardest day of work he could recall.

From breakfast until just before lunch, he cleaned the back of the Taylor's barn. It was a spacious structure with six stalls, three on each side of a central walk. John thought that the size of the barn was a matter of status, not necessity, for there were only two horses and no indication that there had ever been any more.

At the back of the barn, behind John's stall, there was a large area filled with saddles, harnesses, bridles, and a black buggy. First, Wealthy had him move everything to the front of the barn. There she stationed herself with saddle soap and oil so that she could give all the leather a good cleaning as she supervised John's every movement. The removal of old hay, the shoveling of manure, the sweeping of the compacted dirt floor, even the scrubbing of the interior walls—she directed them all and saw each task completed to her rigorous specifications.

When finally at eleven she ordered him out of the last stall, John wiped the sweat from his forehead and breathed an exaggerated sigh of relief.

"Thank goodness that's finished," he said.

Wealthy squinted at the stall. "Hardly finished," she muttered. "But it'll keep until after dinner. Get a drink of water, then take that ax over there and fill the wood box in the kitchen. Ben will be home in an hour, and he likes his dinner on time." She stared implacably at the astonished boy. "Don't stand there gaping at me, you big moose. There's the ax. Now step lively!"

He was clumsy with the ax, so at noon when John and the Taylors sat down for a dinner that was as plentiful as the breakfast was meager, the wood box by the back door was only half full. John slumped over his plate, almost laying on the edge of the table, while Wealthy and Ben carried the conversation.

"What's the news today, Ben?" Wealthy asked.

"Pretty quiet. Everybody showed up except Jeeter. Word is Callie was about to have the baby, so he stayed home to get in the way."

"Good Lord have mercy! I hope they have enough sense to let it go at this one. How a nigra thinks he can support nine children in these times is beyond me."

Ben stopped chewing and looked up at his sister. "I expect it will be us that supports Jeeter's nine head right along. He gets that cabin for practically nothing, and they have a line of credit as long as your arm at the commissary."

"Well, Jeeter and a lot of other folks are about to get a rude awakening with the way this war's going. We'll see how he likes his freedom when he has to work for a wage and pay rent and a grocery bill like whites do. How does he think he's going to get by then?"

"Think!" Ben laughed. "That's a good one, old girl. I've got sixteen niggers working my land, and you couldn't put the lot of them together and come up with one honest-to-God thought—Corey excepted."

"That's our fault, not theirs," John said. The effect was the same as if he had reached out and slapped both of them simultaneously. A forkful of butter beans stopped short of Ben's mouth as he stared in disbelief.

"What did you say, boy?"

"It's true," John answered nonchalantly. "Imagine the reverse situation. Imagine that you'd been whisked off to Africa as a young boy and auctioned to some African villager as a slave. You'd know nothing of the language or the culture, nothing about how to support yourself or a family, except by remaining a slave."

Both Taylors were stunned. White people, enslaved in Africa to the aborigines? They merely stared open-mouthed as he continued.

"Now suppose that after decades of servitude, you and your family were suddenly set free. What have you gained? There'd be no public institutions such as schools or Christian churches to serve as a means of improving your lot in life. How would you go about establishing such institutions? You'd probably be a poor dirt farmer and would only know how to scratch a few ears of corn from the ground or how to hunt for a little meat. That's the black man's situation here.

"I bet there aren't a hundred black people in the whole state who know how to read or write, and I could do both before I was six years old. I think that after the war the new government will step in and provide for the education of black people, and that step will be their first on the road to equality and self-reliance. I think—"

"Enough!" Ben jumped to his feet, rattling the dishes on the table and knocking his chair back across the kitchen. "Your thoughts be damned, boy! If I hear another one of them in my house, you'll be back in Amos Johns' jail before the sun sets!"

"But sir, I only meant to—"

"By God, I said that's enough!"

Wealthy pushed her chair back and stood regally, her hands clasped firmly together at her waist.

"That's quite enough from you, Benjamin Taylor. You have right enough to be outraged at this boy's impertinence, but I'll not sit here and listen to blasphemy in my own home."

"And what do you suppose I've had to sit at my own dinner table and listen to? A mouthful of Yankee rhetoric from some young pup who hadn't the courage to stand and fight for his home when it most counted. And me feeding him while he spews that garbage back in my face? Well, I'll not hear it again! That's your stray, and if you'll feed him, you'll feed him in the barn with the rest of the animals. I'll not have him in the house with me. Do you understand?"

"Yes, I understand," she said meekly. "Now will you pick up the chair and finish the meal?"

"No, by God, I won't. I'll be home promptly at six, and I expect to see a table set for two again."

When Ben slammed the back door behind him, Wealthy sat down and calmly resumed eating. She looked over at John, who sat with his head down, slumping over the full plate before him.

"Sit up and finish your meal, John. You have a lot of work ahead of you this afternoon."

He sat up. "I'll finish whatever you want done in the barn, and then I think you had better take me back to the courthouse."

She scarcely acknowledged that he had spoken.

"It's plain that your brother doesn't want me here, and I'll always be causing trouble between the two of you."

"My brother and I have been fighting ever since I can remember. It's the only way we know."

"I'll not stay where I'm not wanted."

"I want you here, son," she said, and she continued eating.

"I appreciate what you're trying to do for me, but it just won't work. Mr. Ben hates me, and he'll never change his opinion about me. I can't change the fact that I ran away from the war, and that's something he'll never let me forget. I'll be better off going on to Florida."

She looked up at him. "You seem to know a great deal about the future. All I know of it is that your food's going to be cold in the next few minutes. Now, will you hush and eat?"

He took a bite.

"That's better. You aren't a quitter, and neither am I."

"I'm a deserter from the army. That's as big a quitter as you can be."

"You aren't more than fifteen or sixteen," she said. "Had no business in the war in the first place."

"There were a lot of boys my age in the militia."

"They had no business there either. And you talk too much. Finish your food and fill that wood box properly this time."

"Then will you take me back to Amos?"

She looked at him thoughtfully and smiled. "You promised to finish the work in the barn. Will you keep that promise?"

"I will."

"Then I'll take you back after you've fulfilled your promise. Now tell me how you think the government will go about educating the nigra."

Throughout the remainder of the week, Wealthy demanded that John turn to an assortment of work outside the barn. With each new task she made the same excuse. "The things in the barn won't be exposed to the weather. We have to do this before the real cold weather sets in." Then she would coerce John into some minor repair on the house or in some other preparation for the winter weather. On John's first visit to Amos's office, he explained how badly things were going at the Taylor's house since he had moved in.

"Amos," the reverend said, "If John's presence creates dissension between Miss Wealthy and Mr. Ben, perhaps it'd be wise to end the bargain."

"Creates dissension my hind leg," Amos replied. "There hasn't been a day in the last forty years that those two weren't fussing about something. Ben will get used to having the boy around. Just give him a little more time."

Over the next three weeks, John and the Taylors fell into a routine that made life bearable. John stayed out of Ben's way, and although the two of them slept and ate within a hundred feet of each other, their paths rarely crossed. Wealthy insisted that John escort her on long walks each evening, supposedly to strengthen his leg and to familiarize him with the town and the surrounding area. After only a week, Wealthy turned their discussions to her real purpose for starting the walks, and John gradually opened up about his past.

He talked about the good times, of growing up the son of prosperity. Eventually, though, she perceived that he clung to the past a little too tenaciously, and she steered him toward talk of the past few months. He was evasive. She persisted.

"John, I don't mean to sound cruel, but don't you think it's about time you started living in the present again?"

"What do you mean, Miss Wealthy? I only talk about my family because I thought you wanted to know."

"I do want to know about your life, son, but we've been taking these walks for quite a while now, and all you talk of is Atlanta before the war. I know that you need to hold tight to the good times. We all need that security and the hope that we'll live to see happier times. But, it's important that you face up to what happened to you before you came to us."

"Why?" John was suddenly agitated. "I hate what this damned war has done to me and mine. I'm no better than an animal now. Why should I think about the things that have brought me down?"

"It won't do you any good to dwell on it. Nor will it do you a service to dwell on your family. Hold them dear in your memory, so that you'll know how to love a family of your own one day."

"I'll never have a family! You only end up getting hurt."

"You and I both know better than that, John. How could you spend hours telling me about the love you shared with your family and then say such a thing?"

He stopped walking and turned his back to her. He was crying, and she allowed him time to fight the grief that tore at his heart.

"They're all gone, and I'll never have them again, Miss Wealthy. I love them so!" His big shoulders shook, and she put her hands on them, holding him tightly.

"I know, son. Believe me, I know." She fought back tears of her own. "You listen to me. What I have to say isn't easy for either of us, but you have to hear it, and you have to believe it. Your family loves you now just as they did when they were alive. They're with God now, and they know you're here. They still want the best for you, and that means going on with the rest of your life."

John had regained control of his emotions. He turned to Wealthy. "Don't talk to me about God. I've heard about God all my life—about

God and His love. Well, I've seen it firsthand now, and God's love doesn't amount to anything I care to have again."

Wealthy slapped him as hard as she could, but John barely flinched. His expression turned hard, and he stood his ground, staring down at her.

"That doesn't change anything," he said.

"Maybe nothing I can say or do will change things for you, John. If you really believe what you just said, you're probably too far into self-pity to come out again. You took all the good that God had to offer for years. Then when foolish men, who had no better sense than to turn away from God, stole it from you, you blame the whole mess on our creator. Your vision's no better than theirs."

"Didn't God have the power to stop them?"

"He gave us the ability to choose the way we go, son. He won't take that away no matter what men do. Only you can decide what you'll do with your life. That's why I'm telling you to put your family deep in your heart to cherish, but not to live with. You can't have them back in this life."

She turned and walked back toward Magnolia.

"I don't know how to go on, Miss Wealthy."

"Why did you keep going when you left Atlanta? Why didn't you stay and allow yourself to be killed in the fighting?"

"I don't know. Instinct, I guess."

"If that's a name for wanting to live, I suppose it's as good as any. Don't live out your time in misery. If you turn your back on God, that's exactly what'll happen.

"You've suffered terribly, but I expect you to work a little each day to make things better for yourself. If you really want to be happy in this life, you're eventually going to have to reconcile yourself with God."

"Maybe God should make up with me, first. I don't recall doing anything to hurt Him like He's done to me."

Wealthy controlled her emotions. "That's exactly the attitude that you have to overcome," she said softly. "All God's done to you is to sustain you through everything that sinful men have put you through. Be loyal to Him, son. Despite the outward appearances, continue to love the Lord just as you did when you were an innocent child."

The next morning when John awakened, he found a worn, black-bound Bible next to him in the hay. A dark blue ribbon protruded from its uppermost edge. Sitting with his back against the stall, John opened the book to the marked section. In the top margin of the page Wealthy had written, "This book is yours. Search for the answer."

"I've read this before," he muttered. He sat with his back to the wall for a long time, staring at the book. Finally, he opened it to where the ribbon marked the pages and read: "There was a man in the land of Uz whose name was Job, and that man was perfect and upright, and one that feared God, and eschewed evil..."

*   *   *   *

As the town faded behind them John said, "I've read the book where you marked it."

Wealthy looked straight ahead as she spoke. "What did it tell you?"

"That God allows our lives to be destroyed without just cause. I already knew that, though." He expected her to defend the book, but she walked on quietly.

"Is that all?" she asked.

"No. I saw that Job's three best friends stayed by him for a while, but eventually they tormented him more than they helped him. Everyone else who he'd helped over the years turned on him immediately. His wife seemed particularly wise to me."

"'Curse God and die,'" Wealthy quoted.

"Yes."

"When was everything restored to Job?"

"When he acknowledged God's power and wisdom."

"And when he prayed for his friends who had tormented him with their words," Wealthy added. "Maybe his wife was included in his prayers, John—despite her bad advice."

"I guess God really taught old Job a lesson, didn't he? Never mind all the sons and daughters who were killed without cause. Never mind all the needless suffering Job went through. What a wonderful victory for God!"

Wealthy finally stopped and turned to John. Tears ran down her cheeks, and she trembled. "God didn't tell the men responsible for this war to take your family from you. They did it of their own free will. Even Satan had choices to make when he was one of God's own. God didn't tell him to rebel nor to touch Job. Satan did it because he tried to make himself God's equal, and that attitude always brings disaster."

"Why doesn't God protect us from such evil, then?"

"He does protect us, son. He protects what's important—the eternal part of us. I do believe your people are safe with God now. That's something you must come to believe."

"Job isn't going to help me believe it. They were killed without reason, Wealthy!"

"Damn your reason, John! It'll surely damn you if you don't. Read the book with your heart, not your reason. Neither you nor I nor anyone else will sit down and reason life into making sense. Read the story again and again. But understand how Job felt when he went through his trials. Understand how he felt when God finally spoke to him, and when he came to realize how foolish he had been in daring to question God. We come to God as little children come to their fathers here—not knowing much of anything, just trusting."

John turned away from her in confusion. She had no idea how it felt to bury your whole family—had no idea how it felt to be utterly alone in a world falling apart. The heart for argument had gone from him, and he stood, looking into the darkening forest.

XII

As the winter of 1864 changed to spring, the relationship between John Warren and Ben Taylor gradually changed. There was a progressive thaw that led not to warmth, but to a begrudging tolerance of each other's moods and, to a small degree, a respect for each other's abilities.

Prodded by Wealthy, Ben occasionally complimented John on the work he did around the house. He had reason enough to be grateful, for since John's arrival, Wealthy no longer harassed Ben about things that needed a man's attention.

Doors no longer sagged at the hinges, rotten boards on the broad veranda were replaced by freshly nailed pine and given a fresh coat of paint. The wood box was always filled with oak, and fires blazed in the grate each morning and evening. The horses were groomed better than ever before, and every piece of leather riding gear gleamed with a rich coat of oil. To Ben it was all as if by magic, for Wealthy saw to it that every task was accomplished between the time Ben pushed back from the breakfast table at five-thirty and the time he sat down in his easy chair at six p.m. with a cup of steaming coffee.

Ben knew little of the hours of tutelage that Wealthy put into most of the work, but he observed the bond that had developed between his sister and the boy. It was a natural result of the days of solitude and work they shared—two people, the teacher and her student, studying a problem, finding the means to set it right, and then working together until the job was accomplished. Under her vigilant eye, he became carpenter, groomsman, tailor, tinker, locksmith, gardener, bookkeeper, cobbler, and cook.

Most important to John, after two years of necessary neglect, Wealthy made him a scholar again. She had many books herself, but when she thought of some history or classic literature she thought any educated person should read, she found it. She gave John an exacting amount of reading to do daily, and often, as they worked around the house, he and Wealthy discussed his assignments in detail.

Though he and Wealthy grew closer, John's relationship with Ben never went beyond a quiet civility. Occasionally she hinted that Ben should take the boy hunting, but her brother pretended not to understand her meaning. She was afraid that if she pushed the matter Ben would resist acceptance of John as a member of their family even more, and she was right.

The Taylors had immigrated to Georgia from South Carolina thirty years earlier, as the opportunities in the turpentine industry had declined in their home state. Throughout the war Ben had searched out news of South Carolina's fate, and it pained him deeply to hear of the widespread destruction of places familiar to him. John was a deserter, and in Ben's eyes, he was accountable for the ruin of his home state.

Wealthy kept John close to home until the townspeople's speculations of his origins subsided and he was no longer the major topic of conversation.

As Savannah fell to Sherman in December and as the fighting came to a climax in Virginia in the spring, the war again became everyone's main concern, and John was relegated to an item of mere curiosity, unworthy of more than a minute of idle conversation. With attention focused on the war, Wealthy began taking John on shopping trips and various errands around town.

He attended church services each Sunday and Wednesday with Ben and Wealthy. His presence at Sunday morning worship created a mild stir for a while, but they ignored the stares and the remarks about "Wealthy Taylor's young 'un" until the congregation grew used to the sight of John towering over Miss Wealthy as they climbed the brick steps to the church.

He presented quite a dashing figure of a man and soon attracted the attention of several local girls. Miss Wealthy was protective of him and quietly discouraged the young ladies from being so bold as to strike up a conversation with John. He rarely left her sight, and then she made sure that he was in the company of another adult. John was grateful, for he was sure that he would be unable to carry on much of a conversation with anyone his own age—until he saw Jennifer Pace for the first time.

On a rainy Sunday in April, John let Ben and Wealthy out at the front door of the church and returned the buggy to the hitching post. They were late for the service, so the Taylors had gone into the sanctuary before John made a dash back to the vestibule. He barged in with such force that he almost knocked down a young lady standing inside, brushing mud from the hem of her dress. John lunged at the girl, catching her arm in an attempt to hold her up.

"Pardon me, Miss Pace," John stammered. "I was in a hurry to get out of the rain, and I didn't see you there."

"It's quite all right, sir." Her voice was honey and lace. John found it difficult to breathe. "How is it that you know my name?" she asked. "I don't believe we've been properly introduced."

John froze. The truth was too ordinary for this remarkable beauty to hear.

"I first saw you here in this church, and an angel whispered your name to me."

She shivered and averted her eyes from his. She started to speak again, but a young man emerged from the sanctuary and called to her.

"Jennifer, why are you dawdling around out—let go of my sister's arm!"

John drew his hand back as if her arm had grown hot.

"Go into the service, girl," the young man said.

"There's no need to be rude, Roger," she said calmly.

"Mother sent me out here looking for you, so you let me handle this."

She obeyed, but before she let the door swing shut behind her, she turned and smiled demurely at John.

"What were you saying to my sister?" he demanded.

"I almost knocked her down when I ran in out of the rain, and I was apologizing to her," John said.

"Did you have to hold her arm to apologize?"

"No, but I—"

"I don't want to hear it, brother! You let her be. Otherwise you and I are going to have trouble. Is that understood?"

John was shocked by the abruptness of Roger's attack. Jennifer's brother was scrawny and soft looking, and the setting was so unlikely for a confrontation that John was speechless. By the time he could think of a response, Roger had turned and reentered the service.

John took a minute to regain his composure and to allow his face to cool before he entered the sanctuary. When he took his place next to Ben, he halfheartedly joined in the hymn. His mind was on the blonde angel standing across the aisle and one row ahead of him. Jennifer turned slightly and, behind her brother's back, smiled at John. His spirit soared until he recalled his first words to her. *Why didn't I just tell her the truth—an angel! Good Lord!*

By late spring, the once-glorious struggle for independence died on the fields of Virginia, and the scramble for mere survival began. Except for the return of the gaunt and mutilated sons of Clinch County, life went on in Magnolia much as before. The freeing of the slaves in the area became a matter of administration, and the beast of bureaucracy was slow in coming to the county. Ben was unusually moody for weeks after General Lee's surrender, so Wealthy dared not challenge him on matters concerning John. They went about their business as usual.

John met more of the people in town as Wealthy began to send him on errands alone. On one of his required visits to Amos Johns, he was introduced to Clarence Pace, Jennifer's father and the owner of the local bank. At fifty, Clarence had the weak eyes and rounded shoulders of one who had spent far too many hours hunched over ledgers and financial statements. His mouth turned down at the corners in a perpetual frown, and he had an impatient air in the presence of those who were poor. He had a habit of studying and categorizing each person he met as a potential customer. John did not rank high on his list.

By July, John and Wealthy's labors had borne fruit, and there was nothing much left to be accomplished around the house. Wealthy became increasingly anxious for John to work for Ben. She knew that his quick mind and work ethic would win Ben over and then they could become a real family. A chance remark by Mac McLendon one

Sunday after church gave Wealthy an idea of how to persuade Ben to hire John.

"Now that's my idea of how a man should look when he's young and ready to make something of himself," he had said. "If young Warren is looking for work, I have about a half dozen jobs he could fill out at my place. Ben is sure enough letting him go to waste around the house."

From that day Wealthy maneuvered John into a routine that called for him to do his studies whenever Ben was home. He would ride in from the mill precisely at noon to find John stretched out on the veranda, a book in his hands, a cool drink at his side.

In the evenings Wealthy would feed John earlier than Ben, and when her brother went into the barn to unsaddle his horse, the boy would be nodding drowsily over a history or the Bible. Sometimes Ben would find him in deep slumber, the book folded over his large chest. On one such night, he confronted Wealthy at the dinner table.

"Your scholar was asleep at his work again this evening."

"Oh," she said casually, pretending not to notice his tone.

"Oh," Ben mocked. "Is that the best response you can summon? The boy's eating us out of home and hearth, doing not a stitch of work that I can see, and all you can say is 'Oh'!"

"He has quite a bit of catching up to do if he's to enter school in the fall."

"What a bunch of rubbish," Ben muttered. "He's too smart for his own good as it is. I don't think he should go to school."

Be careful now. Let this be his idea. Wealthy said nothing.

Ben stabbed at his food and fumed, his jaw twitching. "The folks didn't have us lollygaging around some schoolhouse when we were his age, and I guess we turned out all right, didn't we?"

"Yes, old dear. We're doing just fine."

Rather than follow his thoughts to their logical conclusion, Ben excused himself from the table and went outside for a smoke.

"This may be harder than I thought," Wealthy said softly. "Time to call in some reinforcements."

She bided her time and three days later she met her reinforcements on the street in front of Harper's pharmacy. As Wealthy and John stepped outside, Mac McLendon and his fourteen-year-old daughter, Kathleen, pulled up in Mac's buggy.

"Well," Mac said, "I see Ben's still letting you work John around the house. Good waste of manpower, if you ask me."

Kathleen smiled at John, then ducked her head. She tugged nervously at her flaming red hair.

"Now there's a handsome pair," Mac said with a wink. "Think we can do a little matchmaking, Miss Wealthy?"

"He'd make a mighty poor catch, Kath, without means to support a girl," Wealthy said.

"I've told you before, I could remedy that. The boy got any drive to him?"

"If he decides to stay on in Magnolia, he'll likely own the county one day. That is, what you don't own of it, Mac. He's thinking of moving on, though. Doesn't seem to be any work to be found."

McLendon hitched his pants and looked Wealthy directly in the eyes. "Just because your brother's fool enough to let such a man stay idle, doesn't signify that I am. With your permission, I'll hire him on the spot."

"Oh, no. That'll never do. I'm all for it, but I insist that you give Ben the courtesy of a little notice."

"All right. Tell him for me tonight, will you?"

"Now, Mac, you know I'm not one to meddle in the men's business. If you want the boy, you'll need to see Ben about it."

He smiled and winked at John as he walked away. "I'll be seeing you, young fellow."

Ben was unusually quiet at dinner that evening. Wealthy tried to draw him into conversation about work, but he ignored her until she began clearing the table. He pushed the chair back from the table and stretched his legs. The muscles of his jaws twitched slightly, and Wealthy knew he was wrestling with a problem.

"What has your mind so occupied?" Wealthy asked cautiously. "You've hardly said three words all evening."

"Just thinking about a proposition that was made today."

"Oh? Anything you'd care to talk about?"

"Not really." As if changing the subject, he said, "Been thinking about getting rid of J.C. Cooper, too."

"Is he one of Nehemiah's worthless boys?"

"That he is. And just as sorry as a Cooper comes. I think he's worse than his old man—always late when he bothers to show up at all, and then he doesn't do an hour's worth of work all day."

"Well, with all these fellows home from the fighting, you should be able to find someone easily enough."

"That's true, but I had more or less settled on someone already."

"Oh? Who is that?"

Ben had expected her to suggest it, had even led her to say the name first, but since she had not, he was trapped.

"Seeing as how I'm supporting him anyway, and he's doing nothing but laying around here reading, I had thought of the boy."

It was all she could do to restrain herself from bounding across the room to hug him. She couldn't resist one final touch. "I don't know about that, Benjamin. John knows you don't care much for him, and just the other day Mac was talking of hiring him."

Ben shot up from the chair and stood glaring at her. "A fine friend Mac McLendon fancies himself, trying to steal labor right out from under my nose! And after I've given that stray a roof over his head and three squares a day. Well, I'll not hear of it. If the boy works for McLendon, he lives off of him, too. Tell that to Mr. John Warren!"

"You've given him a barn roof over his head, and I've had something to do with those three meals a day, thank you. Now I can talk to John, and if you'll move him into the house, it may be that I can persuade him to go with you and not Mac."

"He'll have to pay rent," Ben huffed.

"He'll continue to do the chores around here for his board. You'll not have to raise a finger at home."

"Done." He strode from the kitchen, proud of his bargaining ability and sure that he had saved face in the matter.

Wealthy finished her work, humming an Irish tune she had learned as a girl in South Carolina. All the young men had hungered for her attention back then, and the song brought back pleasant memories.

　　　*　　　　　*　　　　　*　　　　　*

John stood in the midst of a bewildering array of unfamiliar, darkened shapes in the wood yard. The waning moon cast its light over the buildings and wagons around him, but did nothing to illuminate his ignorance. He was so anxious about his first day's work for Ben Taylor that he had slipped from the barn at four in the morning and had ridden out to the mill to look around.

He walked to the sawmill housing and studied the carriage that guided the pine trunks into the jaws of the blade at the far end of the structure. Across the carriage he saw the silhouette of a huge tank which he assumed to be a boiler. He nosed around the equipment for a few minutes, but was able to make only vague sense of what he saw.

The morning air was ripe with the clean odor of cut pine. He inhaled deeply, clearing his mind. To the right of the sawmill sat a high platform with a brick kiln protruding from its center. He had never seen such an apparatus and had no idea what its function was. A dozen barrels were positioned at the lower end of a wooden incline that reached up to the platform some two or three feet above his head.

Evidently, something was emptied into the kiln from the barrels. To John's right was a vat. He dipped his hand into it and felt a hard, cool substance. Picking up a piece, he held it to his nose. It smelled like pine. Sap was taken from the pine tree, heated in the kiln, and came out as crystals. But why did they do that? What did it make? He looked around in exasperation, turning away from the contraption.

"I'll be utterly useless," he said aloud. "Ben will run me off in a day's time."

"Then what you gonna do?" a voice asked.

"Good God almighty!" John whirled around, already crouching to defend himself. "Who is that?"

"Well, it ain't the Lord, that's for sure." The man outlined in the soft glow of the moon made no effort to move toward him. "The question is, who is you? And what you doing prowling around Mr. Ben Taylor's turpentine still?"

"I'm John Warren, and Ben's hired me to start work today."

"Well, he done done it then, ain't he? He sure enough going to get shed of that no 'count Cooper boy. 'Bout time, too." With that said, the man turned and walked toward a shack located on the edge of the yard.

John followed. "Now that you know my name, tell me who you are," he said.

The man paid no attention. "What you doing out here so early, boy?"

"I might ask you the same," John said, irritated at the man's manner.

"You might, but I'm thinking you'd better not." He moved on toward the shack, saying nothing else. John followed silently.

Inside the shack, the man lit a lamp, then labored to set a fire in a small, potbellied stove. He was a little less than six feet tall. His head was covered with a shapeless black hat that obscured his face. A heavy black suit coat covered his bulk except for a protruding paunch of stomach. Underneath the coat he wore a pair of faded overalls. What struck John most about the man were his hands. They were callused and rough, but there was a grace, an eloquence of movement about them that was attractive.

The lamp illuminated a cheap desk littered with papers, a dilapidated cane back sofa, and the cast-iron stove over which the man labored. He scooped some ground coffee into a black pot, dipped water from an oaken bucket, sprinkled a bit of salt into the mixture, and put it on the stove.

"Dip?" He extended his hand to John.

"What?"

"Snuff. You want some?"

"No. Thanks, though."

He packed a generous pinch under his lower lip and stared at the heating coffeepot. After a moment he said quietly, "Name's Stokes, but you just call me Corey." He started to say something else, but a yawn contorted his face. He exhaled loudly and shook himself all over. "This here night work's killing me. I got to get myself some good help," he said, more to himself than John.

"What do you do around here at night?" John asked.

Corey ignored the question. "How old are you, boy?"

"Sixteen."

The old man turned his head and looked at John. "You right growed then, ain't you? You ever turpentined?"

"No, I don't know a thing about this kind of work."

"Mr. Ben, he take care of that." Corey's smile flashed white in the light of the lamp. "Ain't your knowing he's interested in. It's your back. The Cooper boy worked here at the sawmill, but I expect I gonna have you to take under my wing." He looked back to the coffee, took the pot from the stove, and poured out two cups. He handed one to John. "Bet you wonder why a black man got the run of the place like I got."

"Bet I don't," John said. He didn't like the old man's haughtiness.

Corey ignored John's tone. "I Mr. Ben's right hand. Been with him fifteen years now." He blew into his coffee and was silent.

John felt awkward in this strange place with this even stranger old man. He crossed over to the sofa and sat down, leaning forward with his coffee cup on the pine flooring between his feet. After several minutes of silence, he shifted uncomfortably and decided to walk back out into the wood yard. Before he could get up, Corey started talking.

"I come to Magnolia in 1850, and my first stop was the courthouse to register myself as a freed man. Mr. Cowart was the sheriff then, and he said that he was pretty loose with that and to consider myself registered. Said he figured he'd catch me quick enough if I was up to no good. I was pretty slight back then, so he took pity on me and pointed me to Mr. Ben's place. Said I might be able to do a few odd jobs for Miss Wealthy and earn a little to eat that way.

"She put me right to work around the house, chopping wood and washing windows and scrubbing floors and you name it, I done it. I slept in the barn at night for a while, and Miss Wealthy fed me so good that I started to fatten up pretty quick."

John got up and poured more coffee. "Sounds like we have some things in common," he said. "Why did you get moved to work at the mill?"

"Turns out Mr. Ben had been looking for someone to ride herd on the black men working for him. He'd made them an odd situation. Over the years he'd hired some free blacks to work his land, and he'd bought some slaves and let them work for their freedom.

"Mr. Ben built some shotgun shacks for these men and their families, and they all lived together in an area that the whites call Shakerag. He was having a time with some of them men. They was a little too free and was as likely not to show up for work as they was to show up. And when they got to work a lot of times, it wasn't worth having them there. He'd tried a white man as an overseer, but the whites he tried couldn't get used to the idea that them men was free. The more that white overseer beat them and the more he bullied them, the less they showed up for work. The business was suffering for it."

John smiled at the thought of Ben's frustration. "I bet the old man was hell to live with then. How'd you turn things around?"

"Well, all the time I'd been living in his barn, I'd been going out to Shakerag at night and on Sundays, so I knew who ruled the roost and who the chickens was. I knew how the place was laid out, so I told Mr. Ben that if he give me a little ground to build a house on and a little extra help getting going on it, that I'd be the head rooster in about six months time."

Corey went on to tell John that Ben agreed to give him six months to show what he could accomplish. He was surprised when Corey requested land about a quarter of a mile away from the others on the road that led to their church.

Corey began learning the turpentine part of Ben's business. Each day when the work was over, he added on to his home place. On Sundays he sat in a rocker on his new porch as the black women and their children walked by his place to church. He greeted each one of them politely, and when the last of them passed by, he joined them in the small, whitewashed frame church at the end of the road. Only one in ten of the women had her husband with her.

In the first month that Corey was overseer, the black men's attendance at work dropped to an all-time low. Ben became nervous. In the second month, it got worse. Ben became upset. In the third month, they were hardly there at all. The turpentine operation was at a standstill.

"He really hit the roof when he started chewing me out about the situation, and I told him that it was going just like I thought it would. You see, I needed that long to build the best-looking home place of anybody, and I needed that long to ease into a courtship. And them was the two things I needed to turn that work situation around."

"A courtship? What in the world could that possibly have to do with getting a bunch of men to show up for work?" John asked.

Corey smiled and chuckled at the memory. Lucy Bryant was the oldest daughter of Willie and Mary Bryant, two of the most respected people in Shakerag. Lucy was shy, but she was a hard worker. She was thrifty and gifted at cooking and sewing and in the art of making a comfortable home. She was also, by consensus, the ugliest and scrawniest woman in the quarters.

At age thirty-three it looked hopeless for Lucy, but the older women were still working on some of the single older men to take her as a wife. The Sunday afternoon that Corey Stokes came calling on the Bryants caught the whole community by surprise.

Over the next month Corey showered Lucy with flowers, with little gifts that he made, and best of all, with his attention. Lucy and her mama were the first ladies of Shakerag to set foot in Corey's home, and the report they made to the rest of the women was almost incredible. That a man, by himself, had built a home of such beauty and utility as they witnessed was beyond their experience.

At the end of the fourth month of Corey's employment, the resistance of the other men to his leadership reached a peak. But by then, Corey was the most popular man in attendance at the Bethel A.M.E. church, at least among the women. Ben was to the point of exasperation. He needed workers desperately.

In the fifth month, Lucy Bryant became Mrs. Corey Stokes. In the second week of her marriage, Lucy had the ladies of the choir over to her home for a visit. The day after the choir meeting at the Stokes' home, all of the married men employed by Ben Taylor showed up for work, and they were early. By the end of that week all of the men were coming to work and the majority of them were on time every day.

"You know the funny thing about all of that? People thought that marrying Lucy was just a part of the plan I had to get them men into line at work. And I guess it did help me out with the women folks, 'cause they didn't think nobody was ever going to marry that gal. But you know something? I could've picked another girl or two that would've been all right with the community. Truth is, my Lucy had the prettiest soul. That's what I was looking at."

From their marriage in 1851 until her death at age forty-five in 1863, Lucy gave Corey eight children. Their home and their standing in Shakerag grew over the years.

"A couple of years ago, my Lucy passed on, and I took me another wife just last year. Ranetta's a good woman, and at my age, I'm hoping that she's the last woman I need. Now that's old Corey, but I done rambled on a little more than I meant to."

He got up and threw the rest of his coffee out the door.

"Let me tell you something, John. You done bought yourself a heap of trouble here. You know that?" He didn't expect nor wait for a reply. "Mr. Ben done told me you was coming, and I been musing on it. J.C. Cooper and his bunch is ornery enough, and when he come up here this morning and ain't got no job, he gonna be laying for you. You hear what I tell you? J.C. and Ned Worthington and that bunch gonna be laying for you, so watch your step."

John sat up straight. "Do you know Ned Worthington?"

"I know enough of him to know he's a mean one. His daddy had him drinking 'shine before most young 'uns is out of knee pants. I know for a natural fact that he laid up a stock of 'shine last night that'll keep him mean for a week or better."

"Then he's here," John muttered.

"Not many white folks know it, but he's been in the county since before the Yanks took Atlanta. You just mind what I tell you about him and Cooper."

The old man finished his coffee, rinsed the cup, and hung it on a peg near the stove. He picked up an ax near the door and without another word strode out across the yard to the sawmill. John stood at the door watching him go and thought of Ned Worthington.

"He knows I'm here," John said, "and he probably thinks I mean to kill him."

XIII

The first light from the east pushed the cool summer mists from the earth as the rider approached the mill. Corey and John looked at each other, then strained to catch the first glimpse down the east winding road. John hoped that it was not light enough for Corey to see the concern on his face. He shouldn't get all worked up about J.C. Cooper. He could take care of himself. The rider rounded the last bend and emerged from the forest.

"What a way to start the week! The old girl gets me up an hour late, and my newest hand is nowhere to be found! Just what do you think you're doing, boy? My best damned horse is gone, and I figure you're halfway to the Okefenokee, and the old girl is moaning and crying 'til I go off without my breakfast, and here stands you and that grinning nigger like a couple of possum-fed gators and—"

By then Ben was off his horse and into the shack. He stuck his head back out the door. "And stay out of my coffee!" He jerked the door shut with such force that the top hinge popped loose, and the door sagged outside the jamb.

"Come here, boy," Corey whispered. John followed him over to the sawmill. "Ain't no need to get your heart up in your throat. He's like this the start of every week. Next thing he'll do is stick his head back out here and say, 'Stokes, if them shif'less niggers of yours ain't here in ten minutes, you get your black ass on the wagon and round 'em up!'" Corey's impression of Ben's voice and mannerism was flawless. "Watch that door!"

A minute passed, then another. Still, Corey pointed to the door and chuckled gently. An explosion ripped the door from what remained of its hinges and Ben almost fell back into the room from the impact of his foot on the door. He regained his balance and composure simultaneously, glaring at Corey and John, as if daring them even to smile.

"Stokes," he bellowed. "If those worthless niggers of yours aren't here in five minutes, you get your black ass on that wagon and round them up! And take that simpleton with you!" Ben disappeared into the shack.

Corey nudged John and walked toward a corral. "Let's get them hitched, John. Ain't no niggers gonna be here in five minutes." As the two rode out of the lot, Corey shook his head and spit over the side of the wagon. "Where'd he get 'worthless'? He most always say shif'less."

"Kicking the door off the hinges was a nice touch," John said.

When they returned to the mill with twelve men from Shakerag, Ben was standing near the turpentine still, talking to a slender boy of about seventeen. The boy had a taut, grim expression and stood with one fist clenched on his hip. The two were arguing.

Corey nudged John. "Remember that face. Looks like Mr. Ben is giving the word to J.C., and he ain't taking it none too good."

As Corey stopped the wagon, Ben knocked the boy to the ground. Before they could get to him, Ben hauled J.C. up by the front of his shirt and hit him again.

"Mr. Ben," Corey yelled. "Don't do that! Whoa, sir!"

John stepped between the two, holding Ben back with his right arm, his palm flat against Ben's chest.

"Get him out of here!" Ben roared. "If he doesn't get off my land, I'm gonna bloody him up good!"

"You heard him," John said. "Get up and get out of here."

The boy jumped up, glaring at John. "So you're Warren, huh? I've heard of you. The old man took me by surprise that time, but you let him go, and I'll show him a thing or two."

"I'm not letting him go, and you're not showing anybody anything, except your backside down that road."

J.C. sized John up for a moment, then unclenched his fists. "I guess you think you done something—taking my job away—but let me tell you something. You ain't seen the last of J.C. Cooper. I got friends around here, and a lot of them. We gonna take you down a notch or two, big man." He pushed his way through the gathered hands, heading toward the road.

"We've got work to do, so let's get with it," Ben said. "Dewey, get up your boiler pressure. You men working with him get that first log on the cradle. Sam, Wiley's going to be laid up another week or more, so you're back on the still. Make sure you scrape her good before you start the charge. Stokes, I want your crew out on the Bear Creek road today. Where's Jeeter?"

At the mention of Jeeter's name, all of the men except Corey hung their heads, trying to avoid the question and Ben's withering stare.

"Well, where is he this time?" Ben demanded. The men stirred slightly.

"I stopped by his place, and Callie say he ain't come home in two, three days now," Corey said.

A few of the men grinned and winked at each other, trying to stifle their laughter.

"Where is he?" Ben asked, looking around the group with growing impatience. He noticed that among all the smug, jovial expressions, one face stayed dead serious and was quick to single the man out. "Malaciah, you don't seem to appreciate the humor in my question. Where would you say Jeeter is?"

"I expect he's getting a little doctoring this morning."

Several of the men could no longer contain their laughter, and a few echoed Malaciah's assessment of the situation.

"That's the truth!"

"I 'spect he is!"

"Do doctors treat corn liquor headaches now?" Ben asked.

"No, sir." Malaciah said. "But they doctors up cuts, and if that nigger don't stay away from my Sassy, a undertaker be the onliest one do him any good."

"Good lord," Ben said. He shook his head and looked up to the sky. "Load 'em up, Stokes. You can have John here to make up for Jeeter."

Corey directed the loading of a couple of barrels onto the wagon as the men gathered their chipping tools and scrapers. John and Corey climbed onto the wagon seat, and six of the twelve men they had picked up that morning climbed up behind the barrels as Corey pulled out of the lot.

The sun was well up behind the slender pines as they drove down a three-path road west of the mill. At first the men were quiet, each nursing a hangover and spitting cotton alongside the path. When they were a quarter mile from the mill, most of them came alive, joking with each other.

"Malaciah, what you done to Jeeter?" Corey asked.

"I done made a mess out of that nigger's big ass."

"How come you to cut his backside?" Another man asked innocently. The question set all the men into an outburst of jokes and laughter.

"That be the part I seen first."

"Well, how come you see'd that part first?"

Malaciah swung at the interrogator, knocking him off the back of the wagon. "Cause that was the part that was hanging high while he was bouncing on my Sassy."

In the ensuing laughter, two more men fell from the wagon, then ran to catch up. Corey looked over at John and winked.

Another quarter mile down the road, Corey stopped the mules and turned to the men. "Here we be. Malaciah, you and your two be cutting on the south side of the road. Two-Fingers, you be on the other side." The last man only had a thumb and an index finger on his right hand.

"Boy, you get a couple of them eight-times and wait here on me." Corey walked off with Two-Fingers a few paces, talking and pointing out where he wanted them to work. When he came back to the wagon, John was standing by it. Corey looked at him a moment. "You ain't got no idea what a eight-times is, do you?"

"Not the slightest," John said.

"Oh Lord, this is gonna be one long day," Corey groaned. "The buckets, boy. Takes eight buckets to fill up one barrel." John took two buckets from hooks on the side of the wagon and followed Corey off into the woods. "You see them holes cut in the bottom of these pines? You dip the gum out them boxes this way." He took a metal scoop from John and set a bucket at the base of the tree. He inserted the scoop into the tree, parallel to the side of the trunk, and with a deft flick of his wrist dipped into the gum and pulled the scoop to the other side of the trunk.

When he pulled the scoop out to the bucket, a thin stream of liquid trailed behind his hand—a delicate, crystalline necklace looping to the coarse earth. Corey dumped the gum into the metal bucket, scraping the scoop on its rim as he withdrew it. He made another pass in the box, repeating the same motions.

He straightened up and looked at John. "Two things you got to remember. You can't do this job and stay clean. You gonna end up wearing some gum and that's a natural fact. Now, look around you. What you see?"

John surveyed the area. "A lot of trees and brush."

"Them low, pointy things is palmettos. Them bigger bushes is tupelo and gallbladders. They's a bunch of sawgrass in places, so you ain't got no picnic out here. Watch out for snakes. They's rattlers out here that could poison a full-growed mule. One of 'em gets a hold to your leg, and there ain't nothing I can do for you."

John looked around warily.

"That's a time. You keep that look in your eyes, and you gonna be all right. Now, you try this box over here."

They walked a few yards to the next tree, and Corey handed the scoop to John. He made a face as his hand closed around the sticky handle of the scoop. As he tried to emulate Corey's movements, he brushed the front of the box, and the tree's sap matted the hair on his forearm. He looked up at Corey and frowned.

"That's number one. Can't stay pretty dipping gum."

John pushed the metal scoop into the gum and was surprised at the resistance it offered. Corey had made it look effortless.

"Come on, boy. Dig into it. A week or two of dipping, and you'll be able to arm wrestle anyone in the county."

John forced his scoop down, pushed it across the box, and drew up his first load. Pulling it out, he tilted the scoop back too far, and the sticky mass flowed back onto his fist. "Damn!"

When he steadied the eight-times with his left hand, the dried sap on its rim ruptured, covering his palm. He ignored the mess and dipped the box again. After scraping the scoop on the rim, he leaned back on his heels.

"You got it," Corey said. "And from the looks of things, you going to get a whole bunch more of it 'fore this day's over. Work all the boxes right around here. I'll call you from the wagon when it's time to eat."

As the old man lumbered toward the road, gnats swarmed around John's head. Before he thought of the consequences, he raised his left hand to fan his face. The gum on his palm stuck in his hair. "Damn!" he yelled.

      *   *   *   *

For the first time during the month that John had worked for Ben Taylor, he was late. Not late in the sense that anyone but Corey would already be there, but late by his own standards. For the past month he had risen at four a.m. and had ridden the two miles to work, so that Corey could teach him about the various timber operations. Since John worked in Corey's crew, they started with the cycle of turpentine production.

The older man showed John how to hollow out the trunk of a pine tree to form a box. He explained how the sap rose in the spring and again in the fall and demonstrated the technique of scarring the tree to create the optimum flow into the box. Corey was a thorough and deliberate instructor, and they spent most of the month going over the turpentine still. From the making of the barrels in which the sap was transported to the repairing of the copper worm through which the distilled mass flowed, John learned not only how to run a turpentine still, but also how to build and maintain one. And now, on the morning when John was to have his "final exam," he was late.

Ordinarily he let the horse take a leisurely pace, giving himself time to wake up, breathing deeply the clear pine scent of the countryside. This morning he demanded that the horse pick up the pace. His mind was preoccupied with the day's work when he rounded a bend in the dirt path, and he had to rein in hard to keep from running down a shadowy figure standing directly in his path. The figure in the road fell back and sat down awkwardly.

"You durn fool. Didn't you hear me coming? Are you all right?" John asked.

A voice came from behind the man in the road. "Get down off that horse!"

John recognized the voice instantly. He thought of turning back or forcing his way past them.

"I said, stand down."

He threw his leg over the horse's rump and stood in the road.

"Hello, Ned. Is that J.C. with you?"

"Never you mind who's with me. This is between me and you."

"There's nothing between us, Ned. I came down here hoping to find a friend."

"That ain't the way I remember it," Ned said. "Last word I had from you was that you aimed to kill me if I done something I had in mind. Well, I done it, and here you are."

Ned and J.C. stepped closer to John, and he saw that there were two more men behind them. Ned looked healthier, much bigger than when he had last seen him in north Georgia. He was clean-shaven and his hair was cut short. John saw a wild look in Ned's eyes and knew that he meant to fight.

"And now you done took my friend's job. Looks like we just ain't going to get along, Warren."

"There sure are a lot of people out here for something that's just between us."

"J.C. settles his own scores." Ned jerked his thumb back toward the other two. "He comes from a close family."

"That's more'n enough talk, Ned," J.C. said. "If you ain't going to whip him, I am."

"Shut up, J.C."

"I deserted, too," John said. "Things changed a good bit after you took off, so I've got no reason to kill you. Let's talk this thing out. I want to be your friend."

One of the men behind Ned stepped forward. "This kid's yellow, J.C. Let's get him."

The man started toward John, and Ned hit him squarely in the stomach with his elbow. As the man doubled up, Ned caught J.C. by the arm.

"I said he's mine first, and I mean what I say." Ned let go of J.C. and approached John. "I want you out of Clinch County, and right now is as good a time as any for you to go. You know I've been hiding out down here, and you're the only one that knows that's liable to talk about it. Take that horse or walk, but you light out. Florida's that way."

John stood a moment, considering his options. He turned as if preparing to mount, then whirled and hit Ned. As Ned went down, John squared himself in time to meet J.C. head-on. The force of his charge drove them both into the horse. As J.C.'s brothers piled in, John fought savagely in the confusing tangle of bodies. He struggled to regain his feet, but there were too many blows in rapid succession, and it was all he could do to get in an occasional punch of his own.

Ned scrambled to his feet and kicked John in the ribs. Instinctively his hands went to the source of the greatest pain, and they had him. The brothers hauled John to his knees. Ned backed up a pace and hit savagely, striking John on the side of his skull.

"You get out of here while you're still able to go!" he said through clenched teeth.

"Don't hit that man again," a voice from the woods commanded.

Ned and the others looked in the direction of the voice.

"Who is that?" Ned asked.

"This old squirrel gun of mine is going to answer that if you don't let him go, right now!"

The four of them moved away from John, who stayed on his knees.

"This ain't none of your business, mister," J.C. said. "Why don't you just get out of here, 'fore you buy yourself a mess of trouble?"

"Why don't you Cooper boys back up about ten paces and sit down, before you buy yourselves an early grave?" They did as the voice suggested, and there was an uneasy moment of silence before he spoke again. "Can you get up, boy?"

John stood.

"Here's how it's going to be. You Coopers are going to be real still or you're going to be real dead. Worthington, you and my young friend are going to resume your business. Any questions? No? Go to it, then."

John and Ned closed on each other warily, their fists up, muscles tensed. Ned jabbed at John's head, missed, and John had his arm in his grip. John started to twist it, but Ned pounded John's head and shoulders with lightning blows. John threw him to the dirt and followed him down, swinging frantically. Ned grabbed John around the waist, and they rolled over repeatedly, each trying to gain the higher position. John broke Ned's grasp and rolled back, but Ned was up first. He kicked at John's head, missed, and John grabbed his leg and upended him. When Ned was halfway to his feet, John slammed into his left shoulder, and Ned lost his balance. He struggled to right himself, but another blow landed on the back of his neck, and he went down.

John grabbed the back of Ned's shirt and spun him around, catching him in the mouth with his right fist. Ned swung blindly and when he missed, John hit him again on the jaw. He fell sideways, his blood mingling with the dirt and caking his face and shirt. John grasped the front of his shirt and pulled him up again.

"Wait," Ned pleaded. "Had enough."

John cocked his right arm, and with all the strength left in him, he drove his fist into Ned's battered face. Ned twisted backwards, and the force of the blow carried John onto his back. They lay in a heap, struggling for air, Ned face down. He covered his head with his arms and though his voice was muffled, they could hear his pleas.

"Please—stop. Don't hit me again. Had enough."

John pushed up and stood over Ned, breathing heavily. He drew back and kicked Ned in the ribs as hard as he could. Ned balled up, grasping his side, desperately trying to yell, but lacking the wind.

"That's enough," the voice from the woods said. "J.C., I think you'd better get your partner and be on your way. You need to go toward town."

As J.C.'s brothers helped Ned onto his horse, J.C. looked toward the woods. "I've heard your voice somewhere before. Soon as I figure out who you are, you're gonna be one sorry son of a bitch."

"That's strong talk for someone looking down a gun barrel. You better get on from here before I let my finger slip."

When they had gone, a man emerged from the protective tangle of vines and brush. Enough light filtered through the surrounding pines for John to study him as he broke out of the palmettos onto the road. He was slender and a head shorter than John. He walked lithely, reminding John of a deer who glides through a secure part of a forest, sure of his safety. A light cotton shirt and khaki pants hung loosely on him. The man was blonde and fair. He carried a short fishing pole and a burlap bag in his right hand.

"I'm much obliged to you for your help, mister," John said.

"Gray Hampton's the name," the man said. Laying his gear on the road, he extended his hand. John was surprised by the firmness of his grip.

"I'm John Warren. Where's your gun, Gray?"

The man smiled faintly. "I have a cabin on Suwanoochee Creek about a mile west of here. I keep the gun wrapped in a blanket under my bed. Do you want to borrow it sometime?"

"No, I thought—"

"So did Ned and the boys. Good thing for us they didn't call the bluff."

"Thanks for your help."

"Glad I was coming this way," Gray said. "If you go down this road about a mile, it curves down by the creek, and I have a cabin you can see off to the left. I'll be frying some jack fish about sundown if you want to come by."

"Thanks for the invitation," John said. "Look for me."

Gray started on down the road. "See you then."

John watched him go for a minute. "There's a freebooter," he said to himself.

That evening on the ride back to Gray's cabin, he thought of Wealthy and Ben's comments on Gray when he told them he was going out to the cabin to eat with him.

"That's an odd duck you're getting mixed in with, but I suppose he's harmless," Wealthy had said.

"A useless duck, if you ask me," Ben said.

"The poor boy's had no one since his mother passed away, and that was in '57. He was only thirteen or so at the time."

"The old woman was going to take him in, too," Ben said. "But no one could keep him in hand long enough to tame him. He roams the countryside and does as he pleases."

"Maybe you'll be good company for him," Wealthy said. "Let me know if there's anything I can do for him. I just hope he's not living like an animal out there in those woods."

That evening John almost missed the cabin in the fading light. "Hello there," he yelled as he walked his horse through the pinewoods to the front of the place.

"Round here," Gray yelled. "Come on back."

John rounded the corner and there was Gray, dropping fillets into a kettle of hot grease.

"Tie your horse over there and ease the saddle off of him so he can get comfortable. Hope you brought your appetite with you."

"I'm about to starve," John said.

As John helped Gray prepare the food, the two talked effortlessly about their pasts and about the war and politics. It was as if they had known each other for years. The longer they talked, the more they realized how much they had in common. Both men's parents had valued honest discourse, and they had been encouraged to learn what was happening in the world. They had been expected to form and to express their opinions about the events of the day.

They found that most of their ideas about politics and the war were similar, but that they were not offended to disagree with each other. John tended to the practical approach to problems, Gray to the idealistic.

They ate their fill, then cleaned up and moved the kettle off the fire. Gray built the fire up, and they leaned back against some logs to listen to the creek for a while. The night was clear and moonless, and a million stars jeweled the Georgia sky.

"You ever tried any of our swamp fire, John?"

"You mean moonshine? Can't say I have."

"I don't recommend it, but I do partake a little myself, so I offer it to you."

"Yeah, let me try a little," John said.

Gray walked to the cabin and returned with two jars, each half full of a clear liquid. "If you're smart, you'll just sip at it."

They sat in silence again, listening to the creek and the popping of the fire. The first of the liquor went down smooth, so John drank a little more than he should have. When it hit the pit of his stomach, he shivered a little and exhaled loudly.

"Give me a shot of that campfire to cool me off," he said, grinning.

"Take her easy there, sport," Gray advised. "Just a little bit."

They were equally at ease with each other whether they talked or not, so the next twenty minutes heard only the creek, the fire, and the sounds of the night.

"Let me ask you something, Gray. Are you going to live like this forever?"

Gray took a drink and meditated on that one for a minute. "What does 'like this' mean?"

"No family, no steady job, not a lot of ambition, not accomplishing much."

"Well, I'm not going to live forever, but I think my personal forever will roll along about that way. Why? Is there something wrong with that?"

"Not at all," John replied. "If you can get away with it." He reached over to a pile of wood at his side, selected a log and studied it a moment, then tossed it onto the blaze at his feet. He took another shot of moonshine. It was more than a sip, and his eyes watered a little.

"I think I can pull it off," Gray said. "The key thing is the family. If I have no wife or children, then I'm only accountable to myself. That means the ambition and everything else you named only goes as far as I want it to."

"Yeah, but it also means you end up a lonely old man with no one to look after you."

"You and your family would look after me, wouldn't you, John?"

"Assuming I have a family," John said.

"Well, there you have it. All I have to do is to make sure that you have a family, and I'm covered."

"Good point. Gray?"

"Yes?"

"Do you have any more of this swamp fire?"

"Good God, boy. Don't tell me you've downed the whole jar already."

"It's gone, Gray."

"How do you feel?"

"I feel fine."

"Just give the blood a few turns around your body, and then tell me how you're doing, but in the mean time, that's it for you."

John stared at him for a minute. "How old are you, Gray?"

"I'm twenty-two."

"Twenty-two," John repeated. "At that age, you ought to have figured out a few things. Tell me what you've figured out."

"You want answers to life, John, then you read the Bible. It's all in there somewhere."

"That's sure not what I expected from you," John said.

"Why not?"

"Because when I think of reading the Bible, I think of church, and when I think of church, I think of little old ladies and straitlaced preachers, and being prim and proper. Not exactly things I associate with Gray Hampton—poet, philosopher, wanderer, and moonshine drinker."

"And not exactly things you should associate with the Bible either. Little old ladies and men behaving proper and preachers full of moralistic sermons with all the right answers aren't in the Bible. Jesus condemned all the self-righteous religious leaders in his day. But there's a heap of good sense in that Bible, John. And there's certain laws in the world that the Bible tells you about, and it tells you what happens when you ignore those laws." Gray paused for a moment and rocked back on his heels, looking intently at John. "So, what did you hear, John?"

"You said to ignore what people tell me about the Bible and to read it for myself."

"No. That's nothing like what I said. On any given day a straitlaced, prissy, self-righteous little preacher can show you truth and the same for little old ladies. You're the problem, not them. You have to know when you're hearing the truth and when you're hearing lies. And to complicate matters, the very people who love you will tell you lies, thinking they're telling you the truth."

"That's clear," John said sarcastically.

"You're asking me to tell you what I've learned about life, and you want the simple version? You've hit on a lifelong discussion, my friend."

All Gray's talk was beginning to run together, and John was having trouble focusing. "Okay, what else you got for me? Read the Bible. Listen to people 'cept when they're lying or they think they're telling the truth."

Gray smiled. "All right, try this on for size," he said. "Truth is what we're after, because truth sets us free, so the purpose of life is to get free."

John jumped to his feet, staggered, regained his balance, and flung his arms up to the stars. "That's it! Man has questioned his existence from the beginning, and now a South Georgia sage has discovered it all—the meaning of life! Hallelujah! Hallelujah!"

Gray sat back, laughing. "Sit down, John. You and that 'shine are getting mighty noisy."

John paced around the fire. His head was reeling. "Sit down?" He mocked. "No, sir, I shall not sit! This is a momentous occasion. This is historical!"

"This is a drunken, slobbering fool," Gray laughed.

"No, really," John said. "This is sounding pretty good. I think you're on to something here."

"The other important thing in life is to learn to make good animal sounds."

"Is that so, Gray?" John's words slurred. "Why is that? Why animal sounds?"

"To put yourself in tune with nature. To befriend the fellow inhabitants of earth."

"Which animal sounds are the really 'portant ones? Just give me the really 'portant ones, 'cause I may be getting a little drunk, and I may have trouble remembering."

"Okay. Let's go with the cow first."

"Cows 'portant?"

"Very important. There are a lot of them. They're found everywhere men are, and they help sustain us with food. Try some cow, John."

John staggered stiff-legged toward the fire. "Moo."

"No, John," Gray said solemnly. "That's not it at all. Most people make that sound."

John stared at Gray and tried hard to focus his eyes. "Not right?" he murmured.

"No. It needs more of an 'uh' sound. Less of an 'oo'."

John's head was beginning to spin faster. The creek looked as if it were next to the cabin, and suddenly he was feeling sick. He backed up to the log where he had reclined earlier and plopped down unceremoniously, his head hanging.

"How are you feeling, John?"

"Oh God!" John answered without raising his head.

"I expect that grease from the fish has just about got together with the alcohol."

"Muhhhh!" John vomited violently.

"That's it, John!" Gray said enthusiastically. "A perfect cow if I ever heard one."

§   §   §   §

On a mid-October morning, John arrived at the mill at the usual time, but Corey wasn't there. He didn't think much of it at first, but when the old man didn't show up in the next half-hour, John became concerned. He saddled his horse and rode toward Shakerag. The sun had still not risen when he reined up in front of the house. The front was dark, but from the side, John saw the feeble light of a lamp.

Stepping cautiously up on the porch, he hesitated a moment, then knocked lightly on the rough surface of the pine plank door. He waited for a minute, listening intently for some sound. Hearing nothing, he knocked again.

"Who that?" a female voice asked tenuously.

"John Warren," he said. "I work with Corey in the woods." The door opened slightly, but John couldn't see anyone. "Is Corey all right? He's usually at the mill by now, and I'm worried about him."

The door opened wide and from the light beyond, John could just make out the features of a young black woman. She looked to be in her twenties, and she was very pretty.

"Corey not at the mill yet?" she asked anxiously. She looked back into the room. "Zach! Zachary, wake up!" A boy stirred reluctantly on a couch and sat up, rubbing his eyes.

"Your papa not at the mill yet. You got to go out to the place and see if he all right."

The boy stood and dragged on a pair of pants and brogans. John judged him to be about twelve.

"How far is this place?" He asked. "I'll go with the boy."

"The boy'll look to his papa. You can go on back to the mill, sir," the young woman said quietly.

"I'd better go along. Corey might be hurt, and I have a horse to carry him on."

The boy eased past John and started down a path into the woods behind the house.

"Corey wouldn't want you to come. The boy can handle it," the woman insisted politely.

"I've no intention of standing here and arguing with you." John jumped off the porch, mounted the horse, and set off after Zachary. The trail he followed dwindled to the barest trace of a path, then to a mere bending of sawgrass where Zachary had been before him. The

clutter of brush among the pines and hardwoods made riding imprac-
tical, so John dismounted and tied the reins to a tupelo bush. He
heard a faint rattle of bushes further to the west. He followed the
sound for five minutes until he thought he heard running water—
probably Suwanoochee Creek.

John moved cautiously, trying to keep Zachary from hearing him.
When he could no longer hear the rustle of limbs ahead of him, he
stopped. Off to his left he thought he heard voices, faint in the darkness. He turned, and after another five minutes of slow progress
through the ever-thickening woods, there was no mistaking the sound
of talking.

"Don't know if I..." The voice was faint, but it sounded like Corey.
Then came the boy's high-pitched voice.

"...white man at the house with a horse. Said his name..."

"No! Don't bring him...rest a minute, then you can get me home."

John was on the edge of a clearing now, and Corey and the boy
hadn't heard him. He wiped the sweat from his eyes and saw Corey
leaning against an apparatus of some sort with Zachary on his knees
beside him. He stepped into the clearing.

"That's why your daughter didn't want me to come out here," John
said. "You're making moonshine."

Corey groaned feebly and leaned back against it again. John
walked to where the old man lay.

"She ain't my daughter," Corey said. "She's my wife."

John looked closer and saw a trickle of blood at Corey's right eye.
"What in the world happened to you?" He bent over to take a closer
look.

Corey reached up and gently touched the wound. "Had some unexpected customers what was a little short of cash money."

"It doesn't seem to be too bad a cut, but we'd better get you home
for a closer look."

Corey was too weak to resist. He stood with the help of the two
boys, and they headed back through the woods to the horse. Corey
stooped over, and John could tell that his ribs had taken a beating.

Once he helped bed Corey down and assured his wife that he would
recover without seeing a doctor, John hurried to the mill. The sun was

well up into the trees when he arrived, and Ben was standing near the sawmill to greet him.

"Where the hell have you been, and where's Stokes?"

"Corey didn't show up this morning, so I went to check on him. He had an accident and got banged up a little."

"What happened?" Ben asked.

John was surprised by the tone of concern in Ben's voice and the worried look on his face.

"Not sure. His head's cut, and I think he has some bruised ribs. Probably just needs to rest up for a day or two."

"A lot of information you are! I'm going to check on him. The crew is already out in the woods chipping boxes. You catch up with 'em and run the show until Corey's back on his feet. I want that section north of the road finished up by tomorrow."

John didn't see Ben again until that evening when they sat down for supper.

"I couldn't get anything out of him about what happened," Ben said. "He's too old to be fighting, but I swear that's what it looks like to me."

"I'm going to check on him in a little while," John said. "I'll see if I can't find out what happened."

When John arrived at Corey's house he was sitting on the porch, his feet propped up. His pipe scented the air.

"You made a quick recovery," John said.

"My skull bone and sides don't feel like talking no recovery," Corey muttered. "Just feels worser laying up in the bed."

Corey's wife, Ranetta, brought them coffee, and they sat quietly, warming their hands around the steaming cups.

"Are you ready to talk about what happened at the still?" John asked.

"Are you willing to take no for an answer?"

"No."

"Then I don't reckon there's any sense in putting it off. I got into moonshining back when Cable Worthington was alive. He wanted someone in Shakerag to help him out, so we set up the still back in '53. We kept our partnership pretty quiet, so when he died, I kept operating by myself. I built myself a reputation for pretty good stuff, and I sells it right."

"So, some of your white competition decided to put you out of business."

"No, Cable's been dead long enough that if that was it, they'd already took care of that. I was truthing you about one thing the other night. This here was done by somebody with more thirst than they had money or sense. It was Ned and the Cooper boys."

John looked up from his cup, feeling his face go hot. "Ned? I'm going to fix him once and for all!"

"No, you're not," Corey said calmly. "Fighting ain't gonna solve nothing with him. He likes it that way. That boy would rather fight than eat."

"Maybe he'd rather fight someone he knows he can whip, but he doesn't want much of me."

"Pretty big talk, John, but you fight him, you got to whip all the Coopers, too. You just let it lay for now. Chances are they won't come after me again."

"I don't take chances. They got free liquor from you once, so what makes you think they'll ever want to pay again?"

The old man looked down at his coffee. "It's my fight."

"But you aren't equipped to fight it. Even if you could scare them off some way, what would happen then? You get after some whites with a shotgun, and you know what'll happen. You won't be much good to that woman and those children in there hanging from a tree."

They sat quietly for a minute, sipping their coffee.

"Corey, what you need is a partner. A white partner."

"What you got in mind?"

"It's an obvious solution. I need to make more money than Ben pays, and I can work both jobs—pull the same hours you do. I can sell to more whites than you can and handle Ned and the Coopers. Make it my fight, too."

"I don't know," Corey said. "Mr. Ben find out, and it likely we both be looking for jobs."

"Then we'll just have to make sure that Ben doesn't find out."

       ß   ß   ß   ß

For the next five years John was preoccupied with work to the exclusion of everything else. All his waking hours were filled with the work at hand and with anticipation of what he had to do next to build the business over which he had the most control. His social life consisted primarily of church services with the Taylors and the time he spent with Gray Hampton fishing or relaxing at his cabin by Suwanoochee Creek. The money he kept in the barn accumulated. John kept a meticulous accounting of his earnings in a small ledger, and he gained a feeling of strength and control as the amount grew week by week.

As rarely as he withdrew money, he still felt a little pain and remorse when he took money from one of the caches in the barn. He considered putting the money in the bank, but he could not bring himself to trust anyone with the knowledge of how much money he had.

Ben and Wealthy provided the necessities of life—his food, shelter, and clothing. He had no need of tobacco, and what little drinking he did came from Gray or the operation with Corey. After a year of work, the ledger showed a total income of just over five hundred and forty dollars. Only two hundred of that came from moonshine commission.

The second year brought in another six hundred, but he invested four hundred of that into the business with Corey. The liquor sales accounted for two hundred of that, and John was now a full partner.

The third year, as the liquor business began to prosper from better operating techniques and their hard work, John made a total of a thousand dollars. Stokes and Warren, as they now referred to themselves, contributed a little over half of that, and John would never again make as much working for Ben Taylor as he would from peddling bootleg liquor.

At the end of 1870, after five years of continuous labor, John Warren was twenty-one years old. He knew the timber business better than did men twice his age that had worked in it all their lives. He owned fifty percent of a thriving business few people knew he was involved in, and he had a net worth of over three thousand dollars when land was selling for a dollar an acre.

After five years in Magnolia, John began to believe that his life had settled down again. Although the loss of his family still hurt deeply and he was still tormented by the dreams of water, the accusatory voice was no longer there, and the war seemed like a part of his dreams now—very faint, very distant.

But in the year that he turned twenty-one, John Warren learned anew that life is seldom predictable. Eventually he would know that out of great conflict comes great opportunity.

XIV

From Grey Hampton's Journal
Sunday, June 6, 1870

There is no sacrifice so great that a man will not offer himself up to it for the sake of land. He will give of himself day by day, month after month, year upon year to hold, protect, and nurture the land. He will demand that those who follow him do the same.

Through all this sacrifice of time and money and life, a relationship of man to land develops, so that finally one is indistinguishable from the other. The man is no longer mere flesh, bone and blood. The land is no longer simply a mingling of soil, rock, and moisture.

At some indefinable time in the history of a man's ownership of the land, he is judged by his utility of it, and the land is evaluated in terms intimate of the man who owns it. This is the way of man and earth, generation after generation, place upon place, time out of mind.

Land is the sustainer of man's life, the source of his power, and in the mind of man—perhaps in the spirit of God—creator and creation are inseparable. In God, no punishment for sin was sufficient but that a man and woman should be utterly excluded from their place on the earth. No punishment was so great, but that a murderer should be cut off from the earth's yield and be made a fugitive in the land. No punishment for sin was sufficient but that mankind should be wholly separated from the earth by vast and unsearchable waters.

The earth and its inhabitants dwell in the midst of a great cycle. Places diverse in nature and animals arrayed in time exist at some unknowable point along the circumference of the circle, always at the passing point of some epoch, always on the threshold of infinite change. Wise is the man who discerns his place in time, who forsakes the light which is failing and quests for the light which is kindling.

Of the great cycles of place and time, there is none beyond the power of man quite like the transfiguration of land to water or water to land. Where we now witness the ebb and flow of human fortunes—the tide of human society—an earlier world saw storm-bludgeoned seas—the domain of those prehistoric and historic creatures that carried their commerce in a watery world. How can one tell of it when all that remains only occasionally surfaces from the rocks of the present age— shark teeth on a Tennessee hillside, seashells in a south Georgia riverbed?

Who can tell the story of the wandering of the earth, of the great cycle of land and water, of the uplifting of an island or an entire continent, of the cataclysmic crush of a new or extended ocean? Who has seen the land yield to the water or the water to the land? All men witness in part, none witness in its fullness.

A man awakens to the lure and the power of land gradually. He is born and raised in a place as if by chance and for the first fifteen or twenty years of life the land is his birthright, and he takes it for granted. He lives on the wealth of the father and, if that wealth is sufficient, he stays until the land is his, and the transaction is made in the courthouse. For some sons, the wealth is insufficient and they move on, searching out a place of their own.

Some sons are prodigals and go out in search of an idea, and some prodigal sons never return to a forgiving father and the birthright of land. But whether a son leaves his native land for reasons of poverty or duress or for an ideal, he eventually finds his wealth in more land or his ideal in a place.

If his quest for power or virtue takes him to the edge of a continent, he may cast his fortune onto the sea, but the land is never out of his thoughts. He doubles the value of land, for his toil at sea makes land not only home, but refuge.

If a man's travels end on a great plain at the heart of a continent, he looks to see what the earth will yield to him. If it is fruit or grain, he is made a farmer; if minerals valued by other men, he is made a miner or industrialist. If the land yields animals or trees, it shapes him into a hunter, trapper, or lumberman.

Other men and their occupations will grow around him to offer him services and material value, but at the heart of every place there thrives the man who was shaped by the earth. All others are extraneous.

This is the way of man and earth, generation after generation, place upon place, time out of mind.

     s   s   s   s

In his twenty-first year Sundays became important to John Warren, not because he had regained any measure of faith in God, but because it was the one day of the week when he could see Jennifer Pace. In the morning service he rarely heard anything that the Reverend Polk said, so captivated was he by Jennifer. Upon leaving the services he hesitated in his pew long enough to let the Paces get ahead of him in the aisle.

One Sunday in late August as they proceeded up the aisle, Jennifer's father beckoned to Roger and John found himself at her side.

"How are you today, Miss Pace?" John asked.

"Just fine, Mr. Warren. How do you like working for Mr. Ben?"

"The hours are long enough, but I like to keep busy, so it's good."

"You must be terribly tired by the end of the week."

"Yes, I suppose I am."

"I hope you're not too tired to join us at the social today at Lake Verne."

"Will you be riding out with Roger?" John asked.

"No, he and Daddy are leaving for Waycross after lunch. I'm afraid I'll have to impose on someone with a vacancy in his buggy."

"What time will the group leave?"

"Didn't you hear the reverend's announcement during church?" Jennifer asked, smiling demurely.

"Guess I was preoccupied."

"We leave in thirty minutes. We're planning a late picnic lunch. If Miss Wealthy hasn't prepared anything, just tell her that I had some food ready for Roger, and you're welcome to share my basket."

John felt a little light-headed on the way home. He tried to sound casual.

"I thought I might go along with the others to Lake Verne this afternoon."

"I didn't think you cared for such outings," Wealthy said. "Aren't you a little old for those children?"

"No, I think there are a couple of the older boys going."

"Well, I don't have a thing prepared, and I'll hardly have time to make something now. Why don't you wait until the next outing? That will give you time to meet some of the young folks on an individual basis."

"Unless you plan on bringing them out to the woods, I don't think I'll have much time for that. Anyway, I've had an offer to share a basket, so you don't need to fix anything."

"So that's why you and Clarence's girl had your heads together coming out of the service," Ben said.

Wealthy snorted. "You'd do well to pay more attention to Reverend Polk and less to Miss Jennifer Pace. Don't think I haven't noticed."

"That's why he likes to sit next to the aisle," Ben said. "I can't say as I fault him for that. Clarence's girl is a sight easier to look at than old Polk-er face."

"Ben Taylor!" Wealthy exclaimed.

"Just teasing, old dear," Ben said. "You go ahead on your church social, boy." He silenced Wealthy with a stern look.

"Could I take the buggy? I don't know if there'll be enough room with the others."

"You may not," Wealthy said. "The reverend will have to see that you have a place to ride."

They met at the church, and after John was introduced to those of the group he hadn't already met, the caravan of six buggies was off to the lake—the girls in their carriages and the boys in three separate buggies. It was a beautiful day, but it was hot and cloudless, and the travelers were grateful for the slight breeze that stirred.

Lake Verne was situated two miles from Magnolia just off the Griffin Road, south of town. As the caravan turned the last curve on the road, they were looking across the lake, and John was overwhelmed by its beauty. It was an enormous diamond, glittering in the afternoon sun and sprinkled liberally with the emerald hue of water lilies. Ancient cypress rimmed the natural lake and spread across its surface. An area had been cleared on the eastern fringe of the pond and over the years people had built shelters for their outings. There, under the direction of Mrs. Polk, the girls spread quilts on the grass and emptied the contents of the picnic baskets.

Some of the boys explored the edge of the lake while others tussled in the grass or turned cartwheels in an attempt to catch the eye of a special girl. All of them wanted Jennifer's attention, but over the years she had made it clear that they didn't meet her standards for proper suitors.

John remained aloof, looking out over the lake, judging its size and looking for likely fishing spots. By the time the food was ready, it was the middle of the afternoon, and everyone flocked to the quilts, eager to eat.

Jennifer smiled at John as he maneuvered through the crowd toward her. Several boys tried to strike up a conversation with Jennifer, but she scarcely paid attention to them. She brought John into every conversation and turned her attention to him as if he had initiated the small talk.

When the meal was finished, the group dispersed into couples or small groups. John and Jennifer were part of a group of two other couples, but after a few minutes of gossip, they disengaged themselves and wandered off along the bank alone.

"What do you think of the outing, John?"

"Beautiful place," he murmured.

"This is just about the best spot in Clinch County," Jennifer said. "It's so peaceful out here."

They wandered far from the others.

"I suppose you plan to stay in Clinch County permanently, don't you, John?"

"I suppose," he said. "I really have no place else, and I like it here."

"Why is that?"

"Because you're here." The boldness of the statement embarrassed him a little, and John started to turn away from her penetrating gaze.

"You want to kiss me, don't you John Warren?" She looked him in the eyes, her smile triumphant as always.

John glanced toward the others. They seemed preoccupied with small talk and dalliances of their own. He gathered his courage and stepped closer to her. He felt on fire as he stooped to her, and she raised her head. They stood tenuously for a moment, and as he leaned forward, he saw her eyes close. He brought his lips to hers, and they kissed. He drew back and saw that her eyes were still closed. She bit softly at her lower lip. John cradled her head in his huge hands and kissed her again, as delicately as before. Suddenly she stepped back and opened her eyes, tilting her head up to meet his gaze. They stood transfixed for a moment.

"You must think I'm shameless," she said.

"No. Forgive me for not being bold enough." His words seemed frail and clumsy compared to what he felt in his heart. "God, you're beautiful," he finished lamely.

She smiled. "Yes, and so are you."

Too soon, Mrs. Polk called them to pack up and head back to town. They walked back toward the buggies, and John knew that this would be their last moment of privacy.

"I want to see you—to be with you again," he said.

"Daddy and Roger will be in Waycross for several days, so my mother will be your only obstacle. I know you'll think of something," she said.

John made up his mind to do just that. He often used Gray Hampton as a way to get out of the house to tend to the business of Stokes and Warren, so the next night, he made the usual excuse about going to eat at Gray's cabin and left.

Once he was out of sight of the house, he rounded the town in the darkness and came back in on the far side of the courthouse. He tied his horse at the Methodist church and walked across the yard to Jennifer's house. He crouched by an azalea bush until he saw Mrs. Pace in a room at the front. A light shone from an upstairs room at the side near the back of the house.

John picked up two pinecones and crept under the upstairs window. His first throw hit the house and got no response. The second cone hit a pane, and John stared up anxiously at the window. Jennifer peeked out from the side of the window, and John stepped out into the light. She slid the window up.

"Do you know where my mother is?" she whispered.

"In a room, up front, on the other side of the house."

Jennifer disappeared, and John crouched by the azaleas again. In a moment she rounded the back corner. John stepped from the bushes and grabbed her arm. She turned and pressed close to him, tilting her face to his. He stooped slightly, encircled her with his arms, and brought his head down to hers. The kiss was tender and brief, and then she kissed him repeatedly, giggling under her breath. John pulled back.

"Why are you laughing?"

"This seems so odd. I feel as if we've been together for ages, but I hardly know you. My gracious, I've never sneaked out of the house before to be with a man, and here I am behaving as if I have no morals at all! It's so exciting!"

He kissed her again and felt her body relax against him. His right hand cradled the back of her head, his fingers caressing her soft blonde hair. She pulled back, laid her head on his chest, and hugged him as hard as she could. He held her tightly, resting his chin on the top of her head.

"You'd better go back inside now," he said.

"No, no, no!" She held to him tighter.

"I don't want you to, but—"

"Just one more minute," she pleaded.

"I'll be back tomorrow night at this same time. Tell your mother that you're tired and you're going to sleep. Then she'll be less likely to catch us."

"Are you always so logical?" Jennifer released him and pretended to pout.

"I try to be, but you're making it tough."

"Good!" She kissed him once more, lingering. She looked into his eyes, pulled slowly away from him, and ran back to the house. "Tomorrow night! Same signal!"

John waited until she appeared at the window. He waved and crossed the yard back to the street. The air felt fine beneath his feet. As he rode past Doc Williams' house across from the courthouse, he saw someone in the shadows. Not daring to be discovered, he hurried along.

Meeting Jennifer Pace each night after that was a simple matter for John. He appeared outside her window just after dark, so no signal was necessary, and the risk of being caught diminished. They became bold enough to sit in a gazebo in the side yard. John stretched out on a bench that ran the circumference of the structure, lying with his head on the soft folds of Jennifer's dress. She stroked his hair as they talked of the day's events or of their pasts.

At first John was reluctant to speak of Atlanta. He wanted to know about Jennifer, and she told him about growing up in Magnolia, the daughter of privilege and status. She'd interrupt her story to bring John's head up to hers, and they held each other and kissed—passionately and hungrily or tenderly, the barest wisp of caresses.

*   *   *   *

"What dreams do you have for me to interpret, John?" Gray Hampton asked.

John paused in the process of tying a hook to his line and turned in the boat to look at his friend.

"What makes you ask such a thing as that?"

"It occurred to me just now that you and I are the archetypes of the Biblical prophet and king. Don't you think the roles fit us?"

"No question that you're a wild man living off fruit and honey in the wilderness, but I'm a little hard-pressed to identify my kingdom." John went back to the fishing line.

"You're not established yet, but I see it coming. That's another reason I'm a prophet, you see. I foretell the coming of the king."

"I've often wondered how many times the prophets missed on things before they got a prophecy right," John said.

"Blasphemer," Gray retorted. "But you're just trying to elude my first question. I saw the raw nerve I hit."

They continued fishing, drifting with the river's slight current.

"Why did those kings always want the prophets to interpret their dreams for them?"

"They believed that a dream was a foretelling of the future," Gray said.

They found a bream bed and were preoccupied for several minutes, catching fish as fast as they could bait their hooks. When the action slowed, they moved on downstream.

"What makes you think I dream about anything in particular?" John asked.

"I know that your past has been troubling you for a long time." Gray said. "The mind works overtime on that sort of thing and that means dreams. If you want to talk it out, then the jokes are aside. If you don't want to talk about it, that's okay, too."

"I dream about water. There are people in my dreams and things happen, but there's always water, and it doesn't always behave as we think of water."

"What do you mean?"

"Sometimes the water runs up into the sky, and when I look at it close, there's stars instead of rocks in it. Other times I touch it, and it comes rolling down like saltwater taffy. Once, I shot an animal and instead of blood, water came out of the wound and made a river that flowed over me and carried me along."

Once John got over the initial reluctance to talk about personal matters, he opened up to Gray without reservation. In the telling of his dreams, one memory triggered another, and he recalled details he had not thought of for years. They involved unusual water, the wounding or killing of an animal, or a combination of the two.

"I guess I dream every night," John said. "For the first couple of years after my family was killed, I dreaded the night, and I had a problem sleeping. There was always a voice in those dreams, and it questioned me over and over:

'What have you done? Why are you here?' How I hated that voice!"

"Was it saying that you had done something to cause the death of your family? Was that how you took it?" Gray asked.

John hesitated, his eyes misting. "If I hadn't insisted on joining the militia, would things have turned out differently? Could I have saved some of my family?"

Gray was absorbed in what John was saying; paying attention only to the bare mechanics of fishing and steering the boat away from snags along the riverbank.

"For years my dreams were similar—the water, violence, the death of an animal, Job and his suffering—but lately there's something new. Isn't that odd?"

Gray looked up from straightening a hook. "You're dreaming about the Indian couple, aren't you?"

John turned on the boat seat to look back. "How did you know about them?"

"I've seen them, too."

"In your dreams, you mean."

"Yes, of course," Gray said. "I get the feeling that they're ancient people, not someone we'd find in the swamp now."

"I've thought that, too. I dream about hunting with them, and the weapons are primitive—spears mostly, and we never have horses."

"How do your dreams of them end," Gray asked.

John thought for a moment. "It's always the same. We're through hunting, and we return to camp, but I can't get there. The other men go in among their huts, and I can see their wives greeting them, but I'm still on the path. I try, but I can't enter the camp." He threw his line into the water.

"Is that it?" Gray asked.

"The others go into their shelters, but the same man and woman wait for me. They beckon for me to come, but it's no use. I want to, but I can't find the way in, and then I quit dreaming or I wake up. There you have it, Mr. Prophet. What do you make of my twisted dream life?" He expected Gray to joke with him to change the long, somber monologue into some lighthearted conversation.

"You've given me a great deal to ponder, my friend," Gray said as they unloaded the boat. "You've lived with these dreams a long time. What do you think the water means?"

"Wait a minute now. You started all this study. Do you recall the prophets asking any of the kings to do their work for them?"

"You must've tried to figure out what it means, the water and the violence. You must've tried to see if there were other common threads running from one dream to the next. You might be getting close, or you might say something that puts me on the right track."

"Miss Wealthy says the answer to my problems is in the Job story, but I've never been able to find it. It's kind of confusing. There are some things about water and violence in there, but I can't make it fit me."

"That's a start," Gray said. "Water could stand for a lot of things by itself, or it could be part of something bigger. Maybe its significance lies in its source or its behavior. Or maybe it's something simple. Water moves you on through life whatever the circumstances may be."

"That's kind of appealing," John said. "If your troubles would stay on the riverbank, you could just float on downstream and leave them behind. Problem is, my troubles seem to get in the boat with me."

John had given Gray the central image. Of all the pictures of water that one could imagine—rain, oceans, ponds, creeks, storms, floods, lakes—a river was the powerful image significant to John Warren.

       s   s   s   s

Ben Taylor kept his head in the newspaper and tried to ignore his sister. It had been one of those days at the mill when nothing seemed to go right, and he was trying to put it out of his mind.

"You know what the rumors are," Wealthy said.

Ben knew. He knew what the facts were, too, but he wasn't going to tell Wealthy. It would break her heart if she knew for sure that John was a common moonshiner. Although, from what he had been told about the operation, it was Ben's growing opinion that John was an uncommon moonshiner and a good businessman.

"Those stories have been going around for years now," Ben said. "Has anyone ever given you any proof that John makes liquor?"

"No, but then they aren't likely to, either."

"Has Amos Johns ever brought charges against the boy or Stokes, or has he ever found a still that he could connect with them?"

"No."

"Then will you please let me read this newspaper in peace? And will you tell those biddies in the Missionary Union to worry about the heathen more and about John Warren less?"

She stared glumly out at the rain. "Where do you suppose he goes at night? What's so urgent that he'd go out in a downpour like this?"

       s   s   s   s

John stood at the front door of a dilapidated cabin, the rain pouring off the brim of his Stetson, the lightning flashing close behind him. He hated what he was about to do, but it was necessary. Open the door before I'm struck dead for doing this.

"Who's there?" a gruff voice called from inside.

Something about the tone irritated John and gave him the resolve to do what needed to be done. He kicked the rickety door off its hinges. The man inside fell back, cowering amid the clutter of the dimly lit cabin. John stepped inside.

"Get up, Dub," he said calmly.

There was a movement off to his right, and in the shadows he could make out a woman. Three dirty little faces peered out from behind her plump body. She cradled an infant in her arms.

John turned back to Dub. "Get up and get outside." John turned and walked back out into the storm. Dub followed reluctantly.

"Do you like standing out in this rain, Dub?"

"No, sir, Mr. Warren. I'd a heap rather be inside."

"Me, too," John said. "So you can imagine how I feel, having to ride four miles here in the rain and then standing here getting soaking wet, and then I have to ride the four miles back home."

"I don't understand, Mr. Warren. How come you to ride here on a night like this?"

The lightning flashed, and Dub saw for the first time that John had a gun pointed at his considerable gut.

"Your voice is quivering," John said. "You don't have any reason to be afraid of me, do you?"

"I...uh...why you got that piece on me, Mr. John?"

"I figure that's the only way I'm going to get my rightful share of your sales, Dub. Now isn't that a shame, that a man has to ride eight miles in this crap just to hold up his own sales agent?"

"What're you talking about? I send you the money by that boy every week, just like we agreed."

"Either business is way off, or I'm justified in holding this gun on you. Now which is it?"

Dub's voice had a bit of an indignant edge to it. "I don't know what you're talking about."

John stepped forward and hit Dub with the side of his pistol. The man fell sideways into the mud. Although he was still conscious, he made no effort to get up again.

"Get on your feet, you liar, or I'm going to kill you right where you are!"

"But Mr. John—"

"Shut up, Dub. I'm doing the talking now." Dub stood, and John got within inches of his face. "You've done plenty of talking all over this end of Clinch County. Running your sorry mouth about how much money you're screwing John Warren out of. Don't you keep trying to deny it, either. I'm in no mood for your lies, you sorry bastard."

Dub flinched and watched for John's gun to come crashing up aside his bloodied head again.

"Give me one good reason not to kill you right here, Dub."

"Oh Lordy," Dub moaned. "Please, Mr. Warren. My—my family."

"God have mercy on the family that has to depend on the likes of you for their support." John backed up a step. "All right, you listen to me good. You owe me one hundred fifty-six dollars and twenty-five cents, isn't that right?"

"It's more like a hundred and twenty-five," Dub admitted.

"Yeah, that's the figure you've been bragging about, but if you multiply that times twenty-five percent interest, you'll get one fifty-six twenty-five. That's what you're going to pay me, isn't it?"

"Yes, sir."

"You're never going to mention my name again in connection with this business, are you?"

"No, sir."

"We shook hands on that once before, didn't we, Dub?"

Dub lowered his head. "Yes, sir."

"Then let's shake hands on it again, and this time you'd better honor your word."

John extended his hand and Dub took it. John began to squeeze, and Dub's knees buckled.

"You're breaking my hand, Mr. John," Dub yelled.

"That's what I mean to do," John yelled. "You look at those busted knuckles, and you keep your word to me. Do you understand?"

"Oh God, yes. Please stop. Please."

John pushed the man backwards, and he lay in the mud crying.

John walked over to the open doorway of the cabin and sat down. When the crying subsided, he made Dub stand up and the two of them repaired the door and hung it back in place. When the work was done, John called to Dub's wife, and the frightened woman took a step into the light, still clutching her baby.

"Ma'am, I apologize for disturbing you and the children. I wish I could've avoided it. I can't say I'm sorry that I bloodied your husband, because I'm not. I want you to take this money and buy you and the kids some decent clothes. Get some soap and clean them up good. Then get some things for the house. The next time I come out this way, I'd like to see some curtains in the window. Would that be all right with you?"

The woman looked at the money in her hand. She had never seen that much in her life, and she couldn't speak. Her eyes filled with tears.

"I'll take that as a yes. Between you and me we're going to make a man out of Dub. Somebody you can be proud of, so you forget what I've done to him tonight for his sake."

He turned back to Dub. "That's twenty dollars I'm giving her, and its all for her and the children. You still owe me, and it's coming out of what you sell. I expect it to be paid back within two months. Do you understand me?"

"Yes, sir!"

"If you so much as say a hard word to that woman or those children over this, or if you dare to even touch one cent of that money, I'm going to find out about it. When I do, I'm going to come back here and kill you, Dub. Have I ever lied to you?"

"No, sir, you haven't."

John turned and walked out the door.

　　　*　　　　　　*　　　　　　*　　　　　　*

Roger Pace sat alone and miserable at one end of the planks that served as a bar in The Jug. Behind him was the small, dank room with its few boisterous, mid-afternoon patrons, kicking up the smell of stale sawdust as they thrashed about in arm wrestling bouts for beer.

Roger was out of place among these men. Most of them had to work for a living—their sun burnt, rough bodies were silent testimony. He had never faced the necessity of sweat and an aching body. The others hated him for his pale, skinny body and the softness of his hands, but they tolerated him because he bought everyone an occasional round.

When Ned Worthington and the Cooper boys enter the bar, Ned beckoned to the bartender for a drink, then nudged J.C. and pointed. "How about that? Speak of the devil."

Ned strode over to Roger and slapped him on the back. "Roger Pace! This is quite a coincidence. You're just the man I was hoping to run into, if you know what I mean."

A sense of dread and nausea flowed over Roger as he turned to face Ned. "No, Worthington. I don't know what you mean. Suppose you enlighten me."

The bar got quiet. The Coopers flanked Ned, glaring at Roger.

"Mr. Pace, I don't really believe that you want to make our private conversations known to half the clientele of The Jug. Suppose you and I remove us to that table over there. And you bring that bottle along with you."

"Go to hell," Roger said. "I've no business to transact with you."

The Coopers laughed. "You better leave this man be, Ned," J.C. said sarcastically.

Ned rubbed the back of his neck. "That's rather insulting for you to brush me off that way, Mr. Pace. I'm sure you didn't mean it, though." He smiled broadly. "After the business transaction that Ray Black and I made a couple of days ago, I'd think that you'd want to be real nice to me."

At the mention of Ray Black, Roger turned to the bar, picked up his bottle and glass, and headed for the table.

Ned winked at J.C. "Horace, give me a clean glass to drink Roger Pace's liquor with." The men around him laughed. "Boys, get you a bottle, too, and liven this place up a little. It's way too quiet in here."

Ned turned and walked to the table, grinning. Before he could pull back his chair, Roger snapped at him. "How do you know anything about my dealings with Ray Black? And what kind of business do you have with him that could possibly interest me?"

His smile vanished. "You've got this all wrong, Roger boy," he said quietly but firmly. "I'm running this meeting. You just pour the liquor and speak when you're spoken to. Is that clear?" For emphasis Ned reached into the inner pocket of his coat, withdrew a packet of papers, and threw them casually onto the table. The smile returned, and he took his seat. "I have a little problem, and you might be able to help me out." Ned pointed to his glass, and Roger was quick to fill it. "My good friend, Ray, had a cash flow problem. It seems that some gambler ran up some debts with Mr. Black's gaming establishment. This party was slow to pay, which put Mr. Black in a tight spot with some of his creditors."

Ned took the bottle from Roger, poured another drink and settled back in his chair.

"I recently came into a sum of money and found myself in a position to help out our friend, Mr. Black. And, well, Roger, I bet you can guess my problem. I buy Mr. Black's notes at a fraction of their face value and solve his cash flow problem. Here we are, just a few days later, and I may have to call some of your notes to make ends meet. Speaking of face value, Roger—do you value your face? I only ask because it's time for you and me to discuss repayment terms on these notes."

Roger leaned forward. "I'm on a salary at the bank, Ned, and my father isn't about to consider raising it right now."

"We have to come up with a payment plan, Roger. We're talking about a lot of money, and I'm not content to let it ride. You wouldn't operate your bank that way."

"Frankly, Ned, I've never heard of factoring gambling debts."

"There are so many exciting, new things in the world today, aren't there? You're not going to refuse to pay this debt, are you, Roger? Because that would do terrible, terrible things to your face...value."

Roger glanced nervously toward the bar, and the look was not lost on Ned.

"My associates—J.C. Cooper and company," Ned smiled.

"I think I can come up with a hundred a month," Roger said.

Ned rocked back in his chair, looking solemnly at Roger. He took a long drink. "You're in a lot of trouble here, Roger boy, and a lousy hundred a month won't get the job done. That barely covers the interest. No, we're going to have to do better than that."

Roger was shaking slightly, and his voice betrayed his nerves. "I suppose that you've thought of something."

"As a matter of fact, I have," Ned said. "I've thought of several options, but the one I like best is the one where I go to work for your old man."

"What?"

"You'll deposit five hundred a month into an account, beginning the fifteenth of next month. In only four years you'll have paid the principal and all interest. That'll satisfy the debt to me. In order to ensure that your father and other people never learn of your improprieties in Waycross, financial and social, and to serve as indemnity against loss of 'face value', you'll get your old man to hire me at the bank."

"What if I can't persuade him?" Roger asked.

"Then I'll go to him to see if I can't persuade him to honor your obligations," Ned replied. "And then you'd suffer a loss of face value. You really should remember that, Roger. It applies to all possibilities, except the one I told you I prefer. I'm prepared, however, to make your task a simple one. Aside from money, what's nearest and dearest to a banker's heart?"

"You have all the answers," Roger muttered.

"More money!" Ned was pleased with his joke. "That means new business, Roger boy. You tell your old man that along with Ned Worthington comes a hefty increase in business over the next twelve months. It'll begin the second quarter after he hires me, so he'll only have to invest about three month's salary to call my hand on this deal."

Ned poured himself another drink, taking his time, letting Roger grasp what he was saying.

"What's the source of this new business?" Roger asked.

Ned winked. "Family and friends, Roger, friends and family. I'm going out of town for a few days. You might call it a vacation before I put my shoulder to the old banking wheel. I'm counting on Monday being my first day at work."

"Ned, be reasonable. If I can even pull this off, it'll take weeks of discussion with the old man. I have to bring him along gradually."

"You're on my timetable, Roger. Be creative."

"He built the bank himself. He's not going to up and hire just—" Roger hesitated, fumbling for his next words.

Ned leaned forward to pour Roger a drink. "Go ahead. And really insult me good this time. I'm savoring your insults, you self-righteous shit!"

Roger was silent.

"Let's see," Ned mused. "He's not going to hire just some dirt-poor redneck whose old man was a worthless drunk. Is that what you were saying to me?"

"Ned, I—"

"You shut up, Roger. When I'm talking from now on for the next four years, you shut your mouth." He brandished the packet of notes at Roger for emphasis. "For the next four years, I own Roger Pace, and you'd best not forget it. This meeting's over. You get your ass to the house, get sobered up, and start to work on old Clarence. I'll see you on Monday."

Without another word, Roger stood and turned toward the bar.

"Where do you think you're going?" Ned demanded.

"To pay for the drinks," Roger said.

"No, no, no, Roger boy. I'll handle that. You have a substantial note payment coming up in a couple of weeks. You really can't afford it. Now get on home." Ned laughed.

"Sounds like your meeting with Pace went pretty good."

Ned turned in his chair to face J.C. and his brothers.

"Mr. Cooper! Have a seat and a drink, and I'll tell you all about it."

"You said he wouldn't have the balls to buck you about them gambling notes," J.C. said.

"Or the sense. Let me tell you something about power, Mr. Cooper. The man who has it, but doesn't know he has it, doesn't have it. Power's all around us, but you have to have the sense to seize it and the courage to use it. Roger Pace has neither. I have both. And that's the reason I'm going to take everything he has."

"Hell, I know you," J.C. said. "You want everything Clarence Pace has, not what Roger has."

"One step at a time, Mr. Cooper," Ned said. "One step at a time."

XV

Clarence Samuel Pace was a man ideally suited for his position in life. He neither sought nor received popularity, yet he was perfectly civil to those with whom he came into contact, and they were civil to him in return. Clarence did not have intimate friends neither did he yearn for any. As the town banker of Magnolia, he was respected for his business acumen and conservative approach to financial matters. That respect and the proper maintenance of it were the height of his desire.

Years earlier, before moving to Magnolia, he had chosen an appropriate spouse, Martha Rogers, and she had proven to be adequate in the role of respected banker's wife. A quiet, shy woman, she had provided Clarence the perfect family, one son and one daughter, and then she had sunk into his shadow to tend the home, him, and the children.

Both he and his wife cared for their children, but Clarence was much relieved that they were grown to the age when they could be reasoned with on any matter of weight. The only exception had been Roger's proposal concerning Ned Worthington. Why in God's name had Roger been so insistent on hiring him? The prospect of a substantial increase in business was attractive, but who knew if Worthington could actually produce on that promise? There had to be something else to the matter. Worthington was certainly not a name in Clinch County that evoked admiration. It was a name associated with irresponsibility, idleness, and drunkenness, thanks to Cable.

At least Roger seemed to have thought the matter through, reasoning that they would only be risking three months' salary to test Ned's promise of such a large volume of new business.

And so it was that Clarence Pace's desire to see his son make a shrewd business deal allowed Ned Worthington to take his first step toward respectability in the eyes of Magnolia society.

Ned was careful to make good on his opportunity. From the first day of work, he was prompt, and he never consulted his watch as lunch or the end of the day approached. He took his orders to the letter from Clarence and, for all appearances, from Roger.

A week into his employment, Ned was placed in the cashier's cage while Mr. Harvey, the regular cashier, was on vacation. The work bored Ned. Customers were shocked to see him employed by the bank, and the rumor mill ground into action, but through it all, Ned played the good soldier. He looked up from his paperwork one day into the clear blue eyes of Jennifer Pace.

"Good morning, Mr. Worthington."

"Miss Pace," Ned replied, trying to sound officious.

"How do you like banking?"

"I'm afraid I have a lot to learn, but Roger's an excellent teacher, so I have an advantage. How's your boyfriend these days?"

Jennifer's eyes widened, and she glanced past the cashier's cage to see if her father or brother was within earshot. She lowered her voice. "I don't know what you mean."

"Is that a fact?" Ned asked nonchalantly. "Then if a fellow were of a mind to come calling, you would be free to consider him?"

"I suppose so," she said.

"How may I be of assistance, Miss Pace?"

"I beg your pardon?"

"Did you wish to make a transaction?"

Ned's abrupt transition confused her for a moment. "No. No, I—I just heard from Roger that you'd come to work here, and I thought I'd come by to welcome you."

"Well, thank you, but if you'll pardon me, there's a customer behind you, and your father wouldn't want me to keep him waiting."

"Oh, yes. Of course," Jennifer said. She quickly left to hide her embarrassment.

Ned smiled as he watched her cross the street.

Each day after that meeting, Ned made it a point to give Jennifer the opportunity to see him. He went out of his way to leave the bank with Roger, appearing to discuss business on the way to the Pace home. When they arrived there, he positioned his back to the house as they stood out front talking. Occasionally he would see Jennifer in town, and if spoke to her, his tone was flat.

"Good afternoon," he would say. Or if he was feeling formal, "Good evening, Miss Pace." No compliments on her wardrobe or her hair or her rare beauty as she had heard a hundred times before. No attempt to prolong the conversation with meaningless small talk. Just a terse hello and then he would lapse into conversation with Roger.

He had calculated accurately what a blow his coolness was to her pride. Within days of the time he predicted that Jennifer would begin to flirt with him, she entered the bank. Jennifer spoke briefly to Mr. Harvey, then passed through the door to the office.

"Ned, can you tell me where I might find father or Roger?"

"Hello, Miss Pace," he said. "They've gone to Waycross with Ben Taylor to look at some equipment. Didn't your father tell you that he would be gone overnight?"

"Yes, of course he did," she admitted. "But I didn't know they would be off so suddenly this morning."

Ned remained aloof. "Is there a message I could relay to him, Miss Pace?"

"No, it's nothing that important," she said.

"Is there something that I could help with?" Ned asked.

"I don't suppose so. Mother isn't well, and I'd feel better if someone would check on us later this evening. I was going to see if father would get someone to do that. I'm being silly, I guess."

"I suppose you're right," Ned replied. There was a moment of awkward silence. "Was there something else, Jennifer?"

"I'm a bit light-headed. It must be the heat. Would it be an imposition on your bank duties to see me home?"

"I'd feel responsible if something happened," he said.

Jennifer could hardly contain a smile of triumph.

"After all," he continued, "your father's left me in charge of the bank. I'll see if Mr. Harvey will escort you. I'm sure he'll be delighted."

He gestured at the little man to come over to his desk. "But I am concerned about your being alone with a sick mother. With your permission, I'd check on you ladies this evening. What the local gossips don't see won't hurt us."

"Please try to make it before nine, as I'm sure Mother will be asleep by then," Jennifer said.

Ned stepped by Jennifer to the door of the cubicle. "Mr. Harvey, I need you to do something for me," he said. As Mr. Harvey escorted the perfectly healthy Jennifer Pace down the quiet street, Ned stood at the window admiring her gait.

*   *   *   *

Jennifer tried to will the rest of the day to speed away. She fussed over details in the house most of the day until everything looked perfect to her. She decided to receive him in her father's study on the north side of the house, so that they wouldn't be visible from the street. She was patient as long as the work lasted, but when all was ready and the hour passed for the bank to close, she became more and more anxious. Wouldn't darkness ever come? Why did she allow herself to get so worked up? The boy's family simply wouldn't do. Seeing him would only complicate things for both of them. Her father might even object so strenuously as to fire him.

On the other hand, he was a right nice-looking man if one discounted the rough edges—the need of a proper haircut, a little more care of his fingernails, an improvement in wardrobe. All were things she could take care of nicely.

So intent had Jennifer been on bathing and dressing herself and tending to her mother that she let seven, then eight o'clock pass her by. When she realized that it was getting late, her first thought was that he had changed his mind about coming. Her mother ate some soup at eight-thirty, then settled in for the night and was asleep by nine-fifteen.

By then Jennifer was indignant at the nerve of Ned. How could he lead her on this way? Was he so insensitive as to miss the way she smiled at him whenever she was in the bank? Yet here he was trifling with her emotions, abandoning her in her hour of distress.

"I won't speak to him for weeks," she said as she entered the study.

"That'll teach him," a voice said.

Jennifer stepped back, inhaling sharply. Her voice didn't work at first, but he didn't move from behind her father's desk, and she regained her composure.

"Is that you, Ned?" She asked.

"Didn't I tell you I'd come to visit tonight?"

Jennifer sighed in relief. "Yes, and I asked you to come before nine. I did expect you to be received at the front door like a gentleman, not to sneak in like a thief. If my mother comes down here, you'll be without a job." She felt all the frustration and anger of the entire evening coming to the surface. "What do you think you're doing sitting at my father's desk? He won't even let Roger sit there. Why, he'll fire you just for that, if he finds out about it."

Ned leaned back in the leather chair and propped his feet on the corner of the desk, laughing softly. Jennifer gasped at his sacrilege of Clarence Pace's desk.

"Sit down and shut up, Jennifer!" he commanded, pointing to the sofa with a riding crop. She obeyed, perching on the front edge of the sofa.

"Are you still feeling as faint as you were this morning?" His tone was solicitous now. His behavior had her anxious and confused.

"I'm feeling much better now, thank you." Her voice trembled.

"I've frightened you, haven't I?"

Her voice and her submission had betrayed her. She didn't answer, but she bowed her head slightly.

Ned sprang up and slapped the riding crop down on the oak desk. "Answer me!" he yelled.

Jennifer's head snapped up, her eyes wide, her pulse and breathing accelerated.

"Yes, you—you're frightening me now." Why was he behaving this way? She suspected that he was drunk, but she was too intimidated to question him.

He sat again, swiveling from side to side slightly. He played with the whip, rolling it slowly between two fingers.

"There are some things you need to know," he said finally. "Some things I need to discuss with you, and you need to hear me out. Do you understand?"

She nodded.

"Answer me," he said calmly, looking at the whip.

"Yes, I understand."

"Good. I've shocked you enough for one evening. I don't like surprises myself, but, used sparingly, they add a little flavor to life."

Jennifer felt her body tingle. She didn't understand her emotions. They were in such turmoil of frustration and fear and anger and humiliation that she was shocked to find herself excited by Ned's behavior. The whole conversation was unreal to her.

"You'll find that I'm a man who gets right to the point. I have a great deal of ambition, and I am impatient. Those two characteristics make me direct. I also believe that there are many paths to any ambition in life. That belief makes me bold to proceed when other men hesitate." Ned leaned back in the chair again, propped his feet up, and continued. "For example, if I wanted to marry, I'd be patient long enough to survey the prospects and narrow the field to two or three. Then I'd choose the woman I wanted the most, and I'd either win or lose her. If she turned me down, I'd go after the next. Most things work out in two or three tries."

"Is this an attempt at a proposal of marriage?" Jennifer asked.

Ned stood and walked around the desk to stand behind her. He touched her on the neck with the riding crop.

"No. This is an explanation of how I operate. Is the feel of the leather on your neck pleasurable or painful?"

"It's soft," she said. "It feels good."

"But you know that this thing which feels so good is also capable of burning right through your skin. I'm just like this whip, and you need to know that." He walked around the sofa and leaned against the desk. "The next thing you need to know is that I demand loyalty from those who want to associate with me. What are your feelings for John Warren?"

"What do you mean?" she asked.

Ned lashed the whip across his hand, and a red welt appeared as the blood rose to the surface of his palm. He raised it to her, and Jennifer cringed.

"I'll suffer this and more for you," he said. "And you'll have to wound your pride a little in return. I know what happened in the gazebo out there in your yard. I know everything about your meetings with John Warren. Be honest with me."

"I have many suitors. Mr. Warren and I enjoy each other's company, but he's too interested in his work."

"Or he's not interested enough in you."

"I should slap your face for an unwarranted remark like that!"

"You misunderstand me," Ned said. "The man's a fool if he doesn't give you the attention you deserve. I'll never make that mistake. That's the way I feel about you, and I think you should know it. But if you turn me away, I won't be back." Ned stepped back to Jennifer and extended his wounded left hand. "Take my hand and stand up," he ordered. "I know that I've sounded harsh, but it's my way. I make no apologies for that. You're the woman I want. I'm not asking tonight if you'll marry me. When I do ask, though, I won't be patient. You be thinking about it, because I won't ask twice. I've given you fair notice."

He turned to go. Jennifer held onto his hand, and Ned turned back to her. She raised the hand to her face, opened the palm, and gently kissed it.

§   §   §   §

Clarence Pace was studying a list of engineering equipment that was up for auction in Waycross when he became aware of someone standing at his office door. He looked up to see Ned fidgeting with his hat.

"What is it?"

"Do you mind if I come in and close the door? This is a private matter, sir."

"Is this something that you might take up with Roger? I'm busy at the moment," Clarence said.

"This is something that I'd think you'd want to hear yourself, sir. It involves Jennifer." Without waiting, Ned entered the office and pulled the door shut behind him. He sat down and made himself comfortable. "I'll make this as brief as I can, Mr. Pace. Jennifer's seeing a man. I feel terrible being the bearer of bad news, but I felt obligated to bring you the truth."

"I hope for your sake that you have proof," Clarence said, barely containing his anger.

"Sir, my only hope and prayer is that nothing more has happened between John Warren and Jennifer than what I've witnessed."

"John Warren! Oh my God—that stray that Ben and Wealthy Taylor were so foolish as to take in?"

"I was going home late from work one evening, and as I passed your house, I heard voices back in the yard. Naturally at ten-thirty I feared the worst. I couldn't make out what was being said, and I thought that some outlaws were about to rob your home. Imagine my shock when I saw what was going on and who was involved."

"And just what was going on?" Clarence demanded.

"John Warren and Jennifer were in the gazebo. He was lying on the bench with his vile head resting on her lap, and they were talking."

"Is that all that went on?" Clarence asked.

"Yes, sir. At least while I was there. I was embarrassed to witness such a scene, particularly since I knew that this was going on without your knowledge. I didn't stay long, but I did hear Warren trying to talk Miss Jennifer into some things that a young girl shouldn't be thinking about until she's properly wedded."

"What!" Clarence slammed both fists on his desk and glared at Ned. "You heard that without a doubt?"

"Upon my honor, sir. But to the credit of your daughter and the upbringing she's had in a God-fearing family, she wouldn't hear of it. She begged him to stop saying such things and looked as if she wanted to get away from him."

"And you did nothing? What in God's name were you thinking?"

"Just as I was about to come to her aid, she slapped Warren and got away to the house. I started to go after him anyway, but then I thought of how awkward it would be for you if there was a fight in your yard at that time of night. I sure wanted to straighten that scoundrel out, but I had to think about more than my desires. This is better handled quietly."

"It sounds to me as if Jennifer's come to her senses and handled the matter herself," Clarence said, easing back in his chair.

"That's what I thought at the moment, sir, but I wanted to make sure that Miss Jennifer was safe, so I confronted Warren the next chance I had."

"And what did the rascal have to say for himself?"

"Mr. Clarence, I wouldn't repeat to Satan himself the vile things he said to me. I didn't let him get much out of his foul mouth before I knocked him to the ground. He wouldn't fight, but he had the nerve to lay there in the road and tell me that he had every intention of seeing Jennifer again and that eventually he would get what he wanted."

"I'll kill him," Clarence said. "I'll see that he's tarred and feathered and run out of town, and then I'll kill him. Excuse me. I'm going to see Ben Taylor right now about that boy. You've done the right thing in coming to me privately about this matter. I'm indebted to you."

"Mr. Clarence, may I make a suggestion?"

Clarence stopped beside his desk. "Of course, my boy."

"Let's think through the best course here. If you go to Mr. Ben insisting that Warren be run off, Miss Wealthy and Mr. Ben are going to hear Warren's side of things."

"So," Clarence said. "How could he possibly defend his actions?"

"He won't. He'll just deny them or if Jennifer's brought into the matter, he may think of some way to tarnish her honor. I'm thinking of your daughter's reputation, sir."

"You're right, Ned. I must get a grip on my emotions so that I can think clearly."

"What I suggest is that you catch Warren in the act of luring her out of the house. Then there's no way for him to deny what's been going on. Once you've caught him at his game, then go to Mr. Ben and Miss Wealthy and make the boy admit what he's been up to. I don't think you'll have to wait any later than tonight."

"I must admit that this sounds like a good approach, Ned."

"Of course it is, sir. I think it'd be best if no one knows that I'm your source of information on these goings-on. The less talk, the fewer people who'll learn of this indiscretion."

$\quad$ ❧ $\qquad$ ❧ $\qquad$ ❧ $\qquad$ ❧

Wealthy had just finished cleaning the last of the dinner dishes when she heard someone knocking at her front door. As she stepped from the kitchen to the hallway, the knocking became louder, more insistent.

"Just a moment. I'm coming." When she opened the door, there stood Clarence Pace, looking highly agitated.

"Clarence, what's the matter? You're making such a racket!"

"Pardon my impatience, Wealthy, but I need to speak with you and Ben on an urgent matter. Is he here?"

"Yes, come on in. I'll get him for you. Sit in here," she said, pointing Clarence to the sitting room.

When she returned with Ben, Clarence was sitting on the edge of the chair, his fingers drumming on the arm. The men shook hands.

"What can we do for you, Clarence?" Ben asked.

"I've come to the two of you privately to try to handle a problem we have among us. I'll come directly to the point. Tonight I caught John Warren luring my daughter out of her bed and into the gazebo in my own yard!"

"O good Lord!" Wealthy gasped.

"Is Jennifer all right, Clarence?" Ben asked.

"Her mother's talking with her now, so I don't know the extent of this liaison, but we certainly will find out what's been going on."

Wealthy cried quietly, unable to compose herself to ask any questions.

"I agonized over what to do after I caught them outside and finally decided it would be best to address this matter right away by coming here."

"I commend you for your restraint, Clarence," Ben said. "I'm afraid I might not have behaved so well under the circumstances."

"I'm mortified," Wealthy sobbed. "If Jennifer's harmed in any way by John's irresponsibility, I'll die."

Ben started to leave the room. "I'll get to the bottom of this."

"No, wait, Ben," Clarence said. "I want the three of us to talk before you get that boy."

Ben turned and stood at the door.

"I want to hear both sides of this story, Jennifer's and John's, but my daughter's reputation cannot help but be stained regardless of the truth. Some people will assume the worst. Therefore, I'd like John Warren to leave this town. His presence here will only serve to remind people of this episode."

"I understand, Clarence," Ben replied.

"Oh no," Wealthy cried. "Please don't take the boy from me. There must be some other way to set this right."

"Wealthy, I won't have it thought that any young man may deceive my daughter and lure her into depredation without suffering at my hand. It's just unthinkable."

"The whole thing could be entirely innocent," she protested. "Please, let's not talk of punishment until we hear the whole matter."

"I'm going to get John," Ben said.

Wealthy excused herself to wash her face and to try to regain her composure. Her instinct was to protect this boy she had made her own. Clarence heard Ben coming, so he stepped out into the hallway as Wealthy returned.

"He's gone," Ben said.

*   *   *   *

"Hand me another crawfish," Gray Hampton said.

John handed the whole bucket of bait to Gray. "Here, take them all. I'll just paddle the boat for you."

Gray took the bucket, set it on the bottom of the boat, and picked one out.

"That makes you the perfect fishing companion, provided you clean the fish later," Gray said smiling. "I have two questions for you, and I suspect they both have the same answer."

John kept the boat steady in the breeze by holding onto some branches along the bank of the pond. Gray pulled the boat next to a hollow stump and dropped his baited hook inside.

"Why are you so down in the mouth, and why aren't you at work?"

Gray's line tightened and moved from one side of the stump to the other.

"I've put myself in a mess, Gray."

"Who is she?"

"What makes you think there's a woman involved?"

"Pull over there to that big stump. In about ninety percent of the cases when a man says that, there's a woman involved. Five percent of the time it's liquor and the other five it's religion. Who is she?"

"Jennifer Pace," John muttered. He paddled slowly to the stump.

Gray looked up from baiting his hook. "I admire you, John Warren. When you get in trouble, you don't fool around. You get in about as deep as a fellow can get. So you've got Clarence Pace on your tail, huh?"

John looked up sheepishly. "Jennifer's been sneaking out of the house at night to be with me."

Gray smiled for a few seconds and began to laugh. His reaction caught John off guard and broke his sullen mood.

"Old Clarence's going to kill you," Gray said.

John nodded. "I know."

Gray fished the stump and John swirled the paddle in the dark green water to steady the boat. Gray pulled up another warmouth perch. "How serious is this trouble? You ain't got the girl in a family way, have you?"

"No!" John said. "This has been innocent stuff. We kiss a little and talk a lot, but that's it."

"No pledges of undying love, no temptation to follow through on those urges of the flesh?"

John felt his face warm and knew that Gray had him blushing. "Jennifer's a beautiful woman, and I think I love her, but I'm nowhere near ready for a family, and I'll have to have something to offer her before we get too serious."

"How did you leave things with Clarence?" Gray asked.

"Pretty bad," John said, "and I imagine things will be worse with Ben and Wealthy. Mr. Clarence caught Jennifer and me out in the gazebo tonight. He made me promise to go straight home to take up the matter. They're probably finding out that I'm not around right now."

"You have a heap of problems there," Gray said. "What do you plan to do?"

"I thought that some time out here with you would help me come up with something, but so far I've drawn a blank."

They continued to paddle from stump to stump, and from almost every one, Gray pulled a hand-sized fish. After a dozen or so, he leaned back on the bow of the boat to rest.

"The way I figure it, you have to look at the situation from their point of view," Gray said. "First, the Paces. Their daughter's reputation is harmed, and you're the cause. The crime's serious enough to them to warrant the highest punishment. What's the worst that Clarence Pace could do to John Warren?"

"He could keep me from seeing Jennifer."

"Right," said Gray. "This is a small town, so it'll be impossible for him to keep the two of you from seeing each other. You know, church and the like. So, I'd say he'll try to run you off or have you jailed."

"You really think it's that serious?" John asked.

"Do you really think it's not?" Gray asked incredulously. "This is a little kingdom you're living in, boy, and Clarence Pace thinks it's his. You can't mess with the king and get away with it. Otherwise, who'll try it next? You'll have to be made a rather harsh example."

"What do you think Ben and Wealthy will do?" John asked.

"Miss Wealthy will fight for you all she can, but there's a point she won't cross. As long as you convince her that the whole deal was innocent, she'll be on your side, clawing and kicking and fighting. But if she thinks you hurt Jennifer in any way, she'll be the one to lock you up, personally. Ben will make the most businesslike decision. If you're valuable to him in his operations, then he'll fight hard for leniency. If he can do without you, though, he'll get rid of you to keep in Clarence's good graces on all those notes he owes at the bank."

"Assuming you're right on all of that, what do I do?"

"You lie like a dog," Gray said. "You try to convince them that Jennifer lured you out at night. Maybe she told you that she was in some sort of trouble and that only you could help her and that it had to remain quiet. So actually, you were being the gallant gentleman."

"Are you crazy?" John asked. "I can't believe what I'm hearing. I can't try to put this off on Jennifer."

"Why not?" Gray asked, smiling.

"Because she does have a reputation to protect, and because I came to her first and got her to come out. I'm not going to lie about it."

"Well, what does that leave—the truth?"

"Yes, the truth. Is there something wrong with—" He looked off across the pond, trying not to smile.

"Sometimes it's easier helping a fellow see what he ought to do by showing him what he shouldn't do," Gray said. "But when you're owning up to the stupid thing you did, there's a lot to be said for trying to drum up a little sympathy, too. You just can't be obvious about it."

"What do you mean?" John asked.

"Paddle us over to that stump, and I'll give you a few ideas," Gray said. He hooked the next crawfish as John paddled.

Later that evening, when John stepped onto the back porch at the Taylors, Wealthy looked anxiously across the table at Ben.

"Please try to keep calm," she said. She didn't like the way he scowled at her. As John entered the kitchen, Wealthy turned away from him to get another cup of coffee for Ben. She fought back tears.

"Where the hell have you been?" Ben snapped.

John looked down at him. "I've been trying to think about how to straighten out the mess I've made."

"I didn't ask what you'd been doing," Ben said. "I want to know where you've been, because you told Clarence Pace that you'd be right here."

John sat down at the table, and they glared at each other. "I've been out to Gray Hampton's place," John said.

Wealthy returned to the table and sat down. Ben stabbed at the pie on his plate and gulped it down.

"You think you can do anything you want? You think you can lie to people who are trying to help you and not honor your word and just have everybody accept it?"

"No, sir. I was wrong to do what I did, and I want to try to make up for it."

Ben's jaws twitched as he clenched his teeth. "How do you expect to do that?" he yelled.

"Tell us how this whole fiasco started, John," Wealthy said solemnly.

"Jennifer and I first started talking at church and at the church socials. I thought she was the prettiest girl I'd ever seen. I'm lonely for people my age, so one thing led to another, and one night I couldn't sleep very well. I went out for a little walk, and the next thing I know, I'm outside the Pace's. I got her attention by throwing something up at her window, and I told her I wouldn't leave until she came down."

"What happened when she came down?" Wealthy asked.

"We talked mostly. Just got to know each other, talking about our lives and our dreams and such."

"How many times have you met like that?" Ben growled.

"Maybe a dozen or so," John replied.

"And how serious did it get?"

"Benjamin Taylor!"

"We have to know, Wealthy. If the girl's carrying, that'd be a different story than if she's not."

"It's all right. I've done nothing like that. We kissed and hugged some, but that's all. We liked being together with no older folks around."

"That's good enough for me," Wealthy said. "We'll hear Jennifer's side of things later and then make a judgment."

"You make sure you're here tomorrow," Ben said. "There's no legal charge that I know of for what you've done, but I'll come up with something that'll put you right back behind bars if you don't show up for work."

John did show up for work on time the next morning. The day fell into the routine, as if trouble with Clarence Pace was not brewing. The only change in the order of things was that Ben was more than an hour late returning from lunch. Several of the men remarked about his tardiness out of concern for him.

That evening John learned the significance of the change in Ben's routine as he sat in the Taylor's parlor with Ben and Clarence.

"I believe John has something to say to you, Clarence," Ben said.

"I apologize for my behavior in regard to your daughter and in failing to keep my word about returning here last night," John said. "Jennifer isn't to blame. I lured her out of the house. Our physical contact was limited to embracing and kissing, so her honor's intact."

"But her reputation's ruined," Clarence snapped. "And I'll be laughed at as an old fool who can't protect his own. That's a sorry reputation for a banker. This incident could seriously damage my business. Did you ever stop to think of that?"

"No, sir. I guess I didn't," John said.

"Obviously not," Clarence said, "but where you're going, you'll have plenty of time to think about all the wrong you've done me."

John looked at Ben. "Where am I going?"

"To the east of the swamp," Ben said. "I'm sending you and Stokes to work in a venture that I'm investing in over there."

John looked from Ben to Clarence and back. "What if I won't go?"

"Then you'd be out of a job," Ben said. "You'd have to leave town or be jailed for vagrancy."

"Suppose I get another job?"

"Don't you try to push me, boy," Clarence said. "You won't get another job in Clinch County. I'll make sure of that."

"It's your choice, John," Ben said.

John rubbed the back of his neck and thought for a moment. "Can I talk with Wealthy about this?" John asked.

"There's nothing to discuss," Ben said. "Either you'll go or you won't, and you know the consequences if you choose not to go."

John knew that he had no options. "I'll go, but I want to know what I'm getting myself into."

Ben and Clarence exchanged glances, and Clarence shrugged. Ben looked back to John.

"We're going to drain the Okefenokee Swamp and cut the timber off it."

XVI

The waves of the ocean thundered onto the white blade of shore. The shoreline was flat and only a few yards wide at low tide for hundreds of miles in either direction, with the exception of a forty-mile stretch. In this area the ocean floor had weakened a million years earlier when the water had extended fifty miles further inland. Over ten thousand years, the movement of water and the weakness of the floor washed out a shallow saucer forty miles long and twenty-five miles wide.

The relentless movement of water tore at the earth, reducing the soft limestone fragments to sand and mixing the earth with shell and bone. The ocean deposited the mixture along the vast sweep of the shore, but just to the east of the depression the tide piled the sand high, forming a ridge along the forty miles of sunken earth. Another two hundred thousand years passed and the water receded to a point twenty-five miles to the east of the ridge that it had patiently built.

Day by day, year after year, century after century as the water retraced its course, life grew in the saucer left behind. The salt water evaporated in periods of drought, replaced by fresh water running into the area from small creeks on the north and from great torrents in the sky. As the freshwater replaced the salt, those plants that depended on a high salt content died and fell into decay, and new life formed. Slowly, patiently, constantly a new growth arose from the decay of the old. Thousands of years passed.

§　　　§　　　§　　　§

Cau Au Ra stood facing the people, his back to the warmth of the council fire, a blaze that reached the leaves of the surrounding trees. There were only two dozen now, most of them old and too feeble to move beyond the confines of their island in the great swamp. They depended on their leader for sustenance. Among the men, only he had the strength to pursue game and to do the heavier work in the settlement. Only the braids of his black hair were untouched by gray. Only the features of his countenance were unlined and strong.

They depended on his woman, Au Eve, for the continued existence of the people. Among the women only she was young enough to bear children. Only the braids of her black hair were untouched by gray. Only the features of her countenance were unlined and strong. But this couple of last hope was barren. At twenty-five they were almost beyond the hope of children due to their advanced age.

The light from the fire extended a few yards beyond the people, creating an intimate, primal setting for the story. Many there had heard it far more often than Cau Au Ra, but as last of the line of Ruler-Priests, he had been tutored in every detail of the historic journey of their ancient ancestors. He knew it best, and the people loved to hear him tell it.

When his father and grandfather were both living, they had taken him to the sacred place where none of the people went. They were there for eight suns and in the midst of that time, through fasting, incantation, discipline, and the fruit of the earth, Cau Au Ra had his vision of the journey. Like all the Ruler-Priests before him, he participated in it in his spirit and was thus fit to transmit the experience to future generations.

As Cau Au Ra faced the few people left and began the rhythmic swaying walk around the fire that was the prologue for the story that took the night to tell, it occurred to him that he might be the last to tell it. In his ancient language he began. "With one single step, the Fathers of old left that which they knew, the land of their birth, land we shall never know, to travel the earth..."

Only the stars, the night, and the Ah Fin Au Cau witnessed the story that Cau Au Ra, indeed, told for the last time.

$ $ $ $

He held his ground behind the fallen tree, waiting patiently for the sow and her brood to move into the range of his bow. The mid-winter day was crisp but windless, so the hog was not picking up his scent. Silently, he armed the bow and drew a line of sight so that the arrow would strike just behind the foreleg. He hoped to pierce the heart to avoid a chase through the thick tangle of the underbrush.

At the last fraction of a second, as Cau Au Ra released his arrow, the hog took a step and the arrow shattered a rib as it pierced her stomach. The sow squealed in pain and lumbered off, her pigs trailing.

Cau Au Ra bounded over the tree and chased the sound. A few hundred feet into the tangle of grapevines and briars he heard a roar, and the insistent squeal of his prey swelled and died away in the cypress and pine forest of the Ah Fin Au Cau. He heard the pigs scatter. Cau Au Ra advanced cautiously now, for he knew what lay at the end of the trail. He had to be careful, but he also had to get to the sow before the bear had time to devour it.

He saw the bear sitting on its haunches, inspecting the kill, pawing curiously at the arrow. Cau Au Ra set his arrow, took one step into the clearing and pulled back on the bowstring. The arrow struck the animal directly below his sternum. The bear stood to his full eight feet and roared as the second arrow hit him below the first.

Roaring louder, he kicked the dead hog aside and advanced on his adversary. Cau Au Ra reached to his right and picked up a large pine branch. He hefted it to make sure that it was not rotten and watched the bear rush him. His first swing glanced off the animal's massive head.

     *   *   *   *

Au Eve paced as she watched the path. She knew that he had not intended to be gone this long. After the second day of his absence, three of the old men had gone in search of him, but they had no teeth and could not eat the deer for his agility or the bear for his stamina. They searched the major trails, but it was all they could do.

The people tried to console Au Eve, but their inward fears made their words hollow. They were in need of consolation. They could not give it.

On the fourth day of his absence from her, Au Eve was cleaning halfheartedly when she felt him trying to stay on earth until he could reach her for farewell. Her heart leapt up, anxious to find him, but she restrained herself. She didn't want to startle his spirit and send him off to the sky before they could talk one last time.

Au Eve walked calmly down the path. "My love?" she called. "Tender one?"

She heard a groan just around the curve. The fading light was kind, preventing her from seeing the extent of his wounds. He was bathed in blood and the Ah Fin Au Cau. His scalp was half gone, lacerations covered most of his body, and with a dozen broken bones, he had struggled for three days to reach her. Au Eve knelt in the path, desperate to hold him in her arms, yet afraid to touch him, afraid of causing him more pain.

He tried to focus himself on his woman.

"Find water. Clean my face," he murmured. When she hesitated, he touched her hand. "I strove to be with you. I will stay a little longer."

She ran to the hut and returned in minutes with a bowl of water. At first she just allowed the water to run from her fingers onto his face. Then as she could see unwounded flesh, she washed it tenderly with her fingertips.

They sat together, his head cradled by her lap, and looked at each other while he gained the strength to talk. Au Eve felt his spirit slipping away, her heart breaking open. Her tears wet his blood-encrusted hair.

"Shall I live on here without you?" she asked, praying that he would not have it so.

"It saddens me," he said, "but the people must have you, if they have not me."

"But you are the last of your line. The people are undone."

"I saw something on the way here from the bear," he said. "You will be the last of the people. You will tell those who come to Ah Fin Au Cau after us of the people. It is the only way they will know. Don't let the memory of the people pass from the earth. Tell the journey. Then come and join me in the heavens."

"Where will you be?" she asked.

They looked up to the sky filled with the winter stars. It was a clear, bright night. Au Eve searched the sky until just above the pines she saw an exceedingly bright star, one she had never seen before. It was part of Aquarius. She slowly rocked Cau Au Ra, a rhythmic sway like the prologue to the journey.

"O yes, there," she said. "I see you now."

     ❧   ❧   ❧   ❧

The three men settled back on their bedrolls, the day finally done, for a little coffee and conversation.

"This feels good on my old bones," said Corey.

"My young bones, too," John Warren agreed.

The night sounds of crickets and frogs added to their sense of tranquility. John turned to look at his friend, Gray Hampton, who was looking at a million stars overhead.

"What saith the prophet and the poet?" John asked. Gray kept his face toward the stars as he spoke.

"Time is but the stream I go a-fishing in. I drink at it, but while I drink I see the sandy bottom and detect how shallow it is. Its thin current slides away, but eternity remains. I would drink deeper; fish in the sky, whose bottom is pebbly with stars.'"

Gray turned to look at John and continued.

"I cannot count one. I know not the first letter of the alphabet. I have always been regretting that I was not as wise as the day I was born.'"

Gray rolled back to look skyward again. John and Corey looked at each other, and John shrugged. They were struck by the simple beauty of the images of fishing and of a river and of the sky.

"I like that part about the stream, but what do that last line mean, Mr. Gray?" Corey asked.

"I have an idea or two about it, Corey, but I want to hear what John thinks."

"You've got me on that one," John said. "I don't recall much about the day I was born. I don't think I knew much of anything back then."

Gray sat up, cross-legged, to face the others. "You're confusing knowledge and wisdom," he said. "We're at our wisest when we know the least, and that is on the day we're born."

"Knowledge is the accumulation of information," John said, "and it leads us to wisdom."

"So much of what you call information is false that knowledge is the accumulation of prejudice, and it leads us to folly. Don't believe me? Just look at how foolishly people behave, day in and day out."

Corey poked at the fire with a stick to stir it into flames and added wood. "Would it be better to forget everything we done learned?" he asked.

"It would be best never to have learned it," said Gray. "But since we have, yes, we should try to forget it all."

"What!" John said. "You're going way around the bend on this, so don't expect us to follow you. Corey, don't listen to this lunatic. He's a poet with way too many stars in his eyes."

Corey chuckled and poured himself some more coffee. "Sorry, John, but I think I know what he's saying to be the truth."

"O good God, Stokes, not you too!"

"The Good Book says that you won't get into Heaven, lest you accept it like a little child. I thought it was talking about a eight or nine year old, but it could have been saying be like a little baby, not knowing the things of this world at all. This ain't our home, no how," Corey said.

"Be practical," John sneered. "You have to know the ways of the world to get along in it. You forget what you've learned about making moonshine, Corey, and then see how much you miss the money."

"You're too involved in following the stream in this life, John," Gray said. "Don't you detect how shallow it is? That's some of your reason for fighting the water in your dreams. Time is overwhelming you, or maybe it's running past you. Stay in one place sometime and see how eternity remains when the current of time moves on. Every second, past or present, is still only a part of eternity. Drink deeper, John."

"I think I'll do just that." He got up and retrieved a jar of liquor from the wagon. "Anybody care to join me?"

"Probably do my joints some good," Corey said.

"Pass," said Gray.

John poured the clear liquid into Corey's cup and sat down again. "So you think this quote has something to do with my dreams?"

"It may not be the one complete answer, but I think it's a piece of the puzzle. You can associate water with a lot of things, but if not for Mr. Thoreau's writing, I don't know if I'd have linked it to time and eternity."

"I can see that part, but this thing about forgetting everything we've ever learned is beyond me. I can use what I've learned in the past to help me in the present and in the future. Why try to forget it?"

"Sometimes our current knowledge blocks us from getting anything better. If a man thinks he knows it all, when of course he doesn't, then he'll never learn more. If you think you have the capacity to get free or to understand your spirit, then you'll keep working to gain knowledge so that you can. But it's a false trail. You'll never get free by trying to learn how. We get free by being free. Your knowledge encumbers you because most of it is only good for living in this world, or it's wrong."

"How can you say such a thing, Gray? You study and learn more than anyone I've ever known. How can you justify that?"

"I immediately forget what is non-eternal. Those things which are eternal, I make them part of me, so that I no longer have to know them. They are me."

"Just a minute, Mr. Gray. Let me get a big old snort this time, and maybe I can understand that."

"Yeah, me too," said John. They grinned at each other and turned up their cups. Gray shook his head and laughed.

"You both are definitely on the wrong track if you think you can reason this out. You won't understand it by applying what you've learned in the past. The way to make eternal things a part of you has to be revealed to you."

"Revealed by the Holy Spirit." Corey said.

"There you go," Gray said. "He is the one who leads us into all truth."

"And knowing the truth will set you free," John said.

"That's it."

"How's it do that, Mr. Gray?"

"In ways that I probably haven't even imagined yet, Corey," Gray said. "But the first way that the truth has set me free, is that I no longer worry about anything. I have a peace about life that sets me free from that sort of aggravation."

John sat his cup on the ground and leaned forward, looking intently at Gray. "You mean to tell me that you never worry about *anything*?" John asked.

"I'm concerned about some things that I think ought not to be, but I don't worry about them. If there's nothing I can do about some injustice, I let it go."

"And what truth did the Spirit reveal to you to give you that freedom?"

"He showed me that the world is bigger than I am, John, and that it was here before there was me, and that it will be here after I'm gone. He showed me that God is in charge, regardless of what people think."

John snorted and shook his head. "God's in charge of what?" he asked.

"Eternity."

"What would you say if I told you that I disagree? God isn't in charge of a damned thing in this world."

"I'd say that it's too bad that you're not as wise as the day you were born. Maybe you can return to that degree of wisdom one day."

"You wouldn't argue the point with me?"

"John, have you ever seen the Atlantic Ocean?"

"No."

"Do you believe that it exists?"

"Of course."

"How do you know?"

"I believe the people who have seen it."

"Would you try to convince them that the Atlantic doesn't exist, or that it doesn't have a taste of salt to it?"

"No, of course not."

"And why not?"

"Because they've seen it firsthand, and—"

"Because they've seen it, and they know what it's like," Gray finished. "So I won't argue the point of God's sovereignty with anyone, John. You can point out any circumstances you want to, but no matter how cruel the world may seem, God runs it. I've seen the truth of that statement."

"Well, I haven't, Gray, and that's one I'm going to have to see for myself."

s   s   s   s

May 23, 1871

My Dearest Jennifer,

We have finally completed the long haul to the far side of the Okefenokee. Arrived here about noon today, but I could not rest until I had written you.

I regret that I could not invent a means to reach you for a real farewell, but there was simply no path around Ben Taylor or your father. I deeply regret any pain that I may have caused you or your family. My actions were motivated by the genuine affection that I feel for you. My heart longs for you.

My greatest pain lies within the uncertainty of my life. When will I find my way back to you? How can I ever gain your father's trust and approval? Will your affection for me grow cold in this time of separation?

The Okefenokee has captured my imagination as no place else on earth and Jennifer Pace has captured my heart as no person on earth. I could no more tell the Okefenokee of her beauty, than I could her of the beauty of the swamp.

I must leave you for the moment. I don't know how well you know Gray Hampton, but you can trust him wholeheartedly as I do. If you find it difficult to post letters to me, Gray is clever and will find a way. He has agreed to do me the service of passing my letters on to you. Captain Jackson has named our encampment for his daughter; thus you may address me at Camp Cornelia, % Postmaster, Folkston, Georgia. Please write to me soon.

My Greatest Affection,
John

s   s   s   s

May 23, 1871

My Dear Miss Wealthy,

I have sat for hours trying to compose this letter in my mind, that my thoughts might adequately express what is in my heart. I'm afraid that I shall fall terribly short of the mark.

I love you a great deal. Forgive me for letting you down. I know that I have disappointed several people and offended many others, but I know that I have wounded you, and that offense I cannot bear. The others have been a great help to me since I came to Magnolia, but you alone have cared for me as a mother cares for her child, and only the memory of my own mother exceeds the love I feel for you.

Please believe that I only feel the purest affection for Jennifer Pace, and that I have been raised from infancy to respect and cherish ladies of all ages and station in life. I would never take advantage of Miss Pace in any manner. That I have embarrassed her family and compromised her honor are the result of my inability to think clearly of the consequences of my actions. Otherwise, I would never have undertaken to meet her under what I now see were questionable circumstances.

How can I begin to regain your affection and trust? What can I do or say to relieve the pain that I have put in your heart? Please answer me without hesitation and without reservation. Speak bluntly to me, and I shall obey.

I want to share with you the experiences of my day on this side of the world and the beauty of this land, but I cannot address those topics until I have made atonement for the sins of my recent past.

I love you, and I long for your reply.

John

      s   s   s   s

May 23, 1871

Dear Mr. Ben,

First, I want to thank you for the manner in which you have stuck with me. I know that you were under no obligation to keep me on under any circumstances, so I am all the more determined to represent you well in this venture. Perhaps in time and with diligence on my part, I might regain some small measure of trust from you and Miss Wealthy. That is for you to say, but I will be working toward that end.

I apologize again to you for my behavior, and I regret my actions in regard to Miss Pace. If you think that Mr. Pace will read a letter from me, I will also write an apology to him. I would like your direction in this matter.

While I don't want to detract from what I have just said, I think that I should give you my first impression of Camp Cornelia. Captain Jackson had departed for Atlanta by the time Corey and I arrived at about noon. The site selection for the camp seems excellent, and the Captain has left matters in the very capable hands and profane mouth of one Orvis Sweeney. He is a big bull of a man with an enormous gut and hams for arms. Due to his size he is in a perpetual sweat, and he constantly mops his brow and neck. Though the camp he has set up is neat and orderly, his personal appearance is a disaster, his pants riding low, shirt tail half out, hair uncombed, and shirt front stained with peach or tobacco juice.

While there is no evidence of extravagance, the camp has been made very comfortable, with several facilities I didn't expect. There is a common mess hall with a wood floor and sidewalls that can be propped open half way down from the ceiling to catch any available breeze. There was quite a variety of meat and fish for lunch today, so if this is the usual fare, no man should slack his work for a growling stomach.

We will pitch our tent on a pine platform raised three feet from the ground, being about eight feet square. Some of the men who have been in camp several weeks now, have used their spare time to construct cabins that are down right fine. Corey and I will pitch our tent on a pine platform and will be content.

I haven't had the opportunity to speak with Mr. Sweeney about the operation's progress. Just as soon as I can, I will follow this letter with an assessment of where we are on the time scale that you and I discussed.

Thank you again for all you have done for me and for all you continue to do.

John

*   *   *   *

The events leading to John's transfer to Camp Cornelia seemed a blur to Wealthy, now that the move was done. How had she lost her boy so fast? He was her boy, and she loved him as if she had given birth to him. She alternately blamed Ben and then herself for the separation from the one person she loved without condition. Wealthy loved her brother, but there was much that she would change in him, much that she despised. Her boy was perfect in every way.

It all came down to money with Ben Taylor, she decided. John was just behaving like any normal boy who was beginning to notice girls. What was so terrible about meeting the little Pace girl in the evenings? But Clarence Pace had his self-righteous image to protect, didn't he? And Ben Taylor, her flesh and blood, had to bow down to Clarence because of his obligations at the bank.

But it's cost me my boy, and that's too high a price to pay. Everything is just as if he had never been here. But, I've known him now, and I can't stand to go back the way it was before I knew the joy of having a son.

It was my fault. I didn't keep a close enough watch on him. I saw how the girls were interested in him, yet I did nothing to monitor the situation. I should have talked with him about it. What would any mother have done? She would have given her son guidance, of course. Would have arranged for him to see the young ladies under the proper circumstances. I did nothing. I failed my boy, and now they've taken him from me.

And so Wealthy's thoughts went day after day for weeks, back and forth between her brother and herself, laying the blame at the feet of first one, then the other. Day by day she became a little more distracted, a little more isolated from her brother and from her small circle of friends. There was no reason for them to notice any particular change in her personality. They just didn't see Wealthy quite as often. It was a minor thing.

Then John's first letter arrived from Camp Cornelia, and she was so elated to hear from her boy that she seemed quite normal. She was quick to write him.

June 1, 1871

My Dearest Boy,

How your letter pleases me. I would never presume to replace your natural parents, but now that I'm all that's left to you in this world, I do flatter myself with the hope that you would consider me as your mother. I think of you as my son, and I prefer no one, not even Ben, before you.

You ask in your letter what you must do to regain my trust and esteem. Let me assure you that you've lost neither. You, my son, are the most honorable young man I have ever known. You have overcome the worst that life has to offer in the loss of your first family and your childhood. You have persevered and worked hard, and I find it grotesquely unfair that you have been expelled from Magnolia and from the presence of one who loves you as I. I shall never forgive Clarence Pace or my brother for even one minute's separation from you. I constantly worry about you, whether you're properly fed and clothed and rested. I know that you lack a mother's guiding love and sober conversation, so how can I rest?

I have the means of revenge on Ben Taylor, though, and I have the will to exercise my revenge. You see, my boy, Mr. Ben Taylor has a great love for money. That's why you were sent away from me. He had to bow down to Mr. Clarence Pace, or Mr. Pace would take his business from him. As a result, the one person I wanted close to me to give me solace in my old age, as only a loving son can comfort a mother, was taken from me without remorse, without consideration for my feelings in the matter.

So be it. It is now without consultation or concern that I act against Benjamin Taylor. One half of everything he owns belongs to me. Or should I say, to you. I have taken the necessary steps to bequeath all my worldly goods to Mr. John Franklin Warren upon my leave-taking.

I know my brother. He shall take every means possible to deprive you of what is rightfully yours. I give you this letter to keep until the day of my death to prove my intentions in regards to my inheritance and to explain my motives.

As my brother is not above lies to preserve his great fortune, I have made Sheriff Amos Johns my executor. Amos is trustworthy, and I know of his great personal regard for you. I have made all of these arrangements without my brother's knowledge. Please do not refer directly to these actions in subsequent letters to me, as I don't trust Ben for my privacy.

I cherish the time we had together, and I would not have you think of me as a bitter, spiteful old woman. Please remember me as I was when I was bringing you up from adolescence to adulthood. You brought out the best in me.

I love you,
Mother

XVII

John sat up in his bedroll at the clanging of the iron triangle near the mess hall. He was disoriented in the darkness of his tent and in his half wakefulness. Where was he? Who was that snorting and groaning across the tent? O yes, Corey, the swamp.

"Come and get it 'fore we pitch it to the dogs!" a man yelled outside the tent.

"You awake, Corey?"

"A body would have to be dead to sleep through that," Corey replied.

The two men dressed in the dark and then joined the twenty or thirty others trudging toward the lanterns of the dining hall. As they neared it, Corey's pace fell behind that of John.

"Hurry up, Corey, or we'll be at the tail end of the line."

"I ain't so sure I'm going to be welcome in there," Corey whispered.

"I'm welcoming you. Now come on."

As they drew nearer to the lanterns, Corey saw the other black men enter without hesitation, so he went on in.

They stood in a line that stretched ahead of them to the middle of the hall. Several men served the others from a table that seemed ready to bend from its load of food. Two others were kept busy shuttling more food from the cooking area to this table, and they heaped it with eggs and bacon and ham and cathead biscuits with a variety of jams and jellies and cane syrup and thick bricks of butter. Gallons of sputtering hot grits and hot coffee tempted them closer to the line.

The servers worked with the efficiency of an assembly line, so John and Corey were quickly served and seated at the long plank table that stretched almost the length of the hall. All the men who gathered there ate just like they worked. That is, they took it seriously and with a great deal of effort.

"Mind if I join you?" A tall, slender man stood in front of them with his plate and coffee. "Name's Ed Giles."

"Have a seat, Ed. I'm John Warren and this is Corey Stokes."

"Oh yeah, you're Ben Taylor's men. John, you're a fellow supervisor, aren't you?"

"That's right."

"Well, we'd better pray we're on the bread-winning side of this venture and not the theoretical side."

"What do you mean?" John asked.

Ed looked around casually to see who might overhear him. "Our investors have put a heap of money into the start-up, so they're determined that it's going to be a pay-as-you-go project from here on out. The breadwinners are going to be cutting timber over on the swamp side. That's simple. They tell you how many board feet they need a day. You convert that to stumpage, and then you get your ass to work."

"And the theoretical side?" John asked.

"The Suwannee Canal Company intends to poke a ditch sixty feet wide and thirty feet deep through the Trail Ridge, a distance of about six miles." Ed paused for a reaction.

"So?" John asked.

"The Trail Ridge is sand. They don't have the foggiest notion of how to do it."

"Our boss man says the engineers got that worked out," Corey said.

Ed looked around again. "Yeah, they've got the investors believing they know how. Hell, they're being honest. They think they can do it, but I've done excavation work before. It's dicey enough with soil that has some consistency to it. But sand—"

A booming voice from the far end of the hall startled them. "Foremen meet in my office in five minutes. Don't be late." By the time they reacted, all that was left to see was Orvis Sweeney's backside going toward the middle of the camp.

"Fellow don't waste any words," Corey said.

"Sounds like we'd better move it, John. I don't want that big son-of-a-gun on my case this early in the game."

They crossed the compound together to the whitewashed structure set on wooden blocks in the dead center of Camp Cornelia. The other two foremen were right behind them and after introductions they studied the maps of the eastern side of the Okefenokee Swamp.

Sweeney jabbed his pudgy finger at one. "Gentlemen, this here's what they call the Trail Ridge. It's a wall of sand about forty miles long. That's all that's holding this water on the timber over here in the Okefenok, and here's where we're going through it.

"That will be Mr. Cason and Mr. Thrift's job. Warren and Giles will be in charge of the timbering and dredging operation on the swamp side." John glanced at Giles who rolled his eyes slightly and smiled. "As Captain Jackson's man, I'll handle the procurement and coordinate the whole damned show from the camp here. Anything gets in your way then I'm to help you."

"What's the first step?" Ed Giles asked.

"The five of us are going to take a look at both work sites and discuss the particulars today. We should be able to ride the length of the canal site on the trail ridge in pretty good time, but the look into the swamp will be slower going. Tomorrow we'll start cutting timber both ways. My people will keep hiring today."

Orvis looked up at the others and hesitated a moment. "Any questions so far?" When no one answered, he said, "Okay then, let's get saddled up."

*   *   *   *

October 2, 1871

Dearest Jennifer,

A glorious, blue sky covered us on this side of the swamp today. After four months here, we have cut and milled about a half million board feet of cypress and pine from both operations. We have dredged out about a quarter of a mile of canal as of today, and the crews are working now to set up the skidders. This is a device that will enable us to drag heavy logs into the canal from the surrounding areas where we cut the trees.

I am dead tired tonight. I started to go right to bed, but you linger on my mind, and sleep is impossible. How I long for you, to share the passing of another day, to hold each other close. Another day without you seems unbearable, but I must confess that the work we do excites me. It is a grand challenge, and one that only comes once in a lifetime to a man.

The Okefenokee is a place of great beauty, so that anyone who is alive to the majesty can't help but have reservations about the work we are doing. At times and at certain places, the beauty is raw and terrible, but I love it nonetheless.

Today I saw a deer, slowed by some wound or disease, caught by several alligators. The sense of beauty and fitness that I witnessed in the death struggle was strange, but I know what I felt. It was strange and terrible, yet beautiful. As it should be. The strong survive and even prosper. The weak fall. Today we are the strong. Tomorrow...

Jennifer Pace dropped her hand to her lap, still clutching the letter from John. She gazed out of her bedroom window. *How could he say such a thing about the slaughter of a defenseless deer? Where was the beauty in that? Maybe he had a fever from being in that desolate place. Everyone knows how unhealthy the swamp is. Or maybe she just didn't know him as well as she thought.*

He had been gone for more than four months now, and though he wrote to her often, he had made no attempt to come back to see her. *That would be so romantic, she thought, that a man would go thirty or forty miles to see her for only an hour or two and then would have to travel back the same distance to return to work on time. But John hadn't done that, had he?*

She thought back to the night that Ned came to her home months ago and cut the palm of his hand with the riding crop. A scar was there in his hand and would be there the rest of his life.

Jennifer stood and turned to the mirror across the room. She smiled at the image of near perfection there. "Ned would do it," she said aloud. "He would travel that far just to see me for an hour."

"Jennifer," her mother called from downstairs, "Ned is here for you. Are you ready, dear?"

"Coming mother."

Jennifer walked to the chiffarobe, re-reading John's description of the death of the deer. *Who even knew when or if John Warren was coming back to Magnolia? He's probably seeing women over there somewhere, and God knows what else he's involved in. Everybody knows he's mixed up with those nigras in the moonshine trade. He might just be out-and-out crazy.*

She pulled a hatbox down from the shelf, opened it, and added this letter to the rest. Ned is right here, she thought, and he has certainly won daddy, mother, and Roger over to his side. She remembered what he had said once about proposing marriage. He would only ask once. She believed that, now that she had come to know him better, and she believed that this would be the night that he would ask her to marry him—the only night. She placed the hatbox carefully back on its shelf, closed and locked the chiffarobe, and turned to go.

Wouldn't it be romantic? Engaged to a handsome, young banker and receiving clandestine love letters from a madman in the swamp?

     ❧   ❧   ❧   ❧

For the next three months, on into the winter of 1871, the work of dredging the canal into the Okefenokee and cutting the great stands of virgin cypress and pine struggled on. The exciting initial push into the swamp, with timber within easy reach of the equipment, was replaced by months of frustrating failure.

First, the deaths of two men buried in a cave-in on the sand ridge demoralized the men on both operations. Then a man on the swamp side was bitten by a cottonmouth snake and died an agonizing death in full view of John's crew.

There was constant trouble with the machinery on both operations that brought one delay after another. Men were laid off and hired back so frequently that it was impossible for John and the other supervisors to keep trained, competent crews together. More and more the operation attracted the men who no one else in the area would hire. They were plagued by a full week of rain that shut down the Trail Ridge operation and which made the swamp work even more demoralizing.

The first week of 1872 brought Captain Jackson, the organizer and chief investor, from Atlanta to the Okefenokee for an inspection tour. He spent two days with Sweeney and Cason on the trail ridge, and on the third day John took him to the timbering operation in the swamp.

"You ever seen a man top out a pine tree, Captain?" John asked. He stopped poling and let the flat bottom boat drift in the sluggish current of the Suwannee River running through the heart of the swamp.

"Can't say that I have."

"Look over to your right. That looks like our best topper, Ray Newbern, about half way up that tallest pine. He goes up and cuts the top out of it so he can attach a line that goes back to the dredge. Then when we cut in that direction we can attach a rope to the main line by a pulley and use the dredge engine to haul the logs to the canal."

They saw a man clinging to a slender pine, a rope trailing from his side in a slight arc to the floor of the swamp. He threw his harness that encircled the tree up to the height of his shoulders and leaned back to tighten it. He pulled the spike strapped to his left boot loose from the bole, moved as far up as he could, dug it in again, and repeated the motion with his right foot.

"Rather a tedious process, isn't it?" The captain said. "Why is it that we pay those fellows top dollar?"

John looked down at the Captain and suppressed the urge to hit the back of that slick, pomaded head with the pole used to propel the boat. He might be the money behind this venture, but he certainly couldn't be the intellect. Captain, indeed. Though Jackson was trim, he was soft and pink, and John doubted that his title was earned. More than likely it was bought from a needy legislature during the war. Everything about him rubbed John wrong—from his expensive English wool suit to his glossy boots to his perfectly trimmed mustache and nails and his know-it-all attitude.

"By the time Ray gets to the top, he'll be eighty feet up, hanging by a leather strap with those spikes on his boots dug in. He'll take a saw and reach up over his head and cut off the top of the tree. Then—"

"Heights have never bothered me," Jackson said. "Perhaps I'll try my hand at topping a tree a little later."

John bit his lip to keep from laughing. He'd like nothing better than to see the Captain's manicured fingers covered with pine resin and sawdust raining down into his eyes eighty feet up a pine.

"It's not the height that bothers most men, Captain. It's the wild ride when the cutting's done that's the problem."

"How's that?"

"When Ray starts sawing, his motion will set that tree to swaying. It'll get worse and worse until finally the top will snap, and then he'll be riding a bucking horse."

"What does he do then?"

"He hangs on. What else can he do? Prays a good bit, I suppose."

John resumed poling the boat along the black water trail through the cypress and brush. The Captain continued watching Ray Newbern ascend the pine.

"You couldn't pay me enough to do that job," John said. "I've seen a tree snap off underneath a topper before. Had nightmares about that one for weeks. Sometimes when the top snaps, it splits the trunk lengthwise. Makes a mess of a man's chest."

They rode on in silence for a while, watching. Newbern reached a point ten feet below the tip of the tree where he stopped and rested.

"How much longer until we reach the dredge?" Jackson asked.

"About another ten minutes."

"Do you think they'll have it going today?"

"I expect they will, but that's what I thought three days ago," John said. "We really need an inventory of spare parts, sir. All this travel time in and out of the swamp is killing us."

"The money's in the trees, Warren, not hanging from them like fruit. We have to harvest them first to afford a luxury like spare parts."

"Then prevail on Mr. Cason to let me use parts from his dredge. They haven't turned a shovel of sand in the last week."

Jackson whipped around to face John. "There won't be anything coming your way from Cason. I set those bastards straight yesterday about letting a little rain stop their progress, and they're back to it today."

"This is the first sunshine we've seen in a week, sir. I think that Cason was wise not to risk the men's lives. Under good conditions we've already had four men killed in cave-ins."

"Well, four darkies," Jackson said, "if you're counting them."

"I know their families did."

Captain Jackson shook his head and sneered. "I'm going to speak candidly with you, Mr. Warren. You're too soft to be an effective leader. You'd do well to mold yourself after my man Sweeney. I'm sure you've seen him handle people."

"I've seen him bully men and beat them and curse them."

"There you go. The men know that Sweeney's word is law, and they know the consequences for breaking the law. Your men know that there are no consequences for doing as they damned well please."

John felt his face getting hot. "My men work hard for me. I'd put them up against any crew out here."

"The timber you're cutting is the lifeblood of this organization, and we're about bled dry. Sweeney would have had this equipment running two days ago or there'd have been hell to pay."

"You don't know what you're talking about, Captain. Without that gear assembly—"

"I'm the principal investor in The Suwannee Canal Company, boy. Don't you presume to lecture me, or I'll have a talk with Ben Taylor, and you'll be on your way."

John clenched his teeth and looked off into the undergrowth.

"Now we need cash and that means logs rolling out of this swamp—weather, spare parts, and sick men be damned. I want results. You give me those results, or you get out."

From high above them a rebel yell rang out across the vast wetlands. John and the Captain looked up to see Ray Newbern clinging to his pine and describing a wide arc across the sky.

"He thinks he's on a wild ride," John said to himself.

❧   ❧   ❧   ❧

"Howdy there, old timer."

The old man sat implacably and observed the young man standing in the sandy road in front of his cabin. He made no effort to respond.

"My name's Gray Hampton, and I'm looking for a fellow by the name of John Warren. They told me at Camp Cornelia that he might be out this way somewhere."

The old man leaned to his right and spit off the side of the dilapidated porch, then settled back.

"Go right ahead," he drawled.

"What?"

"Go ahead on and look. I ain't stopping you."

Gray looked down the road. "Do you know where I might find him?"

"Yep."

Gray hesitated, expecting the man to tell him where he might find his friend. "Where is that?" he finally asked.

"You're gonna find him right where he is."

Gray decided to play the man's game. "But what if he ain't there when I get there?"

"Then he'll be someplace else. They always are."

"No," Gray said, "I already looked someplace else. He ain't there."

"Then he'll be where he is."

"Where's that?"

"On down that road about a mile and a half, then south 'til you hear 'em."

"Hear who?"

"Him and that old nigger he runs with."

"Good enough. I appreciate your help."

The last red rays of the sun were filtering through the pines when Gray saw a path that led through the underbrush off to the south. He heard the voices when he was no more than two hundred yards into the palmettos. They were faint at first, and he caught only pieces of what was said. As he neared the light of a campfire, the conversation became whole, and Gray recognized the voices of John and Corey.

"I may just stay in here forever," John said. "Nothing dangerous here—not like where there's women."

"Right," Corey said. "Just some gators and a snake or two. Nothing in here but what won't bare its teeth at you when it don't like you or want you 'round. Womens got them sharp teeth they won't show you 'til you most dead."

Now Gray was at the outermost ring of light where he paused to think of how to enter the circle without being shot. Corey sat on a stump at the fire while John paced around the clearing.

"Yep," John said, "women got long, sharp teeth, and this 'shine of ours will bite you, too."

Corey laughed hysterically at the weak pun, laughed until it became infectious and John had joined in. Gray grinned to himself and took advantage of their vulnerability to step into view.

"Who's that?" Corey stiffened immediately, but John laughed harder until he caught his breath.

"Well, if it ain't my old buddy, Gray!" John lurched toward his friend, throwing his arm over Gray's shoulder. "Come on over here, old Gray buddy, and I'll dip you a snort."

Corey remained seated. "How do, Mr. Gray."

"Hello, Corey. Looks like the moonshine business is prosperous."

"You damned straight," John said. "Best product in three counties and a sales bunch that won't quit. Only worry we got is Corey's boy Zachary outselling us at home. Ain't that right, Corey?"

Corey chuckled. "You know we worried about that."

"By God, you're just in time, Gray. We're celebrating." John led Gray to the still, picked up a tin cup and poured his friend a drink from an earthenware jug. "We're celebrating the engagement and the forthcoming marriage of Mr. Ned Worthington and Miss Jennifer Pace. Here's to the happy couple!"

"Seems as if you two have quite a head start on me," Gray said.

"Our heads haven't started yet, but I know I'm looking for mine to any time now," John said. He wavered a moment, then turned up his cup and drained it. "What brings you to Coreyville, Gray? Did I tell you we've decided to name this place after my old buddy, Corey, over there? We're going to build a city. Two post offices, it's going to be so damned big."

Corey and Gray smiled at each other.

"And stores! Good God, you ain't seen the like of stores we're going to have. And this still! This still is going to stay right here in the middle of town. Going to be so much 'shine the horses are going to drink it. What do you think about that?"

"I came to see about you, John."

"Ah hell, there was no reason for you to walk all that way to see about me. You can see how happy I am. God's in charge just like you said."

"Yeah boy," Gray said, "You look in real good shape. I can't wait to see you in the morning."

Corey chuckled. "The whole camp better walk soft then."

John staggered off to the still.

"How did he find out before I got here, Corey?"

"My boy Zachary come over day before yesterday."

"John been drunk since then?"

"No, sir. He's stayed right with the work over in the swamp. He brooded right hard to start with. Picked a fight or two, but he just got 'round to the drinking tonight."

"Women are a mystery, aren't they, Stokes?"

"Yes sir, they surely are that."

"Well, I guess we've got this one to ride out. Unless you think we just ought to knock him out."

They looked over at John who was struggling to drain some more of the mash into a jar.

"Let's just let him rip and roar 'til he gets it all out," Corey said.

"Gray!" John bellowed. "Get over here and help me with this damned thing. It won't hold still, and I broke my jar."

The next morning Gray tended the bacon over a fire while John sat a few feet away, his head cupped in his hands.

"Where's Stokes with that water? I can't get enough to drink."

"You better thank God you have a friend like Corey. If it were just you and me out here, you could hike over there for more water yourself."

John's rebuttal was interrupted by a shout from the road. "John Warren!"

"Oh God," John moaned.

"Who is it?" Gray asked.

"Orvis Sweeney."

"Warren! I know you're close by here," he yelled.

"Why doesn't that old man back up the road just sell tickets. He tells everybody where we are."

"John Warren!"

"What?" John yelled, jumping to his feet. "What the hell do you want?"

They could hear the crashing of the palmettos as Sweeney made his way, bear-like, to them. Minutes later he entered the clearing just ahead of Corey, who entered from the opposite side.

"You need to come see something right away."

"Have some coffee and quit that yelling," John said. "We agreed to take this Sunday off, remember?"

"This ain't about work, and I want to be there when the photographer gets there. Now come on."

"What you got?" Corey asked.

"We got us an Indian," Orvis said. "Or what's left of one. I expect this one ain't seen daylight for several hundred years."

When they arrived at the site, two dozen men stood or sat on the high embankments that flanked the gravesite.

"Well, I'll be," John said. "That hill I told them to dig through turned out to be an Indian burial mound. It looked too big to me."

They dismounted, and John and Gray walked between the men. There on an altar of sand lay a skeleton with his face turned to the sky, his arms rigid at his sides.

"Will you look at that," Gray said reverently. "Either someone was careless digging him up or this old boy took a beating before he died."

Orvis stood at the head. "The boys say they were careful once they figured out what they had. They even poured water on it to wash the sand off rather than digging too close to the bones."

One of the men from the embankment to John's right spoke up. "Look at what's under him, boss. Looks like some kind of hide they laid him out on. Ain't no fur left, but it looks like parchment or leather."

"Whatever it was," Gray said, "it kept the bones from washing away."

"He looks to be your size, Captain," a man said to John.

John looked up. "Right at six foot four, I'd say. You've dug all the way through the mound. Did you come across any other bones or pottery? Anything else?"

"There's a little bit of stuff over here, but a bunch of it crumbled on us. No other bones at all."

The photographer arrived an hour later and did a booming business taking the men's pictures with their find.

"Question is," Gray said, "What do we do with him?"

"What do we do?" Orvis said. "Not that it's any of your business, but this is the shortest cut through this island. We've got a lot of heavy equipment to move, so we're going through here. The Indian has to go."

"We try to move them bones," Corey said, "and they gonna be in pieces. That old skin under him ain't gonna hold up. Let's leave him be, and go a little out of our way."

"Hell, he ain't gonna know it," Sweeney yelled. "What's the difference if he's laid out or bagged up? When I croak, just throw me in a hole and cover my ass up. Move me around every week if you can stand the smell."

"I'd see what the rest of these men think," Gray said. "They look pretty spooked about all this. If you don't handle this just right, you may lose some of your crew over it."

John looked over his shoulder at the men gathered around the burial site and saw that Gray had a point.

"I'm going to talk to these fellows one at a time over supper," he said to Orvis. "Then I'll sleep on it and make a decision by first light."

"It's your show. Just get everything over to the other side of this island by Monday night."

John Warren dreamed. He was surrounded by water. It lapped against his legs, threatening to topple him. He struggled a moment for balance, found it, and began to walk. The way was dark, but in the distance was a faint light, so he headed toward it. Complete silence. As he neared the light, his feet fell on dry ground. It was the island where they were moving the equipment.

Crossing the island, he came to the altar of sand on which lay the remains of Cau Au Ra. A low campfire burned by the altar, and beside the fire sat an Indian woman of perhaps forty years. Her black braids were streaked with silver. Her countenance was lined with years of disappointment and hard work and loneliness. As John approached, she looked up from the fire.

"I waited a time for you, but you did not come."

"Why were you waiting for me?" John asked.

"Cau Au Ra charged me at his death with the duty to tell of the people and the journey, that the knowledge of us would not pass from the earth."

"You lived here in the swamp?"

"We called her the Au Fin Au Cau, and we did not live in her. The bond was closer. We were and are of her." She gestured to the skeleton. "But only for a time."

"What happened to him and to your people?"

"In various ways, the Au Fin Au Cau claimed what was hers, and the sky claimed what was his. Ursus came for Cau Au Ra. At that time the rest of the people were very aged, and they slipped away gracefully."

"And you?" John asked.

She stared into the fire a long time, and John saw tears welling in her eyes.

"I was Au Eve, Mother of the Earth so named, but now I am Tess, so named the Restless One, because I am the last of the people, and I could not ascend to the sky."

"Why are you crying?"

She looked into John's eyes. "I have told you why, but it had no significance for you."

"I don't understand," John said.

"You are too earthly to understand. To understand, you must believe in the Spirit."

"How do you know what I believe or don't believe?" John asked.

"You are discernable," she said. "I don't understand why Cau Au Ra brought you. I choose your friend who walks. He is Spirit-filled. But Cau Au Ra chooses you. It is enough. Will you hear the journey?"

"Yes."

She stood on the other side of the fire from John and began a rhythmic swaying. In a language that John had never heard, but understood, Au Eve said, "With one single step, the Fathers of old left that which they knew, the land of their birth, land we shall never know, to travel the earth..."

Once more the Au Fin Au Cau witnessed the telling of the ancient journey—story that was older than the trees themselves. When the night was waning and Au Eve had completed the journey, she punctuated the telling of it with a silence. Just this once, there was more.

"They are the stars now. They are with the Son."

"The sun," John said. "I don't understand."

"You are too earthly to understand. You must become as wise as the day you were born."

"What did you say?"

"Come to eternity as a little child, John. It is the only way."

"Why are you telling me this? I thought it was your charge to tell me about the journey and the people."

"I am unburdened, and the Spirit moves me, John Warren. Listen. I have told you an earthly story for a spiritual purpose. I used earthly names to help you know, but knowing is not understanding. Only when you no longer know will you understand. And only when you go beyond understanding will you be. You will then be as wise as the day you were born."

John started to speak, but Au Eve held up her hand for silence.

"Know what I tell you, John Warren, and then spend your life forgetting it to make it part of you. Take it into your Spirit, and then you will have it eternally. We must know and then we must be. Most men never are."

The next day John's crew returned with him to the burial site. To the relief of the superstitious among them, John had them cover the site completely. The following day, their road curved around the site, like a river diverted from its course.

XVIII

January 10, 1872

Jennifer,

I suppose you didn't have the decency to write me concerning your engagement to Ned Worthington. Your lack of judgment in this matter is exceeded only by your lack of taste. My God, girl, Ned Worthington! Your father must be ecstatic at the prospect of having such a rogue in the family. But then, I understand that Clarence has washed the boy and dressed him up like a banker. You will all get what you so richly deserve in time.

I must write Clarence and Ben to thank them for expelling me from Magnolia, for in doing so, they have revealed your true lack of character. If I ever see you again, you shall acknowledge me only to the extreme jeopardy of your dignity.

John Warren

Ned dropped the letter to the desktop with the others piled there and leaned back in his swivel chair. He had been reading aloud for twenty minutes, each letter slowly, deliberately, so he took another long drink of bourbon to soothe his throat. He looked silently at his wife.

Jennifer sat facing him, motionless in the straight-backed chair, her eyes downcast, a thin bead of perspiration lining her upper lip. The ornate French clock on the mantel ticked the long seconds off, the only sound in the room.

He finished the drink and leaned forward in the half-light to fill the tumbler again. As he moved to the bottle, Jennifer flinched, her eyes widening.

"You should be wary of me," he hissed. "These letters are an abomination."

She dared not speak. He took a drink.

"I raised myself from the dregs of society to become respectable—a war hero and a banker. Of all the women I could have had, I chose you to be my wife. I spelled out to you the terms of loyalty that I expect from those I choose to associate with. I gave you a proper courtship. I built you the finest home in the county, and now after all I've done, I find that you're corresponding with another man."

She sobbed, tightening her throat to cut off any sound. Silence was important. She shut her eyes. He drank.

"A dozen letters from him here, and just as many in his possession from you, no doubt. What do they say? Did you profess your love to him? Did you come home from an evening with me and write a love letter to my worst enemy?"

She gasped for air and in doing so, sobbed aloud.

"Speak to me, you bitch," Ned screamed, and he backhanded Jennifer, sending her and the chair tumbling backward. He followed.

$$\quad\quad s \quad\quad\quad s \quad\quad\quad s \quad\quad\quad s$$

Corey Stokes understood John Warren better than anyone around him, but John's reaction to Ned and Jennifer's marriage caught Corey off guard. John isolated himself from the rest of Camp Cornelia, except for the necessities of work. He was easily provoked, and when someone made the mistake of crossing him, they paid a high physical price. Where once he had led the crew by the force of his personality and by the respect his sense of fairness had earned, now he led by fear and intimidation.

John was easier around Corey than he was around anyone else, but the relationship with his old friend had changed. Some of the enthusiasm had gone out of John. Some of the old sense of humor was gone. His every waking moment seemed devoted to business. Everything he talked about was money, sales, growth, or strategy.

Corey avoided him, but John was so self-absorbed that he didn't notice. John thought it was coincidental that their paths didn't cross more often, when he thought of Corey at all.

He rode to Waycross once every two weeks to collect from his salesmen along the way and to meet with Ray Black to do his banking. The liquor business did so well that John invested a portion of his savings in local business opportunities and in real estate Ray recommended to him. Land was cheap, the taxes were low, and John made it his policy never to sell dirt.

The production at Camp Cornelia continued to decline to the point that John felt obligated to admit that he and the other supervisors weren't going to be able to turn it around on their own. He knew it was time to advise Ben of his concerns.

August 7, 1873

Dear Ben,

Corey and I are doing fine, and I hope that all is well in Magnolia. We have been working hard, but I am sorry to say that our best efforts are proving to be short of the mark. We have little to show for our labors or your money in reclaimed swamp or in timber cut and hauled. Please tell me that you have not sunk any more funds into this noble, yet doomed quest. Cut your losses while you may.

If there were to be an engineering breakthrough on this project, it would already have come. Many bright minds have been employed against the problem of breaching the Trail Ridge and against securing the breach long enough for drainage into the St. Marys river basin. I see no engineering improvements in the last quarter.

The idea to log tracts by dredge should be abandoned. The dredge is not efficient enough to provide significant cash flow, particularly when its engines are called upon to do two jobs at once.

Morale is down drastically with the mounting failure to produce headway and with this week's deaths. Several men have left, and we've been unable to find suitable replacements. There are frequent fights as the men divide along the lines of for or against continuing the project.

Let me assure you that I am not discussing my observations with anyone here. I am anxious to receive your reply.

Faithfully,
John Warren

P.S. Will you be so kind as to see that Miss Wealthy receives the enclosed pressed sample of fern? She asked if I might search out this particular specimen on this side of the swamp.

If Wealthy ever received the fern, there was no indication from Ben. First, John received a telegram from him.

"Letter on way. Keep own counsel. Work harder."

A week later John had his answer. When he opened Ben's letter, the fern fell out.

August 14, 1873

John,

You must keep the contents of this letter strictly confidential. I would prefer that you destroy it after you've finished reading it. It shakes my confidence in you to hear how pessimistic you have become in regards to the success of our project, particularly since I hear from others that we may be very close to an engineering breakthrough on the canal.

Captain Jackson tells me that his supervisor reports high morale among his men, citing the steady pay and good living conditions as reasons for their contentment. I have no reason to doubt the word of either Captain Jackson or yourself, so I make two observations.

First, the Captain and I are closer than you to the engineers, so what appears to you to be lassitude may in fact be a maddeningly deliberate march forward. Be patient.

Second, Your own negative feelings toward the project may be affecting the morale of your crew. This may be why Captain Jackson and I have two entirely different perspectives on the same animal.

I am in no position to accept weakness from any man who works for me at this time. If you can't get the job done, I implore you to be honest with me. You are yet a young man, and I wouldn't hold it against you if I had overmatched you with the work. I would much rather employ you here than have you bring me down there. Time has passed, Jennifer has married, and I don't think Clarence Pace would object to your return to Magnolia.

The use of the dredge for powering the lines to haul out timber is not much on my mind. I realize that it is inefficient, as do the other investors, but I enjoy what little cash it generates, and none of us will forego it.

John, I do not mean to undercut your confidence, but self-interest compels me to be blunt in this respect. You must turn your crew around, and it must happen right away. I have planned a trip to your vicinity for the third week of the month. You have until then.

Sincerely,
Ben

John tossed the letter on his bed and looked solemnly at the remains of the dried fern on the floor of the tent.

"You fool," he muttered. "Your sister has ten times the business sense you have, and you're too proud to see it." He moved to the table next to his bed and got out a pencil and paper. He would figure some way out. He had to analyze the situation.

Over the next three weeks John's attitude improved considerably. Ben had given him a lot to think about in his letter, and John saw that he had let Jennifer's marriage to Ned sour him on the project. He regained the men's confidence, and they began to make some headway on the dredging of the next half-mile of the canal. Then Ben came.

Ben and John spent the first two days in meetings with the other investors and supervisors, trying to overcome the problems of the operation. The morning of the third day, they went off for John to show Ben the progress on the canal. John stood in the stern of the boat and poled them along.

"I've tried everything I know to do," Ben said. "I'm not telling the other investors yet, but there just ain't no way to come out of this one, John. I've been down before, but nothing like this. I've tried every old friend I can think of, every bank from here to Savannah and back. I even considered selling a part of the land to buy me time on the rest. Nothing's enough."

John poled on in silence for a few minutes while Ben stared into the surrounding brush.

"Have you given up completely?" John asked.

"I'm beat," Ben said in a whisper.

"Then I know of one route left."

Ben looked at John suspiciously. "I've been in this business for three-quarters of my life. I know everyone around here who's connected with the timber business. I know all the bankers, all the brokers, all the buyers—everyone. If there was a way out of this mess, I'd know it."

"Okay." John shrugged. "If you're too smart to listen, that's fine with me. It'd be risky anyway."

"That's a good laugh! Here I sit, a man who took the biggest gamble in the history of the southern timber industry, and you're telling me what's risky!"

"Look, Ben, I'm in a position now that I don't have to sit still for your bullheadedness. And you can just quit twitching that jaw and getting so red in the face. That doesn't cut any ice with me. Now do you want to hear me out or not?"

"Fire away."

John laid the pole down in the boat and sat down. He took a deep breath and exhaled it long and slow. "All right. As I understand it, you need two things—cash flow and the time to make that money work for you."

"That about sums it up," Ben said impatiently.

"Take a partner."

"Who do you suggest? Some carpetbagger who'll take everything I've done these last forty years and put me to work as a clerk in my own business? I've tried everyone I know."

"I was thinking more along the lines of myself," John said quietly.

"Do you know how much it would take to meet the back payroll? I've had to neglect the equipment in Magnolia to keep the swamp operation going. Do you have any idea how much money we're talking about?"

"I've worked up some figures on what the cost of getting back into fighting shape would be, but I want to compare them to what you think it'd take. Let me warn you about something. You aren't going to shock me. I have the financial capacity to make a deal with you."

"It's true about you and the moonshine business, isn't it? How else could you come up with that kind of money?"

John stood up and started poling the boat back toward camp. "Except to assure you that my sources of funding are legitimate, I won't discuss them with you. I'll buy your land and your business from the steps of the courthouse, or we'll work something out right now, but you'd better start talking business. You have some notes coming due on Monday, and that doesn't give us much time. What's it going to cost to keep you solvent for the next six months?" They reached the landing and John jumped ashore to tie the boat.

"Forty thousand," Ben muttered.

"There's a pencil and paper in my tent. Go over there and break it down for me. Don't leave out anything. I don't want any surprises."

When John and Ben entered the office, Sweeney pointed to an envelope next to the lamp on his desk. "Telegram for you, Warren," he said.

John picked it up and opened it.

"News travels faster than me. Regret to inform you, Miss W. has passed on. Return with Ben immediately. So sorry."

Gray

He read the telegram over and over, unable each time to believe what it told him. She couldn't be gone.

"What is it, John?" Ben asked.

He let it drop to the floor of the office, turned, and walked out into the cool of the evening, out into a delicate rain.

§   §   §   §

John stood at Wealthy's grave until only he, the Reverend Polk, and Ben remained. Though the morning was overcast, the early September air was still warm and laden with moisture. The week since his return to Magnolia was a long, numbing blur in his mind, filled with sleepless nights and endless days of meaningless talk with people who claimed to know how he felt.

As far as he knew these were the same people who had held him at arm's length since his arrival in Magnolia. These were the people who questioned his motives for being in their town, who gossiped about the deserter from Atlanta, who snickered at Wealthy's desire to have a son of her own. They were the people who consigned him to sleep in a barn, who begrudged him a job, and who ultimately ran him out of town for a youthful indiscretion.

They knew nothing about how he felt, and he received nothing from them. He sat on the porch and let them talk or stood in the kitchen and drank coffee with them, occasionally agreeing politely with whatever it was they were saying, not knowing what they said, but taking his cues from their faces, their tones of voice.

It was happening even now at the graveside.

"I think that's the way Wealthy would have wanted it. Don't you agree, John?" the reverend asked.

"Yes, sir." He wouldn't be held accountable for a damned thing he had agreed to this week, he had decided. He wasn't obligated to think their way. He wasn't obliged to this God they paid lip service to.

Ben extended his hand to Reverend Polk. "That was a good service, Jedediah. I appreciate everything that you've done for us this week."

"There's nothing I wouldn't have done for you or Wealthy, Ben."

John looked at the reverend. He could stomach him. It was his God he had no use for.

"John and I need to talk, so we'll head back to the house now. I'll see you later."

The reverend realized that he had overstayed his welcome. With an embarrassed nod, he shook John's hand and walked back toward the church.

Ben led the way to the house, walking slowly to let John catch up to him. John followed, but lingered a step behind.

"I miss Wealthy," Ben said, "but I'm sure glad this week's over with."

John said nothing, and they walked on in awkward silence. A slight breeze was kicking up, the barest promise of rain.

"Too much time spent around the house to suit me," Ben said. "I'm ready to get back to work."

They were in the front yard, and Ben walked to the front steps unaware that John continued across the yard toward the barn.

"Percy wants us to come by his office tomorrow to go over the will. Morning or afternoon suit you better?"

"We're not tending to any business tomorrow," John said over his shoulder. "You stay around town, and I'll let you know when I'm ready to get back to business."

Ben stepped off the porch toward John. "Who do you think you're ordering around? You get back here and talk to me."

John stopped and turned to face Ben. "You've got nowhere to turn," he said calmly. "I'm in charge now."

"We haven't struck a deal yet. My circumstances have changed with my sister's death, so there may not even be a deal."

"Your financial circumstances changed for the worse with Wealthy's death, not better. I already know what the will says. I'll either make a deal with you because of my love for her, or I'll buy your property out of bankruptcy court like some other people are hoping to do."

"You're bluffing," Ben yelled as John entered the barn. "She left her half to me. And she had some cash laid back. You'll see. I'll be able to turn it around without you."

There was no answer.

"You hear me, boy. I'll come back without your help. You're not in charge of anything yet."

Ben was still talking when John rode out of the barn. He glanced blankly at Ben as he rode by and promptly forgot him as he turned the horse toward the mill. His mind was on the conversations he had with Amos and Gray on his return to Magnolia. Along with Corey, they were the only people in the world that he trusted, and both of them were convinced that Wealthy's death was accidental. Or were they just trying to spare his feelings? Could any of them have missed signals from Wealthy that she was about to take her own life? John had read her letters repeatedly looking for some clue, but he wasn't sure. There was bitterness at their separation, but she acknowledged that. Wealthy was not a quitter. She knew that they would be reunited one day. She would have held on. He was satisfied that Dr. Williams had not prescribed the laudanum and that he was unaware that she was taking it. It was certainly not an unusual medication for women, he knew.

John met no one along the road, and the ride was pleasant. The breeze stiffened every once in a while, and he breathed in the pine scent and the smell of distant rain mingled with the sandy road. It cleared his head of the mindless babbling of the past week.

When John arrived at the sawmill it was deserted except for the hound that roused itself from the shade of the office building and ambled off into the surrounding woods. The turpentine boiler was cold, and the mill was covered in a fine layer of dust. The mules had been fed and watered, so someone was keeping an eye on things.

He rounded the mill yard. It had been a long time since he'd been here. He'd learned a lot at this place, and he remembered how good those years had been. With Miss Wealthy's love and guidance and with the friends he had made, it had been a healing time for him. Maybe it could do the same for him again.

John found himself back at the office. He tried the door. It was unlocked, and he went in, leaving the door open for the light. The place was a mess. Every part of the room was cluttered with clothing, eating utensils, unfinished food, tools, machine parts, and documents.

"This is where I intend to hang my hat for a while, so I might as well take it back from the roaches right now," he muttered. He stacked the documents on the desk and swept everything else onto the floor. Then he went around the room recovering every piece of paper that looked important.

He went back into the yard, hitched one of the mules to a wagon, and pulled it to the office door. In an hour, everything inside was outside, except for the settee, the desk and chair, the potbellied stove, two filing cabinets, a lantern, and a coffeepot. John put the pot on the stove, sat down at the desk, and picked up the first of three stacks of paper.

"This is as good a place as any to start," he said, and he began the process of reading, absorbing information, and sorting documents. By the time the light began to fade, he had sorted through most of the paper. Unfortunately, it was confirming his suspicion of just how low the company had sunk.

That night John slept on the settee—the first real rest he had all week. He awoke at six the next morning and spent the day wandering the area on foot, getting reacquainted with the land and thinking. Late that afternoon he fished Suwanoochee Creek and caught a half-dozen redbreast for supper. By dark he had a fire going outside the office and the fish filleted and in a pot of grease. The weather had faired up, and he spent the second night by the fire.

John looked at the stars and thought of Corey, his best friend still on the other side of the swamp. He saw the stars that he now thought of as Cau Au Ra and Au Eve. He thought of his family and their time together in Atlanta. What strange twists and turns his life was taking. It all seemed so disconnected. How could he ever make sense of it? Maybe Gray was right. Make the best of it a part of you and forget the rest. How did a man do that?

John dreamed, and in his dream he was an old man. He was at the mill with a great crowd of people, touring them around the site, explaining the operation, and reminiscing about his experiences there.

At first the people were vague shapes, but the longer he talked, the more distinct they became, and he realized that he was with the people he cared for in life. His mother and father were there, his brother and sisters, childhood friends and teachers, aunts and uncles. There was Amos, Corey and his family, Gray, Wealthy, and the Indian couple, and people that he didn't recognize but intuitively knew. And on the periphery, far at the back of the crowd, old and blind and weathered—Ben Taylor.

     ✿   ✿   ✿   ✿

Ben's jaws twitched as his blood pressure climbed. His face was a deep red and his breathing was audible in the lawyer's silent office.

"Damn it, Percy, she can't do that! You can't do that!" Ben sputtered.

"It's a perfectly legal will, Ben."

"I don't care about that," Ben yelled. "The old girl wasn't herself when she changed that will. She was suicidal, for God's sake. Doesn't that give me room for some kind of appeal here?"

"You don't want to make that argument, Ben. Miss Wealthy wasn't herself lately, but she didn't die intentionally. She got confused on the laudanum dosage. Your sister was a good Christian woman. I've talked with Amos. He says that Miss Wealthy told him you'd try to contest this will, and she gave Amos orders not to let you get away with it. Of course, Amos figured she was talking about many years from now—not within two years."

"And just how does the sheriff intend to stop me from getting what's already mine?"

"Amos doesn't want to oppose you, Ben. But he has to tell the truth on the witness stand in a hearing. He wants you to know that he'll have to testify that Miss Wealthy was no different mentally than he'd ever known her to be when she asked him to be her executor."

"This ain't right, Percy. You and Amos have turned against me, and I can't for the life of me understand why." He was quieter now, but angry and miserable.

"I know this isn't easy for you, Ben, but Amos and I haven't turned against you. Put yourself in our places. Your sister was a strong-willed woman, and she was our friend as much as you are. We couldn't turn her down or betray her trust in us."

"It's when events look the darkest that we can expect the greatest opportunities to present themselves," John said.

Ben turned on him. "That's easy for you to say, boy. It's for me that things look the darkest now. I just may have to hand over half of everything I own to you."

"Except the house, Ben. She wanted you to have the house," said Percy.

"I wasn't thinking of you, Ben," John said. "Your time is past. This is my time."

"That's a little blunt, young man," Percy said.

John looked at the lawyer calmly. "Someday, when I'm about Ben's age, some kid who isn't even alive right now is going to say the same thing to me—and he's going to be right. If he's smart, he'll seize the moment just as I'm about to do."

"I'm going to do everything I can to keep you from getting into my business." Ben said.

"You're kidding yourself. You'll delay me a little at best. Isn't that right, Mr. Hayes?"

Percy didn't speak, but Ben saw the answer in his eyes.

      *   *   *   *

That evening as John rode up to Gray's cabin for dinner, he saw an unfamiliar horse. Gray hadn't mentioned having anyone else out to eat tonight. It was probably unexpected company. When he rounded the cabin, he saw Gray standing at the cook fire. "Gray, whose horse is—"

Gray turned at the sound of his voice, and John saw her sitting on the other side of the fire—the most beautiful young woman he had ever seen. She was dark and mysterious, and her eyes flashed in the glow of the fire. She wore riding britches and a silk blouse that gleamed with the firelight. Her legs were long and turned to one side gracefully, her hands clasped around her knees.

"Kath, you remember John Warren," Gray said. "John, this is Kathleen McLendon."

She stood and walked around the fire, extending her hand. Her flame-red hair mesmerized him.

"Hello, John. It's been a long time."

John took her hand, his eyes never leaving her face. "The last I saw of you was daddy's girl behaving in church."

"What do you see now?" she asked boldly.

"A beautiful young woman with terrible taste in dinner companions."

They laughed together, and the mixture of honesty and good humor set the tone for the evening.

"I'll drink to that," Kathleen said. "I admire a man who isn't afraid to flatter me." She picked up a cup and held it out to Gray and John.

"Explain to me again, Gray, how it is that you can be a Holy Ghost, Bible-reading, born-again Christian and get away with tempting innocent young ladies and men with demon drink," John said. "I don't think the preachers go for that."

"They most certainly do not," Gray said. "But to me, taking a drink isn't a sin."

"You don't believe that drinking's a sin?" Kathleen asked.

"That's not what I said, and that's not what I meant," Gray replied. "I said that it's not a sin for me to take a drink. It may be a sin for both of you. It is for most people."

"A sin is a sin," John said. "It doesn't matter who does it. What exempts you?"

"You're living in the Old Testament days. That's when people had to obey all the rules. All the sins were neatly defined and everybody knew where they stood. Too bad for them that they all stood on the wrong side of the law."

"You're getting way ahead of me," said Kathleen.

"What is sin?" Gray asked.

"Drinking is," John said as he took another drink of moonshine.

"Jesus teaches that it's not what goes into our mouths that defiles us, but what comes out. The evil thoughts and words and deeds come out of our hearts through our mouths, our hands, our feet—all over the place."

"All right, then it's okay to drink," Kathleen said.

"No, it's not," said Gray.

"But you just said that it's not what goes in our mouths that defiles us, so liquor must be okay."

"When most people put the liquor in, the foulness is going to come out, so most people shouldn't drink."

"What separates the people who can from those who can't?" John asked. "No wait, let me rephrase that. Why isn't it okay for Kathleen and me, and it's okay for you?"

"It's okay for me because my heart is pure."

John fell off the log he was sitting on, laughing uproariously. Kathleen swatted at his legs. "Quit that," she laughed. Gray sat and grinned at them.

"I'll put the steaks on and we'll work this out over dinner," Gray said. "I'm starving."

They talked far into the night as if they had been friends forever.

The next two days were long and stressful for John. He made the necessary payments on notes at the bank and to creditors to keep the operation from foreclosure. He and Ben rounded up all the employees who had not taken other work, and John paid all of their back wages. By the end of the week, they had done enough maintenance on equipment to get back into production. On Friday of that week, John was surprised to see Gray come walking up to the sawmill.

"I thought you were long gone to the Okefenok," John said.

"I'm headed that way, but I have an errand to run before I take off. It's Jennifer. She wants to talk to you."

"Fat chance of that," John said. "I hope to make it the rest of my days without talking to her again."

"You want some advice?" Gray asked.

"No."

"You ought to hear her out."

"Are you familiar with the word, no?" John asked. "It means—"

"You ever made a mistake, John, and then wanted the worst in the world to make it right? I think that's all she wants."

John looked off into the pines. "How is it that you can change my mind about something so quick?"

"I'm in a hurry to get off on my trip. Eight o'clock tomorrow night here at the mill all right with you?"

"Send her on."

He dreaded the meeting all day on Saturday, anticipating the things she might say and how he might respond. He didn't want to get into this. Why couldn't she just leave things the way they were and get on with her life and let him get on with his? They had made their choices a long time ago.

She was there promptly at eight, and John was shocked by her appearance. She retained the surface beauty of her youth, but the shine was gone from her eyes, as was the perpetual smile from her face. There was an ugly hardness and fear about her that marred her looks.

"I want to thank you for seeing me, John. I know you didn't have to do this."

"Think nothing of it, Mrs. Worthington. Let's keep this to the point. What is it that you want to say?" He saw the wounded look in her eyes, and it pleased him.

"I'll be brief, but will you please call me by my first name just this once. It's a small kindness that I need from you. It isn't much."

"Not much more than I expected of you at one time, but all right, Jennifer. I'll do that for you."

She sat on the settee, looking at the floor, her eyes averted from his as she spoke. "Thank you. I made a terrible mistake when I didn't wait for you, John. I was a foolish, romantic girl who was old enough to know better than to play the games I played."

"Why are you telling me this now? Haven't you and Ned hurt me enough?"

She couldn't speak for a moment.

"Did he put you up to this?" John asked.

"Hardly," she said. She looked up at him. "Ned beats me, John. He abuses me in unspeakable ways, and you're my only way out. I want you to take me back."

He was stunned. He couldn't think of what to say.

"I've tried every other avenue. I've done everything I know to make him happy. I've been the perfect wife. I've accepted the fact that he'll never let me have children. I've even tolerated his infidelities, but nothing satisfies him." Her breath came in desperate gasps, and she dabbed constantly at her eyes with a lace handkerchief. "You're my only hope."

"What does your family say about this, Jennifer?"

She laughed bitterly. "My father's beaten my mother ever since I can remember. He thinks it's the way to deal with women. I thought maybe Roger would confront him, but Ned has a powerful hold on my brother. He didn't even want to hear what I had to say."

"I'll help you get away from him."

She looked up hopefully. "Do you mean that, John? You'll have me back?" She asked.

"No," he said quietly. "I'll help you get out of his house."

"But I have nowhere to go. He'd find me. He'd have them kill me. He's as much as said that."

"Amos will help me. We'll hide you somewhere, so that he'll never find you. I'll pay all your expenses until you can get reestablished elsewhere."

Jennifer stood and backed to the door of his office. "It's you or him. There's nowhere else. You have to help me, John. He's afraid of you."

"I've offered to help you, Jennifer, but I haven't loved you for a long time. I've dealt with the loss of you, and it's too late to go back." He stepped toward her. "Let me help you in the only way I can. I have business associates out of state who can help."

"No. Get away from me! It was a mistake for me to come here." She fumbled at the doorknob. "Please, don't tell anyone I came. He'll find out. Please, don't tell." She opened the door and hurried across the yard to her horse. John followed.

"Jennifer, wait."

"Just stay away from me," she cried. "You'll only cause trouble."

$$\text{\textit{s} \qquad \textit{s} \qquad \textit{s} \qquad \textit{s}}$$

John immersed himself in the process of rebuilding the business and put Jennifer out of his mind. It wasn't too hard to do. He was thinking about another woman.

A month after his talk with Jennifer, John heard that Gray was back from the swamp. That evening he went out to Gray's cabin, and they loaded up the boat. Gray climbed into the bow, and John pushed off into the slow current of Suwanoochee Creek. They rounded a couple of bends, and Gray got the lantern going and the lines adjusted to keep the chicken livers just off the sandy bottom.

"There's not much better than a pan-sized catfish out of this old creek," Gray said.

They were busy for a few minutes pulling them in, but Gray noticed that John lacked his usual enthusiasm.

"How's work going?" Gray asked.

"Okay," John said. He put his pole down and leaned back in the boat.

"My Lord, John Warren not taking the bait to talk about work. What's going on here?"

"I'm just thinking," John said quietly.

"Let's see," Gray said. "It's not about fishing, and it's not work. That leaves women, religion, or philosophy. I'm the philosopher, so it's women or religion."

"I'm confused," John said.

"That doesn't narrow things down between religion and women," Gray replied.

"It's Kathleen."

"What about her?"

"I don't know how I feel about her."

"Maybe your problem is that you do know how you feel about her, but you don't know how I feel about her."

"Yeah," John said. "Maybe that's part of it—a big part of it. Why don't we start there?"

"That's easy, John," Gray said. "I love Kath."

John fidgeted with his bait, keeping his eyes averted from his friend. He felt sick. Gray kept a straight face as long as he could.

"Fortunately for you," he said, "I love her as a sister, not as a potential wife."

"Are you sure about that?" John said.

"That first cookout the three of us had when you came back to Magnolia? That was my feeble attempt at matchmaking. You and Kath don't seem to be getting the message. You'd be great for each other."

"Do you think so?"

"Let's see. There's Kath—a red-haired angel right here on earth, great sense of humor, great intellect, a beautiful woman. There's you—" Gray paused a moment. "Great potential."

John grabbed Gray around the neck and wrestled him over to the side of the boat. "Maybe your scrawny body would make a great splash in this creek!"

Gray's muffled voice came from beneath John's arm. "Now that you've lightened up, maybe we can finally catch some fish." John let him go. "I'm tired of talking about how fortunate you are," Gray said, "so I'm going to give you a piece of advice and a warning, and then we talk only about catfish, and we eat catfish. Agreed?"

"The advice?"

"Don't take Kath for granted. She won't stand for it. If you mean to marry her, then give her a proper courtship and engagement and get on with a wedding."

John nodded. "The warning?"

Gray smiled. "I'll never tell her, but for the rest of our lives I'm always, without fail, going to take her side against you. Don't let her ask my opinion too much."

John hung his head and laughed. For different reasons, each man was thinking that he had to be the happiest person on earth.

§   §   §   §

John and Kathleen were married three months later. Polite society thought the courtship and engagement were scandalously brief and disapproved of Kathleen's decision to hold the wedding at home with limited invitations.

"Poor Miss Wealthy must be spinning in her grave," Mrs. Pace told Mrs. Polk and their circle of friends. The ladies did not have high hopes for a marriage that had started so inauspiciously.

By the end of the summer, John and his crew at the mill finished the construction of Kathleen's new home across the street from her father's. By design it was the largest, most expensive, most luxurious home in Clinch County.

"The Warren place is downright gaudy if you ask me," Ned Worthington told the Reverend Polk. "It takes a petty mind fixed on the trivial things of this world to conceive of columns the size of those."

Most everyone in Magnolia who mattered agreed with Ned. John Warren had come to their town under questionable circumstances. He had deceived certain loving, but naïve, people into helping him. Clarence Pace had the good sense to run him out of town, but here he was again, bolder and brassier than ever. And he had cheated Ben Taylor out of everything he had ever owned, had broken Wealthy's heart and in some way had undoubtedly contributed to her death.

"Mac McLendon had better look out," Ned was telling everyone. "It looks like he's next."

XIX

"Look at old Mac McLendon over there," Roger Pace said. "He's really entertaining the troops tonight." Roger and Ned sat at a corner table in The Jug.

Ned looked at Mac gesturing wildly as he told a story. "He's quite a talker. Your father should be concerned about that."

"What do you mean?" Roger asked.

"I mean that Mac likes to dredge up the past. More and more here lately, it involves your old man."

"What kind of stuff is he saying about my father?"

"He was fairly drunk the night I heard him, but it was something about his wife's death, and how he would probably do well just to get it all off his chest. He said it would probably be worth it just to see Clarence Pace sweat."

"What would my old man have to do with Mrs. McLendon's death? I always heard that she fell down the stairs at their house and broke her neck."

"I can't figure it out," Ned said, "but let me tell you one stranger than that. Mac got wound up another night and started talking about the good old days with my old man."

"The gambling at The Jug and the horse races?" Roger said.

"Yeah. This one night Mac gets to re-living the glory days. I mean, he's got a hundred stories, and he's trying to tell them all. Then, about one in the morning, he's drunk, and he's getting tired, and all of a sudden he gets kind of ill with the world. Says if it weren't for Clarence, he'd still be whipping my old man's ass in them races."

Roger looked puzzled.

"That's peculiar, ain't it?" Ned asked. "What does Clarence have to do with either one of them deaths? My old man bashed his fool head on a tree limb. Still, if I was Clarence, I'd want to know that Mac

McLendon is shooting his mouth off. Could get hard on a man's reputation."

Over the next few days it was evident from Clarence Pace's increasingly surly disposition that Roger had done Ned's work well. Several times a week Clarence sequestered himself in his office for hours at a time. When he came out, he said a terse "good evening" and ignored any attempt to catch his attention. Business suffered, but Clarence didn't seem to notice. To Ned, that was the highest confirmation that his plan was exceeding his expectations.

"The old buzzard's in a haze," Ned bragged to J.C. Cooper. "I bet he hasn't had a good night's sleep in three weeks. Roger can't show his face in that office without getting his butt reamed good."

"How are you getting along with him?" J.C. asked.

"No problem. I stay clear and keep the business coming in. Matter of fact, I'm the only reason the doors stay open, and Clarence knows it. You can never catch him or Roger there."

"Sounds like it's going your way. What's your next step?"

"I've got to help the boss out," Ned said. "The way I see it, Mac McLendon's the cause of all his problems. If I can help Clarence eliminate him, he'll be on easy street."

"Yeah, I guess that's right. But, if old Clarence were to blame for getting rid of Mac, I guess that would eliminate a problem for you, since you've got Roger under your thumb."

"It could work out that way," Ned agreed, "but Clarence isn't that big of a problem. There's someone else who needs to pay for the death of Mac McLendon."

    *   *   *   *

John stepped into The Jug, filling the door with his large frame. His eyes adjusted to the dimness as he scanned the room for Mac. His search was brief and he strode over to the bar. "Time to come on home now, Mac. Finish off that last glass, and I'll see you off."

Mac backed off. "Hold on there. A McLendon knows when it's time to ease on, and I ain't for easing yet. I'll let you know when, though, if you think I won't keep you out too late to suit your wife."

"I'm not trying to tell you the proper time for leaving, but Kathleen is waiting dinner for you. I thought you'd want to make her happy."

"Well, let me tell you something then, boy." Mac stabbed his finger into John's chest for emphasis. "You're a damned fool. Any man knows you can't make a woman happy."

John was struggling to stay patient. "Yeah, Mac. Now come on home with me. It'd make me happy."

"Ha! You think I worry about making you happy?" Mac bellowed. "You'd attempt to give me orders?" The stout Irishman swung from the heels and caught John with a glancing blow to the right shoulder, knocking him against the bar.

"That's enough, Mac. You've had plenty, and I'm getting enough, so we're leaving."

"I'll go out the door with you," Mac said, " but I'll be back in here shortly. Right after I whip your tail."

"Come on then, you hardhead," John said.

As soon as they were outside, Mac struck the classic fighting pose, his knees bent, torso erect, and his arms half-extended, fists up. The tavern emptied as they circled each other, and the bets shaped up.

"When I've thrashed you, I want you to get on that horse and get home to your wife," Mac said.

John stood his ground and said nothing.

Mac struck at him with a jab. John dodged, landed a blow on Mac's jaw, and watched the older man go down in a heap. When he didn't move, a groan went up from the losers, and the crowd dispersed.

The next morning after Kathleen saw John off to work, she went to see how her father was. She hated it when they fought, but she was determined to do something about Mac's drinking, and she knew that she would need John's help to do it.

"I don't guess you'll be content 'til your big oaf of a husband kills me in a barroom brawl," Mac said.

"If you'll stay out of the barrooms, my husband will stay out of the brawls."

Mac rubbed his jaw tenderly. "I don't want to talk about it. My jaw's killing me. I don't want to talk about your blamed husband."

"I knew a time when John was all you could talk about," Kathleen said.

"That was before he started screwing people I care about," Mac yelled.

"Both you and Ben Taylor drive a hard bargain when it's you doing the driving. Let the other fellow outsmart you and that's taking unfair advantage."

"You're not that hardhearted, Kathleen McLendon, that you have no sympathy for Ben Taylor. The man's reduced to a pittance in his old age, struggling to keep a roof over his head," Mac said, softening his tone.

"My name is Kathleen McLendon Warren, now. Tell me, Papa, what have you been able to do to help Ben?"

"Not a thing, and don't think I haven't tried. He's a stubborn, over proud man."

"I don't suppose he's told you that John offered him a job doing pretty much as he pleases, and that he turned it down flat."

"Kathleen, can you imagine working as a hired man at a business you once owned? It would be the worst humiliation I can imagine."

"Uncle Ben can have his pride, or he can have people's sympathy, but I don't believe he can have both."

"I guess that all depends on how big a person is, Kathleen. I thought you were a bigger person than that. I guess I don't know much about this new woman, this Kathleen Warren." Mac turned away from his daughter, his arms folded across his chest, and stared out the window.

Kathleen sat motionless and fought back tears. She loved her husband and her father, but there was a great distance that separated the two men. Kathleen stood and walked to the door, hesitated, then turned the glass knob and walked out. Mac stayed at the window, watching her go.

"Don't make me choose between my pride and your sympathy, Kathleen Warren," he said.

§   §   §   §

"All right, all right. I'm coming," Mac bellowed. "Quit that infernal racket, beating down a man's front door like that!" He was surprised to see John standing at the door. "What do you want?"

"I want to talk to you a minute without getting into a shouting match or a fight. Last night was the last straw for me, Mac. I mean to get some things settled with you, so that we can get on with living."

Mac pushed by him and went to sit in the rocking chair on the veranda. "I don't care much for that tone of voice, but I'm a fairly patient man. Go ahead and get things off your chest."

"How did you get home last night, Mac?"

"That sounds like a question you already have the answer for, so why don't you just go ahead and give it to me?"

"I'll have to do that, Mac, because you don't have any idea. I rolled you over your saddle out at The Jug and brought you in like a dead man, which is what you're going to be if you don't quit drinking."

"And did your bringing me home have anything to do with this sore jaw I've got today?" Mac asked.

"You see? That's exactly what I'm talking about. You get out here on a bender. Kathleen worries and finally sends me out after you. When I catch up with you, we always end up in an argument, and then you want to fight."

"What's your point?" Mac asked.

"You can hear all sorts of stories about us in Magnolia. It has to stop!"

"Old women and idle preachers spread that sort of gossip. Don't let it bother you."

"It's not me that it bothers, Mac. It's Kathleen, and I mean for you to quit embarrassing my wife."

Mac jumped up from his chair. "I've loved my daughter since before she was born, and if anyone's embarrassing her, it's you!"

"What?" John yelled. "Your drunkenness causes all the trouble. How can you stand there and try to turn this back on me?"

"Number one, Mr. Warren, don't try to change me. I'm an Irishman, for God's sake! I'm going to have a drink now and again. Number two, get control of your wife, man. A woman doesn't tell her men folk when to come home. A man comes home when he's damned good and ready, and the woman is glad to see him in the bed the next morning. And number three, when you've come to fetch me in the past like Kathleen's little boy, you've probably used that insulting tongue of yours on me, and I stand up to you like a man would."

John breathed heavily through his nose, his jaws clenched. "I did-n't come to trade insults with you, Mac. I came to make peace and to get us out of this vicious circle. You have to quit drinking."

"Go to hell. Who appointed you to run the world?"

"It's for your own good. I'm just trying to help you," John said.

"You're just trying to help yourself," Mac countered. "I've watched you operate. You drop in here from God knows where, get Wealthy to take you in, and then how do you help Ben? You take everything it's taken him a lifetime to build. I suppose you think I'm next. Well, my property may not be as easy to come by as Ben's. As a matter of fact—"

John hit Mac in the jaw and staggered him against the wall. He recovered and lunged at John, his momentum carrying them off the veranda and into the bushes below. John got out first. He untied his horse and mounted as Mac continued to thrash around.

"You look like a fool," he yelled to Mac. "But no bigger a fool than you talk like. I'm going to remember your accusations." John turned his horse and rode away.

"Come here, boy. I'm not through with you!" Mac yelled.

John rode on, and as the hoof beats receded in the distance, Mac pulled free of the bushes.

"I need a drink," he muttered. He eased along sideways between the bushes and the veranda until he came to the front steps. As he walked into the house, he cursed John under his breath. In the kitchen Mac took a bottle from a cabinet shelf. He pulled the cork on it and took a long drink. Mac rubbed the left side of his face.

By ten that night, three empty pint bottles sat side by side on the kitchen table. Mac's head was hung over the edge, and he was barely able to focus his eyes to see his brogans. He had the worst case of indigestion that he could ever recall.

"Son of a bitch is turning my daughter against me," Mac brooded. "My own flesh and blood embarrassed by me. Idolized me when she was little, she did. When I raised her right by myself. Got to get him away from my girl. He's just after my property."

As Mac sat trying to convince himself of these things, a sound pen-etrated the haze of whiskey in his head. He stood to answer the door, but found it much easier to sit again than to walk. He tried to focus on his options, but found it difficult to concentrate on much of anything.

"What is that damned noise?" he said. "If ye be man or beast and can make your way in here, come ahead!"

*   *   *   *

John rode past his house headed west to the mill. Mac's remarks about his treatment of Ben Taylor and his supposed designs on Mac's property stung. He had been too hard-nosed, could have softened things up a bit, but didn't the old man realize it was for his own good? He's drinking himself to an early grave and making me look like a heel in the process.

When he arrived, he was relieved to find the mill deserted. He was in no mood for company. Entering the office in the dark, John fumbled a moment until he found the lantern. It felt light, and he searched for more coal oil and the matches. He found the fuel container, but knocked it over in the dark.

"Lord," he said softly. "What a day this is turning out to be."

When he finally lit the lantern and cleaned up the smelly mess, he sat down to work on his billings for the sawmill. Over the next two hours he accomplished very little as his mind wandered back to his confrontation with Mac. He became weary and nodded off at his desk.

*   *   *   *

No one in Magnolia smelled the smoke or saw the flames that began in Mac McLendon's kitchen until the house was beyond saving. The Reverend Polk's dog finally woke him and his wife with its incessant barking. Pulling his pants on over his nightgown, he ran to the church and rang the steeple bell until he saw people on their way to the fire.

The men began a bucket brigade from a neighbor's well, but its only purpose was to contain the fire. The intensity of the heat kept everyone back, and the men at the head of the brigade were doused to protect them from burning. They took on the demonic qualities of the fire as steam rose from their bodies and the brightness behind them made the men appear in silhouette to the growing crowd.

Amos Johns circled the house, searching for Mac. When he came to the front of the house again, Ben Taylor was there trying to help Kathleen locate her father in the crowd.

"Has anyone seen Mac?" Amos yelled above the roar of the fire.

Ben shook his head.

*   *   *   *

John Warren dreamed.

He stood on the bank of a river, a shotgun in his hands. On the other side a doe and her yearling stood on the edge of a sandbar and drank. John waited patiently in the heat, not daring to move, barely breathing. Sweat rolled into his eyes. He waited for minutes that seemed like hours, until the buck appeared through the undergrowth at the tree line, cautiously nosing the air, barely moving his magnificent head. Sensing no danger, the deer eased down to the sandbar, reconnoitered one more time, and drank.

He inched the weapon to his shoulder, painfully slow. Carefully, he lowered his head to sight at the chest. Steady. Blink away the sweat. Wait until he raises his head. Hold it.

"Bust him, boy!" the sergeant shouted. "What are you waiting for? He's nothing but a damned deserter. Shoot him!"

John's concentration was so great that he never moved, even though a whole army of men urged him to shoot. He blinked away the sweat, and when his eyes focused again, he was sighting on Ned's chest. He held his aim where it was.

Ned motioned for John to cross over the river, and the men behind John broke out into laughter and jeers.

"What you gonna do, boy?"

"You gonna join that traitor, John?"

"You gonna let him go?"

"Last chance, Ned," John yelled.

Ned waved a farewell to John.

John squeezed the trigger.

At the close range from which John fired, the shot pattern was tight when it tore into Ned's chest. He crumpled to the sand, and from the wound there issued a torrent of water that engulfed John before he had time to lower the rifle.

The soldiers moved away to the north, unmoved by what they had seen. The flood that poured from Ned's chest obscured him. John moved calmly with the current, at one with the movement that carried him south.

Bells rang somewhere in the distance.

John woke in his office as the Reverend Polk sounded the fire alarm in Magnolia. He sat at his desk confused until he could reconcile the dream with reality. He checked his watch and walked outside. The church bell could only be tolling trouble. He saw the glow of a fire in Magnolia and raced to his horse, fearing for Kathleen.

John arrived in town in minutes to find Mac's house burning. As he dismounted he saw Kathleen and pushed through the crowd to her. She was crying too hard to speak.

"Where's Mac?" John yelled above the noise of the crowd and the conflagration.

Kathleen shook her head, but still could not speak.

"My God. They can't find him, can they? Stay here. I'll see what I can do."

John ran to where Amos stood in the yard. The Sheriff turned to face him, and John saw that there was no hope. Tears ran down Amos' face.

"Are you sure it's him?"

Amos looked back into the fire. John tried to follow his line of sight.

"If I'm not mistaken, that's what's left of him right there." Amos pointed to the back door of the house. To his horror, John saw the charred outline of a man lying outstretched toward the back door.

"It'll take a while for this fire to die down," Amos said. "I'm going to try to break up the crowd and get a few men to stay with it the rest of the night. Why don't you get Doc and Brother Polk to help you with Kathleen?"

John closed his eyes and swallowed hard. "What am I going to tell her?"

"You ain't going to have to say much, son. Just put your arms around her and hold on tight. Now go on. She needs to know."

John walked back to Kathleen, and the people around him faded from his consciousness. She came quickly to him. She had composed herself in the last few minutes, and now she stood before her husband, resolute. "I expect my father is dead."

He nodded.

"I'd like to hear it from you, John, so that later on I'm not harboring false hopes."

John looked down for a moment. When their eyes met, his voice was firm."Your father's dead, Kath. There's no mistaking it." John put his arm around her, and they made their way home.

As they moved away from the crowd, the Reverend Polk's wife turned to a neighbor. "Did you notice that Mr. Warren smelled strongly of coal oil? I wonder how this fire started?" she said.

     s   s   s   s

Clarence Pace sat slumped behind his desk. The dark bags under his eyes saddened his expression even more than the deep frown at his mouth. He was unshaven and unwashed.

"He has to know, Clarence. There's no telling what he might slip up and say unless he's aware of the stakes."

"What's this all about, Ned?" Roger asked.

"I'm telling him, Clarence," Ned warned the older man. "He needs to know."

Clarence stared at the floor.

"Your father and I went to Mac's house last night. We wanted to straighten him out about his loose talk at The Jug."

"Good God!" Roger whispered. "What happened?"

"He came at me," Clarence said quietly.

"He was drunk," Ned said, "and he was raising hell because we'd come by so late and disturbed him. Then we told him that we didn't appreciate his verbal attacks on Clarence, and he went out of control."

"How did the fire start?" Roger asked.

"We're not going into all the details, Roger!" Ned snapped. "Have a little consideration for your father. This is a nightmare for him."

Roger fell silent. Ned paced.

"All you need to know is that your old man killed Mac. Whatever happens, you just remember that, and you keep your mouth shut."

"What if Amos questions me?"

"Use a little common sense, man! Tell him it was two in the morning when all the commotion woke you up, and you don't know anything about it."

Ned turned to Clarence. "You have to get home and get cleaned up, and, above all, you have to quit moping around. It's one thing to have people think you're saddened by Mac's death, but if you get too far down, they may get the message."

Clarence looked at Roger. He started to say something, then stood to leave. Ned grabbed his arm as Clarence passed. "Not a word of this to anyone—either one of you. People are going to speculate. 'Poor old Mac,' they'll say. 'Drunk again and knocked a lamp over and couldn't save his home, but he died trying.' Ain't that the way you gents got it figured?"

"Yeah," Roger said eagerly. "That's it."

"That's it, ain't it, Clarence?"

"If you say so, Ned."

"Well, I say so." Ned thrust Clarence away from him. "And that's damn sure what this group had better say."

＊   ＊   ＊   ＊

"State your full name for the record, sir."

"My name is John Franklin Warren."

John sized up the district attorney, William Edwards. He appeared to be in his mid-thirties, and though his hair was completely gray, his face was unlined and his whole body was animated. He was all business, and his Waycross associates at law had a standing bet on when he would next be seen smiling.

"Mr. Warren, do you know why you've been called to testify before this grand jury?"

"This is an inquiry into the death of Mac McLendon."

"Indeed it is, Mr. Warren, but that isn't the question I've put to you. Do you know why you, in particular, have been called to testify?"

"I make no presumptions, sir."

Edwards frowned. "Could you render a simple yes or no, Mr. Warren?

"No, sir."

"Do you mean to tell this gathering that you haven't heard the rumor that you may be charged with the death of George Edward McLendon?"

"No, sir. I mean to tell this gathering that I find it difficult to render a simple yes or no in matters that may tend to hang me."

"Then you have heard such a rumor?"

"Yes."

"And what do you reply to this rumor, Mr. Warren?"

"I make no reply to rumors, sir."

"Mr. Warren, did you have a hand in the death of Mr. McLendon?"

"I did not."

Edwards turned his back to John and walked slowly toward the jurors as he spoke. "What is your relation to the deceased?"

"I was his son-in-law."

"And is your wife Mr. McLendon's sole heir?"

"To my knowledge."

"What do you stand to gain from Mac McLendon's death, sir?"

John stared at the district attorney's back.

"I've asked you a question, Mr. Warren."

"I'll answer your question, sir, and I'd remind you that not all disputes or insults are resolved in a courtroom."

Edwards whirled to face John, his face already reddening with indignation. "Is that a threat on my person, Mr. Warren?"

"My wife will inherit all of her father's—"

"I've asked you an altogether different question now. Did you just threaten the district attorney of the Alapaha Judicial Circuit in the presence of this grand jury?"

John continued to look Edwards in the eyes. His tone remained even, and he sat with one leg crossed over the other, his hands resting on his lap. "No, sir. I did not threaten you."

"What would you call your previous remark about solving disputes outside the courthouse then?"

"I'd like for the court recorder to read aloud that remark, and what you said just before that."

"Mr. Warren, have you ever threatened a Clinch County citizen with death?"

"Mr. Edwards, I'm finding it difficult to follow which question I should answer next."

Edwards balled his left hand into a fist and planted it firmly on his hip. His tone was imperious. "Answer my last question, Mr. Warren."

"In the late war, sir, I threatened many men with death, as did every man who bore arms."

"Don't evade my question with generalities, Mr. Warren. Have you ever told a citizen of this county that you'd shoot him specifically?" He jabbed at the air with his index finger.

"Are you interested in particulars, Mr. Edwards?"

"A yes or no will suffice."

"Yes."

"And did you fully intend to carry out this threat, sir?"

"Under a given—"

"Just a yes or no will suffice in this instance, also, Mr. Warren."

"I must limit my answer to yes or no. Is that what you're saying, Mr. Edwards?"

"Yes, that's what I'm saying."

"Then my answer is yes."

"Mr. Warren, do you come from a violent background?"

"How do you mean that, sir?"

"I mean have individuals in your family committed acts of violence, such as assault or murder?"

"Not to my knowledge, sir."

"Why do you guard your answers? What do you have to hide?" Edwards advanced toward the witness table as if stalking prey.

"I resent the implication that I'd perjure myself, Mr. Edwards."

"To hell with your resentment," Edwards roared. "You aren't above suspicion, and your mask of piety will not deter me from my duty."

"You push the limits of my patience, Mr. Edwards." John uncrossed his legs and leaned forward as if to rise.

"And what will be my punishment for exceeding your standard of forbearance, Mr. Warren? Need I fear for my life as Mac McLendon? Will you beat me in public, as you did Mr. McLendon on two separate occasions?" He was within a few feet of the table, his arms folded across his chest.

John calmed himself and sat back. "I'll not dignify such drivel as this. Do you have any pertinent questions for me?"

"Yes, sir, I do. I'll give you a great dose of pertinence. Have you and Mac McLendon ever quarreled publicly?"

"Yes, sir, we have."

"And did these quarrels ever escalate to blows?"

"They did, but only when—"

"Were you alone with Mr. McLendon at any time on the night of his fiery death?"

"I was."

"And did the two of you quarrel on this occasion?"

"We did."

"And did that particular quarrel turn physical?"

"Yes, it did."

"And what was the outcome of the fight, Mr. Warren?"

"Mac knocked us off the porch. He fell into the shrubbery, and I left to avoid further trouble before he could untangle himself."

Edwards stopped and returned to his table. He looked down at some papers, flipped through them a moment, then looked up as if he were surprised that there was anyone else in the room. He smiled. "That will be all, Mr. Warren."

*   *   *   *

When John entered their bedroom, Kathleen stood at the window with her back to him. She leaned against the draperies and stared at the blackened ruins of her father's house, the place that had been home to her for twenty years.

John slumped in the damask chair on the opposite side of the bed. Neither spoke for several minutes, trying to make sense of the events of the last several days. John broke the silence.

"Kathleen, I want you to ask me anything that might be on your mind. Anything at all."

She continued staring out the window as she spoke. "I shouldn't have to ask you such a question. What sort of marriage do we have if I don't know you any better than that?"

"I think we have a good marriage, Kath, but if we're going to keep it strong, you're going to have to be certain that I didn't murder your father. I'm not sure that you know that in your heart yet."

She didn't answer, so he walked to her and put his hands on her shoulders.

"I want to look into your eyes, Kathleen."

She turned to him.

"I didn't kill Mac. I had nothing to do with his death. He was alive when I left the house that night, and I didn't come back until you saw me at the fire. That's as plain and honest as I can say it to you. I'll have to prove my innocence in the courthouse, but that's as good a testimony as anyone can hope to get from me. Belief or disbelief, well, that's going to have to come from you and from a jury."

"Don't expect any quick answers from me," Kathleen said. "I know that our marriage is at stake, and I'll try with all my heart to believe that you're innocent, but I have to know for sure, John."

"That's all I ask, Kath." He stepped away from her. "Amos has come to pick me up," he said quietly.

Panic flickered across her face. "What can I do?" she asked.

"Nothing for now. I've hired a lawyer from Jacksonville, and I'm sure he'll want to meet with you. Just be patient and hold on for a rough ride."

"Do you want me to accompany you to the jail?"

"No. Amos is embarrassed enough to have to arrest me, so I'll go quietly, and we'll see what happens. Just stay put." He leaned down and kissed her cheek. He heard her crying as he left the room. He paused at the top of the stairs to compose himself before facing Amos. He could see his friend pacing below, anxious to get this over with.

"Just like old times, isn't it, Amos?" John said loudly as he descended the stairs. "Seems like only yesterday you were arresting me for vagrancy."

"Don't make light of this, John," Amos replied. "I'm having enough trouble as it is."

"I don't mean to give you a hard time, Amos. Let's go. I have a few questions for you on the way to the courthouse."

They were out the front door and on the way down the dusty street before John spoke again.

"What do you figure they have on me?"

"As an officer of the court, I can't answer that. As a friend, I can tell you that their case looks fairly weak to me. They can show that you and Mac quarreled the night of his death, but that looks like it to me."

"What about my reason for killing him? Can't they show that Kathleen stands to inherit a large sum of money?"

"Yes, I suppose so. But I think the district attorney will be careful not to drag the innocent lady into the mud. He'll try to avoid the implication that she conspired with you to murder her own father."

"So they'll have to prove that I planned and carried out Mac's murder without her knowledge."

"That's what I think," Amos said.

"Well, we'll see what my lawyer thinks. He's due here tomorrow."

"Due here?" Amos asked. "You're not using Percy?"

"This is over Percy's head," John replied. "I took the recommendation of a business associate and hired a fellow out of Jacksonville."

"Anybody I ever heard of?"

"A fellow by the name of Harris Teeter. Do you know him?"

"Only by reputation," Amos said. "I understand that he's quite a show horse, but I also understand that he hardly ever loses."

"Sounds like my kind of man," John said.

XX

He was dressed in a white linen suit with a sky blue shirt, white suspenders, coal black boots, and a white Panama hat. From beneath the back of the hat boiled a mass of black curls, but in front, the hairline stopped halfway on top of his head. His cheeks ballooned beneath two slivers of eyes. The effect had been calculated long ago, and he cynically referred to it as the "southern gentleman". He had several stock outfits with which he manipulated people's impressions of him and several personalities that were calculated to do the same.

Amos Johns read the business card:

> Harris Rabelais Teeter, III
> Attorney-at-Law
> 1 Ellis Street
> Jacksonville, Florida

He looked up at the elegantly dressed gentleman standing before him, as if midgets appeared in his office daily.

"What can I do for you, Mr. Teeter?" he asked though he already knew.

"I believe a client of mine is incarcerated here, Sheriff, and I'd like to spend some time with him—a Mr. John Warren."

"I've heard a great deal about your success in the courthouse, Mr. Teeter, and it never occurred to me that you might be a midget."

"I appreciate your forthrightness, Sheriff Johns," Harry said. "It never occurred to me that you might be a giant. But size aside, I suspect it's my father you've heard of, and he's quite normal-sized."

Amos liked Harry right away. "How about you, Mr. Teeter? John Warren's a friend of mine, and I know he didn't kill Mac McLendon. Are you good enough to prove it?"

Harry walked to the wall opposite Amos' desk and straightened a picture. He could barely reach the bottom of it. "You're asking the wrong question, sheriff, and you're asking the wrong man."

"Set me straight."

"I've been in town for a couple of days, doing a little homework. The correct question is who killed Mac McLendon? The correct man to ask that question of is you. If you can't answer it, I firmly believe that, right or wrong, the good people of Magnolia are going to hang John Warren. Could I see him now?"

As they entered the hallway to the cells, John looked up from some paperwork Kathleen had brought him.

"Amos, have you heard anything from that shyster lawyer down in Jacksonville yet? Damned if I don't think he's going to be content to let me hang!"

"Uh, John—"

"And who's this? You take to arresting children now? Come on in and have a seat, son. If you're lucky we'll have you a lawyer here in a month or so."As he drew closer, it became apparent to John that this was no child. "Amos, why are you bringing a midget in here?" John paused for only a second. "He's my lawyer, isn't he?" He slumped back on the bunk. "Oh God."

"Now John, I think this man will work out just fine."

John jumped up to the bars. "What makes you think that? I'm going to be the laughingstock of three counties, right up until the time they hang me. That's not just fine with me!"

"Quod timemus subito nos invenit," Harry said.

"Will you quit jabbering! Speak English!"

"That which we fear will come upon us suddenly," Harry said. "It's Latin, Mr. Warren. I'm Harris Teeter III, the attorney whom you have engaged. Don't be concerned by my lack of stature. I rarely lose a case. You see I have an excellent brain, which I use to the full advantage of my clients. I've overcome my limitations, sir. May I help you overcome yours?"

John looked at Amos, then back to Harry.

"What are my limitations, Mr. Teeter?"

"Well, sir, for one thing, you're in jail." First Amos, then John and finally Harry began laughing at the absurd simplicity of the statement. "Sheriff, would you mind letting me in the cell? I need to get acquainted with my client."

In the cell with John, Harry removed his hat and coat and arranged them neatly on a table in the corner. He made himself comfortable on one end of the bed, folded his hands on his stomach, and closed his eyes. "Tell me your life's story, John," he said.

"Where would you like for me to start?" John asked.

"Tell me your family's background before your birth. Then start with the first day you can remember. I'll steer from there."

John looked at him uncertainly.

"I assure you I'm awake and I'll hear every word—meditation. Helps me visualize your life."

John rolled his eyes and began to tell Harry his life. By sunrise the lawyer knew more about him than any living person. But the odd thing to John was the feeling that he knew Harry better than he had known another person for a long time. He had complete confidence in him.

"Where do we go from here, Harry?"

"After some rest I have a little more research to do around town, but based on what I've already seen and on what you've told me about Mac's death, I'd say we had better be finding out who the killer is."

"But there's no eyewitness," John protested. "There's no evidence that I killed Mac. All they have is a set of circumstances."

"I'd rather they did have something more concrete to work with," Harry said. "I could turn an eyewitness inside out. Make him look like the biggest liar in the south. But circumstances—they're too subjective. I can tell a jury all day long that the circumstances don't prove anything, but in their minds—different story. And a good prosecutor will just keep stacking circumstance on top of circumstance, until your twelve peers will convince themselves that the murderer couldn't have been anyone but you. Do you understand?"

"Yes, I guess I do."

"All right. You rest up, because Amos and the two of us are going to begin solving the murder this evening. First, though, I need a bit more information."

     ⚘   **⚘**   **⚘**   **⚘**

That evening, Harry returned to the jail from the boardinghouse accompanied by Mrs. Leggett's son, Ralph. As Harry greeted Amos, the boy sat a large wicker basket on the floor next to the sheriff's desk. He pulled a blue-checked tablecloth from the basket and spread it over Amos' empty desk. He set a table for three and loaded the desk down with fried chicken, mashed potatoes and gravy, coleslaw, pickles, bread, and tea.

"Sheriff," Harry said, "will you be so kind as to let John join us here for the evening meal? Mrs. Leggett insisted on taking care of us this evening, and she's done such a fine job with the special touches that I just couldn't see us dining in that cell."

With that, Ralph lit an incense candle and placed it in the center.

"Well, I'll be—I wouldn't want John to miss this," Amos said, smiling. "Besides, I want a witness. You sure this came from Birdie Leggett?"

"That will be all, Ralph. Thank you so kindly," Harry said, and he flipped the boy a silver dollar.

As they ate, Harry told them who he had interviewed that afternoon and the gist of each conversation.

"Now, gentlemen, the next order of business is to eliminate everyone who didn't murder Mac. Once we've accomplished that, we'll know who did kill him, won't we?"

"Sounds simple to me," John said.

"Why, Mr. Warren," Harry said in mock indignation, "you sound skeptical of my method."

"Don't you think Amos and I have been trying to figure out who did this?"

"Ah, but you and the sheriff have two flaws which are almost impossible to overcome in an examination of this sort."

"And those flaws are?" Amos asked.

"First, your unwillingness to eliminate suspects. Second is your inability to suspect the right people. I'm from the outside, therefore I'm objective and can do both of these things for you. All you have to do is correct my observations as we go."

"How do we start?" Amos asked.

"I need to make some notes as we work, sheriff."

Amos took a sheet of paper and a pencil from the desk drawer and handed them to Harry. The attorney pushed back the tablecloth, and across the top of the page he wrote the words family, friends, business associates, and drinking associates. In a column down the left side of the page he wrote passion, power, money, and politics.

"All we have to do is match the man with the motive. Given Mac McLendon's small sphere of influence I don't think this should take over an hour."

"The man with the motive, huh?" Amos mused. "You're eliminating all women, then?"

"Unless you or John can give me some likely female suspects, I am."

"Mac doted on women," John said. "He thought they were all angels, and he looked after them like they were daughters. I think it's a man, too."

"Very well," Harry said, and he crossed off "family" from the top of the page. "Aside from John the only family is a daughter, so that eliminates one category."

"What about his brothers and sisters?" John asked. "He left them a long time ago. Maybe one of them finally caught up with him and killed him out of anger."

"Flaw number one is your unwillingness to eliminate suspects—too unlikely. Let's move on. From my interviews around town it seems that everyone liked Mac. They respected him, but the only friends I'm aware of are Ben and you, Amos. Am I missing anyone? Perhaps someone in Waycross or Valdosta?"

"Mac had hundreds of friends," Amos objected. "Why'd you think he only had two?"

"It's been my observation, sheriff, that a man has only two or three real friends in a lifetime. On rare occasions he marries one of them and then life is exceptionally fine, but for the most part it's two or three. The rest are just drinking buddies, if you know what I mean.

"I spent a night or two at The Jug, so I remove drinking associates as a category. No one there had the spine, the initiative, or the intelligence to kill Mac. There's one possible exception, but he appears in another category anyway."

"That leaves business associates," John said, as Harry crossed out another category.

"The most fertile field," Harry said. "When you consider the motives for murder, every single one of them and various combinations of all of them apply to business. Who first comes to mind when you think of Mac and business?"

"Clarence Pace," Amos said.

"Very good, sheriff," Harry said. "You see how much better this works when you don't labor at it? Clarence Pace and by extension Roger Pace, my candidate from The Jug, and Ned Worthington."

"Now I can think of three other fellows I've known to have business differences with Mac," Amos said. "Two from Waycross and one from this side of Dupont."

"Keep them in mind if you like, but now you have to learn how to suspect the right people. I believe we have all the suspects needed. That's Ben Taylor, you, Clarence Pace, Roger Pace, and Ned Worthington."

"This is craziness, Harry," John said. "You've just run right past a whole town full of people you hardly know. Think of how easy it'd be to over look a hundred clues that would lead you to a hundred people other than those men."

Harry jumped from his chair to stretch. "You know the advantage of this system, John?" he asked. "You can always start over—no harm done. We can add a hundred suspects if you want to, but this trial starts tomorrow. If Amos doesn't get busy with his investigation, your time could be running short. Let's consider motive a moment. I've talked with enough people to know Ned Worthington's motive, and his is the strongest of all—revenge for the death of his father."

"And Roger is good accomplice material, but that's about all he'd be worth," John said.

"Except for one problem, I'd say that Ned is our man," Harry said.

"What's the problem?" John asked.

Harry motioned toward Amos, who looked as if he were a thousand miles away.

"Sheriff, you're too quiet," Harry said. "Which of our three suspects has put you into such deep thought?"

"I have to check out a couple of things," Amos said. He stood and motioned John to the cell. "Time to act like a prisoner again, John."

"Can you tell me what's on your mind?" Harry asked.

"Not just yet, but within the next day or two. You go ahead with the trial and stall a bit when you can."

"Amos Johns, Ben Taylor, Clarence Pace, Roger Pace, and Ned Worthington," Harry recited. "Can I narrow the list any?"

Amos stared down at him a moment. "Ned Worthington or Clarence Pace," he said.

"Can we prove it?" Harry asked.

"It's doubtful."

❧   ❧   ❧   ❧

As Judge Sylvanus Hitch entered the bench in the Clinch County courtroom in Magnolia, there was far too much murmuring and laughter to suit him. He had known this was going to happen. It was inevitable. It was bad enough that the defense counsel was a midget, but his client was well over six feet tall, which only served to heighten the comic effect. He knew how he was going to handle this. He banged his gavel, and the report echoed in the high ceiling of the room.

"I want some decorum in this court!" he snapped. "A man is on trial for his life today, and I will not have a spectacle made of these proceedings. Is that understood?"

The crowd of two hundred fell silent.

"I believe in meeting situations head-on, so let's get to the heart of the matter. Mr. Warren is very tall. His attorney is very short. Many of you obviously find that humorous. I do not, and I will not tolerate anyone in this courtroom who disturbs the order of these proceedings with inappropriate laughter and unnecessary talking." The judge turned his attention to the lawyers. "Gentlemen, are you ready to proceed with your opening statements to this jury? Very well, Mr. Edwards for the people."

"Thank you, Your Honor."

The prosecutor stood and walked directly in front of John Warren. He stood there with his hands on his hips, glaring contemptuously at John, his brow furrowed in intense concentration.

"The people versus John Franklin Warren!" he finally yelled. "The people of this great state, the sovereign state of Georgia, have found reason to stand against the treachery of John Franklin Warren, who stands before you—a jury of his peers. He is accused of the vile murder of one of our own—our dear, trusted, respected George Edward 'Mac' McLendon." He turned and walked to the jury as if he had found something that they would be interested in seeing.

"We have the evidence, ladies and gentlemen, to enable you to find John Warren that which he truly is—guilty of the murder of Mac McLendon. I will endeavor to present that evidence to you in a clear and concise manner, so that you may do your duty with a clear conscience, knowing that you have protected your family and your neighbors from John Warren." He spit the name out as if the taste was too vile in his mouth.

"There he sits, a man so possessed by avarice that he betrayed the trust of those who took him to their bosom when he was at the ebb tide of his life. He has wrongfully wrested from those who nurtured him their very livelihood, putting them under more strain than they should have to bear. Indeed, more strain than poor Miss Wealthy Taylor could bear, and now she has taken her rightful place with the saints."

The district attorney paused and turned to face the jury. "Kathleen McLendon married John Warren in the faith and trust of a good woman. His unfaithfulness to the Taylors had yet to come to light. But this poor woman had innocently taken a viper to her bosom. Ladies and gentlemen, look at John Warren. Doesn't he look like a solid citizen? Were the Taylors and Mac and Kathleen so wrong to trust appearances? Be careful of this high-priced, big-city lawyer who John Warren has bought to aid him in escaping his just punishment. Be careful of this stranger among us."

At this reference to him, Harry raised his head from some papers he had been pretending to read. He sat erect and bobbed his head up and down slightly, nodding to the jury and smiling broadly.

"The people of the state of Georgia are prepared to prove in this courtroom that John Warren carefully planned the murder of our beloved Mac McLendon, and he carried out that cold-blooded murder in the most vicious, most painful manner possible. He wasn't content with merely murdering Mac. He punished him with the very fires of hell! Can you imagine what it's like to be burned alive! Oh Lord, have mercy on Mac McLendon. Give him a special place among your angels for what this John Warren did to him here on earth!"

With that, the district attorney could not go on. He hung his head in despair and tried to compose himself. The ladies throughout the court were dabbing at their eyes and trying their best to contain their sobs of anguish, lest they raise the ire of Judge Hitch. The men were indignant and were considering ropes and good, stout oak limbs.

"Your Honor," Mr. Edwards said meekly, "I find that I cannot continue, and I yield the floor to Mr. Teeter." He collapsed in his chair and mopped his face with his handkerchief, spent by the effort of persuading these good people that Satan was in their midst.

"Mr. Teeter, you may proceed."

"Thank you, sir," Harry said cheerfully. As he struggled to get out of the huge chair, backside first, his rump hit the table, tipping over a glass of water. John lunged to catch the glass, but he was too late. The papers on the desk were soaked, and the glass rolled to the front edge of the desk and off, shattering on the floor.

The people on the first rows directly behind Harry and John coughed and laughed behind their hands, straining to avoid irritating the judge. They were too late. Judge Hitch glared at Harry. Harry grinned up at him foolishly.

"I'm terribly sorry, Your Honor," he squeaked. "It seems the hurrier I go, the behinder I get."

The people on the back rows were straining to see, some going so far as to ease up out of their chairs, craning their necks to see this funny little fellow who claimed to be a lawyer.

Judge Hitch hammered his gavel. "Quiet! You people in the back sit down this instant." The room immediately fell silent. "I warned you— all of you—that I'll not have a bunch of shenanigans in this court. Mr. Teeter, I'll thank you to be more careful, sir. Bailiff, get this mess cleaned up so we can proceed here. Mr. Teeter, get on with it!"

"Yes, Your Honor. Good morning, ladies and gentlemen," Harry said politely. "The purpose of an opening statement is to set the stage for the case an attorney will make on his client's behalf, and I intend to do just that. But since I'm new to these parts, I think you also want to know a little about me."

A couple of the men on the jury and some of the gallery grinned at the emphasis that Harry put on the word "little". The judge shifted uncomfortably. Harry kept a straight face.

"My name is Harris Teeter III, and I'm from Jacksonville, Florida. Some of you may have noticed that I'm a midget."

The crowd couldn't contain themselves on that one, and the judge had to pound his gavel to calm their laughter.

"Mr. Teeter, will you please restrain yourself from such remarks and get on with your opening statement?"

"Yes, of course, Your Honor. Ladies and gentlemen, in this great land of ours, we're presumed to be innocent of evildoing until it's proven beyond a reasonable doubt that we have indeed committed a crime. This is a principle of law which prevents many well-meaning but overzealous guardians of society, such as the district attorney here, from hauling your fathers, your husbands, your brothers from your homes at night and throwing them into a dungeon there to rot away the last of their days."

Harry stood a calculated distance from the jury box so that those on the back row had to labor to see him, leaning one way or the other.

"As well-informed people, you realize that there are citizens of the world who do not have such protection. Do you recall that we are only a generation or two advanced from a people who lacked that presumption of innocence? God has blessed us with such a defense from our own government. Now the government, represented by Mr. Edwards, wants to strip one of you of that safeguard. Today it is John Warren who suffers, but who of you will be next?"

Harry pointed at first one juror, then another. "You sir? You ma'am?" His brow was furrowed, the look of concern for these dear people unmistakable in his eyes. "Mr. Warren is getting a trial, so he has the presumption of innocence,' Mr. Edwards would say. But in his opening statement, the district attorney has already convicted Mr. Warren of the murder of Mr. McLendon, and also of the death of Miss

Wealthy Taylor. In fact, ladies and gentlemen, Mr. Warren loved both of these dear people, and he mourns their passing as all of you do. Mr. Edwards conveniently forgets that Miss Wealthy Taylor died accidentally at a time when John Warren was over fifty miles away, trying his best to save an investment for Ben Taylor, a fact that Miss Wealthy acknowledged in writing to Mr. Warren."

Harry paced away from them, his head down and shaking slowly from side to side.

"If Mr. Edwards will try to deceive you on one count, he will attempt to deceive you on all counts. John Warren had nothing to do with the deaths of either Mac McLendon or Wealthy Taylor. The district attorney means well, I think. He is persecuting—I mean prosecuting Mr. Warren with zeal. But ladies and gentlemen, what about our right to be protected from persecution?"

He turned to the gentleman sitting at the jury foreman's position. "The government can only describe a certain set of circumstances to you, placing Mr. Warren here on this day, there on this night, quarreling with Mr. McLendon then, fighting with him now. Let me ask you an interesting question, sir. If one of your in-laws turned up dead, could I easily show this court some time when your relationship with that person was less than sterling silver?" Harry paused, and there was a nervous shuffling and murmuring in the court.

"I'll take the group's response as a definite yes. Put simply, ladies and gentlemen, the government has only a case of circumstances against your neighbor, John Warren. Protect him as you would protect yourself, for that may be precisely what you are doing."

Harry returned to his seat and climbed nimbly up into it.

"Is the per—prosecution prepared to call its first witness?" the judge asked.

"We are, Your Honor. The people call the Reverend Jedediah Polk."

As the Baptist minister made his way to the stand, John leaned down to Harry. "That was good work once you recovered from the accident with the water glass."

"Accident, my hind leg," Harry whispered. "This Edwards is pretty good. If I hadn't put on that little show, they'd have hanged you after the first five minutes!"

After the first day's session in court, Harry was content with their position. The prosecution had undeniably made a few points in establishing that John and Mac fought frequently and in the financial benefit that John and Kathleen would get upon Mac's death. Edwards was careful to exonerate Kathleen in all of his implications of murder for money.

Harry knew from his interviews around town that some of the prosecution's witnesses could be turned to his advantage. The Reverend Polk told of some bragging that Mac had done about his "fine son-in-law" just days before his death. Another man, one of the regular patrons of The Jug, admitted that Mac McLendon was quick to argue and fight with all comers when he was drinking.

Things were going fairly well in court, but Harry knew that ultimately how he handled the trial would be beside the point. John's survival depended on Amos Johns.

*　　　　　*　　　　　*　　　　　*

Sara Worthington put a coffee mug in front of Amos and sat down across from him. She was a masculine woman who had learned long ago what it took to survive in South Georgia with no husband and an ungrateful eldest son. She dressed in a denim work shirt with pants and heavy brogans.

"My boy ain't killed nobody, Amos. Them murderers is just reaping what they sowed, and you ought to know that for the truth. If you'd a spent as much time looking into my husband's death as you are Mac McLendon's, you'd a found out that he ain't hit no tree limb by accident. Clarence Pace and McLendon murdered him."

"Sara, we've been all over this. I investigated everything I could in Cable's death, and there was no evidence that it was a murder. Mac and Cable were both drunk, and you know how they loved to race those horses at night."

"That's my point, sheriff. They knew every turn in that road. Cable wouldn't of hit no tree limb. He got the best of them two in that business deal and was getting ready to take a bunch of their property, and they weren't going to have that."

"Sara, there's no record of any business deal between Cable and Pace and McLendon. Let it go, and let's deal with today. Do you know where Ned was the night that Mac died?"

"His fancy wife says he was home in bed with her. Now who'd dare dispute the word of a Pace?"

"I've heard that Mac and Ned had some run-ins at The Jug here lately. What can you tell me about that?"

"Not much. I've got a fellow that runs the place for me, so I don't go there much when the crowd's there."

"What have you heard, Sara?"

"They argued some over cards. Nothing unusual."

"Did Ned threaten Mac?"

"No, sir! He never done that. If he couldn't get along with Mac on account of his Daddy's death, I'd have told Mac to stay away from The Jug. That's what I'm telling you, Amos. The boy was reconciled to it."

"If you think Clarence killed Mac, why are you letting John Warren stand trial? Why haven't you spoken up?"

"What did you say when I spoke up to you, Amos? I've got nothing but my opinion to back up what I'm saying. Nobody's going to listen to me. Nobody around here wants to believe that Clarence and Mac were able to murder Cable, and that includes you. I'm telling you, sheriff, if you want to save John Warren's hide, you'd better open your eyes, and you'd better figure out a way to pin this murder on Clarence Pace. He done it."

Amos finished his coffee and started for the door. "It was him or Ned, and I mean to find out who. I'm not letting John hang for something he didn't do."

"Well, you ain't hanging my Ned neither."

"Then you'd better help me come up with a way to get Clarence to confess, because there's no evidence anywhere on these murders."

❧   ❧   ❧   ❧

Clarence Pace sat upright in his chair. He glanced nervously at the door to his office, then back at Amos Johns.

"What can I do for you, Amos?"

"I'm a little surprised that you're not over at the trial, Clarence."

"People depend on the bank being open. Besides, from what I hear, the outcome seems pretty sure."

"Oh? And what do you hear?"

"That Warren is guilty. I hear that the district attorney has spent the week making a good case that John killed Mac for his property. It's no secret that he and Mac didn't get along, and the size of Mac's assets make for a pretty good motive, wouldn't you say, Amos?"

"No, I don't buy that, Clarence. John's doing all right in business for himself, and Kathleen was going to inherit everything, anyway."

Clarence glanced at the door. "Do you, uh—do you have any other suspects?"

"Yes, as a matter of fact, I do." Amos looked the banker directly in the eyes. "I've narrowed it down to Ned Worthington—and you." Amos had never seen the color drain from a man's face so fast.

Clarence fought for control of his emotions. "Well! That's a hell of a thing to tell a man. Why would I want to do something like that? Mac was a good customer of mine."

"You always relate things to business, don't you Clarence? Of course, it wouldn't be honest to say that Mac was a good friend of yours, so I guess a good customer is the next best thing."

"Mac and I got along just fine. Why would you say we weren't good friends?"

Amos looked at Clarence steadily, wondering if he should proceed. "I don't think Mac could get over the fact that you got Alice pregnant."

Clarence sprang up behind the desk. "That's outrageous! How dare you come in here making accusations like that and saying that I murdered Mac! I think you'd better leave this bank!"

Amos kept his seat. "Clarence, you'd better sit down and calm down, before I have to calm you."

They glared at each other.

Amos leaned forward and slapped his hand on the desk. "Sit down, Clarence!"

The banker collapsed into his chair.

"Now, Clarence, more people know about your affair with Alice than you think. By the time she told Mac, it was too late for him to pretend to himself that the baby was his. That's what he'd have done, you know, to protect her. So the best thing for you to do is to be honest with me. Otherwise, I'm going to forget about Ned altogether and just concentrate on you."

Clarence's face was pale, his lips drawn tight. "So you think Ned killed Mac to avenge his father's death. How do you intend to prove it?"

"I have to place him at the crime, but the fire pretty much took care of any physical evidence. That means I've got to have one of two things—either an eyewitness who saw Ned at the murder scene, or a person who can testify that Ned was not where he claims to have been."

Amos watched quietly as the light came on in Clarence's head. "Listen," Amos said, "I've got a few more stops to make, a few people to see who might have had indigestion that night and went for a late night stroll. I'll just keep looking, and we'll see what turns up."

"I'll be in touch, Amos, should I come up with anything."

"You do that. I'm pretty sure that hanging is a painful way to go."

*   *   *   *

As the trial entered its second week, Harry tried to hide his concern from John and Kathleen, but not from Amos. The district attorney was as good at assembling the pieces of circumstance as Harry thought he might be, and he knew that the jury was rapidly being persuaded that John was Mac's murderer.

"This trial is winding down, Amos. I've done all the foot-dragging that I can do, so my advice is to go ahead now with your measure of last resort."

"What do we do if it doesn't work?" Amos asked.

"There's the appeal process," Harry said, "but the judge has run a tight ship, so I'd have to be pretty inventive in coming up with grounds for an appeal."

"A long shot, huh?"

"They don't get any longer."

"All right," Amos said. "I'll see if I can't arrange to bump into Ned this afternoon. Clarence has had plenty of time to get through to Jennifer if he's going to be able to get her to testify against Ned."

*   *   *   *

Ned motioned Clarence out to the cashier's cage. "Come here. I want to show you something." When Clarence reached the cage, Ned pointed across the street to the courthouse. Roger was just entering the front door.

"So what?" Clarence snapped. "Roger's going to waste time watching that trial." He turned and went back to his office.

After Ned had locked up for the day, he came into Clarence's office, closed the door, and took a seat.

"What do you want?" Clarence said.

"I want to talk with you for a few minutes. I know that this whole Mac McLendon affair has been a terrible strain on you, but I want you to calm down. It won't last much longer."

"Come to the point, Ned."

"My wife told me some very distressing news last night, Clarence." Ned looked down at his trousers and calmly brushed away some imaginary lint from his knee. "It appears to me that our coalition has fallen apart. That's too bad, because I thought we were within one day of hanging John Warren and getting you completely off the hook."

"Me?" Clarence said. "Don't you mean us? You had just—"

"One day!" Ned screamed. "You spineless old fool! We had it made, and you let Amos Johns shake you up, and then you turned on me. You betrayed my trust!"

"Ned, he was going to come after me. He was going to convince your mother to—"

"You leave her out of this, Clarence." Ned was calm again. He pulled a pistol from beneath his coat and leveled it at Clarence's head. "You don't even think about my mother, or I'll put you out of your misery."

Clarence was so despondent that the gun didn't even shake him. "You'd be doing me a favor, Ned. This whole thing is unraveling. We're both going to be ruined."

Ned smiled and lowered the gun to his lap. "No, it's just you. Jennifer's going to say what I tell her to say. I guarantee it. And Roger wasn't going to the trial. He was going to talk to Amos."

"My son wouldn't turn on me."

"He has no choice, Clarence. Don't feel hard toward him. There are some men in Waycross who will hurt Roger if he doesn't turn you in.

I'm the only person in the world who can stop them. That's why it's important to your wife and to Jennifer and to Roger that I stay alive and out of prison. You're the only one who will be ruined. So it looks like you have a choice. Do you want to spend some time in Amos' jail and go through a trial and tell people about your past affairs, and explain what really happened to my old man? Or do you want to do what's best for everyone concerned?"

Clarence stared into space for a moment. "What do you have in mind?"

"In order to protect your family, you're going to need to write a confession. You'll need to say that you acted alone when you murdered Mac. Otherwise, people may begin to ask too many questions that I can't answer."

"You're going to let John Warren get off the hook?"

"Got no choice. I don't like it, but I'll have other opportunities to bring Warren down." Ned lay Clarence's pistol on the front edge of his desk and backed slowly to the door. Clarence sat staring at the gun.

"I'd say you have about ten minutes to think this over before Amos hears Roger out and gets over here to arrest you. Make your farewell letter short." Ned turned to go and then looked back. "And when you get to hell, tell my daddy hello for me, will you?"

Ned slipped into the courtroom and sat down on the last bench beside Roger Pace. "Anything interesting going on?" he asked. Roger shook his head.

XXI

From Gray Hampton's Journal
Sunday, August 31, 1890

The object of this life is freedom—freedom from sin, freedom from suffering and pain, freedom from worry and the anguish of bad or destroyed relationships, freedom from all that is earth binding.

The most liberating knowledge that a man can get is that his time in this life is brief. The most liberating choice that he can make is to believe that there is a loving God who will provide for him forever, beginning with some time preexistent to his making that choice.

Thus freed from the constraints of time and want, he has only one bond left to slip—the most difficult to escape. He must get out of himself. The Lord Jesus said it this way: Deny yourself, take up your cross, and follow me. It isn't what most of us want to hear, but it is what we have to do. It is an action we must take, for clinging to life keeps us bound to it. Let it go.

When we get out of our selves, a miracle occurs. God takes us from mere existence to living. We go from dying a little, day by day, in a finite world, to living infinitely. When is eternity? For the eternally alive, it is now.

My aim is to convert myself more and more into spirit and less and less of flesh. By my last breath here on earth, I hope to be almost transparent. It is my hope of heaven that the spiritual body we're promised is light and airy, and I believe that is so. I'm weary of weight, and I long to fly.

So what is the sum of the matter? There is not life and death, only life.

Life is the substance, death only an apparent change in that substance. There is little comfort in this truth for one who has suffered the loss of a child or a husband or wife, but it's the truth nonetheless for the suffering of separation.

The object of life is freedom, I say. Freedom from many things, yet also freedom to one thing—the unchanging life of unity with the Creator, not equality—unity.

§   §   §   §

On November 29, 1859, Dr. Homer Mattox deeded ten acres of land that was adjacent to the Atlantic and Gulf Railroad to the County of Clinch for the establishment of a town intermediate to the railroad's Waycross and Valdosta stations. There was no greed or egotism involved, and it quite surprised the good doctor when those people who initially moved to the area insisted on changing the name from Railroad Station number eleven to Homerville in his honor.

The new town was situated eight miles from Magnolia, and it prospered over the course of the next five years. In early 1860 Dr. Mattox provided the means for city government by the construction of a city hall. A general store was built across the road from the railroad depot, then a blacksmith shop and stable, then another retail store or two. The Methodists started services in Homerville in 1860, then the Baptists in 1861.

As Homerville grew, Magnolia declined. By the time Harry Teeter revealed the events that led to Clarence's suicide, the people of Magnolia lost faith in their leaders. The men they had known and respected all their lives—Mac McLendon, Clarence Pace, even Amos Johns to a degree—had turned out to be more clay than gold.

In the early 1880s John and Kathleen started their family. A daughter, Celia, was born first in 1882, then two years later a son, Harry. In November of 1887 another daughter, Rosalie, was born. John was spending so much of his time at the mill and out of town on business that Kathleen teased him that Rosalie must be a doll, because she hadn't seen enough of him to have a real baby.

Kathleen devoted herself to the raising of the children, John to his work, and both of them to each other, to the exclusion of all others except Gray Hampton and Corey Stokes. Their relationship had survived the ordeal of Mac's death and the trial, and their dependence on each other, their mutual admiration, and their love deepened and grew stronger at the places where it had almost been severed. As they drew closer together, they felt more and more isolated from the people of Magnolia.

By the time they were in their thirties, John and Kathleen Warren had grown into the handsome and distinguished couple that they would be for the rest of their lives. Their business trips to New York and other cities gave them sophistication enhanced by the lack of importance they attached to it. With Mac's considerable land holdings added to what John already had accumulated in Clinch and Ware counties, the Warrens were headed for their first million.

John considered the money a by-product of the achievements that were his primary interest. He yearned to build his company, Southern Timber, into a successful organization—one that would support his family as well as others and one that would support his descendants for generations to come.

Rosalie turned three in September of 1890. Immediately after the birthday celebration, John left for Waycross on business. Early on the morning of his second day there, he received a telegram from Gray Hampton.

"Urgent you return home. Kath needs you now."

John dropped everything and rode the thirty miles home. Gray met him five miles out of Magnolia.

"What is it, Gray?"

"Rosalie is missing."

A chill went over John. "Let's keep moving, and you give me any details you can," he said.

"There's not much to tell yet. Kath put the children to bed last night, checked on them a couple of times, and when she woke up this morning about six, Dolly Girl was gone."

Amos Johns and the Reverend Polk met John outside the house.

"Kathleen is with the doc and Mrs. Polk inside," Amos said.

"What's being done, Amos?"

"I've just finished checking around the house. I've got a few things I want to look at with you. Other than that, I've got a search going on, and I'm trying to see if some of my regular lowlifes are accounted for—at work, at home, wherever they usually are this time of day."

"Thanks, Amos. Get Stokes for me, will you? Come on, Gray."

They went into the house and found Kathleen with a half dozen or so people in the library. They rushed to each other and embraced, crying freely. Gray ushered people out of the room until only he and Doctor Williams remained.

"Where's my baby, John?" she asked. "What does Amos say? Oh God, I don't know where she is. She must be cold and scared and—"

John held her close and whispered to her. "Be quiet just a moment. Cry it out, but don't try to talk just yet."

He felt her shaking. He saw the doctor for the first time over Kathleen's shoulder, and he held up a medicine bottle and a glass of water. John continued to hold her close as he spoke to her.

"Amos is doing everything he can do, and now Gray and I are going to help him. I want you to take what Doc Williams has for you."

"No," she said firmly, and she looked up at John. "My children are scared and confused, and they need me right now. I'll not be sedated at a time like this."

"Kath, we don't know how long this is going to take. Get rested now, so that you can be stronger for the children."

"I'm as strong as you," she said. "I'll run my home. If you want someone sedated, then you or the doctor can take that damned medicine." She pushed away from John and took a deep breath. "Get Amos Johns in here. I want to know exactly what he's doing to find Dolly Girl, and I want to know what you're going to do. Then I'm going to be with Celia and Harry while you do it."

John nodded. "It's the only way to go. Gray, would you ask Amos and Corey to come in? Doc, you might as well have a shot of that nerve relaxer. You'll need it if you're going to stay here with Kathleen."

When Gray came back, he had Amos, Corey and the Reverend Polk with him.

"John, I've asked Jedediah to pray for us. We need to keep the Lord involved in this situation." Gray watched all the old objections coming to John's mind, but he knew that John would yield for Kathleen's sake.

John kept his eyes on Gray. "Go ahead, reverend," he said. As the minister prayed, John Warren hardened his heart.

*   *   *   *

Jeeter and Samuel sat in the shack in the dark. They were cold and miserable, but a fire, any kind of light, might attract someone's attention, and they most definitely could not afford that.

"He ain't coming back, is he?" Samuel asked. He almost choked on the words.

"No, nigger," the reply came slowly from the darkness. "He ain't coming back. We on our own."

All the anger was out of Jeeter for now. He even felt a little remorseful at having beaten Samuel.

"How's your head?"

Samuel touched his swollen jaw, the broken nose, the cut lips. "It's okay. Most everything's pretty numb."

They sat silently for a few minutes.

"Jeeter, I'm sorry for the little girl. I ain't used to riding no high-spirited horse, and she was scared and twisting and turning, and I tried to hold on to her—"

"Just hush up about that. She dead and buried now, and it's over with."

Samuel cried in the dark, softly, to himself at first, then louder and louder.

"Oh God, Jeet. Mr. John Warren gonna do terrible things to us. He gonna peel our hides, 'fore he kills us."

Jeeter knew the truth of it. He turned to one side and curled up into a fetal position. There was nowhere to hide. There wasn't even going to be the money that they had been promised. Damned, stupid Samuel, Jeeter thought. The little girl wasn't supposed to be hurt. He dozed off to sleep to the sound of Samuel's crying and to his own thoughts of suicide.

"Get up slow, boy."

Jeeter was startled by the voice and by the sharp pain in his ribcage. His eyes opened and his head cleared to see a man standing over him, a shotgun in his face. Light streamed through the open door. He sat up and there was Samuel behind him, cringing against the wall.

"Get back against that wall and sit up."

Jeeter saw leg irons in the man's hands and realized that this would be his last opportunity. He leaped toward the man, and Amos Johns knocked him unconscious with one swing of the shotgun.

When Jeeter came to, it was still daylight. A chain around his neck pinched him and pulled his head down almost to his knees. His arms circled behind his legs, everything in chains. A rag jammed into his mouth and tied into place forced him to breathe through his nose.

Samuel sat with his wrists and ankles chained together, silently watching Jeeter.

"The sheriff done dug that little girl up and took her to the under-taker," Samuel said. "He say he be back for us at dark."

Jeeter thrashed around and tried to communicate with Samuel.

"I think I know what you're saying, but I ain't doing nothing no more, so you just take your rest. I ain't taking that rag out your mouth, and I ain't trying to get away. I'm fixing my mind on the Lord, Jeeter," Samuel said calmly. "You better do that same thing." Samuel hummed softly to himself, some spiritual song that he'd heard half his life.

"Lord," he said aloud, "this here's Janie's Samuel. I ain't lived good, Lord, but then I ain't telling you nothing, am I? I'm sorry in my heart for all the gambling and the drinking and the pure out cussedness. I'm powerful sorry I hurt that little Warren girl—God, I know you're more'n me. And I know that Jesus is yours, too, and that He's up in Heaven with you. Save me, Lord! And save Jeeter, too! Help us, Lordy!" Samuel could barely get his words out for the tears.

Jeeter thrashed on the dirt floor of the shack, gnawing at the rag and rolling on the chains that bound him.

*   *   *   *

Amos returned to the shack just before nightfall. Without a word, he stood both men on their feet, adjusted their chains so that they could walk, and led them outside. As he mounted his horse, he spoke to them.

"I want both of you to know that it's all I can do to stop myself from killing you right now. If you try anything stupid on the way back to town, I'll enjoy shooting you down. Now get walking."

It was almost midnight by the time they arrived at the courthouse. Amos locked his prisoners in, leaving their chains on, and walked to John's home.

John was on the veranda, slowly rocking and staring out into the night. "Do you have him, Amos?"

"Yeah. There's two of them, and I have them in the jail."

John inhaled deeply, then exhaled. "And my Rosalie is dead."

Amos' eyes closed at the words. "Yes. I've taken her to Russell's."

"I'd better get Kathleen," John said.

"Can't you let her rest until morning, John?"

"There's no rest for us now, Amos. She'll want to be with her baby. Can you keep your prisoners until morning without a lynching?"

"Yeah. I'm thinking about going on to Valdosta with them. You know how word gets around on this kind of thing."

When word circulated that John and Kathleen had been seen entering the funeral parlor, it didn't take people long to assume the truth. Amos hadn't realized the word had spread so quickly, and he found himself trapped in the courthouse by a group of men gathered outside.

They milled around in front of the courthouse for a half-hour or so, smoking and speculating on whom might be inside with the sheriff. When their spokesmen entered his office, Amos wasn't surprised to see Ned Worthington leading the pack.

"Good evening, gentlemen. You're out awfully late." He sat on the corner of his desk, a shotgun in his lap.

"We're not in the mood for humor, Amos. You know why we're here," Ned spoke up. "We want some answers about the Warren girl."

"Rosalie is at the funeral parlor, Ned. If you really wanted information about her, you'd be over there."

"Damn it, Amos. Who's in those cells?" Ned snapped.

"Those cells? You think it's more than one person, do you, Ned?" Amos looked steadily at him. "You boys don't need to get all worked up about this. I have everything under control."

"Now hold on here, Amos," Ned almost yelled. "You're our representative for law enforcement, and we have a right to know what's going on."

"All right. Listen good, because I'm only saying it once, and then I want everyone out of here. Rosalie was taken from her home shortly after midnight on Tuesday. After all the searching you men helped with, I got a tip this afternoon. I followed up on it, and I found the two men who are in custody now hiding out in a cabin south of town. Rosalie was buried behind the cabin. I chained the men so they couldn't escape, brought the girl in to Russell's, then went back and brought the suspects in."

"That's good work, Amos," Ned said. "Let's go ahead with a little justice."

The half dozen men with Ned backed him up, so Amos stood up with his shotgun held chest high.

"Boys, it's time for you to go on about your business. I've filled you in, so get home before this gets nasty."

"We ain't in the mood for that neither, Amos," J.C. Cooper said. "Either you get them animals out here, or we'll get 'em ourselves."

"Over my dead body, J.C. I've been sheriff for nigh onto forty years, and I ain't lost a prisoner yet. Don't mean to start now." He leveled the shotgun at a point between J.C. and Ned. "This old scattergun will take out two or three of you on each barrel, so you boys make up your minds who wants to die first."

"You're not making any friends here, sheriff," Ned said. "Why are you threatening us? Those killers need hanging."

"My patience is gone. You fellows get going by the count of three. One—two—"

They backed toward the door.

"All right, you win." said Ned, "But you can't stay awake for too long. We're going to make those niggers pay."

"I never said who it was, Ned. How did you know their color?"

"Let's get out of here, boys," Ned said, and they all filed out.

As soon as Amos heard the door to the courthouse close, he pushed the desk back several feet and lifted up three sections of the floor. Cool, earthy air rushed into his nostrils like deliverance. He fetched Samuel and Jeeter from the cell, leaving their hands chained.

"You fixing to give us up, sheriff?" Jeeter asked.

"I'm the only chance you have, Jeeter, so you shut up and listen. I aim to get you boys to Valdosta where that mob can't get at you. If we sit tight, they're gonna try to take you. I'd have to kill a few of my friends, but they'd get me and then they'd get you."

"I know that's right," Samuel said.

"They probably have a man at the back door, so we'll drop under the courthouse and see if we can't pick a spot to come out. You men know where Ben Taylor lives, don't you?"

They nodded.

"I think Ben will help me out with horses, so if we get separated, you get to the backside of his house, and I'll meet you there."

Amos ducked down into the hole. Jeeter and Samuel followed. As they crawled back to the middle of the structure, they could hear the angry voices of the men outside. Over them all, they heard Ned and J.C. justifying their reasons for wanting to take the prisoners.

"We'll go out right here. It's wide open out there, so if they're going to see us, ain't nothing we can do about it. Just walk normal and follow me."

They crawled out and immediately started for the north side of the Baptist church. Amos fought the urge to run, and they progressed as if they were walking to a store on an afternoon errand. There were twenty or thirty men listening to Ned, and each time they shouted in agreement, Amos flinched. Finally they reached the shadows of the church, and from there, it was simple to get to Ben's house undetected. The three of them slipped around to the barn.

§   §   §   §

At the funeral home, John walked back to where Kathleen sat with their daughter's body. He stood beside her for a while, his hand on her shoulder, and looked at Rosalie. He didn't want to forget her. It wasn't something that he could say to Kathleen, but he knew how terrible he had felt the first time he could no longer recall exactly what his sisters' facial features had been.

It was odd. You cared for someone as much as humanly possible, and you saw them hundreds, maybe thousands of times, but before long, their faces, the sound of their voices were no longer with you.

"I'm worried about Amos," he said. "That crowd's growing, and it's getting louder by the minute."

She looked up at him and smiled faintly. "I'm okay for a while. You'd better see about him."

He squeezed her shoulder and leaned down to kiss her cheek. Then he leaned over the casket, kissed his daughter's forehead, and walked from the room.

He decided to check on the children first and to get Gray to go over to the courthouse with him. He was almost home when he heard Ned Worthington shouting to the men gathered outside.

"They're gone! There's boards pulled up in the sheriff's office. Surround the building. See if they're still under there!"

John hurried on to his house. "Gray!"

"In here, John." Gray met John in the foyer.

"Are the ladies still here?" John asked.

"They're in the kitchen. The kids are fine. Been asleep for hours now."

"Amos has made a break for Valdosta with his prisoners, and that crew out there has just got on to it. Let's saddle up." They hurried to the barn.

        s   **s**   **s**   **s**

"I said we aren't taking any chances," Ned yelled at the men. "We're covering every road out of Magnolia, and that's final. Ben's missing two horses, so the niggers are riding double. If one group picks up a trail, they fire three shots and then everybody can head in that direction."

"We're wasting time here," J.C. yelled. "Now get!"

The four groups of six or seven men saddled up and headed off in the directions that Ned assigned them. The group that headed east to Waycross failed to see John and Gray standing next to the court-house.

"They have a pretty good plan," Gray said, "so what are just two of us going to do?"

"Let's give them a head start, and then we'll go toward Valdosta. That's the way Amos has gone."

They walked back to the horses.

"What are we going to do if they catch up with Amos?" Gray asked.

"He's been at this business for as long as we've been alive. If they catch him, he's going to kill about half of them to start with. You and I are going to react to the circumstances. There's no telling what we may do. Is your God going to let you kill another man?"

They mounted up and rode west, about a half mile behind Ned and the seven men who rode with him.

*   *   *   *

The sheriff and his prisoners came back onto the dirt road a hundred and fifty yards from where they had left it.

"Maybe that track will slow them down a while before they realize that we came back to the road," Amos said.

"Why don't we strike off across the country, sheriff? They won't know which way we gone."

"There'll come a time for that, Samuel." Amos said, "But the longer we can stay on this road, the faster we get to Valdosta. They'll give us plenty of notice that they're coming."

Only another seven miles passed before Samuel and Jeeter understood what Amos meant. Samuel heard the sound first. It was so faint in the distance that he thought it was his ears playing tricks on him.

"Listen," he said. They could just make out the sounds of the men behind them, the faint pounding of hooves and the occasional raised voice.

"All right," Amos said, trying to conceal the anxiety he heard in his own voice. "Time for some hide-and-seek. This way." He headed north off the road into a stand of pines choked with brush. He had only gone about ten feet into the woods when he heard a crash behind him and the other horse raced off toward Valdosta, still on the road.

Amos wheeled his horse around so fast that he almost ran over the stunned Samuel, who lay half in a tupelo bush beside the road.

"Damned fool," he yelled at Jeeter. "You're going to get us all killed."

He extended his hand to Samuel and hauled him up on the horse as they sped off after Jeeter. Amos rode about a hundred yards or so, then slowed down to listen. He couldn't hear Jeeter out in front of him, but the men behind them sounded closer.

"I think he's off in these woods somewhere, Mr. Amos," Samuel said quietly.

"Yeah. We're going to have to hide, too. They're about up with us." Amos eased the horse off into the woods, looking for any sort of natural defense line. The terrain was so flat that he knew a thick clump of bushes or a fallen tree was the best he could hope for.

"Look here, Ned," Amos heard someone yell. "They started off in here, and it looks like there was a scuffle. Then they took off down the road again."

"All right, I want two men here to block them from going back to Magnolia. I want you two searching the woods to the south, you two on the north, and J.C. with me. Let's go."

Amos found his defensive position, and he and Samuel dismounted. He knew that his only hope was to kill one or two of his pursuers in order to demoralize the others. He didn't want to think of them as his friends and neighbors now, couldn't afford to. In rapid succession, three shots sounded from the north side of the road.

"We got one!"

"Hey boys! Over this way! Come see who we caught!"

Amos knew they were heading back to the road with Jeeter. "Samuel, I have to get Jeeter, and I may have to move fast when I get back here, so I don't want to chain you to this tree. You have to trust me, because you don't have a chance without me. Will you be here when I get back?"

"Yes, sir. I'll go with you, if you could use my help."

"You just hold it here." Amos ran toward the sound of the men.

They saw him coming across the road and, thinking he was one of them, they yelled to him. "Look here, one of them killers is Jeeter!"

Amos never slowed down. He shot one of the two men as he approached. The other man and Jeeter stood stunned, giving Amos time to get to them. He hit the white man in the head with his pistol as the three of them fell. The sheriff rolled over and came up on his knees with the pistol on Jeeter.

"Last chance, Jeeter. You get back across the road, or I'll kill you right now. I got no time to argue with you."

Amos stood and walked toward Jeeter, who scrambled to his feet and started toward the road ahead of the sheriff. They crossed and had barely made the brush on the south side when the others rode up and dismounted. Amos and Jeeter moved further into the woods as the men stopped by their wounded companion.

When they reached the fallen tree with the thick bushes behind it, Amos shoved Jeeter. "Get down behind that tree and don't get up 'til you're ready to die," he said. "Samuel? Where are you?"

"You looking for this, sheriff?"

The voice came from off to his right, and Amos recognized it as J.C. Cooper. He turned slowly. Samuel's head was held up close to a pine tree by a chain pulled around his neck. His waist was secured by rope. J.C. and Ned flanked Samuel, each with a gun on Amos.

"You just drop that gun, Amos, and you won't get hurt," Ned said. "All we want is that other killer chained up to this tree here across from his partner."

Amos aimed for J.C. first, but by the time he got his gun up, both men had shot him. They walked cautiously to his body, and J.C. poked him with the toe of his boot. When Amos didn't move, Ned picked up his gun.

"I'll get Jeeter fixed, and you pull the sheriff over there, so we don't have any explaining to do."

Ned walked to the fallen tree where Jeeter hid and pointed his gun into the shadows. "Get up, boy, or I'm going to wound you pretty bad." He cocked his gun.

Jeeter stood. "Why don't you just shoot me and be done with it? I might tell some of them men who put us up to taking that girl."

Ned hit him in the mouth with the butt of his pistol. It stunned Jeeter, but he kept his feet. "You ain't saying nothing, or when I get through with you, I'll have to pay a visit to your family," Ned said. "Do you hear me, Samuel?" he yelled. "That goes for both of you."

As they chained Jeeter to a tree facing Samuel, Ned shot into the air to signal the others. They were there in a matter of minutes.

"Are we missing anyone?" Ned asked.

"George Davis," a man answered. "He died over there where the sheriff shot him."

"That means that these boys have more white man's blood on their hands," Ned yelled. "You men think about that! You think about that little girl asleep in her bed, and you think about George Davis' family. And where's the sheriff? Hell, I bet they've killed him. Now you tell me that these sons of bitches don't deserve to die!"

"Let's hang 'em!" the men yelled.

"No!" The cry that came from Jeeter was half anger, half fear. "No. You don't kill me!"

"Call on the Lord, Jeeter!" Samuel yelled at him. "Quit that hollering and give up the ghost, brother."

Jeeter raged. "You dirty white men! We don't do what you say, and you kill us. We do what you say, you kill us!"

"He still take you, Jeet! Then they can't hurt your soul. Tell the Lord you turn away from your—"

"Hang them, Ned!"

"Yeah, get them chains off and hang them!"

"You hear me, Jeeter?" Samuel yelled. "Repent! He'll still have you!"

"Hanging's too good for these child-killers," Ned yelled. "Listen to me!"

The men began to quiet down.

"Listen to me. These niggers around here have to be kept in order. Otherwise, they're going to be in your house or my house next. I'm not going to have it. These two are going to be an example!"

"Burn them!" J.C. screamed.

"That's it," Ned agreed. "Let's get us up some wood. Any nigger that comes by here is going to see why you don't fool with white people!"

The men fanned out into the area and were quick about gathering the wood. They brought it in and piled it until the small branches and sticks came up to Samuel and Jeeter's knees. As they worked, Jeeter cursed and screamed, and Samuel pleaded quietly with him to call on Jesus.

"Take His hand. Quit that nasty talking here at the last minute of your life and just trust the Lord. I done it, and I got a peace about this."

The higher the pile of wood grew, the louder Jeeter howled and the more incomprehensible he became.

"Pray for these men that's killing us, Jeet. They gonna know what a mistake they made in a day or two."

"I'll see them in hell," Jeeter screamed, and he spit at the men. "I'm gonna be waiting on you when you get to hell!"

The men tormented him, hitting him with the stout pieces of wood they brought for his pyre, cursing him as he cursed them.

Samuel's love wounded them. They kept their distance from him, throwing the wood at his feet, avoiding his eyes, and darting back to the safety of Jeeter's hatred.

So consumed were the men by their deadly labor that no one noticed the convenience of the containers of camphor oil J.C. produced. As they threw the last of their wood at the feet of the prisoners, J.C. circled the trees, drenching first the men, then the piles of branches around their legs. He worked quickly and silently at Samuel.

"Help this man, Lord." Samuel whispered. "Help him get free of hate. Help this man, Lord."

The words burned J.C., and he moved quickly to Jeeter to salve his wounds.

"You're gonna see my face the rest of your life, you white bastard! You gonna wake up screaming in the night, seeing me 'til you in hell with me!" Jeeter screamed and howled, and Ned and J.C. screamed back, mocking him, hating him completely. The men laughed and screamed in an increasing frenzy until finally all was ready.

Several of them made torches of pine resin knots, and their fires imparted a ghostly glow to the proceedings. Gradually the noise lessened, even Jeeter quieted, until the predominant sound in the forest was the hissing of the pine knots and Samuel's persistent, quiet prayers. Ned walked to the apex of a triangle with Samuel and Jeeter and addressed the vigilantes.

"Gentlemen, I congratulate you on your conduct this day. You have restored honor and justice to Clinch County. You have given notice to the weak among us that you will stand firm in a time of crisis. I'd like for us to stand silent for a moment to honor our fallen friend, brother George Davis."

After a few seconds, Ned raised his head and looked at the men bowed at his bidding. He savored the moment. "Having found these men guilty of the kidnapping and death of Rosalie Warren, and having found them guilty of the creation of the ensuing mayhem of this evening, and having found them guilty by association of the deaths of George Davis and Amos Johns, we find it fitting that they be executed."

"If it's fitting that they be burned, then it's fitting that I do it." John and Gray stepped from the shadows. John took a torch from a man close by and walked toward Ned. "Didn't you say that these are the men who killed my daughter?"

"These are the ones," Ned replied.

John walked to a point between Samuel and Jeeter. He looked for a moment at Jeeter. "You're the one who's been doing all the cursing and carrying on, aren't you?"

"What you gonna do the day you die?" Jeeter hissed.

John turned to Samuel. There was no fear in the doomed man's eyes.

"Did you take my child from my home?"

"Yes, sir. We did that."

"Why? I want to know."

"We was going to get money from you. She wasn't supposed to die. I couldn't hold on to her, she was fighting me so."

"She fell under the horse?" John asked.

Samuel was crying now at the memory. "Yes, sir. I don't think she suffered none, 'cause she was gone by the time I got to her. I took good care of her after that."

John was crying now, the tears streaming down his face silently. "You took her from her mother! You took her from me, and then after you killed her, you're telling me you took care of her! I want my child back! I want her back! You don't know what she meant to me! Oh God!" John yelled, and he fell to the ground, pounding the torch to put it out, pounding out his torment and despair, trying to put out the murder in his heart. "God!"

"Kill them, damn you!" Ned yelled. "Get revenge for your child, man!" Ned threw his torch at Jeeter and grabbed John's torch before he could extinguish it. The pyre caught up with a burst of flames that engulfed John, Ned, and Samuel. The camphor oil that soaked Samuel ignited a second ball of fire, and Samuel's body sustained it. Jeeter screamed and lacerated himself trying to pull his head out of the chains that held him mercilessly in place. He cursed and pleaded and suffered so that the men around him grew silent and began their suffering long before even Samuel had thought they would.

John straightened up from the ground in a halo of smoke. He looked at Samuel until Gray reached him and pulled him away from the flames. Samuel's head was bowed, his eyes closed.

Gray walked him to the road, away from the stench of burnt hair and flesh, away from the terrible sounds. The last of Jeeter's screams had died away in the night air, and Gray and John sat in the sandy road, their backs turned to the hellish punishment in the woods. John stared into the dark. They sat there until the fires were no bigger than campfires, until the other men walked back to their horses near the road and headed for home to a good breakfast or a few hours of rest. They sat there in the road until Jeeter and Samuel no longer resembled men, but unrecognizable shapes that seemed to flow from the trees themselves.

As the first hint of day spread through the tops of the pines, Gray stood. Somewhere close by he would find the corpse of Amos Johns, and once he and John had transported it back to Magnolia, the work of this night would be finished. Only the consequences would ripple on through eternity.

XXII

The winter of 1890 was sullen and gray for the Warren family. It seemed to rain every other day, a bitter, cold rain that stung the flesh and wearied the soul. Their home had lost most of its vitality—the raw, powerful emotion and energy happy children and contented parents bring to a home.

John often awoke late at night to find Kathleen gone from their bed. Sometimes he found her trying to get Celia back to sleep. More often, Celia would be asleep beside him, and Kathleen would be in the girls' room on the floor beside Rosalie's bed, crying quietly.

Each family member endured the days in his own way. It was difficult to tell that Rosalie's death had affected Harry at all. Whatever energy remained in the Warren home that winter, he supplied. Were it not for the increasing number of fights that he was involved in at school, there would have been no evidence that he was hurting.

John buried himself in work and, without realizing it, gradually distanced himself from his family. With the loss of Rosalie and Amos Johns, there was too much death and he began to relive those last, terrible days in Atlanta. The old dreams haunted him more frequently than they had for the past twenty years and he found his respite in work and in avoiding sleep.

Kathleen suffered in silence and grew stronger. From her childhood she had been prepared for the suffering of this hour. Her father had loved Kathleen as he knew how, but his alcoholism had stranded her emotionally and she had learned to accept a love that transcended what people had the capacity to give.

At a very young age, Kathleen had found that church was much more than somewhere you were forced to go and that the Bible was

much more than a book filled with stories of strange and faraway people and places. While her friends were interested in the stories,
Kathleen believed what she was taught about God's love and the
peace that He offered because she desperately needed to believe it.
She needed to have a peace about being left alone at night and having to care for herself. She needed to feel a love that went beyond convenience and congeniality.

She had come to the Lord as a child, not knowing any better than
to believe, and now that she was an adult, she received her suffering
as a gift. She could not rejoice in it, but better than her husband, better than her children, she could receive it.

Beginning the week of Rosalie's death, Celia was unable to stay a
whole night in her own bed. Every night she woke her parents with
her screams, and most nights she could not get back to sleep until
she was securely pressed against her mother.

Kathleen tried to talk with Celia about her dreams, but she claimed
not to remember what scared her so. Finally the screaming stopped,
but only after Kathleen and John let her go to sleep with them. John
could move her, but before morning she was back. They tried doctors
from Waycross and Valdosta to Jacksonville, but no one had any success in treating her.

Christmas came without Rosalie, and the family had no enthusiasm for it. The Warrens merely survived that winter.

      *   *   *   *

In the spring of 1891, on a sunny Sunday morning, John had Gray
keep the children, and he took Kathleen for a ride in the country north
of Magnolia. As they rode, John pointed out where he had spent the
night in the woods twenty-seven years earlier on his way into
Magnolia that first cold November day. For the first time since Amos'
death, John could speak of his friend.

They rode in silence for a long time, holding hands and enjoying the
quiet country around them. The pines towering above them swayed
gently in the breeze. Birds skittered from bush to bush along the road
and entertained them with their bright colors and songs. John
stopped when the sun peaked in the sky, and they spread a blanket
for a picnic.

"Kathleen, I didn't stop here by accident. There's something I want to show you."

"I thought you seemed distracted. What is it?"

"We own all this land around here, further than you can see. This is pretty close to the center of it. I'm going to move the operation here, and if you'll agree to it, I'd like to move the family here as well."

Now that he had said it, John was relieved. He had agonized over this decision for months, and he needed her cooperation.

"What if I don't agree?" she asked.

He shrugged his shoulders, unable to speak for a moment. "I can't bear the memories that are in Magnolia anymore."

She put her arms around him. "You'll get no argument from me, John. I feel the same. When we move, there are two things I want."

"Name them," he said.

"I want my home to look like Dad's house, and I want Rosalie brought close to me."

They spent the rest of the afternoon walking the area that John already had his men clearing for the business. He showed her where they would locate the sawmill and turpentine still. He told her how the Atlantic and Gulf Railroad to the west of this site would eventually spell the end of Magnolia. It was good business sense to get close to the railroad. They walked the boundaries that John had in mind for their home site.

"It looks as if you're planning to build your own town," Kathleen said.

"Our home will be the only one here, but I plan to build a wall around the whole area." She studied his expression for a moment. He was serious. "As the business continues to grow, so will the odds that someone may attack us again. This is Sanctuary, and that's what I intend for us to make it."

"I'll listen to what you have to say on this matter," she said, "but I'll not stand for a prison for the children."

"I'll have the wall meander over a broad enough area that you'll scarcely notice it from any one point inside. We'll plant evergreens and magnolias to hide it. We can begin to plan it all out today."

"Let's be sure to include a good-sized nursery in those plans," Kathleen said.

"For the plants, you mean?"

"No, for a baby," she said.

It didn't take long for John's men to circulate the news that he was moving his entire operation close to Homerville and that his residence would follow. The belief around Magnolia was that John intended to ruin the place that had brought him so much sorrow. That belief was accurate.

At first he just encouraged his men to relocate to Homerville. Then he offered a small tract of land to those who would move. When only the sentimental were left near Magnolia—attached to a plot of ground or other family members—John gave them an ultimatum.

"If you stay near Magnolia, I have no use for you in my operation." He didn't lose a man, but Magnolia lost six white families and eleven black ones. Almost a tenth of its population shifted to the vicinity of Homerville within the year.

The children were involved in the plans for the move to Sanctuary. Celia and Harry were old enough to understand what was going on, so the excitement and the activity of the remainder of that year brought the family out from under the painful cloud of Rosalie's death.

Sightseeing trips to John's construction site became popular diversions for people in nearby towns. These people were a source of concern for John, the opposite of what he aimed for in the building of Sanctuary, and were it not for Kathleen's intervention, he would have run them off.

"This is all private property, you know," he said to her one night. "That's exactly why I chose this spot, so far off the main roads."

"Let them satisfy their curiosity," Kathleen said. "They'll continue to come until they do. Once the wall's in place, they'll grow tired of it."

The ten-foot-high brick wall that was started that summer took two four-man crews another seven months to complete and proved Kathleen right. Once there was nothing but red brick to see, the crowds thinned, then died away altogether.

Charles was born in November of 1891, and in March of 1892, John and Kathleen moved their family into Sanctuary. Kathleen did not consider the move complete until they had laid out the family burial ground, and the headstone for the first little grave was visible from her bedroom window.

Kathleen taught the children at home, so for the next three years, the Warren family rarely ventured beyond the walls of Sanctuary. John did more traveling but his travel was strictly business. He preferred to stay at home.

When he was out of town, John had a half dozen armed guards posted around the grounds. Some of them traveled with Kathleen or the children whenever they were away from Sanctuary. Kathleen disliked the restrictions, but she felt better about the safety of the children, and she learned to live with it. The boys thought of the men as playmates, and Charles thought that every little boy had traveling companions. The guards unnerved Celia.

The move to Sanctuary improved Celia's ability to sleep. Her room was downstairs, adjacent to her parents, and within six months, she was sleeping through the night.

John and Kathleen were elated by the change. They believed that the worst was behind Celia and that she would soon be back to normal. That was before they noticed her quiet time. Sometimes it occurred in bed just before she went to sleep and went undetected. Other times, her parents didn't distinguish it from her shyness and quiet nature. But quiet time was different.

On a Sunday afternoon in July, John left for business in Savannah and Kathleen had just put Charles down for a nap. Harry was playing soldier with the guards, so Kathleen went to one of the rockers on the veranda to read while Celia played with her dolls nearby.

After an hour of reading, Kathleen put down her book and rubbed her eyes. Celia had not spoken to her dolls for quite some time. She sat perfectly still with her back to her mother.

"What are you and the girls doing?"

There was no reply and no movement. Kathleen walked around the dolls to face her daughter. "Celia?" She reached down and took her hand. "Come on, sweetheart. Let's go inside and rest a while." Celia's hand was limp, almost lifeless.

Kathleen panicked. She managed to carry Celia into the house and to the bedroom. She dropped her on the bed, and realized her facial expression was unchanged. Celia blinked occasionally, staring at the ceiling or somewhere far beyond it.

Kathleen ran to the wall and sent one of the guards for Doctor Mattox. By the time she reached the house again, Celia was back on the veranda playing with her dolls. Kathleen approached her daughter slowly, not wanting to startle her. She smiled. "I dreamed that I was in heaven, Mama."

John and Kathleen tried a doctor in Boston and two in New York. They all had seen similar cases, and they all said the same things. The periods of distraction would lengthen, and they would occur more frequently. Eventually the Warrens would lose contact with their daughter altogether. There was still a great deal of mystery to the brain, a lot of research still to be done. No one could help them. Since they had the means, they were told there was no harm in keeping her at home, but most people institutionalized such family members.

John and Kathleen started regular trips to the beach that year in the desperate hope that a change of scenery—the salt air, the water, something—would have an effect on her condition. John found a hotel on the beach in Fernandina, Florida. It was huge, the rooms spacious and airy, with a large porch on the ocean side.

They went intending to stay a week. At the end of the week, John left two men to guard the family and went back to Sanctuary to arrange things for his absence for the rest of August. He would go on two and three-day business trips, but he spent at least four days of each week at Fernandina.

The days were devoted to the children. Most of them were spent on the beach, playing in the surf, building castles in the sand, or burying John up to his neck in the loose sand just above high tide. The boys liked to fish or lower crab traps into the surf from the hotel pier.

Some days they went exploring inland or to the ruins of the old fort on the northernmost end of the beach. They rode bicycles on the hard-packed sand of the beach at low tide, and in the late evenings, boiled shrimp with other families at a pavilion near the hotel.

The evenings belonged to John and Kathleen. The children were too tired to complain about bedtime, and once they were tucked in and the guards in place outside their rooms, John and Kathleen were free to roam together.

They rarely went far from the hotel, but they took long walks on the beach and had quiet conversations on the wide porch. Their relationship deepened and strengthened as they mourned their losses and rejoiced in their blessings together. Late one night they lay in bed, Kathleen with her head on John's chest, listening to the surf as their hearts resumed a normal pace.

"Are you looking at the moon, John?"

"Yes. See how it makes a path on the water?"

"Isn't it lovely? Could you have made a stranger world than this one?"

"What do you mean?"

She hesitated a moment. "This world hurts us so. It seems to wound us at every turn for the sport. Then, just when you've grown to resent life the most, it gives you love and the moon on the sea. Why? Why is the world like that?" She was crying softly. He wanted to know the answer for her, but it was still tangled up inside him, somewhere between his head and his heart.

They fell asleep like children in the moonlight.

Despite the change, constants remained in the Warrens' lives. Corey built a new home close to Sanctuary and moved his family there. Gray Hampton remained on Suwanoochee Creek, and it was a simple matter for John to get away to fish with him. Corey and Gray's friendship with John remained the same, and each was a source of strength and good counsel to the other.

The other constant in John's life was Ned Worthington. Until this latest move by John, Ned's plans had fallen rather neatly into place. First, Roger under his thumb, then Jennifer in his bed, then Clarence out of the way, and that took care of the Paces. He had thought he was set for life. The opportunity to put Amos Johns out of the way had been a pleasant little bonus. But always there was John Warren to contend with. He couldn't get rid of him.

Ned's old enemy seemed likely to spoil everything he had built up with this war of attrition on Magnolia. What good was the bank when the people were moving toward the railroad and Homerville? He decided that Dr. Mattox needed a bank if his town was to grow, and Ned had decided that he was just the man to provide that service. He had only a few minor obstacles to overcome.

The first obstacle was money. Having taken everything that Clarence Pace had once owned, Ned was disappointed to discover that it didn't amount to much. Most of what Clarence had was in cash, and between his wife and children, there had always been plenty of places for that to go.

The second problem was political. With Magnolia's decline, Homerville and Dupont were contending for the county seat. Ned had to bet on one of them, and he had to make sure that he bet on the winner. Should he move the bank to Homerville or Dupont?

On the night of October 8, 1895 the citizens of Magnolia were rudely awakened by the barking of a dozen agitated dogs and by the clanging of the Methodist church bell. The courthouse was burning. The building was constructed of heart pine and, like Mac McLendon's home years earlier, it was gone in a matter of hours.

The citizens stood in an early morning haze doubled by the smoke that boiled off of the ruined records of their lives. They were dismayed to look at this black hole in the heart of their town. But when they learned that the bank was the only other repository of much of the vital information concerning their property, they would be appalled at the black hole in the heart of Ned Worthington.

On November 1, 1895, Ned announced that he had just received a charter for Worthington Bank and Trust. The office would be located at the intersection of Dame and Church streets in Homerville, Georgia opening on Friday, December 1, 1895. On February 2, 1896 by an act of the Georgia state legislature, the seat of Clinch County government was moved to Homerville. Cynics in the county claimed that Ned had made excellent use of the cash he had generated by the burning of the Magnolia courthouse.

*   *   *   *

John stood at the window at Sanctuary watching his children play. He was amazed at the passage of time. Rosalie was gone almost six years. He admired Celia, at fourteen as beautiful as her mother. Harry was carrying considerable baby fat at this age, but John realized that it wouldn't be long before his son would be his height. If Charles hoped to see six, John thought, he had better learn to stay out from under his brother. The boys were chasing each other around a cedar tree, and Celia was starting to wander off.

"Harry's getting too big to roughhouse with Celia and Charles," John said. "I think its high time I put him to work at the mill."

"My baby," Kathleen whined in mock fear. "It may be a little early for Harry to be consorting with the likes of some of your men, but he is awfully bored with the younger ones, and he looks and acts older than twelve. What would you have him doing?"

"I haven't given it much thought, but don't dress him in anything you're proud of. There's not much clean work around there."

"Don't make things too tough on him the first day out. Give him a chance to enjoy the business."

John smiled and nodded.

The next morning at five o'clock, John and Harry left Sanctuary on foot for the half-mile walk to the mill. Harry was eager to get there and stayed two steps ahead of his father.

"Let's get some things straight before we get to the place, Harry. Most of the men out here have been with me since way before you were born. They like things the way they are and don't want to think about any change. You're nobody's boss, and I don't want the men to think of you as the boss's son. I want them to think of you as another hand. Are you with me?"

"Yes, sir." Harry understood his father, but he had little enthusiasm for what he was saying. They were getting close to the office.

"One more thing, son. You're not to do as the others do. You have to maintain your dignity. You have to be better than them even though they tell you what to do. They'll curse and tell disrespectful stories about women and chew tobacco and drink liquor, but you're to stay above all that. The day may come in twenty or thirty years that you run the place. If you start being one of them on this day, they'll run you on that day. You wait out here with the men. You can tell them you're going to work if they ask, but it'll be best if you keep your mouth closed more than you talk." John turned and entered the office.

"Look here, boys. We done got us a new boss today."

Harry turned to see Joshua Tomlinson standing a few feet away, his hands defiant on his hips. Joshua spit his tobacco juice toward Harry who instinctively jumped back.

"Looks like he don't care for a chew, Joshua," Burl said.

"Nope," Joshua said, grinning. "Takes a man to chew tobacco. This boy couldn't stand it for a minute, could you, boy?" Joshua rubbed his chin. "Of course, I did have my first chew about ten. How old you, boy?"

"Old enough to handle a little tobacco, you old turd," Harry said.

All of the men, Joshua included, laughed. He turned and grinned at the crowd behind him. "Well, all right then. Come on over here, and I'll cut you off a bit."

When John walked out into the yard to assign the day's work, everyone was laughing again.

"What's so funny this morning?" he asked.

The crowd of men parted, backing away from the horse trough. Harry was on his knees holding onto the trough with both hands. His face was ashen over a puddle of vomit.

"New boy's breakfast didn't agree with him, boss," Joshua said.

"Well, Joshua," John said, smiling, "you get him a shovel and as soon as he gets rid of that mess, take him with you to the turpentine woods. I expect sunshine and fresh air will do him wonders." John turned to the other men. "All right, let's get this show on the road. Corey, you got your crew picked out?" Joshua helped Harry up from the trough, and together they staggered to the tool shed.

❧   ❧   ❧   ❧

Starting that summer, Harry worked every day. During the regular school year Kathleen insisted that he spend the week under her tutelage, so he was restricted to working weekends from October through May. For several years Harry was torn between the two activities. He preferred to be outdoors with the men, but the work was difficult and boring. He preferred the physical ease of his mother's classroom, but that work was also difficult and boring.

One thing he knew—while it was impossible to get away with anything under his mother's discipline, work at the mill covered a wide territory and his father was away on business so often that it was simple to get out of a lot of the work.

By the time he was fifteen, Harry had all of the laborers convinced that he had the authority to fire them whenever he desired. His bluff kept their mouths shut when they were witnesses or accomplices to his escapades. He had also managed to compromise several of the foremen by catching them in some indiscretion or by inducing them to participate in one with him. By the end of his third year at work, Harry could come and go as he pleased, so long as his work assignment didn't place him with Corey or Burl.

He had barely turned fifteen when he and two of the young black men were teamed up to work the turpentine woods east of Sanctuary. On their second day in the section, the two boys grew anxious as noon drew closer.

"What's the big secret today, boys?" Harry asked several times.

They evaded the question all morning until an hour before lunch. They couldn't stand it any longer.

"Harry," Leon said, "how old is you anyway?"

"I'll be sixteen in February."

"So you be fifteen," Leon said. Harry nodded.

"You ever had any poontang?"

"Any what?" Harry asked.

"He ain't," Herman said.

"Poontang, man. You know. You ever had you a woman?"

"Oh, that," Harry said. "Well, yeah. Sure I have."

"No, he ain't," Herman said.

"I bet I have, Herman!"

"Yeah? Who it was?"

"A gentleman doesn't tell who he's pleasured."

The other two broke down laughing. "You pleasured that hand of yours," Herman laughed. "That's all you done pleasured."

"Yeah, a gentleman who ain't had none don't tell nothing," Leon echoed.

"I damned sure have!" Harry snapped.

They quieted down. This was, after all, the boss man's son they were teasing, and at six feet three, his size was intimidating.

By the time he was fifteen, Harry had all of the laborers convinced that he had the authority to fire them whenever he desired. His bluff kept their mouths shut when they were witnesses or accomplices to his escapades. He had also managed to compromise several of the foremen by catching them in some indiscretion or by inducing them to participate in one with him. By the end of his third year at work, Harry could come and go as he pleased, so long as his work assignment didn't place him with Corey or Burl.

He had barely turned fifteen when he and two of the young black men were teamed up to work the turpentine woods east of Sanctuary. On their second day in the section, the two boys grew anxious as noon drew closer.

"What's the big secret today, boys?" Harry asked several times.

They evaded the question all morning until an hour before lunch. They couldn't stand it any longer.

"Harry," Leon said, "how old is you anyway?"

"I'll be sixteen in February."

"So you be fifteen," Leon said. Harry nodded.

"You ever had any poontang?"

"Any what?" Harry asked.

"He ain't," Herman said.

"Poontang, man. You know. You ever had you a woman?"

"Oh, that," Harry said. "Well, yeah. Sure I have."

"No, he ain't," Herman said.

"I bet I have, Herman!"

"Yeah? Who it was?"

"A gentleman doesn't tell who he's pleasured."

The other two broke down laughing. "You pleasured that hand of yours," Herman laughed. "That's all you done pleasured."

"Yeah, a gentleman who ain't had none don't tell nothing," Leon echoed.

"I damned sure have!" Harry snapped.

They quieted down. This was, after all, the boss man's son they were teasing, and at six feet three, his size was intimidating.

"There was a woman and her daughter came to stay at our house a year or so ago," Harry lied. "Either one of you coons ever been up to Sanctuary where I live?"

"No, sir."

Harry's confidence grew as he put them in their place. "I was out by the moat late one evening, and I was wrestling one of my pet alligators, when all of a sudden that gator spooked and swam off real quick like." Harry had their full attention. "He was one of the little six-footers, and he wasn't giving me much of a match, so I just let him go. And then I saw her. She was beautiful."

"Who she was, Harry?" Leon asked reverently.

"She was the Princess of Europe, and the beautiful woman inside my house was her mother, the Queen of Europe!"

"For sure!" Leon whispered.

"Where Europe be, Harry?" Herman asked. "That anywhere near Sank Sherry?"

"Don't think on that," Leon snapped, and he swatted at Herman. "What'd that Princess of Europe do, Harry?"

Harry looked around the woods and leaned closer to Herman and Leon. "She took off every stitch of clothes she had on, and I saw her titties and everything." He sat back, smug and satisfied.

Leon and Herman looked at each other.

"Did you ride her?" Herman asked.

"Ride her?" This was a new concept to Harry. "Hell, yes. I rode her. That's how you pleasure a woman, ain't it? I rode her all over the place. Used her hair for a rein. She was a little puny, though, so her back gave out quick, but she liked it. Said there weren't nobody in Europe like me. Why do you boys want to know all this, anyway?"

The two of them jumped up and pulled him toward the woods.

"We didn't think you'd ever had a woman, so we got you one."

"What? Hey, let go. Where do you think you're taking me?"

They pulled Harry along, laughing as they went.

"The womens, Harry. They gonna meet us down by the creek."

"What women? Who're you talking about?" He tried to hold back, but they tugged him along.

"You don't know them," Herman said. "Don't worry about that."

They heard them before they reached the creek and saw their clothes scattered along the bushes near the bank. Herman and Leon ran headlong into the creek, each grabbing his mate as they tumbled into the water, laughing and shouting.

One girl remained with her back to Harry, who stood frozen on the edge of the water. She turned and beckoned for him to come to her. It was the first time he had seen a woman without clothes.

XXIII

John had been in the room for the better part of three days, leaving only for the necessities, and then only for minutes. In all that time, Corey had been still except for the gentle, almost imperceptible rhythm of his breathing. He hadn't been conscious since the stroke.

John sat beside the old man's bed, holding his hand, thinking of all the good things that those hands had done. He had never known them to be lifted in anger or spite. They had ever been graceful, powerful hands that spoke eloquently of the man.

He watched the tired, weathered face for the least encouragement of awareness and smoothed the white cap of hair with his hand. Where had their time gone? How was it possible that Corey was eighty years old? He prayed as well as he knew how that Corey could hear him one more time. There were a few things he needed to say.

Ranetta or the children came into the bedroom with him often. They would sit and talk softly for hours at a time, mostly about Corey and something that he had done for someone, some act of kindness or love.

On the fourth day of the vigil, John knew that Corey would not be coming back. The thought came to him early in the morning, long before sunrise. He had been unable to sleep, and he was the only person awake. John took up his old friend's hand and leaned close to him.

"I have to believe you can hear me. I need to think that." He looked hopefully at the peaceful face. "I want you to know that I love you. I couldn't think of how to say it before."

John took a deep breath and tried to sort his thoughts, to make Corey understand. "Respect, Corey. You know, I needed your friendship and your belief that I was worth something right when—"

Trust. Respect. Love. The mere words failed to express the experiences, failed to tell fully the time they had spent together and what it had meant to John. He stood, reached over his old friend and hugged him, laying his head on Corey's chest for a minute. That was better. It wasn't words that he needed. John sat back in the chair.

"I want you to rest easy, Corey, so I'm telling you what I'm going to do. You and I never had to put any business arrangements on paper, but I understand the need to spell things out for this next generation. I'm going to set things up so that your family has a legal half-interest in the businesses, with the notion that Leander, Harry, and Charles will run things. I'm not sure exactly how it's going to be done, but I'm putting some thought to it, and then I'm going to run a bunch of lawyers and bookkeepers at it. You know I'll get it fixed, don't you? I'll watch out for Ranetta and the children, but you know Ranetta. She's not going to need a whole lot of help from me or from anyone else. You always were a good judge of women, old man."

Ranetta stood in the doorway, smiling.

"He was a pretty good judge of friends, too," she said. She had rested, bathed and freshened up for the last hours with her husband. She had on Corey's favorite dress and her hair was fixed the way he always liked it.

"I hate to lose him," John said.

"Me, too," she said. Ranetta walked into the room and sat on the bed at Corey's feet. She patted the quilt. "I surely do."

They sat together, looking at Corey, saying nothing for a time.

"He'd say that it's just for a little while," John said, "and not to worry about it."

"That's right, John. Shortly, Corey'll be with the Lord and there won't be no more trouble for him. Then a little time and I'll be there with him, but I'll miss him all the same. You know, between now and then."

"Is that really how it is, Ranetta? Do we really keep living with God?"

"How do you want it to be, John? If I give you a choice, what would you choose? Go to hell and burn forever, go to sleep and never wake up, or live forever with God and the people you come to know and love here in the world?"

"But how do we know—"

"Shhh!" She held her index finger to her lips. "Choose one."

He looked at Corey. What a simple, good life he had led.

"Choose, John." Ranetta whispered. She stood by the bed. "Choose," she said.

＊　　　　＊　　　　＊　　　　＊

Over the next five years as Harry grew to manhood he learned his father's business from the "mud-end up," as Joshua Tomlinson put it. At age twenty Harry resented his father's methods. Southern Timber flourished over the years at the outset of the twentieth century, and Harry saw no reason why he shouldn't be in charge of some part of it. Here he was, the son of the wealthiest man in South Georgia, and he didn't even know the net worth of the family.

Harry had decided that it was time for a showdown with the old man. What did he have to lose? If push came to shove, he had money in the bank and was prepared to go out on his own. On the other hand, he had everything to gain if only his father would listen to reason.

Besides, he'd had it with Sanctuary. The place was closing in on him. He didn't have any friends, he never went anywhere, he never did anything but work. His courage was as high as it was going to get. Harry knocked on the office door.

"Yeah. Come on in," John yelled. "Hello Harry. Is there a problem in the wood yard?"

"No, sir. I just need to talk to you for a minute."

"Well, if there's not a problem, couldn't this wait until after work?" John went on with his paperwork.

Harry almost lost his nerve. "No sir. This won't wait."

John looked up again and stared at his son. He leaned back in his chair and gestured. "Okay, have a seat. What's on your mind?"

"Mind if I smoke?" Harry asked.

John sighed. "Go ahead, if you must."

"I must," Harry retorted. He took his time rolling the cigarette. "I'm ready to make a change," he said.

"What kind of change do you have in mind?"

"A lot of change, but let's just start with work. I want to run part of the operation."

"Run it! What makes you think you can run this place?"

"That's the attitude I expected," Harry said angrily. "You won't even hear me out!"

"Hold it just a minute!" John said. "I don't have to hear you out on a damned thing. You listen to me, and you listen good."

Harry took a drag on his cigarette and glared at his father through the haze.

"You're years away from running any part of this outfit. I've talked to you about the sloppy work you're putting out, and I don't see any improvement. If you can't do the little things right, what makes you think I'm going to put you in charge of anything big?"

"I'm bored with this nigger crap you've got me doing. Besides, who can please you? If it's not done your way, it ain't right."

John quieted down. "First, you know that word offends me. I'd appreciate it if you wouldn't use it. Next, if something isn't done the right way, it's evident, whether it's my way or not. But in almost forty years, I've learned most of the right ways to do things in this business. Why can't you accept that and let me teach you? You're only twenty. You've got all the time in the world."

"I'm ready now," Harry said. "If you won't let me run part of this business, then help me start something of my own. I've got money saved up, so I'd just need a little help."

"You don't have the judgment for it yet."

"I'm not asking you for the moon." Harry looked away from his father and took another long drag on his cigarette.

"The amount doesn't matter." John said. "I'm not going to help you fail at anything. I'm trying to bring you along in this business, but at the hardheaded, know-it-all rate you're going, it'll be another twenty years before you're ready to run anything bigger than your mouth!"

"I'm trying!"

"You're trying to stay drunk and screw everything in the county! I know about every time you've sneaked off in the middle of a job to go lay up with some whore or to get drunk with the boys!"

"You ought to know! It's probably your liquor I'm buying!"

"This conversation is over. I've got work to do. You show me some good work and some good judgment for a year or two, and then we'll talk about a change."

Harry stood up. "I'm not waiting any damned year." He dropped his cigarette on the floor and ground it out. "Thanks for your time." He snatched the door open and slammed it behind him.

By the time John arrived home after work that evening, Harry had packed and gone, and Kathleen was in tears. John slumped in the chair in their bedroom that evening. Kathleen sat on the edge of the bed.

"I suppose you think this is my fault," he said.

She shook her head from side to side, unable to force words past the knot in her throat.

"Well, I think it is—not that I should put him in charge of anything. He's not ready for that. But I should have put a stop to his nonsense. I should have held him accountable for the poor work he was putting out."

"He's just at that age, John. It's not only you. We're both suffocating him." She wiped at her eyes. "Damn. I have to quit this squalling." She took a deep breath and exhaled. "It's work and it's living at home and it's constantly having to be John Warren's son instead of being Harry Warren. There's no point in trying to blame ourselves or each other."

John walked to the bed and embraced her.

"I love you," he said.

"And I love you. But I want my baby back. He wouldn't tell me where he was going tonight. What will become of him?"

"He didn't tell you, because he probably didn't know. He has money, but I don't think he'll stray too far. Harry's about to find out that he's not quite as independent as he seems to think."

The day after Harry left, John took his thirteen-year-old son, Charles, and his best friend, Leander Stokes, to work at the mill for the first time. Along the way, he explained to the boys how the men who worked at the mill didn't like change.

   *   *   *   *

After the death of Corey, John felt responsible to help Ranetta with the younger children. He loved Corey's family as his own, and he wanted to be involved in their lives.

The whole Warren family was particularly partial to Leander because of his friendship with Charles and because he reminded them of Corey. Leander was solid, dependable, and quiet by nature. Even at fourteen, he applied himself wholeheartedly to whatever he undertook, determined not only to be the best at the moment, but to be the best that anyone had ever seen.

John and Kathleen appreciated the positive effect that Charles and Leander had on each other. Though they competed with each other at work and at play, they were so evenly matched that winning or losing was only a matter of the smallest degree. After a footrace or wrestling match they rarely failed to grin and tease each other about who was the best. The most severe test of their friendship came at the end of that first summer they worked at the mill.

John was helping Burl sharpen a saw blade when he heard a commotion and looked up to see a crowd of men gathered around a fight. They hurried over to break it up and John was shocked to find Charles and Leander rolling in the dirt and throwing punches at each other.

"Burl, get Charles," he yelled. Burl reached down, grabbed Charles by the collar and snatched him up as if he were an infant. John caught Leander as he scrambled after Charles and pinned his arms to his sides.

"Fight's over," John yelled. "You men get back to work. Burl, let's get these two in my office."

The crowd broke up with some men joking and sparring with each other as they went.

"Are you two going to behave, or do Burl and I have to escort you?"

"I'm all right," Leander said, "but it might not hurt for you to stay in between us for a while." Charles nodded in agreement.

"I appreciate your honesty, gentlemen. Okay, Burl, it looks like I can handle it from here."

As they walked to the office each boy brushed the dirt from his clothes and tended to little cuts and scrapes.

"This is a real shocker," John said as they entered the office. "The two musketeers fall out with each other? What in the world?" John looked from one to the other, but they both stood with their heads down. "Well?"

"It's kind of hard to explain," Charles said. "Kind of confusing."

"I don't have all day, boys. This is all family here as far as I'm concerned, so let's just spit it out."

"Turns out we're not as much family as I thought," Leander said bitterly. "Or maybe some of us are a little too close."

"I told you that's bullshit," Charles yelled.

"I heard what you said, but what you meant is that we're not good enough. The Stokes are just the nigger side of the family."

They advanced on each other, but John was already up and around the desk between them. "Sit down," he yelled, "and I mean both of you."

They sat in the chairs that faced John's desk, still glaring at each other. John leaned against the front edge of the desk. "Both of you talk to me, not to each other. I'm the one in the dark. We're going to start with you, Leander. Who is too close in this family? And don't talk to me in riddles."

He didn't hesitate this time. "The rumor is that you and mama—" His voice broke.

John was stunned. He looked at Charles, then back to Leander. They both had their heads down again. He had better go slowly here. What was that Leander had said about not being good enough?

"I think you know that your mother is above that sort of behavior." John looked at him, refusing to speak again until the boy looked up.

"Yes sir, I do." He looked John in the eyes. "But everybody has their weak moments."

"That's right, but I'm telling you point blank the rumor is wrong. I love your mother like I loved my sisters, not in a sexual way. I would never do anything to hurt my wife, either."

"It's not the rumor that bothered him," Charles said. "It's what I said."

"You don't know what's bothering me, so don't go putting words in my mouth."

"I just meant—"

"You may think you're better than me because you're white, but I know who I am."

"Hold it right there," John said. "What's he talking about, Charles? What did you say?"

"I was just trying to show him how dumb the people are who are spreading that rumor, and I said that Aunt Ranetta knows how things work."

"You said she knows *her place*. That's what you said. And I know what you meant by that. The rumor can't be true because my mama isn't good enough for your daddy."

"I didn't mean any such thing. Who's putting words in whose mouth now?"

"What did you mean, son?" John asked.

"I was just saying that Aunt Ranetta knows that white people and black people aren't supposed to be together that way. If she wants to be with a man, she'll pick a black man. What's wrong with that?"

"Nothing's wrong with her wanting to be with a black man if that's who she loves," John said. "But what if she loves a white man and he loves her? What's wrong with that? They're still two people in love, aren't they?"

"Other people won't have it," Charles said. "That's what's wrong with it. Their house would be burned and they'd be killed." Charles' tone was quiet. He wasn't arguing, but stating what they all knew was the truth. "We can't even go to school together, Leander. I don't like that, but it's the way things are. I don't see you trying to come to my school, so I guess you know your place, too. Don't you?"

"What choice do I have?" Leander asked. He was calmer now, but his voice was edged with bitterness.

John looked at the two boys he loved so much and his heart ached for them. They had been sheltered from society this long by their wealth and by their isolation in the countryside. John saw for the first time that he could no longer keep them from the world.

"Listen to me, boys. The Stokes and the Warrens are one family in my sight. That's my choice. Corey was my brother, Ranetta is my sister, and since Corey is gone, Leander is my son. That's the way I choose for it to be. I want you two to be brothers, but I can't force you to think that way. I believe you do, though, and I can encourage you. That's my choice, and if the rest of the world doesn't like it, they'll have to do whatever they're able to do with me. But they better expect a fight if they think they're going to burn me out or kill me or mine."

"You are my brother, Leander," Charles said. "I'm sorry I offended you."

Leander stood. "I just need some time to myself. I—"

Charles stood and put his arms around him. The two hugged each other and cried. John thought of Corey on his deathbed years ago. He remembered how the words he wanted to say had failed him and how he had felt when finally he had quit talking and had simply embraced his friend. John smiled at the boys—wise beyond their years.

     ß   ß   ß   ß

When Harry left Sanctuary early in 1904, he was grateful to his father for two things. First, the old man had forced him to save most of what he had paid him over a seven-year period. Second, half of that money was in an account that Harry could access without John's signature.

There was a lot he could do with four thousand dollars, but the first order of business was to have a little fun. He figured that after a dozen years in a place like Sanctuary, he deserved it.

The hotel at Fernandina where they had spent several summers was for families and old folks, but he had always wanted to go to Jacksonville from there. It was the closest thing to a city in the area, and Harry wanted to buy an automobile. He wanted to be in a city and drive up to a dance hall with the best-looking woman in town and a backseat full of liquor.

Harry was an instant hit with the smart set in Jacksonville. He was a big, good-looking fellow with a wavy brown pompadour and a million-dollar smile. His suits were right, the new Peerless was right, the free-flowing booze was right, the all-night parties in town and at the beach were right, and the money was definitely right.

It only took Harry's new friends six months to help him go through the four thousand dollars. He didn't realize his financial condition until a day in mid-October when he couldn't square the account at the end of his daily poker game. He didn't have the cash and Benson, good sport that he was, had to refuse Harry's bad check.

When Harry threw a fit, it was Benson's sad duty to inform him, in front of the others, that his last two checks had bounced and that he foresaw a similar fate for this one. Would Harry mind terribly, Benson wanted to know, straightening out this whole mess and paying the one hundred and fifty dollars he owed the poker bank?

Harry informed Benson that when he finished with those bastards at First National, he would not only have his "yard and a half," but also a bank officer's head on a silver platter. By the time they finished with Harry at First National, he figured that his best option was to borrow some money from his latest flame and make himself scarce. Unfortunately for him, she made it very loud and very clear that he had wormed the last cent from her he was ever going to see.

There was no question in Harry's mind as to his next stop. All he had to figure out was how he was going to get the other four thousand that his father had tied up with his signature. He would work that out before he arrived in Waycross. Ray Black would help him.

One week later, Harry sat in Ned Worthington's office in Homerville, studying the tops of his dirty shoes. It was late, and the bank was closed for the day. Ned stood with his back to Harry and poured two whiskeys.

"I hate to say it, because he's a friend of mine, but Ray Black can be a real prick when he wants to be."

"Isn't there something I can do, Mr. Worthington? I mean, it is my money."

"There's nothing you can do to get to that money without your old man's signature, but there's something I can do to help you out." Ned smiled and handed Harry his drink. "Tell me, Harry, what do you intend to do with this money?"

"I moved out of Sanctuary, and I need a place to stay. I intend to go into the timber business for myself."

"I see," Ned said. "What have you been doing since you left home?"

"I spent some time in Jacksonville. A man's got to see a little of the world before he settles into the old grind."

"And did you have a good time there?"

"Extremely good. You might say I left them laughing," Harry said smugly.

"Tell me about your business venture, Harry. If I like what I hear, I'll put up four thousand dollars. We'll call the money with Ray Black's bank my collateral. How about that?"

"Sit back and relax, Ned. You're going to like what you're about to hear."

§   §   §   §

Harry looked up from the hub of the wagon wheel he had been tightening. "What do you want?"

"I want you to come back home," John said. "I guess I was wrong about the way I brought you along in the business. Let's try to work this out, Harry."

"It's a little late for that, isn't it? Now that I'm running my own out-fit, I don't think it's likely that I'm going back under your thumb."

"I'm not talking about that. I'm willing to let you run part—"

"You don't understand, do you? Look around. I have a business. I don't need to run part of anything. I'm running all of this."

"You're doing business with the wrong man, son. You can't trust Ned. He's been out to get me for forty years now and you're—"

"It always comes back to you, doesn't it? The whole world revolves around the great John Warren! If Ned goes into business with me, it can't be because I might be a good bet to make money. It's got to be a way to get at you. Is that it?"

John looked intently at Harry. "That's it. He's using you to get at me."

"Get off this property," Harry scowled, and he went back to work at the hub.

"Watch the company's debt load, Harry. He's going to get you so far into debt that—"

"Are you deaf, old man? I told you to get in the saddle and get your ass off my property. I mean now!" Before Harry could move, John pinned him to the wagon. Harry struggled for a moment, but his father was too strong.

"Listen to me, Harry. You run with the wrong dogs long enough and you end up with fleas. But you'll always be my son, and I'll always have you back. Don't let your pride or Ned Worthington tell you any different. It's never too late to come back to me, son."

John let him go and got back on his horse to leave. "Your mother wants to see you more than anything else in this world, Harry. I'm going to be out of town until Sunday. Why don't you come out to Sanctuary and surprise her?" He rode off before Harry could reply.

*   *   *   *

Ned held his glass up to Harry's. "Here's to Warren and Worthington Timber Company," he said. "Long may confusion reign among our enemies."

The Jug was deserted now—only the two of them and the bartender remained. Harry drained his seventh bourbon in the past three hours and slammed the glass to the table. "Damned right." He tried to focus Ned's face. "Who are our enemies?"

Ned smiled and sipped his drink. "Anyone who dares to compete with us."

Harry poured himself another drink. "You got that right. Let's start with my old man. Let's run him out of business first. Let that old son of a bitch work for me for a while. See how he likes that."

Ned took a long thoughtful pull on his cigar. "I'm afraid that won't be possible. He's a little too powerful for us—too many assets."

Harry leaned forward on the table. "There ain't no horse that can't be rode, ain't no cowboy that can't be thrown." He leaned back and took a drag from his cigar, smiling broadly.

"What do you mean?" Ned asked.

"I mean I've thought it through, and I know how we're going to run everybody out of business, my old man included. It'll take a little time and a lot of money, but we can damned sure do it."

Ned smiled again. "I don't know how, but if you say so I believe it. That's why I jumped at the opportunity to be your partner."

Over the next three months Harry put together the saw mill operation to the northeast of Homerville. At first he tried to include Ned in the decisions, but Ned's response was always the same. "You're the expert, Harry. I know the bookkeeping side, so I'll take care of that, but running things and making deals is what you do best. I trust you, partner." Ned's only advice was that when it came to equipment, Harry should buy the best.

"You have to spend money to make money," Harry agreed. His strategy to run the small time saw mills out of business was to deprive them of work by running the price up that they paid for timber by out-bidding them at every opportunity. He expanded his operation rapidly adding new equipment each month until Warren and Worthington Timber operated five sawmills in various locations in two counties.

On the rare occasion that their debt and margin of profit entered Harry's mind, Ned assured him that he was on the right course. "Old Lester McCall threw in the towel yesterday," Ned informed Harry. "He's the third wildcatter to go under in the last eighteen months and guess who repossessed his equipment."

"I know McCall's operation," Harry laughed. "You might as well let that pile of junk sit out in the woods and rust."

"That's exactly what I intend to do. A few saw mill carcasses here and there might remind people what they get when they screw around with us."

§   §   §   §

Ned heard the door to his office close and when he looked up, John was closing the blinds at the window that looked out onto the banking floor. Ned pulled open a desk drawer to make his revolver accessible.

"What the hell are you doing in my office?" He asked. "You know you're not welcome here."

John walked to the desk, and Ned eased his right hand into the drawer next to the gun. John settled into the wingback chair in front of the desk.

"I'm here to make you a business proposition, Ned. You like to make money, don't you?"

"I don't deal with the devil, Warren. He'll find a way to get his pound of flesh every time."

John smiled. "I'm sure you know what you're talking about when it comes to the devil, but you're going to listen anyway."

"What makes you think that?"

"If I have to get up and whip your ass, I'm going to make you eat that gun you've got your hand on. Then, when you've had enough, you'll listen. I've got all day, and I'll beat you until all you can do is listen."

Ned leaned back in his chair and folded his hands in his lap. "I just had the office cleaned, and I'd hate to get blood on the rug. My answer to your proposition is no. Now go ahead and tell me all about it."

"I want to buy you out of Warren and Worthington Timber, and I want you to stay away from Harry."

Ned laughed. "All right, I listened. You have my answer. Now get out."

"How much do you want?"

"I want you to get the hell out of my office."

"Two hundred thousand dollars."

"Screw you. Get out of here."

John's face reddened. "Five hundred thousand."

"You can't buy your boy back. I've got him in my hip pocket, and he doesn't even know it."

"A million dollars. Come on, Worthington, you can't get him deep enough in debt to screw me out of that much."

"Well, I'll give it the old college try. That's all I can do."

"Name your price."

Ned shook his head in disgust. "I don't understand how you've done so well financially, because you're pretty damned stupid if you think that Warren and Worthington Timber has anything to do with money. Our relationship has never been about money."

"What's it been about, Ned? Tell me that. I tried to do right by you when I first came to Magnolia, but you chose to be my enemy. Why?"

"Maybe it had something to do with that threat you made to kill me if I deserted from the army. Did I take that wrong?"

"We were kids in the middle of a war. We said and did a lot of things we regretted later."

Ned stood and walked to the door. "Maybe you did, but I didn't. The plain truth is that I never have liked you. Never will." Ned opened the door and walked out into the bank with John close behind.

"You're turning Harry against me, and I want it to stop. What's it going to take?"

"Are you threatening me, Mr. Warren?" Ned asked loudly. The bank employees and several customers turned toward them and stared. "I'm in business with your son, but that's no reason to threaten my life. Now if you don't leave these premises immediately, I'll call for the sheriff."

John looked around the bank and saw the fear on everyone's faces. "Did anyone hear me threaten Mr. Worthington?"

Two ladies backed out the door and onto the boardwalk and fled. The employees tried to look busy. John looked back at Ned.

"Are you going to leave peaceably, Warren?"

John leaned toward him. "This isn't over." He strode from the bank.

"If something happens to me, these good people will know who is responsible," Ned called after him. He turned to the people in the bank. "Please excuse me, but I'm shaken by Mr. Warren's threats of violence. I'll go to my office and try to regain my composure."

As soon as Ned closed the office door behind him, he fell back against it laughing softly. What a great turn of events! Warren had better not be so sure that he couldn't run the tab up over a million dollars. Harry was so gullible that he would sign any piece of paper that Ned shoved in front of him. He only needed one huge project for Harry to mishandle in order to cap off all the little disasters he had caused since they had started their company.

He knew that he would have to be patient. It would take time to get Harry as deeply into debt as he intended to, but he enjoyed seeing John worry. He was in no hurry.

      *   *   *   *

The year 1911 rewarded Ned's patience. The Hebard Cypress Company of Pennsylvania had been in operation in the forests of South Georgia for several years with an extensive timber and sawmill operation. When the company announced its acquisition of over four hundred thousand acres of the Okefenokee Swamp and intent to harvest the cypress and pine from it, Ned knew he had his project. Such a job had broken Ben Taylor years ago. What a shock it was going to be for Harry when he realized that he alone was responsible for the debt of Warren and Worthington Timber.

Throughout the year the Hebard family and their investors occupied themselves with preparations to invade the Okefenokee. An elaborate survey was completed. At a cost exceeding one million dollars, construction began on a narrow gauge railroad into the heart of the great swamp and on a huge sawmill operation near Waycross. The Hebard's interest was in the high yield cypress trees, so they let out bids for other companies to harvest the yellow pine and extract turpentine in areas that were to be cut years later.

The day after Harry Warren won and signed the first contract with the Hebards to harvest pine trees along the railroad right of way he received a note from his mother. It was an invitation to dinner at Sanctuary to celebrate Charles' fall enrollment at the Georgia Institute of Technology and the acceptance of Leander Stokes at Oxford in England. Harry readily agreed to come. He couldn't wait to see what his father would say about his success with the Hebards.

Kathleen was happier than she had been at any time since Harry had left Sanctuary. Her whole family, Ranetta's family and Gray were all together again.

Harry looked for an opening to announce his successful bid with the Hebards, but with the focus on Charles and Leander he feared that his news would fall flat. Typical, he thought. He had something significant to tell, and they weren't even going to give him a chance with all this small talk. It served them right. Let them find out from someone else. The evening passed quickly for everyone except Harry. When he finally made his excuses about needing to go, John walked Harry out to his automobile.

"Aren't the roads around here still pretty rough for this thing?" John asked.

"Come on into the twentieth century, Pop," Harry grinned. "It won't hurt."

"I think I'll wait a little while longer. I wanted to thank you for coming, Harry. It meant a lot to Charles to have you here, and to your mother and me."

"No problem."

"How's your business going?"

Harry studied his father's expression for a moment. "You know about my bid with the Hebards, don't you?"

"Yes, I do."

"I expected you to bid against me. Why didn't you?"

John looked back toward the house. "I have more work than I can say grace over. Besides, I helped a fellow go broke in that swamp one time."

"We ain't going broke this time. The railroad is the way to go—not trying to drain something that big."

"I agree," John said. "Harry, a good businessman always has a fall-back position. He never really expects to have to go there, but if things turn sour, the smart ones always know what they're going to do to save some of what they have. They won't lose it all on any one venture."

"Sounds pretty chicken shit to me," Harry said. "No guts, no glory."

"Is that your motto, son?"

"That's it."

"Then I'm your fall-back position. If things go wrong on this contract with the Hebards, I want you to talk to me. Nobody has to know but us."

Harry climbed into the car. "Nothing's going wrong with the Hebards."

John walked around and shut the door for Harry. "Nothing had better go wrong, Harry. The talk is that this job is make it or break it for Warren and Worthington."

"Says who?"

"People who are in a position to know, son. You didn't so much bid that job as you bought it."

"Ned and I just might have an angle that you know nothing about. Our pockets may be a little deeper than you figure, too."

John backed away from the car a step. "Ned taught me a lot of what I know about fall-back positions. He knows what his looks like, and you're not in the picture. I have a business proposition for you when you're in a position to consider it. I won't humiliate you if you need to come to me."

"Don't hold your breath," Harry said. He started the Peerless and drove away.

*   *   *   *

The old black gentleman patiently waited outside John's office at the sawmill. He was tall and slender, and he moved with the deliberate grace and ease of one who had learned the old lesson that life would move at its own pace, regardless of what he did.

John stepped out into the morning sun and strode over to him. "Yes, sir. What can I do for you?"

He took off his old, sweat-stained felt hat and grinned. "You don't recollect who I am, do you, Mr. John?"

John looked at him carefully, then smiled. "I sure do, George Bryant, but I guess it's been twenty years since I've seen you." John offered his hand.

"More like thirty," George said. "I was down in the back, and I had to miss Corey's funeral, or I'd a seen you there."

"What are you doing with yourself these days?"

"Not too much. I still does a little for Mr. Ben, but you know Magnolia done dried up and blowed away."

"Come on in the office over here, George. I've got a fan going, and we can get a little relief from this heat."

"I'm much obliged, but I need to say my piece and then get on back. Mr. Ben wants to know if you could be persuaded to come have the noon meal with him tomorrow."

John was caught off guard by the invitation. He didn't think that Ben Taylor ever wanted to see him again.

"I have a good bit to do tomorrow, George. He didn't say if any other day would be just as good, did he?"

"No, sir. Say to tell you if tomorrow ain't no good not to worry with it. Truth of it is, though, he ain't got that many tomorrows."

"You tell him I'll be there, George."

"Yes, sir. I'll do that. Thank you, Mr. John."

He watched George mount Ben's buggy. It was the same one he had cleaned and polished over forty years earlier.

The next day John left Sanctuary on horseback a full hour before he needed to. As he rode, old memories caught up to him, and he wondered how he could be in his sixties so suddenly. This was how he had come into Magnolia the first time. There was the road he had taken to Gray's place so many times. He remembered the wild ride out there the night he went to tell Gray that Kath had accepted his proposal of marriage. He remembered the terrifying ride back into Magnolia the night the church bells signaled the death of Mac McLendon. If Kathleen were right and Ben had asked him to lunch in order to settle something of the past, John knew that he would be in tune with that conversation by the time he arrived in Magnolia.

One old memory fit another, and he thought of Ben, then the swamp venture, Jennifer Pace, his dream of the old Indians. He hadn't thought of that for years. Funny, they seemed like a memory now and not just a dream. Which were memories and which were dreams? Year by year, it was getting harder to tell.

John rounded the curve into Magnolia and stopped the horse. *My God, he thought. Where's the town? His old home should have been there, straight ahead. And beyond it, Doc William's home, and beyond that the Methodist church.*

Through the pines and the gallberry bushes and the wiregrass, he could just see the soft, crumbling foundations of some of those structures. This must be something like what Au Eve saw when she was the only one remaining, John thought. The crumbling remains of what had once been a whole world to her. He thought of Kathleen and Celia back at Sanctuary. "It isn't going to last," he said aloud. "It never does. This world is not our home."

He completed the curve and there ahead of him stood the only remaining piece of a substantial part of his life. The barn was weeds and charred wood. The beautiful yard with its multicolored flowerbeds that he and Wealthy loved so had gone to seed. The proud house was gray and feeble, part of its roof peeled away and several rooms ruined, lit by the noonday sun.

On the porch sat Ben Taylor, as feeble as his house, rocking and smoking a pipe. John lifted his hand in greeting, but Ben didn't acknowledge him. As John rode closer, Ben looked in his direction, uncrossed his bony legs and stood, reaching for the post at his left. John was shocked at his appearance. Ben's hair was thin and white and his face was scant skin over bones. His shoulders were stooped and John estimated that he carried no more than a hundred and thirty pounds on his six-foot frame. The upper half of his body shook with the effort of standing.

"Hello, John," he said cordially.

John couldn't answer until he cleared the lump in his throat. "Hello, Ben. Thank you for having me out." John dropped the horse's reins to let him graze. He stepped up on the porch and when Ben offered his hand, John shook it gently.

"Have a seat and rest a minute from your ride." Ben gestured to a rocker next to his. "You're not in a hurry to eat, are you?"

"No, sir." John said. "I'm in no hurry."

"What's that?" Ben cupped his hand at his left ear.

John raised his voice. "No, sir. No hurry."

"Good. Good. Have a seat. George Bryant's helping me out around here. You remember George, don't you—Stokes' brother-in-law?"

"Yes, I remember him."

"He's a good fellow. Can't cook worth a damn, but George is all right."

Ben fooled with his pipe for a while to get it refilled and tamped and lit again. He was so quiet and preoccupied that John thought the old man had forgotten that he was there. John looked at the remains of Magnolia, listening to the wind in the pine boughs high overhead.

"You know the advantage of being blind, John?" Ben said suddenly. "I can still see Magnolia. I can see everything the way I remember it, including you and me. I asked you to come out to Magnolia today because there's some things I want to clear up with you before I die." He hesitated a moment, as if to recall the starting point of a speech he'd rehearsed. "Did you know that I had found out about Wealthy's will before she passed on?"

"No sir. I had no idea."

"Well, I did, and I hit the ceiling. She and I had it out good, but she wouldn't budge an inch. My sister loved you like you were her own son, and I didn't understand that until years after she died. Did you feel that way about her?"

John felt the tightness in his throat again. "She was my mother," he said, "and I miss her still."

"Well—" Ben just nodded his head and smiled slightly. "You know, you and Stokes held that swamp deal together about six months longer than I expected. I knew when I sent the two of you around to Camp Cornelia that I had the two best foremen over there. My only mistake was in ignoring your warnings that the thing was coming apart—that and not working with you to salvage what we could. I was just too proud to think that a younger man could show me anything about business."

John was reminded of his relationship with Harry. "I was too hard on you, Ben. I didn't know much about mercy or compromise back then."

"Hell, I wouldn't have had any of that. I'd have thought that meant I was weak." The old man chuckled to himself and leaned back in his rocker for a minute's rest. After a while he sat forward and fumbled for his tobacco. He began to work on his pipe again.

"About ten or fifteen years ago, when Magnolia started going down, old Jedediah Polk used to have a lot of time on his hands, and he'd come over to visit. He was getting on in years, and the Baptists were content to let him finish out his time here. He and I would sit here, rocking, and we talked about everything in the world. Gray Hampton would come by sometimes, and we'd philosophize to the wee hours. Them two know that Bible, so I had to start studying it just to keep up with their conversation. You know I'd always let Wealthy drag me to church, but I didn't put much stock in it. Usually had my mind on business."

"I'm the same way, Ben. Kathleen does the dragging in my case, but I'm traveling on business a lot of Sundays."

"Well that's a habit you need to get out of, son. You're a good businessman. Look out at Magnolia and then figure out where you need to invest your time and your money. This life is awful temporary, but it has a way of fooling you. It has a way of looking permanent, don't it?"

"Yes, sir. It does."

"John, I—I guess I'm fumbling around here awful bad at what I want to say, but a lot of what Jedediah and Gray taught me just kind of sank in. I ain't going to be able to say it to you. I suppose you'll have to feel it more than hear it. My Bible is just inside the door there on a stand. Fetch it, will you?"

John got up and stepped inside the door.

"George reads it to me most every day now that my eyes are gone."

John sat back down and balanced the timeworn book on his knees.

"Turn it to Job, chapter nineteen, and start reading at verse twenty-one. You know, Job is the book that all of us turn to in our afflictions to try to make some sense of them."

"Here it is, Ben. *'Have pity upon me, have pity upon me, o ye my friends, for the hand of God hath touched me. Why do ye persecute me as God, and are not satisfied with my flesh? Oh that my words were now written! Oh that they were printed in a book! That they were graven with an iron pen and lead in the rock forever!*

For I know that my redeemer liveth and that he shall stand at the latter day upon the earth: And though after my skin worms destroy this body, yet in my flesh shall I see God.'"

"I know that my redeemer liveth and that he shall stand—" the old man repeated. "For a lot of years, John, I didn't know or care that my redeemer lives. I wouldn't have admitted that I needed redeeming from anything. Too proud...Too arrogant...Too busy. Turns out, those were the very things that I needed to be redeemed from. Now turn to Chapter forty-two and read verse ten."

John turned the pages. Funny how different the words seemed with the passage of so much time. The same ideas that Wealthy showed him in vain appeared clear and true and simple coming from old Ben, as if John had known the truth of them all his life.

"Looking back on my life, John, I'm shocked at how dishonest I was with people. Most of it was arrogance. I thought I knew best in every situation so I'd try to bully people in the direction I wanted them to go, and I'd tell them that it was for their own good. At times I was dishonest with some folks because I was worried about what other folks would think. That's a fool's game. We're all so changeable in what we think from one day to the next that it don't pay to worry about it."

Ben was quiet again. He puffed on his pipe.

John read, *"'And the Lord turned the captivity of Job when he prayed for his friends: also the Lord gave Job twice as much as he had before.'"*

"When he prayed for his friends," Ben said. Tears welled up in the old man's eyes. "Read about Job's friends sometime, John. They were proud, arrogant men who worried a lot about what other people thought. All the time that they were trying to help their friend, they were wounding him terribly."

Ben reached up and with a trembling hand wiped the tears from his eyes. "Could we have been friends one time, John? Now that I'm blind I see Magnolia as I think it was, but my memories and dreams have become hard to separate over the years. Maybe it wasn't that way at all."

"You can see fine, Ben. We depended on each other despite our faults. That's what friends do, you know."

The old man nodded and struggled to regain control of his emotions. "I've been praying for you, son, because Jedediah and Gray helped me see the need for redemption. It was offered to me, and I accepted it."

John nodded.

"You think about praying for your friends. It's not so much for their benefit as it is for your own good in the long haul. Maybe you'll even be restored from your plenty, like Job and I were restored from our losses."

XXIV

By the end of 1911, the Hebards' plans and the wise use of their investors' money began to pay off. Crews had spent the year girdling the massive cypress trees so that the trees had lost some of their weight and their resistance to the crosscut saw.

The track for the narrow-gauge railroad had progressed several miles into the Okefenokee, at some places on an elevated roadbed, at other places where the water was deep, on a low trestle several feet above the water.

Much of the timber cut in the early stages was used for cross ties and pilings, but as the year passed, more and more of the cypress was brought to the massive sawmill which had spawned the town of Hebardville near Waycross. The pine trees were processed at a smaller mill further into the swamp at a high place that became known as Hopkins.

In the early going, Warren and Worthington Timber was doing well with the pine harvest. The terrain was relatively high, the weather held, and the timber moved through the mill quickly due to the easy access to the railhead. All of that meant quick cash. Given his company's prior debt load and the nature of his contract with the Hebards, to Harry the cash was only a little less vital than air to breathe.

If only he had known seven years ago what he knew now about running a business, he wouldn't be in the mess he was in. The last round of notes that Harry renewed at the bank had staggered him, particularly when he considered the ones that were coming due in the next thirty days. There was no end to it.

Then there was the Hebard contract. Ned had insisted that they lowball it to ensure getting the business. He had even agreed to less than advantageous payment terms on the premise that they would be on this project for fifteen or twenty years.

"This is your way out of all that debt, Harry," Ned assured him. "This job is going to pay the bills and then a little for a long time to come. We can stay tough on the other work we bid, keep our prices up and really make a killing."

In June of 1912 Charles came home for the summer break from Georgia Tech. He was a hit with the young ladies of Homerville with his blond hair and blue eyes and his solid, slender frame of six feet one.

John was impressed with Charles' eagerness to work in the business that summer and pleased with his suggestions regarding the layout of the mill and its collateral businesses. Privately, the two of them had lengthy conversations far into the night on ways to keep the business lean, yet efficient. Publicly, John liked to say that after a year of college, his son had learned just enough engineering to make him dangerous.

Sanctuary was Celia's whole world. The family was thankful that she had not drifted permanently into the other world where she spent so much time. She helped her mother direct the maintenance of the household and the grounds. She preferred working with the gardeners to the cook or the maids, and whatever the season, there was much to be done in the gardens of Sanctuary.

Leander knew that Celia loved to work outdoors, so he sent her illustrations and designs of the formal gardens in London and the surrounding countryside. She and Charles spent hours together that summer, planning and sketching, then implementing sections of their grand design for the grounds. Kathleen loved to sit in the library with them, doing needlework and listening to them work together, sometimes giving her ideas or approval to their work. It was a good summer, a hopeful summer for the family, marred only by the absence of Harry.

In late August Charles moved back to Atlanta for the fall quarter at Tech, and all of Sanctuary and the mill seemed less alive. John found himself looking for Charles to ask his advice on some matter before he could remember that he was gone.

Harry had seen Charles only once during the summer when his brother had come to the job site in the swamp. Harry was relieved. He didn't really have the time or the desire that summer to show some college boy how to run a timber business. He was having enough problems as it was, topped off in mid-August by an ominous telegram from the Hebard Company.

Urgent we meet. Be at Hopkins mill site Saturday, 14 August 1912 at 1 p.m. sharp.

George Hopkins, the general superintendent the village had been named for, had signed the summons.

To make matters worse, as of noon Ned had failed to come as he had promised Harry he would. He watched nervously at a few minutes before one as the Hebard men filed back to the dining hall. There was still no sign of Ned. Precisely at one o'clock a man emerged and motioned him in. All the top men of the Hebard Company were there seated on one side of a table.

"What is the next order of business, gentlemen?" The speaker was a well-groomed, distinguished man about sixty years old who spoke with a hard, but not unpleasant, northern accent.

Mr. Hopkins looked solemnly at Harry as he approached the table. "Warren and Worthington, contract timber cutting, Mr. Hebard."

The older gentleman looked up at Harry. "Ah, yes. The younger Mr. Warren." He took a file folder from one of the other five men seated at the table and studied its contents.

Mr. Hopkins indicated a chair across the table from him. "Have a seat, Harry."

They all sat quietly as Mr. Hebard studied the file. Harry watched him and grew more anxious each time the man's brow furrowed or a frown appeared on his face. Finally Mr. Hebard looked at Hopkins. "Is this the only contract with this company, George?"

"Yes, sir."

"No addenda?"

"No, sir."

"All right. You may proceed."

"Where's Mr. Worthington, Harry?" Hopkins asked.

"He was detained in Homerville at the last hour," Harry lied. "I believe that there was a grave illness in his immediate family."

"It's disappointing that he couldn't be here," Hopkins said. "I want you to convey that message to him. And, of course, give him our sympathy for the grave illness in his family." His tone of voice was most unsympathetic.

"I'll be sure to do that, sir."

"Let me come straight to the point," Hopkins said. He gestured to a man on his left, and the man pushed a piece of paper across the table to Harry. "This is our notice to your company that unless we see substantial progress in the next thirty days, we're going to exercise our right, per our contract, to replace Warren and Worthington as a subcontractor on this project."

Harry was unprepared. He had thought that this was going to be a shouting match with Hopkins and some of his foremen. Lose the contract? It couldn't be that bad.

"Replace us? You can't do that. What have we done?"

"It's what you haven't done, Harry. I catch more complaints from my foremen about your outfit than about any other three companies out here. I don't intend to put up with it."

"We've had our share of problems, but it's been things that nobody could have foreseen. We've done the best we can under the circumstances. What are they complaining about?"

"This meeting is to advise you in writing that we're putting your company on probation for thirty days. We're not here to discuss the details. The problems are all documented in your notice there. You read them over and then you and the foremen and I will meet tomorrow and get squared away. If you improve your performance over the next thirty—"

"I don't think we need to improve as much as your foremen need to get with it. My men tell me that they can't get any cooperation out of them. What are you going to do about that?"

Before Hopkins could reply, Mr. Hebard spoke up. "Son, we have about another eight hours of work to get to today, so we're going to have to wrap this up with you. I've listened patiently while you've sat here making your excuses for poor performance and your partner's absence. Now my patience is gone." He paused a moment, his steel gray eyes fixed on Harry, his face placid but his jaw set firmly. "I've been through years of meticulous planning on this project. I've sought out the best timber men in the world to work for me. I've put millions of dollars at risk for my own family and for other investors to take on this challenge. I really don't care to sit here and listen to how tough your circumstances are."

Hebard never raised his voice. His tone was business-like and factual, without a trace of sarcasm or doubt – nothing to give another man a handhold for rebuttal. Harry nodded meekly.

"When you took on this job, you should've anticipated some tough times. Hell, I've never done a job when reality matched the plans exactly. Now, you have a list of our complaints. Study it, talk to your people about it, and fire a few men if you have to. Then get with Mr. Hopkins tomorrow morning. I want to wish you the best over the next thirty days, because it's in my best interests that you turn things around, but let me warn you about something." With his elbow on the table, he pointed his finger at Harry. "Nobody short of God is going to hold this project back, and I already know what I'm going to do to catch up if I have to fire you." Mr. Hebard stood and extended his hand to Harry. "Thank you for meeting with us, Mr. Warren."

Harry nodded feebly and trudged out into the hot afternoon. The sun burned him like the humiliation he had endured from Mr. Hebard. He was sick to his stomach, and he wanted desperately to be alone.

The next morning Harry and his foremen met with Hopkins and his superintendents. The meeting was tense and loud, consisting primarily of charges and countercharges of incompetence and laziness. After two hours of arguing, Mr. Hopkins called a halt to the meeting. He summarized the Hebard Company's expectations of Warren and Worthington, warned his men to cooperate with Harry's men, and dismissed both groups.

"Them sons of bitches are bluffing, boss," one of Harry's men said as they left. "Ain't nobody else able to cut as much cordage as us, and can't nobody cut what they're saying we have to do to catch up."

"I'm going to talk to Ned," Harry said. "We're going to have to put on another crew. If you'd heard Mr. Hebard yesterday, you'd know that this is no bluff. You two have to work with their foremen, and you have to make peace with them. Push our men harder. We have to show Hopkins some improvement right away." Harry got into his Peerless and started it. "I'm counting on you boys to pull us out of this. I should be back here with help in two or three days."

The foremen stood watching him drive away.

"We're working for a real pistol there. You know it?" One said.

"That kid's about to lose his butt," said the other.

"Well, if he's counting on me to pull him out, he can go ahead and kiss it good-by."

When Harry arrived in Homerville that night, he was dirty, tired, and a little drunk. His only desire was to fall into bed, until he saw the light on at the bank.

"Son of a bitch can't help me out with the Hebards, 'cause he's too busy counting his money."

Harry pulled up next to the bank, staggered up to the side entrance, and slapped on the door with the palm of his hand. The street was deserted. "Let me in, you bastard, and quit making up those fake notes. Worthington! Open this damned door!"

Harry heard the bolt click as the door was unlocked, and he snatched it open. Ned stood in the entry with his pistol aimed at Harry's head.

"You wouldn't kill the golden goose, would you, Ned?"

"Of course not, Harry. But you never know when it might be the wolf at the door."

Harry pushed by Ned and walked into his office. Ned locked the door and followed him. Harry poured himself a drink. "Where were you today?" He snapped.

"Have a drink, Harry." Ned laid his pistol on the desk and leaned back in his chair. "How about pouring me one while you're at it?"

Harry threw back his drink, poured himself another one, and sat down. "Pour your own drink. I asked you a question, and I want an answer."

Ned folded his arms and smiled. "I was here, Harry. I've put in a lot of hours yesterday and today, trying to restructure your debt. See these promissory notes?" Ned leaned forward and picked up several pieces of paper. "That's why I'm down here at this late hour. I'm doing all I can to keep you afloat."

"So you can pile more debt on the heap? The name of the company is Warren and Worthington, you know. Aren't you trying to restructure our debt? Aren't you trying to keep us afloat?"

"Harry, it's late, and you're upset. Why don't we both get a good night's sleep, and we can take this up tomorrow. I want to hear all about the meeting with Hopkins."

"The meeting was with Hopkins and Hebard, and I can sum up the damned meeting," Harry yelled. "In thirty days we're off the job. That was the meeting! There was five of them and just me to face 'em. They didn't like—"

"I should've known you couldn't handle a little pressure. You let those bastards push you around and now you've lost the only job that could keep this company going."

"I've done the best I could under the circumstances. No thanks to you, I've managed to keep this business going for seven years."

Ned laughed and shook his head. "No thanks to me? What a fool you are. If I hadn't pumped money into this bottomless pit for all those years, how long do you think you'd have held on? We're at the end of the road, kid. If you've lost the Hebard job, I have no more use for you. I'm calling your loans, and I'm going to skin you and your old man good."

Harry lurched up on the edge of the leather chair near the desk. "What do you mean? My old man's got nothing to do with this. If you call the loans, it's your problem and mine, not his."

Ned turned to the credenza and poured himself a drink. He was smiling. "You damned fool," he said, turning back to Harry with his drink. "The first few notes for Warren and Worthington have both of our signatures, but those are the ones I've applied all the payments to. I guess I have about a thousand tied up in the business now." He sipped his whiskey and watched Harry's face. Harry's ruddy complexion paled.

"You can't do this, Ned. We're partners."

Ned laughed. "You think I can't? Go ahead, boy. Take a guess at how bad I've screwed you."

Harry closed his eyes and shook his head slowly, fighting the tears.

"No?" Ned said. "How about one hundred thousand?" He laughed. "No. That wouldn't even be close. Two hundred fifty thousand?"

Harry opened his eyes, and the tears flowed down his cheeks.

"Still too low," Ned said in a deadly serious tone. It was the next best thing to doing this to John Warren.

"You can ruin me, but you can't touch my father," Harry said.

"You keep right on underestimating me, boy. Your old man isn't going to let you and me drag the Warren name through the mud, but if he doesn't ante up somewhere between a half million and a million dollars, that's exactly what we're going to do."

"You're out of your mind. The old man isn't going to pay you that kind of money just to keep me out of bankruptcy."

Ned stared at Harry. "You may not care what other people think of your name, but I'm willing to bet this bank that John Warren does, and I've known him longer and better than you ever will."

"You're not getting away with this," Harry said.

"We'll see about that," Ned replied.

As he turned his drink up, Harry reached across the desk and picked up Ned's pistol. Ned slowly lowered his glass. "You planning to use that on you or on me?"

"Looks like you underestimate me, Ned. I'm not the suicidal type. Can't stand pain." Harry gathered up the promissory notes from the desk, stuffing them into his coat pockets.

"They're going to hang you, boy. It won't take a bank auditor thirty minutes to figure out what's missing, and then you'll be the obvious suspect. Put the gun down, and we'll work this out."

"How will we do that? You'll agree to give up a million dollars? That's not likely. Maybe I'm crazy, but I think a million dollars is worth killing for."

Harry raised the gun to Ned's forehead. Ned pushed his chair back into the corner and threw his arms up to shield himself. Harry leaned forward to get closer, and being careful to avoid Ned's arms, he put the pistol barrel close to his right temple and pulled the trigger.

*   *   *   *

John first suspected that something wasn't right about the investigation of Ned's death after the first two weeks. He chided himself for taking that long. What else should he have expected with J.C. Cooper as sheriff? He promptly and discreetly hired his own investigator and met him at a Jacksonville hotel bar. They sat at a secluded table with drinks between them.

"Be specific about the sheriff's investigation, Mr. Warren. What is it that you mistrust?"

"There's nothing that I do trust about J.C. Cooper. I guess the main thing that bothers me is that everything is too quiet. We're a small community and everyone talks. But you don't hear much about the investigation into Ned's death. I think that the sheriff and Ned's family are out to pin this death on my son."

The detective steepled his fingers in front of his round face. He looked too young to have much experience, but he had come highly recommended by John's attorney, Harris Teeter.

"From what you've told me, you and Harry ought to be prime suspects, yet you haven't been questioned by Sheriff Cooper?"

"Cooper has been after Harry hot and heavy, but he hasn't contacted me at all. What do you make of it?"

"Could be that it's conclusively suicide and there's no reason to look further. But if that's the case why don't they just say so and why do they continue to question Harry? Could be that your sheriff is ignorant of procedure. Doesn't know how to conduct an investigation or bring things to a head." He hesitated and stared blankly across the room.

"You're holding back," John said. "What's the next option?"

The investigator took a drink, looking at John intently. "Have you had any contact from blackmailers?"

"No," John said.

"Could be that your son did kill Worthington and somebody is going to make you pay to keep it hushed up. Hope for the best, but expect the worst. That's my motto," the man said. "I'll report to you weekly."

John stayed patient that week, but when his investigator's first report didn't produce much information, he decided to call on J.C. Cooper. When John entered the office at the courthouse, the sheriff was reared back in his chair with his boots propped on the desk. He cut a piece of chewing tobacco from a plug and popped it into his mouth.

"Aren't you going to offer me a seat, J.C.?"

He gestured toward the chair in front of his desk and wallowed the chew around in his mouth. "Sheriff Cooper to you," he muttered.

John sat and crossed his legs, resting one arm on the desk. "I suppose you know why I'm here."

J.C. stared at him a moment. "Nope. Don't know any such a thing."

"I want to know what you're turning up on Ned."

The sheriff leaned to his left and spit. He righted himself and looked at John. "He's dead."

John grabbed the bottom of J.C.'s boot and pushed. He went crashing backwards in the chair and by the time he scrambled to his knees, John had him by the front of his shirt.

"I'm a taxpayer, and I'm not getting the respect I think I deserve from a public servant. You do realize that you're a servant, don't you?"

"You're in big trouble, Warren. You can't attack a county sheriff and get away with it."

"Unless somebody walks in that door, it's going to be your word against mine. You're going to have a better case against me if you don't start talking, though, because I'm going to mess your face up pretty bad."

"Hold it," J.C. yelled. "Ned shot himself and there's no doubt about it. That's why I ain't pushing things."

John hauled him to his feet and picked up the chair.

"Why do you keep after Harry, then?"

"Just trying to be sure I ain't overlooked nothing. He's the most likely suspect if it was a murder, wouldn't you say?"

"When does the district attorney intend to lay the matter to rest?"

"I reckon you'll have to take that up with him. I've made my report."

"I intend to do just that, and they had better not tell me they're waiting on any paperwork from you."

Before John could make the trip to Waycross, he received the second report from his investigator and there didn't seem to be any point in seeing the district attorney. He needed to see Harry.

At dusk John rode into the mill yard at Warren and Worthington Timber and tied the horse's reins to a post outside the office. Seeing no one around, he walked to the office and rapped at the door.

"Anybody in there?" He heard something crash to the floor inside. "Harry, are you all right?" John hesitated, then made up his mind, reared back, and smashed the door open. A shaft of fading light from the doorway fell on Harry as he stood from behind his desk. He wiped at his wet shirt and looked up at his father. "Thought you were one of them." He grinned sheepishly.

"One of who?" John walked to the desk, frowning at Harry's obvious drunkenness.

"Sheriff or his deputy. Damned Roger Pace and his sister won't let up. Keeps them on my ass, questioning me every other day."

"If it's driving you to drink, maybe they have good reason to be after you."

Harry stopped his futile attempt to groom himself and looked at John. "My own father thinks I'm a murderer? That's a hell of a note."

John took Harry by the arm and led him toward the door.

"What are you doing? Let me go."

"Come out in the yard. There's something I want to show you."

"Let me go," Harry yelled, but John already had him down the steps. He pushed him across the yard, and Harry fell. John picked him up, half dragging his son and shoved him into the water trough. He pushed Harry under. When John pulled him back up for air, Harry sputtered and yelled. "Cut it out. What the hell do you think—"

John held him under this time until Harry struggled hard.

"Going to drown me. Stop. Please."

John shoved him under again and Harry continued to fight until John brought him up again.

"Are you ready to talk sense to me?"

"Yes sir." Harry coughed and water ran from his mouth and his nose. He gasped for air. "I'm all right now. No more water."

John stepped back and Harry sat up in the trough, pushing his hair back out of his eyes and coughing to clear his lungs.

"Start talking. I want you to tell me what happened between you and Ned."

Harry glared at John. "You know what happened. He took me for a ride in our little business venture."

"Is that why you killed him? Over money?"

"Killed him? I didn't kill him. He shot himself."

John backhanded Harry. He recoiled and jumped up in the trough with his fists clenched.

"Come on," John yelled. "Get out of there and let me teach you a lesson. I'm fed up with your bullshit, Harry."

Harry stood there breathing heavily, staring at his father, his fists loosening.

"That's what I thought," John said. "You're a murderer and a coward." John walked to the steps of the office and sat down. Harry climbed out of the trough.

"What do you care if I did kill him? The man was your enemy. Looks like you'd be glad to be rid of him."

"We were enemies because Ned chose it to be that way. My grievances with him have been over things he did to people I care about. He usually did those things to get at me. But all that's beside the point, son. I'm concerned about you, not Ned."

Harry crossed the yard to his father, but stood so he didn't have to look him in the eyes. "You don't have to worry about me. They can't prove a thing."

John's voice was quiet, weary. "Listen to yourself. You've killed a man, and all you're concerned about is not getting caught."

Harry whirled around. "Why do you keep saying that I killed him? How do you know? You weren't there when he died."

"I've had it investigated. My man has been more thorough than the sheriff has, and everything he's shown me says you killed Ned. You were probably drunk when you did it, but you pulled the trigger."

"So what are you going to do with your information? Are you planning to have me hanged?"

John stood. Tears welled up in his eyes. "No. I'm going to sacrifice my integrity for you. I'm going to protect you from the law of men, Harry, but I don't know how to save your soul." John wept.

*   *   *   *

Two days later John stood in a formal parlor waiting for Jennifer Worthington's maid to announce his presence. He had misgivings about this visit. Why had she summoned him? The sheriff's investigation was complete, and the district attorney had ruled Ned's death a suicide. In general people accepted it as fact and went on with their lives.

The room was elaborate but sterile when he compared it to his home. There were no family portraits, no items on tables or shelves that looked as if they had any sentimental value. The room looked impeccable to the point of being unused.

"Hello John. Thank you for coming."

He turned and Jennifer stood just inside the entrance. He hadn't seen her for years, but like the last time, he was shocked by the change in her appearance. Her face was lined and hardened by age beyond her years, her mouth turned down by too many ruined expectations, her eyes wrinkled to a squint by a vision that never saw hope.

Her once-golden hair, now streaked with gray, was pulled back severely against her thin skull. The soft, luminous skin that he recalled from their youth was pale parchment against the solid black of her mourning clothes.

"Could I offer you a drink?"

"No, thank you."

She dismissed the maid with a glance, and the girl slid the oak doors together as she left the room. Jennifer moved deliberately, her back erect, hands clasped in front of her, to a decanter at a side table.

"Please make yourself comfortable. I realize you're a busy man, but this won't take long."

As John sat, she poured a dark amber liquid into a cut glass tumbler, took a drink, and then refilled the glass. It occurred to him that this wasn't her first drink, though it was barely two in the afternoon. She turned and sat at one end of a velvet divan as far from him as she could get. She took another drink."I'm sorry about Ned," John said. "There was no love lost between us, but I never wished him dead."

She bowed her head as he spoke and her shoulders shook. He thought she was crying, but when she looked up there was a sneer that she used for a smile these days.

"You think I give a damn about Ned. That's rich. You know how he treated me, so let that bastard burn in hell with my father. I hope there's a special corner for wife-beaters." She drained the tumbler. "I owe your son a debt that I can never repay."

"What debt is that?" John asked.

She inhaled deeply and stared at John. He had the impression that she was savoring the moment.

"I think you know as well as I do that Harry murdered Ned." She watched his face.

He returned the steady gaze, willing himself to stay in control. Slowly he shook his head from side to side. "No, I don't know anything of the sort. I've talked to the sheriff and the district attorney, and they both tell me that the shot was self-inflicted."

She returned to the side table and poured another drink, her back to John. "You do realize that the sheriff depends on Roger and me for most of his income, don't you? The county pays him so pitifully that he really comes as a bargain."

John stood and walked halfway across the room to her. "It's general knowledge that you control J.C. What's your point?"

"I decided when the investigation would stop and what the sheriff would report to the public," she said. "Ned is a suicide because I say so." She turned to John as she drank. "Quit playing games with me. The sheriff kept bumping into a private investigator, and it's not too hard to figure out who employed him or what he found out. The boy is a damned murderer, John, and you know it."

"What do you want from me?"

She peered at him over the top of the glass and when she brought the tumbler away from her lips, the sneer was there.

"Let's see. What do I want from the all-powerful John Warren? Love? No, it's way too late for that" She moved to the fireplace. "What then—money? I have more than I'll ever spend and no one to leave it to. Revenge?" She looked up at John and raised one eyebrow.

"You want to hold this over my head."

"My life has not been very pleasant since I married, so I'm used to short rations. If I caused your son to be hanged so soon after experiencing my husband's death—why that would be too much pleasure at once. That would be ecstasy."

"My God, Jennifer, you can't mean that. The liquor's doing your talking."

"It may be, but you're going to see how much I mean what I say. You're going to think about me day and night for a long time. Who knows when the sheriff will turn up shocking new evidence in the death of Ned Worthington? Could be a year. Could be ten years."

"I feel sorry for you. You're like a wounded rattlesnake striking all around, trying your best to take others with you as you die. But with Ned gone the worst is behind you. Why don't you make peace with the world? Finish out your life with some happiness."

"Your concern for me is so touching. Maybe you're right. Maybe I should clear my conscience, go ahead and have them hang Harry and start attending Sunday school and church regularly."

John turned and walked to the doors.

"Kathleen and I could start a sewing club," she called after him. "We'd have so much to talk about, so much in common."

He reached the doors and hesitated a moment.

"Your son is a killer, and he goes free only as long as I say so," she snarled.

He slid the doors open and walked out.

Jennifer hurled the tumbler after him as he went.

"Don't lecture me on how to be happy," she yelled. "We'll see how happy you are while you're trying to protect your guilty son from people who know the truth. Let's see you contain a wounded snake, John."

*   *   *   *

The bank's new president, Roger Pace, soon had business back to normal. Everything was in as good a shape as could be expected, considering the amount of paper that Ned had burnt prior to his death.

Harry Warren verified that to the best of his knowledge, the notes that the auditors had found amounting to fifty thousand dollars represented Warren and Worthington's entire indebtedness to the bank. With what the company owed other creditors, John felt particularly relieved that his eldest son's business education had cost him only eighty thousand dollars.

By early 1913 John's company had more than made up for the time lost by Harry's company on the harvesting of pines along the main railroad line all the way in to Billy's Island in the middle of the Okefenokee. To soothe the feelings of the other investors in the project, John paid each of them additional money to make up for Harry's shortcomings. He felt that it was necessary to pay them extra, particularly since he insisted that Harry be put in charge of his timbering operation.

Aside from monthly trips to Sanctuary to report on the progress of the work to his father, Harry lived at the job site. He didn't like it, but he knew that it was too early in his time back in the business to argue with John. For the first weeks that he was back with his father, the investigation of Ned's death was going on, and Harry felt more secure in the swamp.

In the summer of 1913 Charles came home again, and it was as if he'd never left. He and Celia resumed their work on the gardens of Sanctuary, and John immediately updated him on the year's changes in the business. After a week at home, Charles was anxious to see the swamp operation. John had to go to New York the next week, so he sent Charles to the swamp while he was gone.

Charles drove from Sanctuary to Hebardville to spend some time studying the cypress mill that was now running at double the capacity of only a year earlier. From there, he took the railroad into Hopkins, and the next day, all the way to Harry's headquarters on Billy's Island. Charles was astonished to see that an entire town of about a thousand people had sprung up in the middle of the swamp.

"Oh, yeah," Harry said. "Word is we're getting a moving picture house here before long—how about that? Mary Pickford plays to the gators. Guess what we already have!"

"Let's see," Charles mused. "It's something that caters to one of your vices, or you wouldn't be excited about it."

"Right."

"A bar."

"And they said college would be a waste of time for you. But this is not just any bar. The Jug!"

"You're kidding."

"Nope. One of the regulars over at the original Jug started up a joint here. Apparently, he wasn't bright enough to come up with a new name, so he just used the old one."

"Who's the owner?"

Harry grinned. "Me."

"I'll have to stop by one night while I'm in town," said Charles. "Although I'm still having trouble believing that there is a town out here."

"Tonight's as good as any. Let's go."

"There's still a good bit of daylight left, Harry, and I've been want-ing to get to the job site. I've got an idea about—"

"No more business today, little brother. I've got an idea, too, and it involves a woman and two blankets in the bottom of a boat. She has two sisters to choose from, but first a whole lot of liquor has to flow. What do you say?"

"I don't think Dad would go for that, Harry. After work, okay, but not now. "I think I'll just settle in at the boardinghouse and then scout around the island a little."

Charles was quick about putting his bag away. He'd loved the swamp from the time of his first boyhood trips. When he had first been allowed to come along on a trip with his father and Gray, he was ten and Harry was sixteen. Now, as Charles walked Billy's Island, he remembered that first trip.

They rode their horses from Sanctuary on a maze of roads and paths, across fields and through dense tracts of forest. Charles was utterly lost, but his father and Gray knew the terrain without question. What he did not realize was that his father owned most of the land they traveled to the swamp.

As the light faded on Billy's Island, Charles heard ragtime piano playing somewhere down the path he was on, and he knew that he was headed for the new version of The Jug. He turned to his left and headed across the heart of the island, through a stand of pines. As the piano faded with the light, Charles heard the tenor of the frogs and the profound bass of the alligators far ahead of him.

That first time in the swamp when he was ten, they had left their horses at Hamp Mizell's fish camp that morning and canoed as far into the swamp's interior as they could go. He was in the canoe with his father at the stern, and they glided down the trails effortlessly. He was sure he had been a nuisance at first, pointing out every obvious sight in a high-pitched squeal. The raw majesty of it was too much to contain the first time, and so it spilled out of a boy or a man, often in a torrent of words. To Charles, the Okefenokee was a natural frame of earth, air and water, a woven tapestry, softly elegant, that he could feel with his eyes. He remembered patting the overhanging leaves, the trees and stumps, the black water beside the canoe with the palm of his hand.

"What are you doing, son?" John asked, genuinely interested.

"It's soft, Pop. I just want to pat it a little," Charles said. *He half turned in the canoe to look at his father. "Don't you like to feel it?"*

John looked at his son with a new appreciation. "Yes, son, I do."

Now Charles walked on across the island in the dark. In the distance he heard a truck engine, moving away from him. It was a sound that he did not care to hear in the Au Fin Au Cau. He hadn't thought of that name for years now. He preferred it to Okefenokee. Au Fin Au Cau. It was a softer sound that matched the prairies of wind-blown grass, the islands of lush pine needle carpet, the mats of earth that trembled at the touch of a foot.

Charles had heard that word, Au Fin Au Cau, for the first time in their camp, deep inside the swamp.

"This place is ancient," his father had said. "Most everywhere else we know is touched and changed by the hand of man, so this is as close as we're going to come to the past." He'd paused a moment. "This may very well be what this place looked like a thousand years ago. Maybe a million years ago."

Charles' mind reeled as his father spoke.

"This place was once called Au Fin Au Cau, Land of the Trembling Earth, by the Indians who lived here. I know two of them who lived here hundreds, maybe thousands of years ago. You see those two stars, right over there? The one on the right is Cau Au Ra. On the left is his woman, Au Eve."

His father had told him the story of the journey as well as he could remember it. Charles was enraptured by the story, and he was astonished to find at the end, that Harry had gone to sleep.

Charles reached the other side of Billy's Island as the full moon began to break over the tree line. The piano and the truck were silent now. A breeze stirred the hot night air. He inhaled deeply and drew in the moist smell of the swamp.

Charles had made five more swamp trips with his father and Gray. Each year he asked John to tell him of the journey and though the story remained the same, each year's telling had its own distinct memory for Charles. Maybe it was because John added some previously forgotten detail. Maybe it was that Charles attached a new significance to some part of the story, saw something at one age that he was unequipped to see at a younger age.

That was twelve years ago. Now a young man, back in the Okefenokee to play a small part in changing that which was the link to the ancient past, Charles longed for his father's vision. He longed to see Cau Au Ra and Au Eve. He turned away from the moon to look at the two stars that his father had shown him. They were in eternity now. He walked back to the boardinghouse in the moonlight.

XXV

Charles pounded on the door to Harry's room. "Harry, get up!" He thought he heard a stirring inside. "Come on, Harry. The locomotive is leaving in a few minutes."

He turned the doorknob and pushed. There was a little resistance, but when he pushed the door harder it swung open, and Charles could see Harry's pants wadded up behind the door. The room was strewn with clothing, cans of half-eaten food, newspapers, and liquor bottles. It smelled of sweat and stale cigarettes.

Harry lay face down on the bed, his arm dangling off the side. A large-busted woman lay next to him, her peroxide blond head propped on her hand and her elbow jammed into the pillow. She was attractive in a brassy sort of way. The sheet was pulled over her lower half, and she made no effort to cover the rest of herself.

"You must be Charles," she said nonchalantly. "You're even better-looking than I thought you'd be."

He looked away from her as soon as he could.

She laughed slightly. "You sure do make a lot of noise early in the morning, little brother."

"Harry and I need to get going, or we're going to miss the locomotive out to the job site."

"Harry don't work on Sundays, dear. It's against his religion." She found that enormously funny and had to lay back on the pillow from the exertion of laughing.

Charles smiled. "Would you be so kind as to cover yourself so I can get him up?"

"Honey, if I can't get Harry up, can't nobody get Harry up." She shook the bed with her throaty laughter.

Charles laughed in spite of himself. He turned to see if Harry was awake, and she had most definitely not covered herself. Exasperated, he walked to the bed and threw the sheet over her.

"This looks like a lost cause. Tell him that I've gone out to the job site, and that I'd appreciate it if he would come on out just as soon as he wakes up."

"I'm telling you, you can forget it. He won't show up today. Don't you want to know my name?" She asked.

Charles had reached the door. He turned back to her. "Why? Are you somebody I'm going to see again?" He asked.

She raised up in the bed again, indignant. "I'm your brother's intended!"

Charles looked at Harry and shook his head. "Then I'll wait for the formal introduction." He closed the door behind him.

Charles didn't like most of what he saw at the job site that day. As he walked, he took notes of the inefficiencies he observed, of the needed repairs, and of the worn-out equipment. The more he wrote, the angrier he became. It was evident that Harry was spending most of his time at The Jug or shacked up with some woman on Billy's Island. On the train ride back to the island Charles lectured himself on the need to control his emotions when he talked with Harry that evening.

After a bath and dinner he walked the short distance to The Jug in the dusk. Unlike the rest of the week when the piano and the crowd could be heard all across the island, the bar was quiet on this Sunday evening. Only a faint light peeping around the doorframe and from beneath the eaves betrayed the presence of its occupants. Charles tried the door. It was locked, so he rapped at it.

"Yeah?"

"This is Harry's brother."

A husky bearded fellow with a long scar near his left eye opened the door. "Come on in." When Charles entered, the man locked the door back and stood there with his arms folded.

The place was rough. A row of planks served as a bar, several shabby pictures of women in various stages of undress hung on the board walls, an upright piano occupied a corner, and a few tables with dirty tablecloths were scattered at random. The floor was compacted dirt with a thin layer of wood chips. Harry and a few men sat around one of the tables, playing cards. The air was thick with smoke.

"Hey, little brother! Honor system on Sundays. Liquor's behind the bar. Two bits go in the till. Nickel for the smokes." He turned back to his cards.

Charles poured himself a drink, paid, and joined the men at the table. Harry folded his hand and looked at his brother. "Charles, this is everybody. Everybody, this is the pride and joy of the Georgia Institute of Technology, my brother, Charles. How'd it go down in the salt mines today, old boy?"

"We missed you," Charles said.

Harry glanced back at him as he dealt the next hand. "'Tis the Sabbath, young Charles," he said, "so we're not talking business right now."

Charles sat patiently, sipped his whiskey, and watched them play cards for the next couple of hours. Harry kept up a running conversation, commenting on the card game and telling stories, picking at one man, then another.

By eleven o'clock Charles was beginning to tire and there was no evidence that the game was waning. By eleven-thirty his patience was gone. When Harry got up to stretch and to get a refill, Charles followed him to the bar.

"What time does this game end, Harry? You and I need to talk."

"This is a weekend, son, and the old man is out of state. It busts up when it busts up."

"That's no good," Charles said. "These jay birds don't work for us, so they can do as they please. You're going to be on that cattle car with me before the sun comes up, so you've got to get some sleep."

Harry leaned back against the bar and poured another drink. "And just who the hell are you?"

"I'm the only Warren our foremen have seen in three days, that's who."

"So? Are those bastards complaining? I can fix them if I need to."

"They don't need fixing. You do. They're doing a good job on their own, but they need some things, and you're the one who's responsible to see that they get what they need."

"Well, pardon me, *Dad*! Am I not living up to your expectations?"

"Pour you one for the road, Harry," Charles said. "We're not discussing this in front of your drinking buddies."

Harry pushed away from the bar and past Charles. "You got that right. We're not discussing this at all. Deal 'em up," he yelled on his way back to the table. Charles was right behind him. "You boys play all night if you want," he said, "but Harry's through."

Harry turned on him suddenly, but Charles was ready and caught his brother on the chin with a hard right that sent him stumbling back into the chairs and the card table. The men scattered as Harry went down.

"Get up, Harry," Charles said calmly. "I'm going to give you whatever you can tolerate."

Harry shook his head and looked at the men around him, then at Charles. "They teach you that at Tech?" It had been a long, three-day drunk, and he was too tired to get up. "Game's over, gents. See you tomorrow night."

They filed out sullenly. Charles helped Harry up, and they righted the table and chairs.

"What's going on here, Harry? Why aren't you tending to the business?"

"Look, I took one long weekend. Our men are able to keep the work going without me over them every second."

"There are decisions to be made that only the head man can make. Any other way and pretty soon your foremen are at each other's throats. You have to be there seven days a week, Harry—like it or not."

"Thanks for the lesson, professor. Let's go. You've put the quietus to this joint."

Harry locked up, and they walked to the boardinghouse. As they went to their separate rooms, Charles slapped his brother on the shoulder. "I'll get you up about four-thirty."

"Oh boy," Harry said as he slipped inside.

The next morning Charles dreaded trying to wake Harry up. He decided to get an early start, so as soon as he got out of bed, he put on his pants and opened his door to the hall. There was Harry, ready to go and smoking a cigarette. He held it out to Charles. "Breakfast?"

After Charles finished dressing, they joined the others at the train.

"Harry, about last night—"

"Don't mention it, kid. We just got a little too much to drink. I've had my share of one punch fights. It's a new day, and I'm sure you'll see my point of view."

"I hope so, Harry."

The sun wasn't up yet, and it was already hot and humid. After they had checked in with the foremen and discussed some problems with them, the two brothers began a tour of the items that Charles had listed in his notebook. As they went, Charles added to the notes he had already made. The more he wrote, the more defensive Harry became, until by the end of the day, they were barely speaking.

"We need to stay out here tonight, Harry, so we can go over my notes without a lot of distractions. We can look at these items first-hand before it gets dark."

"Just what do you think you're doing, Charles?"

"Dad sent me out here to look the job over so I could advise him on improvements. These notes are the basis for my report. I hope to tell him that you and I are well on the way to implementing about half of these ideas by the end of the week."

"Mind if I take a look at those?"

Charles handed his notebook to Harry, who turned and strolled away, reading as he went. Charles followed him. After a few minutes, Harry stopped and snapped the leather cover of the notebook in place. He turned and smiled at Charles. Then, without a word, Harry reared back and heaved the notebook as far out into the surrounding water and brush as he could. Charles took a step forward, watching in disbelief as his work dropped out of sight.

"We're not staying out here tonight, Charles. As a matter of fact, the main line is running to Hebardville tonight, and you're going to be on it. You're getting your ass out of this swamp altogether. Do you hear me?"

Charles charged his brother and hit him chest high. His momentum carried them back until Harry fell, and they both went down in the sand, throwing punches wildly. Finally, Harry kicked Charles away from him and regained his feet. He let his brother up. "We can keep on if you want to, but I'm warning you, this ain't last night when I was tired and about half drunk. If you push it today, I'm going to hurt you, boy."

"You had no right to throw that notebook away," Charles yelled, his chest heaving.

"I'm running this job, Charles. The old man had no business sending you out here to spy on me."

"I'm not here to spy. I'm here to help you."

"You're a college boy. All you have is book knowledge. You ain't had to make a payroll. You ain't had to bring a job in on time. If I listened to ten percent of that crap you had written we could shut down this job before the end of the week. There's nothing you can tell me about running a timber operation! Nothing!"

"There's nothing I can tell you about running one into the ground, you mean. I can recreate my notes, Harry, and the minute that Dad gets back from New York I'm going to lay it all out to him. That's what he's paying me to do, and I'm going to give him his money's worth. If you can't take the truth and get this place in shape, you'd better be ready to explain why."

Harry laughed at Charles and shook his head. "Go on, run to Dad. I can stand up to him any day." Harry walked toward the locomotive. He didn't like the way this was shaping up. Charles had one more year at Tech. He and the old man thought too much alike. Where was that going to leave him the day the business changed hands? He needed a drink.

s   s   s   s

Four days later, John stood in the middle of the deserted job site in the Okefenokee. The rest of the men had taken the locomotive back to Billy's Island, leaving only John, Harry, and Charles at the railhead. John turned to Harry who was leaning against the back of a wagon.

"Could it be that Charles was doing as I instructed him to do?"

"Yes, sir," Harry said quietly.

"Could it be that he has some ideas with merit that you ought to consider?"

"Not many."

"Then there are some? A yes or no will do nicely."

"Yes."

"Aha! Now we may be getting somewhere." John looked over to where Charles sat on a stump. "Can you put yourself in Harry's position for just a minute?"

"Not without a fifth of liquor and a cheap whore."

"Now you see what I'm saying?" Harry yelled. He started toward Charles, but John stopped him with a look. "That boy has a smart mouth on him, and I don't care to take that from some schoolboy who don't know jack about business!"

"Sit down, Harry!" John said. "What's wrong with you two? Just look at this place." John gestured at the job site. "There's a lot that's right about it, but there's a lot of room for improvement. That tells me that you two have some ability, but you boys aren't working together. I'm sixty-three years old, and I don't expect to live forever. I may go another day, or I may last another twenty years, but one day somebody else has to run this business. I'd like for it to be the two of you as partners." He pointed at Harry. "One with the practical experience who's taken the hard knocks." He pointed to Charles. "One with the formal engineering background. It's a perfect combination if both of you will just admit that you need the other fellow."

They stared at the ground.

"Charles, you need to develop some diplomacy. Put yourself in the other man's place. Some things they tell you in the classroom may not work exactly like a book says. If he has any sense, the man who wrote the book would make adjustments on the job."

Charles said nothing.

"Harry, you have to admit that some good things can come out of a book. Men write books to reach a bigger audience with their ideas. It's just as foolish never to touch one as it is to stay with your nose in one all of the time. And your bigger need is for discipline. You need to stay out of the barrooms and out of the cathouses. There are a hundred details to tend to every day in a business, and you're the man who has to see that things get done."

He walked away from his sons in silence.

"We're going to try this again," he said, "and if there's a repeat of last week's fiasco, I'm going to clean house. You don't fight in front of the men. If things get that bad again, the two of you load up in a boat, go to one of these other islands, and just beat hell out of each other.

But not in front of the people you're supposed to be leading. Am I clear on that?"

They mumbled their agreement.

"Well, damned if I'm going to take that for an answer," John growled. "Harry, I'm talking to you. Look me in the eyes when you talk to me."

Harry stood up and looked at his father. "I've got it."

"Charles?"

"Yes, sir. No fighting in front of the men."

"Thank you, gentlemen. Now you two take me around this job site again and tell me about the improvements you intend to make."

Over the next three weeks Harry and Charles cooperated with each other at work to the point that the swamp operation became the most efficient unit in John's business. At first they would have very little to do with each other off the job, but over the three weeks, Charles became lonely enough to mend those fences, too. He approached Harry as they were unloading at the boardinghouse from the train one evening.

"Thought I might stop by The Jug tonight," he said.

Harry looked up in surprise. "It's a public bar."

"Will you be there?"

Harry chuckled. "When have you known me to miss a night?"

At seven that evening there was a knock at Charles' door. When he opened it, there stood Harry with two women. One of them was the woman Charles had found in bed with Harry several weeks earlier.

"This is Daisy and this is Ruthalee. Take your pick, little brother!" Harry said with a grin.

"Harry's a real kidder," Ruthalee spoke up. "He and Daisy are practically betrothed. I'm yours, sugar!"

Charles looked at Harry to confirm his good fortune. Harry raised his eyebrows and grinned. Ruthalee looked to be well acquainted with chewing tobacco and a hard day's work in the sun. He held out his arm, and she moved to him eagerly. "Let's go kick up our heels!" She squealed.

The Jug was packed when they arrived, but they found room at a table at the far end of the bar. As soon as Charles finished his first drink, Ruthalee dragged him out to the dance floor, where they stayed for the next half-hour.

Several times Charles looked through the crowd and the cigarette haze for rescue from Harry, but each time he saw his brother and Daisy talking, gesturing and shaking their heads.

After a full hour, Ruthalee gave Charles a break. "I got to go to the can, sugar. How about getting me another double, and I'll see you right over there." She pointed toward Harry.

Charles fought his way through the crowd to the bar, bought the drinks, and elbowed back to their table. Harry excused himself to get Daisy and himself another drink.

"Long time, no see," Daisy yelled over the noise of the crowd.

"Yeah," Charles yelled. "Here, have a drink."

"As I recall, the last time we did see each other, you saw more of me than I did of you."

Charles wagged his finger at her. "Shame on you."

She sipped at her drink. "If you got 'em, flaunt 'em. That's my motto." She nudged Charles and pointed to the dance floor. "Will you look at that shit? Our dates are dancing."

"Thank you, Lord," Charles said quietly.

"Listen," Daisy said, "this is a good chance for us to discuss something. You need to talk some sense into your brother."

"You're telling me? We've been trying to do that for years."

She lit a cigarette and took a drink. "I'm serious."

"Does this have something to do with what y'all were arguing about," Charles asked.

She looked at him. "I'm carrying," she said, "and it's Harry's baby. He told me he'd marry me, and now he's trying to back out."

"No!" Charles tried to look shocked.

She looked at Charles solemnly. "Don't try to fake it for my benefit," she said. "I know I ain't the first, but this time is going to be different."

"What's going to be different this time?" He asked.

"My last name is Skinner. Have you been in the swamp long enough for that to mean anything to you?"

Charles looked at her in disbelief. He turned to look at Harry, dancing as if he hadn't a care in the world. "You're not really a Skinner, are you?"

She smiled and nodded.

He had heard tales of the Skinner family since his first trip to the swamp. The Okefenokee part of the family had originated when a renegade Creek Indian had bartered otter pelts for Bertha Skinner, the obese, unmarried daughter of a Waycross general store owner.

In one generation the Okefenokee Skinners had made a reputation for meanness that was unexcelled in South Georgia. To say that someone had "gone to see the Skinners" was to acknowledge that person as missing and presumed dead.

"They've never actually found any of the bodies, have they?" Charles asked.

"Never," she said. "You know, Charles, you really should talk to Harry if you care anything about him. I'd purely hate it if my papa had to kill him."

Charles watched his brother jitterbug with Ruthalee. Daisy was right. He had better have that talk with Harry.

s   s   s   s

In the spring of 1915, the family traveled by train to Atlanta for Charles' graduation from Georgia Tech. The morning of the ceremony, John woke Kathleen at sunrise.

"Are you up for a tour of the big city?"

"No," she grumbled. "I'm up because you're tickling my neck with your whiskers. Go away."

"Want me to tickle your fancy, instead?"

"I'll take the tour."

They dressed and had a leisurely breakfast in the hotel coffee shop. For the next several hours they drove the town, sightseeing. Over the years of business trips to Atlanta, John had watched the city change and grow, so he could show Kathleen how the new order had sprung from the old. As their time waned, John turned the car to the Oakland Cemetery.

"I want to show you where I had my family re-interred years ago."

When they reached the cemetery, John parked near the main gate. "Let's walk back to the gravesite from here. I'm a little stiff from all that riding."

As they walked, she held out her hand to him. Both of them were content to stroll silently, speaking only to point out an especially beautiful group of azaleas or dogwoods.

"My mother and father would've loved you, Kath."

"And I would've loved them. I wonder if we'd have met if they had lived and you had never left Atlanta. What do you think, John?"

"I think those are some mighty big ifs."

"That's no answer," she said. "That's just commentary. You can do better than that."

They came to the graves and sat on a white granite bench, facing the five slabs of matching stone.

"It was never going to be any different, Kath. They were always going to die young. I was always going to love you. We were always going to sit here and wonder if things could be different."

"Oh, I hope not," she said. "I've always been one for spontaneity, you know. I wouldn't have life all planned out ahead of our time like that."

"I'm talking about God's perspective, not ours," he said. "We're like characters in a story. We know nothing about what's next, but the author? Once he's written the story, he knows it all, and he can turn the pages—past and present and future. Its all eternity to him."

John stood and walked to his mother's grave. "It's hard to believe that fifty years have gone since I last saw them."

She joined him and slipped her arm around his.

"This life is so quick," he said. "Why do we struggle so?"

She reached up and kissed his cheek. "To see our youngest graduate from Georgia Tech. He was just born yesterday, you know."

John smiled at her as they walked from the gravesite. "Was I getting too profound for you?"

"Way too profound."

"And you say your one-day-old son is about to graduate from Tech?"

She tossed her head haughtily. "Yes."

"What amazing children you have, Mrs. Warren!"

"Excellent breeding, sir."

They strolled from the cemetery. "Why, thank you, madam. I certainly did my best."

She slapped him on the shoulder and laid her head against him as they walked on to the car.

That evening, after the graduation exercises, the Warren family attended a reception for the graduates. John and Kathleen stood at one end of the ballroom with Charles, watching the couples dance.

"I was concerned that Celia would be too reserved to let any of the young men entertain her," Kathleen said. "How many dances is that for her?"

"How many have there been?" John asked. "I don't think she's missed one yet."

"Look at Harry," Charles said, smiling. "Daisy had better put a reserved sign on him."

"Neither of them have missed a dance either," Kathleen said, "Yet they've not been with each other the whole evening."

An older gentleman, using a cane to balance as he approached, interrupted their conversation. "Good evening, Mr. Warren. Will you favor me with an introduction?"

"Professor Gordon, allow me to present my parents, Mr. and Mrs. John Warren. Mother, Professor Gordon taught me everything I know about Euclidean geometry."

"Which is considerable," the professor said. He took Kathleen's hand and pressed it lightly. "Mrs. Warren, may I compliment you on your rare beauty and on your rare son."

"You certainly may, sir."

"Mr. Warren." He shook John's hand robustly. "You must be exceptionally proud of your young man."

"Indeed I am, professor."

"Well, I expect he'll show them a few things about engineering over there. It's a tremendous opportunity for a man just out of school, and I know of no one more qualified or more deserving than young Charles."

John and Kathleen looked at the old man quizzically.

"I'm sure Charles will distinguish himself," John said, looking at his son, who avoided his parents' gaze.

"No doubt. I have thoroughly enjoyed my association with Charles. He has a first-rate mind, mingled with a zeal for life that made him a pleasure to instruct. Full of surprises. Just full of surprises."

"That's Charles," Kathleen said.

"Well, it's past time for me to retire for the evening. I still need to speak with several of the men and their parents, so I'll have to excuse myself. Mrs. Warren, it's been a delight."

When the old gentleman had limped away, John turned to his son. "I'm a little tired myself. Would you mind bringing the car around, and I'll talk to Harry about getting the others back to the hotel later."

The ride to the hotel was tense and silent. They didn't know how to broach the question the professor had raised. Back in the suite, Charles was frustrated from trying to devise the perfect explanation.

"I was going to discuss my plans with you after the reception. I didn't feel as if you were going to be very receptive, and I wanted us to enjoy this time together first."

"Didn't think I'd be very receptive? Hell no. I'd say that I'm not going to be very receptive to anything but what we've planned for the last four years!"

"John," Kathleen said quietly.

"Don't 'John' me! We're up here dining and dancing, celebrating to take this boy home and all the time, he's sitting here with other ideas. And Kathleen, you know as well as I do what 'over there' means."

"I don't want him in Europe with a war going on, John, but we have to listen to what his plans are."

"I don't have to listen to his plans, because he can cancel anything these eggheads have planned for him." He turned to Charles. "Is old Professor Senile going to war with you?"

"John!"

"Well, is he?"

"No, sir, but there are other Tech graduates going. I'm not the only one."

"You can bet the farm he's not, and neither are you. What the other men do is their concern. I need you in our business, and that's all I want to hear about it."

Kathleen started to speak, but Charles held up his hand to her.

"Dad, tell me something."

"What?"

"I'm twenty-four years old, not fifteen. How do you figure to stop me from doing whatever a reasonable adult wants to do?"

"There's nothing reasonable about going to a shooting war. Believe me, I went to one about five miles from here one time. You want no part of it."

"I'm going as an engineer, Dad, not a foot soldier. They want me to help tackle some of the logistical problems the Allies are having. The whole thing has to be kept quiet since we're not involved in the war yet."

"Well, some of those logistics are going to involve the front lines, and I'm telling you not to be naive. A bullet or a bomb doesn't care if you're infantry or engineer corps."

"You still haven't answered my question. How are you going to stop me?"

"Georgia Tech set this up, and they had damned well better call it off, or these sons of bitches have seen the last penny they'll ever get from me. And I intend to be in the president's office first by-God thing in the morning saying just that. I think that should make you pretty unwelcome on this little jaunt."

"Is that what your mother should've done when you wanted to defend Atlanta?" Kathleen asked. "Should she have gone to the governor and used her influence to bring you back to supposed safety?"

"That was different, Kathleen, and you know it. I was defending my home. This isn't even our fight. The Germans can have the whole continent as far as I'm concerned."

"It's a small world, John, and it's getting smaller every day. Maybe when Charles talks of going to Europe, he thinks he's helping defend his home, too. But the circumstances are beside the point. Charles is doing what he thinks is right. I hope that we can convince him that he's wrong, but that's the only way we should stop him from going. Your mother resisted the temptation to embarrass you for what she probably thought was your own good, and you're alive today because of her decision to do what was right, not what seemed safe."

John looked out the window, afraid for his son. "Nobody is shooting cannons into Sanctuary, Kathleen. I want the boy to be safe."

"We both do, but we want him to be a man, too, and that's what he's trying to do. Come sit here by me, John. Let's calm down and let Charles tell us why he thinks this is the best thing to do. Because if you go yelling at the president of this college tomorrow, I'm going to be right behind you—writing these sons of bitches a check for a half million dollars."

By September of 1915, Charles was studying his first supply routes with a British engineer corps in France.

        *   *   *   *

Kathleen stood at the end of the dining room table at Sanctuary with her glass in her hand.

"First, I'd like to welcome Ranetta and all of the Stokes family to our home. Thank all of you so much for coming tonight. Then, I'd like to welcome Leander home and tell him how much we love him and how much we've missed him. I also love your British accent, sir. I think it's very sophisticated."

They laughed, and there was scattered applause around the table.

"I apologize for the absence of Harry and Daisy, and we all continue to pray for Charles, so I'd like to include them in this toast to Leander."

Leander smiled, nodded at Kathleen and raised his glass.

"To our next generation, the future of the Warrens and the Stokes. May you continue to build on the foundation set in place by this generation, and may you have and give love and peace all along your way."

They raised their glasses and drank.

        *   *   *   *

That night Harry and Daisy sat on the porch of the company house on Billy's Island. Their son, J.E., was asleep inside. Daisy lit another cigarette and propped her feet on the porch railing.

"All I said," Harry repeated, "was that it wouldn't have killed you."

"Well, my daddy would've killed me if he'd known I was sitting down to eat with a bunch of niggers. Makes my skin crawl."

"Your old man is half Indian. There's a hell of a lot of people who wouldn't let him in the house. Besides, the Stokes family makes more money than your old man could count. What do they care what he thinks about them?"

"Their money don't make them white," Daisy snapped. "And any time your mama insists on filling the house with them, you can just plan on getting me and J.E. out of there."

"Suits me," Harry said. "Damn, it's hot! I'm going down to The Jug for a drink." He got up and stepped off the porch.

"Hey, that ain't fair! You can't leave me here by myself."

He rolled his eyes. He was hoping to see a certain young thing at the bar. "Come on, then."

"What about the baby?"

"He sleeps like a true Skinner. He'll never know the difference."

Daisy slipped on her shoes and bounced down the steps after Harry.

&   &   &   &

In October of 1915 Leander Stokes turned twenty-four. He was a good-looking man with light brown skin who was much in demand at church socials and dances. At six feet, he was trim and muscular. Like his friend, Charles Warren, he had begun college later than most of his contemporaries, and so as he began his business career, Leander possessed a maturity that served him well.

He had a great deal to learn about how his half brother, Zachary, had organized the business after Corey's death. Although Leander had four brothers or half brothers working in the business, it was generally accepted in the family that the leadership would pass from Zachary to him. It was not a popular notion with all the brothers, but Ranetta made sure that it was understood and accepted all the same. Leander recognized that Zachary and Ranetta had done a remarkable job of conserving what Corey had built up. The family's land and timber holdings were far greater than he had realized when he had left for college four years earlier.

The family that had sprung from Corey and his wives did not live extravagantly. They lived comfortably and quietly, and they stayed to their own. By 1915 all nine of the girls in the family had completed their schooling and had married. Most of them had moved to surrounding towns, some as far as Jacksonville and Savannah.

Two of Leander's half brothers had become ministers and had removed themselves from the business altogether. They loved their whole family, and these two, Artis and Artemus, were determined to move their family away from the liquor business. Zachary could not be swayed to divest the stills, but the preachers had a fervent belief that they could get Leander to see the wisdom of moving the family out of an immoral business. Leander quietly assured them that he would be willing to listen to them when he was in the leadership position, but he reminded them that Zachary was currently the head of the business, and he refused to do anything that would undermine his eldest brother's position.

"Brother Zachary is almost sixty years of age," Artis said. "Don't you think it's time you exerted your education and your influence with your mother to take the reins of power?"

"No, sir. I'm sorry to have to disagree with you, but I believe I should submit to Brother Zachary's authority until such time as he and Mother and the Lord see fit to raise me to that position."

The ministers found it difficult to argue with Leander's respect for authority, so they continued to lobby him to rid the family of its liquor trade at some future time.

Leander contented himself with learning the existing business and with forming opinions on any new directions that he should take the family in the future. Both tasks served to occupy his mind fully throughout the remainder of the year and on into 1916.

§　　　　§　　　　§　　　　§

From the time Charles left for Europe, John immersed himself ever deeper into the business. For months he was upset at Kathleen and Charles for their defiance of his wishes in Atlanta, and he refused to discuss his feelings with his wife. To fuel his resentment, the sawmill at Sanctuary and the whole swamp operation suffered a series of problems, primarily with equipment. John convinced himself that none of it would have happened if Charles had been where he was supposed to be.

To the men who worked around him every day, John was distracted, his mind prone to wander. It was uncharacteristic, and it worried those who knew him best. They found out, though, that if it was even suggested that some time off might do him good, John reacted in a way that was not good for a man's career or his digestion.

Harry came into his father's office one Monday early in 1917 to discuss the week's schedule. It was unusual that John completely ignored him.

"Are you still going to Atlanta at the end of the week, Pop?"

John sat at his desk, turning his coffee cup, moving it an inch at a time, engrossed in the process. At first, Harry thought that his father was pondering his question.

"I think the Hebards and the other investors are due in on Friday. Is that when you're planning to get there?"

John turned the cup.

By the time Harry got him home and Dr. Mattox arrived from Homerville, John was talking quietly with Kathleen.

"I don't remember what I was doing or how I got from the office to here."

"How do you feel?" The doctor asked.

"Like I've been working in the woods for three days, nonstop."

"Good," Doctor Mattox said. "You should be too tired to argue with me. You've had a light stroke, and you have to stay away from work for a while. I want you to have complete bed rest, and I want Kathleen to wait on you hand and foot. Is that such a bad prospect?"

"Depends on what you mean by a while," John said.

"I don't want to be guilty of giving you another attack, so let's just say until I come back day after tomorrow."

John closed his eyes. "I probably won't even wake up by then, tired as I am." He was asleep almost instantly.

"How long will he need to stay away from the mill, Homer?" Kathleen asked.

"We'll have to watch him close, but I'd say for at least a month—maybe two."

"Oh, Lord."

"I know. You're going to have your work cut out for you, but maybe between all of us, we can rein him in. Get Celia to spend lots of time with him. Nobody runs a father like a daughter."

Over the following days John was in no condition to argue about staying home, but as the days turned into two weeks, he became increasingly belligerent.

"Harry's doing fine running things," Kathleen said. "If you'll behave, I'll let him come report to you in another week."

"I feel fine, and I've got to get out of the house. I promise you, I'll take it easy. Four hours and right back home."

"How about two hours?" she said.

"All right, two hours. Would you call Leander and ask him to meet me at the office while I get dressed?"

When Leander arrived at the mill, John was leaning against his Cadillac, talking with Harry. "We're going for a drive, Harry," John said. "I'll see you tomorrow." He threw the keys to Leander. "Would you mind?"

John directed him to drive south and rolled down the window as they pulled away from the mill.

"I'm sorry that I haven't had much time to talk with you here lately," John said. "I appreciate your coming by while I was laid up. Do you hear anything from Charles?"

"Yes, sir. I had a letter from him last week. Seems to be doing well and enjoying his work."

"Doesn't seem like much of a war when a fellow sets up house-keeping in Paris," John said.

Leander laughed. "Been thinking of going over, myself. Those French women favor black men, you know."

"Son, I'm so old I've forgotten why we chase women." John pointed to the surrounding pine forests. "Do you have an idea of the land I own? I mean, do you have a picture in your head of the extent of it?"

"No, sir. I've been studying what's in the Stokes' name for the last six months, so I know a little about your land where it adjoins ours. That's about it, though."

After five miles, John told Leander to pull over, and the two of them sat talking while the dust settled around them. It was early morning. The October air was cool and invigorating, and the pinewoods were peaceful.

"Come on. I want to show you something down this old three-path road. It's too rutted to drive, and the walk will do us good."

They walked slowly down the road. "Gray Hampton stopped by the house the other day," John said. "We got to talking about the bad old days, and I haven't been able to get this place off my mind since. Right about this curve is where I first met Gray. Had a hell of a fight with old Ned Worthington here while Gray kept some of the Coopers off of me."

"What was that all about?" Leander asked.

John kept walking. "That is a long, long story. Maybe I'll tell it to you one day, but not this day. I want to show you something else."

They walked on until the road stopped at a clearing. The weeds were rank, but Leander could see the remains of a shed on the fringe of the clearing, and here and there were scattered the moldering remains of a stack of wood or a wagon reduced to rusted fittings and rotted frames. Leander started to say something, but stopped when he saw the expression on John's face and the tears in his eyes. He realized that this place was sacred to John.

"I first met your daddy right over there. It was before sunup. I'd come out here early from Magnolia, because it was my first day on the job, and I didn't know nothing about nothing."

They walked around the old mill site, and John showed Leander how things used to be. He told several stories about the men who worked here and how they had grown to respect each other. John was proud of the fact that he now had men working for him whose fathers and grandfathers had worked with him at this place. After an hour John was tiring, so they started back to the car.

"Mr. John, I want to thank you for bringing me out here today."

"Old men like to rattle on about old days, son. I hope it wasn't too big a waste of your time."

"Nothing that involved my father or you is a waste of my time. If you don't mind, I'd like to come back out every once in a while. Just to be where he used to spend a lot of his time. See what he saw, you know?"

John was slowing down now. They were almost in sight of the car, and Leander was beginning to worry about him. His eyes were glassy and his face was pale. His shirt was drenched with sweat.

"You come out here any time you want to, son. As a matter of fact, I made your daddy some promises a few years back that I've been working on here lately. I need to get you some surveys and maps, and we need to come out here to—"

"Mr. John!" Leander caught him by the arm and helped John to the road. John was blinking rapidly, his speech slurring.

"We need to...surveys...maps and—"

"You just lay down here. Lay still and I'll get the car." Leander sprinted for the Cadillac, his heart racing.

XXVI

"Doc."

"Yes, John."

"I want you to clear the room now, yourself included, and I want you to send for Kathleen. You've done a good job, and I'm going to recommend to her that she pay you." John chuckled to himself and lay back to catch his breath.

The doctor smiled. "Why, thank you, John. I'll fetch her for you."

As the doctor gently pushed the men from the room, John muttered, "You old goat. You're supposed to have some pity and tell me there's no charge."

Doctor Mattox winked. "I have to make a living, John."

Kathleen entered the room a few minutes later, sat on the bed beside him, and held his hand in hers. She was too close to tears to speak.

"You know, Kath, I never thought I'd end like this. Quiet. At home in my own bed with the person I love best."

She could no longer contain the tears.

"Kathleen," he said softly. He smiled at her. "Let the tears flow, but not for too long. I want to reminisce with you a little."

He pulled his hand from hers to wipe the tears from his own eyes.

"With the life I've led," he continued, "I fully expected to get it outdoors somewhere. Shot in the back or snake bit in the woods or some other nonsense like that. This is a real blessing to spend my last hours with you."

"I love you," she said.

"I know you do, and I've never taken your love for granted. I know it may have seemed that way to you in the amount of time I was away, but I always tried to deserve your love."

"You did a pretty good job." She managed a smile.

"That's better," John said. "Let's not make our last visit here miserable. Let's just enjoy this time together like we have the rest. Agreed?"

"Yes," she said firmly. "There's no sense kidding ourselves or wishing for more time."

"Spoken like a true McLendon." John said.

"You brought up reminiscing, so I have a quiz question for you," Kathleen said. "What did I give you for our twentieth wedding anniversary?"

John thought for a moment. "That would have been in 'ninety-four. We moved in here in 'ninety-two." It came to him, and he grinned. "The first trip to Fernandina. A month of sun, fun, and the best sex a man could ever hope for!"

"John!" Kathleen blushed. "Not so loud!"

"You brought it up."

"I was thinking more of the companionship. I had you away from business, politics, and everything else for a while. I just couldn't get enough of you."

The conversation went on far into the night. The two lovers traveled back over forty-two years of life together and tried to leave none of it unexplored. The pain and joy of birth, the love shared between a man and woman and their children, the agony of losing a child, and the failures and successes.

Kathleen realized that she was doing most of the talking, so she stopped and reached down to kiss him lightly.

"I'm going to sleep for a while now," John whispered. "Will you sit and hold my hand?"

She nodded and kissed him again, caressing his cheek with her fingertips.

"I know you must be ready to get some sleep, but you'll have time for that here shortly. I love you, Kath."

"I love you, John Warren."

He slept without dreaming.

§   §   §   §

In the year and a half that he had been in Europe, Captain Charles Warren had attained more engineering experience than most Georgia Tech graduates did in five peacetime years spent stateside. He was grateful for that experience, but he hated the price people were paying to make it possible.

He was also embarrassed that it had taken America so long to enter the war. He had given up trying to explain or to defend his government's position. It just didn't wash with the French or the English. Finally, in April of 1917, the Americans announced their involvement in the war. Charles figured that it wouldn't be long before he would be able to return home.

He was concerned about his father. Since the last stroke, his mother's letters had become increasingly urgent. She wanted him to ask for at least a month's leave. First she wrote that it would be a comfort to his father, then she said that it was necessary for him to come home. Finally, it was imperative that he came right away.

None of his arguments had any effect on his commanding officer. "Sorry, son, but good engineers are at a premium over here right now, and you're one of the best. War's tough on the ones who wait at home, but we have a job to do."

On the evening of April twenty-fifth, Charles was sitting by an open window of a farmhouse where the corps of engineers lived. The air was cold and a soft rain pattered on the leaves of an oak in the front yard. He was trying to compose yet another letter to his mother and father. How do you say, for the fifth time in as many months that you can't come home before your father dies? He was so engrossed that he failed to see the courier until the man stood at the window and spoke.

"Captain Warren?"

"That's right."

"Telegram, sir. I'm to wait to see if you'd like to reply, sir."

Charles looked at the man and reached to accept what he did not want. "Do me a favor, private." He tapped one corner of the telegram on the table in front of him. "Come in, dry off, and pour you a cup of coffee. The kitchen's at the back of the house. I'll call you."

"Yes, sir," the private said gratefully.

Charles sat for a long time, staring at the paper, thinking of his father. He took out his pocketknife and slit the envelope. "Regret to inform you..."

When he could think clearly again, he sat his notebook in front of him, looked out at the rain for a minute, then wrote. "John Warren was life blown all out of proportion. He lived in epic times, from the War Between the States until his recent death, and it seems that he was a man suited for his era..."

    *   *   *   *

In mid-May Charles was back at his apartment in Paris for three days. He slept late the first morning, trying to shake the fatigue of the past several weeks and the news of his father's death. He awoke at ten and lay in bed another quarter of an hour, praying not to think, but thinking nonetheless. By eleven he had coffee and a croissant and had dressed to pick up his mail and to run errands in the cold, misty rain.

It was the first thing he saw when the postmaster shoved the stack of mail across the counter. There were several postmarks smeared on the envelope, making it impossible to tell when it had left the States, but there was no mistaking the solid, meticulous handwriting of his father.

Charles let his other errands go and walked back to his apartment. He put on another pot of coffee and while it heated, he looked through the rest of the mail, glancing from time to time at the letter. He poured a cup of coffee and settled into the chair at the hearth. He slipped the blade of his knife around the flap of the envelope so as not to cut it. It was the last time he would hear from his father.

April 21, 1917

Dear Charles,

I know that you will be shocked to get a letter from me, but drastic times call for drastic measures. It is evident that you are needed where you are, which speaks highly of your abilities and of the quality of your work. I am very proud of you.

Still, there are some things I want to say to you before I depart. Perhaps this way is even better than a conversation, for now you will have the written words to test against the passage of time. The things that do not make sense to you today might be of help or encouragement when you are older. I love you very much.

Most of my life was lived in turmoil. You know my early circumstances—blessings of family and social position and suddenly the loss of everything. It seems I've spent the rest of my time here on earth trying to overcome the loss of my family and my birthplace. All along the way, there have been people who were willing to help me. All of them were well intentioned. Some of them saw the need I had, but they didn't have the capacity to help me. Others were able to help, but I refused to let them.

The truth I've learned in life is this. It is God who heals us. He has chosen to perform that miracle, whenever we need it, through the love of our friends. Both through what they give to us, and through what they allow us to give. A wise man once told me that we only get two or three real friends in this life, and that if we marry one of them, then life is especially fine. He was right. My life has been especially fine. In the years to come, listen to your mother and to Gray. Try to discern who your friends are. They will be few, and they will be precious.

Here is a truth that you already know. The world is a confusing place. It wounds us at every turn and is full of lies and false hopes. It's our place for a time, though, and during that time, we often come to love it. That's all right. Love this world for the truth and the beauty and for the sake of the people who are in it, but don't cling to it. Live every day that God gives you. Live a long, useful life, but realize that ultimately, this world isn't our home.

We see passageways here, Charles, and the one we choose takes us to eternity, all the way to the stars. My way looked like a river. You will know yours when you see it. My prayer for you is that you will have the wisdom to see your way much sooner than I saw mine. Eternity begins for you when you find your way, and there is a peace in eternity that I want for you. I'll see you there.